H. E. BATES
SPELLA HO

H. E. BATES
SPELLA HO

This edition published in Great Britain 1989 by
SEVERN HOUSE PUBLISHERS LTD of
40–42 William IV Street, London WC2N 4DF.
Originally published in Great Britain 1938 by
Jonathan Cape Ltd.

First published in the U.S.A. 1989 by
SEVERN HOUSE PUBLISHERS INC, New York

British Library Cataloguing in Publication Data
Bates, H. E. (Herbert Ernest), 1905–1974
Spella Ho.
I. Title
823'.912 [F]
ISBN 0–7278–1736–1

Distributed in the U.S.A. by
Mercedes Distribution Center, Inc.,
62 Imlay Street, Brooklyn, New York 11231

Printed and bound in Great Britain
at the University Printing House, Oxford

BOOK ONE

SPELLA HO: 1873

CHAPTER I

THE day before his mother died, in the winter of 1873, Bruno Shadbolt made three journeys to Spella Ho, hunting for coal. The house stood like a huge shell, empty and desolate, on the bare hillside above many tough little copses of oak and haw that were characteristic, at that time, of the lower land. Built in the 'twenties, squarely, out of the white soft limestone of the locality, with immense blood-veined corner-stones of iron, the house shone that afternoon as though with frost against the distances of a sky that was full of unfallen snow. In the shelter of the copses and more still under cover of the house, there was an odd suspense and silence over things: trees rigid as iron, clouds like lead, the few birds going over on dumb wings. It was the middle of January, and it seemed like the dead core of the year.

Bruno was then twenty. The Shadbolts had reckoned, for some years, to have and lose a baby almost every year. That made him the eldest boy of a family of five. His mother was forty-three. Already an old woman, worn out by miscarriage and childbirth, she was dying of consumption, though no one called it that and there was no one with her. They called it, when they called it anything at all, a decline. It was a mysterious thing and no one, least of all the Shadbolts, could do much about it. Bruno had no name for it, did not understand it. He understood only one thing: that the house was cold. He had tacked new sacking over window-holes, and had bunged up door-cracks, but it was no use. All that day his mother had moaned and muttered that one single complaint, like a dirge: it was so cold. She would tell him repeatedly that it was the coldest day she had ever known. At last she made him feel her hands. As long as he lived, for the next seventy-five years, he never forgot the horror of them. It was as though her hands had died before the rest of her body. The coldness clung to them like some invisible and terrible sweat. Her fingers seemed to paint his own with some peculiar weak moisture of agony. It struck down to his heart. That decided him to go for the coal.

The coal belonged to Spella Ho, the house, and originally there had been fifteen tons of it. He knew this because, a year before, he had helped to load and cart and stack every lump of it. His father, Matt Shadbolt, had had the job: the last good job he had had and the last good job, now that the house was empty, he would possibly ever get. His father ran a carrier's van, Tuesdays and Thursdays, to Thrapston and St. Neots, both market towns down towards the coast, making up the rest of the week with odd jobs of all sorts, carting lime, coal, offal, dead pigs, leather, tar, even coffins, anything. He was a small man, talkative, smart, a steady and occasionally violent drinker. He had had the coal job out of sympathy: fifteen tons of it to be carted up the three miles from the wharf on the river to Spella Ho and stacked there under the north wall by the gardens, out of sight, in his own time, and almost at his own price. The job took, counting the days they could not work, more than three weeks. At the end of it there had been left a cart-load of sweepings-up, more dust than coal, which the Shadbolts took home and burned. Up to that time Bruno had never seen coal burn.

As he went across the fields to Spella Ho, that afternoon, for the first journey, wearing across his shoulders like a cape the sack he had brought, he was obsessed by one thought and one particular idea. He was not excited. He was obsessed by the simple fact that coal meant warmth and that warmth, in turn, meant life. His mother was cold, ill; how ill he did not know, but his idea was warmth could cure her. He could take enough coal from Spella Ho, every day for the rest of that winter, to keep her hands from that awful coldness, and no one would know. No one would miss it. And it was quite possible that, in spring, as a result, she would get better.

As he went up the slope to the house, under the big elms of the park, keeping close to the iron fence of the covert of young fir, it began to snow. The stillness and the suspense of the afternoon were, in a way, suddenly unlocked, gently and without violence but in some way ominously, and the snow began to spill down like quiet feathers. The land was deserted. Below, on the edge of the road, the Shadbolt place was a scab of stone and thatch. The grey-cream mud-plaster stood out almost bone-coloured, with the darker patches of hazel-ribbing where the mud had flaked away, against the surrounding clutter of the place; dark horse-hovel, muckle, a rough little stack of coarse grass and nettle, rain-flattened, and the wired-in run for the hens.

He had not seen anyone about Spella Ho for weeks, almost months. He looked at the house, more out of habit than anything, every day of his life. For six months, after the bankruptcy of the Colworths, two caretakers, man and wife, had lived in, and he would see the slow dark coal smoke of their one fire. The house had fifty chimneys. They were arranged in four great vault-like blocks above the flat roof-leads, impressive, monumental and, against the dark snow-sky, in some way symbolical of the whole useless emptiness of the place.

At the back of the house, behind the walled-in gardens, was a paddock where, in the heyday of the place, shetlands and hunters had grazed. Beyond, wedged in between the wall and back entrance, was a yard of flagstones. Here the coal was stacked like a black wall. Bruno took the sack off his shoulders and filled it with lumps of coal about the size of turnips. It was simple: so simple that, for one moment, he was uncertain. Then he stood still. He looked about him and listened. He looked at the house; windows and doors and chimneys all had the same empty deadness as the land itself. Nothing happened. It was all dead and silent, as it must have been for a long time and as it would be, perhaps, for a long time to come. He could see here and there, at the windows, tatters of curtains. The sun had blistered the paintwork and now snow was falling on it in calm dead flakes. He took the sack in his hands but he could not lift it, and he set it down again. He took out four or five turnips of coal and then managed it, swinging the sack up over his shoulder. Bending, he walked off. Then, at the gate of the yard, he looked back, fascinated by the enormity of the house shining almost like snow itself against the indigo darkness of the coming snow, and there were two things, then, that were beyond his comprehension. He did not understand how or why any human soul could live in a house so large; or how, having lived in it, anyone could leave it empty and forgotten and unprotected.

He took the coal across the mile of fields to the Shadbolt house and hid it all, except for two lumps, under a heap of coarse hay in the yard. The two lumps he took into the house. The Shadbolts lived, ate and died in one room. His mother was dying in that room. She was sitting in a rocking-chair, rocking herself gently backwards and forwards. He startled her as he came in. She jerked up her head in alarm and he saw her, at that moment, as he had never seen her before and as he never had time to see her again, as an old woman. She was not washed. Her grey uncombed hair hung about her face like an old dog's. She was too weak to smile and she must have been almost too weak to see, because when he put the lumps of coal on the grey remains of the fire, she made no comment. All the time, because he felt she must be tired, he said nothing. The coal was freckled with snow, but it was so dry and the room so cold that it did not melt until after he had blown the fire a bit and the first coal flames had broken out, yellow and orange. His mother watched the flames in a trance. She had eyes like little mottled pebbles. They seemed hard and dead and yet burning. They were characteristic of her whole self: she was so bitterly cold and yet burnt up by sickness; she was dead and yet just alive. After watching the flames for a moment he left her and went out. It was already mid-afternoon and he reckoned on making at least another journey.

He made it in about an hour. He brought back the same quantity of coal, hid it as before, under hay, but in a different place, and took another two lumps into the house. The fire was burning strongly and he could feel the new warmth of the room as he went in. But he was struck most by the change in his mother. She was in a state verging on hysteria.

"Where'd you get that coal? Where'd you get that coal?" she said. "Bruno, where'd you get it?"

"Ah, what coal?" he said.

"You nicked it," she said. "You bin nicking it."

"It's outa that lot we carted up to Spella Ho. Them sweepings up. I bin raking out behind the stable. I found it."

"We used that up."

"Only the slack," he said. "We got a lot left yit. Ten or a dozen lumps."

"You bin nicking it," she said, excited. "You bin nicking it from Spella. You bin nicking it. I seen you. I seen you go up and now I just seen you come back. You bin nicking it and now you're telling lies, top on it."

"Who's telling lies? I never bin near Spella, for weeks."

"You bin up Stella twice sartnoon, I sat here and see ye. You bin nicking that coal from Spella. Now take it back."

He did not say anything. He stood with the two lumps of coal in his hands. The fire was burning beautifully now, with rich heat, the flame-light dancing on the walls and the ceiling. He stood firm, sullen, stocky. His long breeches, of dung-coloured corduroy, were only half length. His legs, squat and very strong, filled them right out. They had been too short for him for more than a year.

"You git every bit of that coal and take it back to Spella. Go on git every bit of it and take it back."

Not speaking, he went over to the fire and put on it the two lumps of coal he was holding.

"Yes and them too! Take 'em off. Take 'em off afore they git alight. Go on take it off."

Sullen, he took the coal from the fire. A small cloud of smoke lingered about each lump like a puff of dust. He set his face, so that its already thick squat lines seemed foreshortened.

"Ah, and you can pouch," she said. "You can pouch but it won't make no difference. Go and git every bit o' that coal and take it back to Spella."

He went out. He hated her and yet at the same time he was afraid of her, and afraid for her. Outside it was snowing hard, out of a darker sky. He found the first lot of coal and uncovered it and put half in the sack. That was all he meant to take. He was about to cover up the rest with hay when, by some chance, he looked at the window, and there she was, watching him. Her face, close against the window and doubly white with the light reflection of snow, looked unearthly. It was a dying face, and for one moment he was scared of it. As he watched, her lips moved, making motions of insistence, telling him to do what he had not done. "Go on," he knew she was saying, "Go on." So, very slowly, he uncovered the rest of the coal and put it, lump by lump, into the sack.

Then, looking up, he saw her still standing there, and he knew she had not finished with him. Her lips were not moving now. She was pointing. He knew then that she must have watched his every movement of his second journey from Spella Ho across the fields and into the yard.

Beaten, he found the second lot of coal and put it all, except one lump, into the sack. He left the lump under the hay, never uncovering it. All the time she watched him. He filled the sack and shook it down and then, knowing that he could never carry it, tied the mouth with a rope, so that he could drag it along. Then at last she seemed satisfied. Yet, even in satisfaction, she still stood there, awful and inexorable in her sick whiteness and the dumb expression of her honesty.

Somehow he could forgive everything else, but not that. It had seemed so right and sensible to get the coal for her; it seemed so idiotic to be taking it back. Honesty was a kind of lunacy. He despised it. His mother was honest; his father was, and always had been, dishonest. His mother was dying; his father was in one of the fifty pubs of St. Neots. Dishonesty, cheating somebody for twopence here, somebody for a sack of potatoes there, a dishonesty that was second nature, kept his father easily alive. A too-inexorable devotion to honesty, a paying back of every crumb and apple and farthing and farthing rush-light that she borrowed, was, he felt, helping to kill his mother. That burned on his mind, like a scar, the difference between good and evil.

The snow was already an inch or two deep and the sack, as he pulled it, made a dark snake track across the white fields to the empty house. It was still not dark, but it was more silent. The snow softened all sound. It was settling now on the roof-leads and on the drooping branches of the big evergreens about the house and on the coal. He dumped the coal and folded his sack and snow began to fall at once on the new coal. He put the rope in his pocket. Standing still, he wondered for a moment what to do. He looked at the house. Whiter than ever now, it also seemed larger. Against and under the falling snow, it had a particular grandeur, no longer forlorn. Then he remembered that he had never seen inside it. He put the sack over his shoulders and walked across the yard and looked in at one of the windows. He could see the white painted panelling of a corridor, then at the end of the corridor an open door, then beyond that the wall of a room and on the wall the reflection of light and snow.

He walked round the house until he found a broken window. He found one on the east side. He knocked in the rest of the glass with his elbow and then put his arm in and unfastened the catch. He climbed in and shut the window behind him.

He was in a small room, though to him it seemed a large room. It was panelled in white wood, with candlesticks like bullocks' silver horns on the two larger walls. The floor, polished once but now misty with disuse and damp, was the colour of coffee: some fine firm wood that took the sound of his footsteps like a tight drum. He went out of that room and found that it opened into another, much larger, but with the same panelling of pure white, the same candlesticks of bullocks' silver horns. Only the floor was different: the same wood but now inlaid, in a central circle and for a width of a yard round the walls, with squares and parallelograms of rose, black and green. The fireplace, still frowsy with dead ash, was enormous, the dogs in the shape of arms that were like negroes' iron fists clenched. He looked round him, twice. He felt he had to be sure that things were actual. So he took his slow second look at everything, fixing with ponderous determination every detail on his mind: the colouring of the floor wood, the fireplace, the dead ash, the gilt crust on the ceiling, the dust bloom on the mantelpiece and the ledges of the windows, the mice turds whiskered with mould, the silk shine, almost like snail-slime, of the pink bell-rope, and finally the snow falling beyond the windows. Then he went out. He went from that room to another. Leaving that, he began to go with the same fixed deliberation into every room downstairs. He had no emotion: no surprise at all. His one idea was to see everything, as though he had been sent to survey it all by a very particular authority. He went down into the kitchens, and he took away with him the sourish smell of grease and damp, of the queer sick smell of the last food that had been cooked there, the ice-cold floor of stone slabbing, the scoured paintwork, the bits of soap still left by the sinks, the dust-thick cobwebs skeined across the great dressers. From there he went, finally, into the hall from which the stairs circled up, serpentine-fashion, with steps of eight feet width and iron balustrades figured with grapes and wheat ears held together by iron ribbons and the great blood-coloured banister of mahogany swinging up out of sight. He stood with one foot on the bottom stair for a long time, looking up. He took in the details with the same sharpness and extreme deliberation as ever. It was getting darker now and it seemed as though he were standing at the bottom of some upturned well, with the ceiling reflecting, like a dome of water, a vague collection of painted cherubim and seraphim, fat as little pigs. He went up, at last, to look at them, taking every step at the same pace, his hand on the banister, feeling its apple-smooth polish. Like that he walked up the whole flight until he could look almost horizontally and not up at the painting on the ceiling. The balustrade ran for a short distance along the great second-floor corridor, and he stood with both hands on it and stared at the painting. Just below it a great double window dropped almost to the floor. It was like an immense glass panel of falling snow, and the cast-up snow light made the cherubim and seraphim seem whiter and plumper and alternately more angelic and more pig-like than ever. He looked at them steadfastly; he saw, without emotion, their little butter-ball bellies, their stiff marble wings. He tried to get the drift of the picture: there was a man, a sort of god, bearded, in anger, and another, helmeted, holding a spear. There were women. The light was failing quickly and the painting was not clear and for some time the women baffled him. He was looking, unconsciously, for skirts, for the big ballooning dresses of the time. Then suddenly he saw that the women were wearing nothing. They stood out strong and nude and white, clear soft symbols of love and flesh. He looked at them for a long time and with his first emotion: un-belief. He stood magnetized by it. And he stood there, staring, trying to get it straight, held by his own emotion and the sight of the three nude females on the ceiling, until he could hardly see.

He walked slowly, at last, along the corridor. One emotion aroused, he began to feel others: wonder, a slow amazement, and above all a curious sense of attachment to the empty desolation of room after room. There was something about the forlorn dampness of them, the dead echo of his own feet in them, the gloom of their constant silence and the occasional sight, beyond their windows, of falling snow, that he liked without being able to explain why he liked it. He missed nothing. He got impressed on his mind every bell-rope, the bits of split moulding where screws had been torn away, the continual mice turds, the dust, the skewed cane-coloured blinds, the bits of spidery curtains, the spiders themselves that he frightened across white or emerald or yellow walls. In one room somebody, a child perhaps, had drawn figures with charcoal on the wall. The unfaded shape of the bed-board was outlined, slightly whiter then the rest of the room, on the painted panelling. The scribbling was just beside it, as though a child, perhaps, had lain in bed and had amused itself, out of boredom or devilry, by drawing the figures of dogs and elephants, a cow, a human face, a woman's most likely, with its night-cap. Beneath these were two lines of writing; but, since he could not read, he did not look at them. It did not even occur to him that they could be read.

There was another room, with a mirror that had never been taken away. It was fixed to the wall, with a spray of three gilt candlesticks on either side. He had a look at himself in it. That was something else he had never seen; a mirror. He saw himself in the too-short cow-muck coloured corduroys; the high lapelled, also too-short jacket, out at elbows; the string-tied kip boots, too small also, which seemed to be looking at him out of their split laceholes. He looked at himself without moving. He was stolid, thick across thighs and shoulders, ugly, in some way impressively ugly. His face, with its thick crude lines, coarse wiry hair, and large mouth, gave him the appearance of a slightly refined monkey. He looked at himself, as he looked at everything else, with solid, unmoved, indefatigable determination. It was a pose so fixed that it became, in time, quite dreamy. That brought out a momentary softness of his large grey eyes, so large and motionless that they were fascinating.

That room was his last. He had seen everything. There was only one thing he wanted to see again and that was the picture of the women on the stairs. Going down, he stopped to look at it. It was almost too dark to see. Yet, looking up, he saw the distinct pale-cream shapes, without detail, of the nude figures. That was enough. They were, a reality, and he went downstairs, satisfied, with an idea that he could and would, some day, come and see them again.

He got out the way he had come, shutting the window carefully behind him, and then out through a little arbour-garden, where tussocks of christmas rose were blooming, almost sea-green against the snow whiteness. The snow was falling heavily and silently on the empty garden. A thick crust of it lay on the long white empty rows of forcing frames, another already on the little olive hedges of box. The gates into the garden were locked. He climbed the twelve-foot wall and walked along it, all fours, monkey-fashion, until he could drop down on the coal on the far side. As he slithered down on the heap, coal and snow clattered down with him. In a few seconds it was silent again: an enormous silence of snow-softened emptiness, of the deserted gardens, of the great house without a soul inside it.

He walked down across the fields without looking back. He walked at a fixed pace, thick legs wide apart, arms swinging low and with a heaviness that, almost mournful, seemed beyond his years. He walked with head down, eyes on the snow.

It was only when he got to within fifty or sixty yards of the Shadbolt place that he looked up. He looked up, then, for one thing: a light. He could not see it. The house was in darkness and he knew, then, what to expect. They would be sitting there in the dark, the whole family, Maria, Walter, Else, George, his mother, waiting for his father. His father was a man who could not bear the darkness.

As he reached the door of the house he looked back. It was still snowing, faster now, and it was more silent. Looking back, he could see Spella Ho. He could see it white and square, above the long slope of white grass, under the whitening trees. He looked at it for about ten seconds. Then he went in. But in that moment, going out of one darkness into another, it occurred to him, for the first time in his life, and with the first impulse of consciousness, that somewhere, between himself and that enormous house, something was wrong.

II

IT was as he had expected; they were sitting in the room, in darkness, waiting for his father.

They were waiting, also, for him. At first, since the fire was almost out, he could see nothing. He could only feel them about him in the cold darkness of the small room. Then, as his eyes grew used to the darkness, he saw the five figures: his mother, still in the rocking chair; the two little boys, George and Walter, sitting on the floor; the two girls, Else, thirteen, and Maria, the eldest, eighteen.

"How is it?" his mother said. "Does it snow all the time?"

"Thick," he said.

His sisters were sitting on boxes. Maria turned her box over, length-wise, so that he could sit with her. He felt the thick coarse serge of her skirt as he sat down.

"Your father ain't in," his mother said.

He did not speak. He was thinking of the one lump of coal still left under the hay. Had she seen it?

"Wheer you bin?" George said.

"Scaring rabbits," he said.

They sat in silence. It was not only cold, but he could feel thin draughts, like wires of ice, skimming across the hairs of his neck. His hair had been cut with a basin, bob-fashion. It hung over his ears in thick rat-tails and it seemed, soon, as though he were wearing icicles of hair. At the windows, three panes out of five, there were sacks, enforced by slats of wood, bits of cardboard, nailed on. A piece of cardboard, loose, flapped and slapped in the wind. He could smell the snow. As he drew in his breath it was like drawing up into his nostrils two needles of ice, and once, as he stretched out his hand, he could feel Maria's hands in her lap, like frogs.

Soon his mother spoke again. Her voice was so feeble now that at first he did not catch what she had said. Then he heard her begin to sing. Then he knew what she had said. He got up. At the same time Maria and the rest got up.

His mother was singing, in a voice tender only because of its extreme weakness, the hymn "Sun of my soul, thou Saviour dear". She sang for a few moments by herself; then Maria joined in, then the children, then himself. Then one by one they fell into line and began to march round his mother, Maria leading, in a small circle in the darkness. All the time she led the singing, and all the time he could hear her hand tapping the beat on the chair-frame.

They sang the hymn through once; then they sang it completely through again, without stopping the march. Then they sang "O for a thousand tongues to sing". They sang that through twice, not stopping the march again. After that they sang two other hymns, repeating them and still not stopping, always beating their feet on the floor in time to the music. Then they went back to "O for a thousand tongues to sing". And gradually, as they sang, Bruno began to feel warmer. The blood trembled in his feet. He could no longer feel the cold cutting like wires of ice across his neck. Like this they went on for almost an hour, singing and marching in the small dark room, his mother leading and beating. Their blood warmer, they got worked up and sang almost, but never quite, with joy.

At the end of an hour, Shadbolt had not come. Mrs. Shadbolt stopped the singing and they stood still, in the strange dark silence, to listen for the sound of cart-wheels. They could hear nothing. Then Bruno went to the door. He stepped out into the snow and was surprised to find, then, how deep it was and how fast it was still coming down. Out in the yard, away from the shelter of the house, he was caught up in a furious vortex of whiteness. He was blinded. Somewhere in the yard the wind was lifting a loose plank, cracking it apart and shut again. It was the only sound.

He went back into the house and shut the door.

"Ain't he coming?" they said.

He said no, he was not coming. His mother rocked for a moment in silence, the creak of the chair like a stiff bough in the wind. Then she began to sing again, this time "O for a faith that will not shrink", and the children, one by one, joined in, Bruno last. Then, as before, they began to march round and round his mother, she leading the singing in her weak soprano that was now weaker than ever. They sang the hymn through, as always, twice. Then they sang another, and then still more, until almost another hour had gone by. At the end of that time his mother suddenly left off. She seemed tired. The children sat about on the floor and the boxes, in a silence that now seemed strange after the singing. Then, as they sat there, inactivity brought on, for Bruno, the stabs of hunger. He had eaten nothing since midday. The meal had been, then, of bread and boiled potatoes: the small potatoes, less than the size of pigeons' eggs, that they called pig-potatoes. They ate them whole, jacket and all. They had four potatoes and a piece of bread each. His mother had nothing.

Now, when he felt hunger, the fact did not mean much. He was not only used to hunger, but inured to it, as a man becomes inured, at last, to a sound that has once disturbed him. The meal of potatoes and bread was good. He knew of nothing, except rabbit, bone-pie, suet lumps, boiled bacon, with which to compare it. And just as he was inured to the fact of hunger he was inured also to the fact that God would, in time, do something to dispel it. This was, and always had been, his mother's creed. They had been brought up to this. God was watching them; God would provide. They must trust God. Bruno did not disbelieve this, but they fed so often on pig-potatoes that he conceived the idea that God, in his mercy, presided over one vast celestial pig-sty, with many fields of potatoes.

After a short time they sang again, this time sitting down. Then his mother said a prayer. Her voice was so low, now, that the children could scarcely hear her. She seemed to be talking into herself, into her flat exhausted breast, as though she felt that God were now extraordinarily near her. She prayed in a voice that was not her own, a voice made delicate and strange by weakness and the special nature of her pleading. She prayed for some time for Shadbolt. "Guide his hand in the darkness, O Lord, and the snow." Then she prayed for the nag. "Guide thou, O Lord our Redeemer, the feet of the horse over them bridges. Keep him on the right path and the straight path, for Christ's sake." Then she prayed, for a time, with growing incoherence, for themselves, for things in general. Then, gradually, she went off into some rambling meditation, no longer coherent, of words and half-words, that had no meaning, except that they were a declaration of her faith. Then she ceased altogether. She sat as though asleep, motionless and noiseless. The children sat quiet too.

Suddenly she fell out of the chair. Except for Bruno, the children sat momentarily paralysed. He sprang up. "Git a light! Light the candle Maria, light the candle!" He lifted his mother up in his arms and was surprised to find how light and frail she was. He seemed to have, suddenly, an enormous strength. He put her back in the chair, unconscious, her eyes wide open. The two little boys were crying and when the candle came, with its tallow stink, he could see the scared white faces of all of them, thin-shadowed, as they bent round her.

"Git a blanket off the bed and wrap her in it," he said

to Maria. "Git some water. Rub her hands." He made for the door.

"Wheer you going?"

"I'll be back."

He went wildly and blindly across the yard. The snow, furious, fell in flat lumps across his eyes. He edged sideways like a crab. He got to the haystack and it was better there, under the shelter of it, and he could see. He tore away the snow from the hay, still like a crab, scrambling to bury itself. Then he pulled away the hay, feeling with both hands for the hardness of the coal. At last he got the coal. He wrapped it clumsily in great handfuls of dry hay and ran into the house.

His mother had not come round. He put the hay in the fireplace and then began to break up a box with his feet, ponderously, making sounds like small gunshots. The hay smoked and he piled the broken wood on it, blowing it with his mouth. Suddenly the flame sprang up, from smoke to hay and then from hay to wood. He broke up the coal with his feet and hands, and then gradually, with extreme care, he put the coal into the flames, watching it, until at last there was a great glow and the room itself seemed alight.

"Git the kettle and put on," he said.

Maria went into the little back wash-house for the kettle. The three children were crying.

"Git the kids to bed. Tek 'em up wi' the candle."

With the children and Maria upstairs, he sat alone with his mother, watching her with one eye and the kettle with the other. The room was full of light. It fell full on his mother's staring immobile face. "Why don't she come round?" he thought. "Why don't she come round?" The predominant emotion in his heart was not fear, but anger. He knew, more subconsciously than not, that she was dying. He had known that all afternoon. He accepted the fact of her dying stoically. But against the reason for her dying he felt, as he bent over her, trying to rouse her to consciousness, an immense unformulated anger that filled his heart like pain. It had no reason in it. It was directed against nothing and yet against everything: against her and her faith and the futility of her faith, the singing, the cold, her honesty, the fact of his having to take back the coal to Spella Ho, against Spella Ho and finally against himself. It was so huge that he could not shape it, so terrific that, for a moment or two, it seemed stronger than the notion of death itself.

At last Maria was down and the kettle was boiling and they were rubbing his mother's hands. They drew her, in the chair, close to the fire, so that her feet were against the flames. The room was full of leaping orange light. Then she came round at last, her eyes splitting darkly open in the dead vacuity of her face, she looked at the flames as though she and they were part, now, of another world. She did not speak. She sat with a queer resigned look of almost happy disbelief.

It was a look that never quite left her. They gave her sips of hot water. Then Maria made a little bread sop in a cup, and she ate that. They tried, all the time, to get her to say something, to ask for something, as though they had everything to offer. She sat dumb. In a little while she sicked up the bread. That seemed to be the last of her strength. They rubbed her hands and held them by the fire and bathed them in the warm water, but it was always the same. It was as though she were already dead.

They sat up all night, he on one side of her, Maria on the other. Shadbolt did not come. The fire went slowly out. About midnight she asked for some more water. It was still warm in the kettle but she could not drink it, and it dribbled like weak spittle out of her lips.

All the time the anger in his heart continued. It remained huge and ungovernable, but as the night went on it formulated itself a little. It began to be directed, clumsily, against his first conscious notions of injustice. What kind of injustice it was, who was responsible for it if anyone was responsible at all, he did not then know. It was still connected somehow with the cold and his mother, with Spella

21

Ho and the coal. It had something to do with the snow and his father. Beyond that it had no reason.

Between midnight and six o'clock he must have fallen asleep. When he roused himself his mother was not in the chair. Maria was asleep, clinging with both hands to the rockers. He got up. His mother was lying on the floor, half-way to the door, as though she had dragged herself up, in the night, to look for Shadbolt again. It was so dark, still, that he stumbled against her dead body.

He woke Maria. They lifted his mother and laid her in a corner of the room and covered her face with the blanket. It was dark and they did not say anything.

He went outside, determined to make another fire. He stepped into a world sunk in snow. It lay in huge crusts on the roof of the house and the hovels and the haystack. He sank into it up to his knees. A low wind was blowing it off the branches of the trees in little bitter dusty clouds. In a world of death, wonderfully silent, it was still dark, but in the east the light was just coming over Spella Ho.

CHAPTER II

Up to that time he had lived an existence in which thought had played very little conscious part at all. He could not read or write. The boundaries of his world made, almost, a straight line. Beyond St. Neots at one end and Northampton at the other there was, for him, and as far as he cared, nothing but space. He had never thought of going beyond these limits. There had been a time when his mother had held him, as a child, and in fun, upside down, asking him if, beyond the upturned horizon, he could see London. He would say yes, and he knew that London was a town, because she told him so.

He had not worked, regularly, at any rate, and for two reasons. First, his father claimed him. Shadbolt was a man of ideals, refreshed daily by the thought that his luck, always out, had turned at last. "You stay where y'are.

Along o' me. Content yourself. We're on a big thing. Bloke in St. Neots." He kept Bruno about the yard, feeding and cleaning the pig, burying the privy refuse, cutting the nettles. He took him with him in the small hooded carrier's cart, to fetch lime from the kilns across the river, offal from slaughter-houses, skins from the tanneries down on the river to be brought up to the little dark thick-windowed shoe-factories in Castor. Castor was a place, then, of six or seven hundred people. The Shadbolt place lay about three miles outside it, to the north-east. Shadbolt had a bad reputation. "What's yourn's your own. What's other folks's is yourn if you can git it."

Bruno had not worked, apart from this, for another reason. He had had jobs, rook-scaring, dockpulling, harvesting, but he had never kept them long. He was not liked. This was something else of which he was aware vaguely, but not consciously. He did not notice it much. What he did notice was that he did not like other people. That, in the end, was the same thing and because of it the jobs never lasted long. Out of work, he made the journeys with Shadbolt to the markets; they picked up eggs and cabbages and fruit and rabbits and sometimes boots in Castor, one day, and delivered them the next. They took passengers, women mostly. The passengers sat on the side seats, facing each other, under the canvas, with their feet on the parcels and sacks of cabbage and boxes. They always talked a lot, shouting question and answer through the front flap to Shadbolt. Shadbolt did not like passengers. Passengers had eyes; passengers talked. He could have got on very well, a lot better, without passengers. It was not that passengers did not pay; it was only that, when they were not there, other things paid better. And where, with the regular twice-a-week run and the regular passengers, business ought to have been good, business for a year or two had been very bad. Passengers heard things and they had now, for a long time, taken either to travelling with their stuff or not sending their stuff at all.

In his turn Bruno did not like passengers either. He

23

made a point of never speaking to them. He sat silent, almost morose, in the front seat of the cart; or, when the time came, he climbed into the cart by the two iron steps at the back, foraged among the clutter of boxes, feet and parcels, got the thing he wanted, and lumbered out. The passengers paid at the end of the journey. He took the money. Standing at the rear door, he waited with outstretched hand. At the age of twenty he could not count the money. Since the passengers did not know this, it never mattered. Shadbolt could count it. All Bruno had to do was to see that nobody missed paying. With that on his mind, he stood at the door like some obdurate monkey, with great pouched lips and half-lowered eyes that seemed lost in primitive reflection. He looked mournfully, impressively ugly, speechless, never moving, never giving the women a hand. It was as though he were not fully aware of life, even of existence. Out of the money Shadbolt gave him a penny.

There were several things he could buy with a penny; a mug of small beer, a ha'penny loaf and cheese, a bun, a meat faggot. One week a woman, getting off the cart, dropped a penny. He put his foot on it, instinctively, and stood with his foot on it, for nearly ten minutes, without a change in his expression of obdurate gloom, until the search was given up. With the twopence he bought something he had wanted to buy for a long time, a pork-pie. He crammed it madly into his mouth as he came out of the shop. Later, he was very sick. Fed for so long on a diet of bread and potatoes, he could not stomach the pastry and the rich white meat.

Shadbolt was a master-mind. By a system of forgetfulness, cajolery, pure cheating, slick talk on doorsteps, he managed, somehow, to get paid, quite often, at both ends of the journey. He managed even to get paid for things he had not brought and for things he had not done. He managed, about once a month, to lose something, a parcel, a dozen eggs. "Goods carried at Owner's Risk *by Order*. M. Shadbolt", he had painted inside the cart. This covered him, and in times of protest the old system of slick cajolery saved him. In times of desperation he pointed to the order printed in the cart. "*By order*. See that? That's legal. If I lost every blamed egg in the cart it wouldn't matter. If I lost every blamed packet it wouldn't matter. *By order* means it's legal. Means I ain't responsible. See? It's the law. Well, I'll git off. See y' some other time. On a deal. Big thing."

Bruno had never had his father's gift for words. He spoke with dull reluctance, with physical difficulty, as though the huge lips could not frame the syllables. It was as though they were a heavy trap-door operated from the brain by some clumsy device of string and pulley. Every now and then the dull mechanism between brain and lips struck and refused to function, leaving him with open speechless mouth. Then suddenly the pulley did work and he spoke. He spoke then with double deliberation, with the intense slow emphasis of someone who has thought for a long time.

In the same way his mind took in the impression of things. It worked with the heavy almost comic clumsiness of some ancient camera. It made a slow sombre exposure and then, as though to make sure, a second. Then, somehow, the impressions were locked away, the same picture, doubly taken, as fixed and permanent as though chiselled into rock. This gave him the air, almost stupid, of looking at everything twice. Because of it, he never forgot anything.

There were two things he could not understand about his father. Both concerned money and both were, in reality, the same thing. With the passengers' fares and the money for the carriage of goods on the long journey, to St. Neots, Shadbolt would have by noon a pocketful of silver, ten shillings, twelve, occasionally fifteen. The pubs, from noon to mid-afternoon, accounted for about a third of that. Bruno sat in the cart in the market square and, sometimes for two hours, watched for doors of pubs to open and let Shadbolt fall out. Shadbolt had a way of going into one pub, going out by the back door and appearing finally from another. Bruno knew that his father, then, always had money left, because Shadbolt could never get up into the cart and Bruno helped him, and all the time Shadbolt had one thought in his mind: his money. "Is me money all right? Av I still got it? Feel. Feel in me pocket. It's there, ain't it? It's there all right?" And Bruno would feel in Shadbolt's pocket for the money. After that they still had to pick up goods, calling at twenty or thirty shops or houses. This took about two hours. In that time Shadbolt sobered a good deal. They ended up, always, at a house by the river. Bruno had it imprinted imperishably on his mind: a small yellow-brick house with lace curtains, number six, in a row of ten. It had a canary in the window in a basket cage. Shadbolt went into this house by the back and stayed, generally, about twenty minutes, but often longer. By the time he came out, in winter time, it would be dark and in the darkness Shadbolt groped about with half-drunken stupidity for the cart, until at last Bruno helped him up again. But by that time, for some reason, the fact of the money no longer concerned Shadbolt. This never troubled Bruno until one day, heaving his father up by the buttocks into the cart, he put his two hands on Shadbolt's two jacket pockets and felt them empty. The problem of his father and that house was one of the few things, before the death of his mother, that he had consciously tried to work out. What happened in that house and what happened to that money?

It was not until after the death of his mother that he found out. He found out by accident. About three weeks after the death of his mother he sat in the cart, in the small dark street, waiting for his father to come out of that house. He sat there for longer than he ever remembered sitting there before, for almost an hour and a half, before he began to wonder what was the matter. It was raining and his hand slipped on the greasy buttocks of the horse as he climbed down from the cart, and the horse shuddered with misery. Round at the back of the house he could see a light shining down on the wet cobbles. He went round to the small back-yard and found the window where the light was. The paper blind was drawn but he could see into the room through the side-slits, and there in the room he could see his father, with a woman. His father had his coat off. On the table stood a big glass oil lamp. The woman was in her chemise and on the table lay a pair of large mauve corsets, terrifically ribbed. She was a large woman, fascinating and dominating to look at, with black pigtails that were handsome but somehow unpleasant. She and Shadbolt were talking. The window was cracked across the bottom pane and after a moment the boy could hear, more or less, what they were saying. After a time he saw that they were going through a repetition of the same argument. "I gotta git back," Shadbolt would say. "I tell y' I gotta git back."

"Why? What for?"

"I got stuff to take. I got the kids."

"Kids. Ain' they old enough to take care o' theirselves? Ain' that gal old enough?"

"Yeh. But then they's the stuff."

"Stuff. I tell y' if y' stop here I can git y' job as coach-man. A smart job. Tips. Free beer. Livery an' everything. All you gotta do is stop here."

"For good?"

"Well, you can't be in two places at once."

"Ah, I dunno," Shadbolt said. "I dunno. I dunno's I couldn't be pulled for it."

"Pulled for what?" she said. "Talk sense. You go back there and what y' got? That rabbit-hutch, the kids, no woman. You go traipsing all over the show for next to nothing. You got the horse to feed. Kids to keep."

"You come here and live."

"What? Me?"

"We can git married. We can smarten the place up."

"Talk sense."

Shadbolt stood silent, in a maze, trying to make a decision. Suddenly the woman put her large white arms on Shadbolt's shoulders and pressed her enormous bust up to him. She took the end of one of her pig-tails in her hand and rubbed it softly across his skinny neck, like a brush. Shadbolt seemed bewitched. "Well, stop one night," she said. "Stop just for one night. Matt. Duckie. Stop like you did that night it snowed."

At the window the words had for a moment no effect on Bruno. He stood staring and listening, unmoved, as though they had not been spoken. Then the woman did almost the only thing which, at that moment, could have moved or impressed him. She repeated what she had already said.

"Go on," she said, "stop like you did that night it snowed."

The repetition of the words struck right down into Bruno's consciousness. He made a decision before he felt there was any need for a decision. He walked straight out of the backyard into the street and got up into the cart. He took the wet reins in his hands and drove off. He drove the twenty miles home, sitting with his long arms across his knees, his eyes fixed on the greasy lamp-yellow frame of the horse and beyond them on the solid darkness and rain. He sat with tremendously solid, apparently emotionless immobility. All his emotions were really part of one: hatred. But where he had once felt the emotion vaguely, against nothing, he now felt it solidly, with direct force, against his father. He felt it all at once to be part of his life. It was somehow linked up with his anger at the cold, his mother's rigid honesty and with her death. With it he felt the peculiar necessity of obtaining, against somebody or something, some kind of revenge. He did not then understand it. It was simply there, a force and a reality, and driving home alone, in the darkness and the rain, he was fully aware of it for the first time.

He never saw his father again for more than twenty years.

CHAPTER III

IT was the first important decision of his life. It was responsible for a problem. "How are we gonna git through?" Maria said. "Bruno, how can we git through?" She was frightened. She saw, before them, a hard time. To him it was immaterial. Things had been so bad that they could, he felt, hardly be worse. Slowly, solidly, he evolved plans. "I'll kip on wi' the Thrapston round. I can do what he done. And 'stead o' St. Neots I'll go Northampton. That ain't so fur, and it ought to be better." At the back of his mind was a single thought. It generated the power necessary for the initiative he had to take. It drove him out of apathy into resolution. His father had another woman. For a long time, possibly for years, his father had been going to the house with the canary in the front-room window. He had gone in with money and had come out without it. The woman's whole physical life, her great white arms, her huge bust, her actual voluptuousness, had been built up and sustained by Shadbolt's money. It had been built up out of the life that should have been his, Bruno's. That was wrong; somehow he had to set it right. Not now, perhaps. Not for ten years; perhaps not even for twenty years. But it would come.

"I'll go Northampton Wednesdays and Saturdays," he said, "for a start."

So, on the first Tuesday, he made a tour of Castor, with the cart. He had wanted to paint up on its cover, "Northampton market: Wednesdays and Saturdays," but neither he nor Maria could form a letter. He went to every shop and house in Castor, telling how he would start, in the morning, on the first of the regular runs to Northampton, and had any one anything to send and did anyone want to go? That solid, systematic tour took him till late afternoon. At the end of it he had nothing to show except a box of duck eggs and some tobacco for a woman lying in the infirmary, to be delivered with a message, "Tom's well and Hannah's expecting in July." People were suspicious. Where was his father? What was the idea? He went back to the Shadbolt place, to the scraggy tumbled down hovel and the miserable damp room, in despair. He stabled the horse, gave it a handful of the coarse pulled-out hay from the stack and then stood in the yard, trying to think. To go all that way, fifteen miles and back, for one parcel, for threepence, for nothing: where was the good of it? Yet he knew he must go. He had taken his threepence carriage money and with it he had bought a loaf and a quarter of red cheese. That act had finished him.

Thinking, he stood looking at Spella Ho, huge, white, in some way desolate as ever, with its dead chimneys lifted above the wintry trees. And suddenly, looking at the chimneys, he thought of something else: the coal.

Darkness was already falling and after waiting for a little while he found a sack and, as he had done on the day before his mother's death, went across the fields to the house. In his mind was almost precisely the same thought as on that day; but where he had then been obsessed by the thought that coal meant warmth, he was now obsessed by the thought that coal meant money. He must have money. There was a gap in his life and it had, somehow, to be filled up. Money would fill it; the coal would make money. He saw nothing wrong in that. If his father could go into the house with the canary and give away the money that ought, by right, to have been his mother's and Maria's and his own, then he could go to Spella Ho and take the coal, and one act would do something to balance the other.

All about Spella Ho it was quiet again in the stormy winter air. As before, he filled the sack with coal, his mind slightly on edge at first, then quite calm. It was almost dark. The enormous shell of the house towered up sepulchrally among the still bare trees. Nothing stirred at all. He dragged back the coal across the dark fields and hid it under the cart seats, ready for morning. Then he found another sack and went back to Spella Ho and filled it and dragged it home, like the first, in the darkness. It began to rain as he came home and he felt secure.

It was still dark when he drove off next morning. He drove without the cart-lamps, not seeing a soul. He sat with the same fixed immobility as ever, one thought in his mind: to get rid of the coal, to make money. It was raining slightly. As it got lighter he could see the sullen fields sloping away to the river. He could see the steel ridges of the ploughed land, and here and there some park wall, built of stone almost orange with iron. He rested the horse outside Northampton and gave it a feed of hay from the nosebag. It was about nine o'clock. He drove on in the rain to the infirmary.

He went into the stone building. He found the old woman from Castor in a room with four other patients. She lay in a small hospital bed, propped up, with her nightcap on, looking like a white cockatoo. She was in a temper. He set the box of tobacco and duck eggs on the bed and said: "Tom's all right and Hannah's expecting in July and here's the bacca and the duck eggs."

"Who the bleedin' hell said anything about duck eggs?" she bawled at him.

"They did. They sent 'em."

"Well, you take 'em back! I never said anything about duck eggs. It's that damn fool of a gal o'theirn. She's deaf. I said for Jesus Christ's sake send me some bacca and a new pair o' legs. *Legs!* Not eggs! I don' want the damn duck eggs! They taste sat-on to me! Take 'em back."

"All right," he said.

He took the lump of tobacco out of the box and put the box of eggs under his arm and began to walk out. She called him back.

"Here!"

He went back and stood by her. She was a furious little woman, grizzled and tough and shrill as an old bird.

"What?" he said.

"You never washed yourself this morning," she said.

He stood silent.

"And I'll tell ye' another thing. You never had a mossel o' breakfast."

He still had nothing to say. She said: "You take and git yourself a wash and look a bit decent. You look like some blamed hooligan. And take them damn duck eggs too and sell 'em or do summat to git yourself some vittle. And what's that whip in your hand?"

"It's a horse whip. I drove in from Castor."

"You'd feel it round your arse," she said, "if you were one of mine. Coming out mucky. You can't help your face, but you can keep it clean. You'll git a lot further if you're clean."

That was all she had to say. He went out of the hospital. He got up into the cart and drove on into the town. He was puzzled. What was this about keeping clean? He looked at his hands. The skin was like tree bark, deeply fissured with marks of dirt that had bitten in until they were like old scars. His nails were like claws, long and tough, split and broken, with semi-circles of old dirt blacker than the smears of coal on the flesh. He turned his hands over, as he drove, and looked at them, first one and then another, and then both together. They were hands of extraordinary ugliness and size, with thick crude fingers. They sprang from powerful short wrists. He pushed back his sleeve. His arm was stained by old rivulets of sweat from the elbow downwards.

He took the cart and put it into a dead-end street behind the market place. He took the box of eggs and walked round the market. Eggs were scarce.

"How much are eggs making, missus?" he said to a woman on a stall.

"More'n folks can afford."

"Give me a shilling for these 'ere duck eggs," he said.

"How many?"

"Eight," he said. "They're good eggs."

"You say so. How do I know they ain't month old an' more?"

"They're good eggs, I tell you," he said. "I fetched 'em in yesterday."

"Sixpence," she said. "Folks ain't gone on duck eggs."

He walked away. He had set his mind on a shilling. A shilling was life. He would get a shilling or nothing. He took the duck eggs back to the cart. Supposing he washed? He thought about it for a moment; then he went to a house and asked the woman who answered his knock for a bucket of water for the horse. She gave him the water and he lifted the bucket into the cart and there, under cover of the canvas, tried to wash himself. Without soap, the water was harsh on his arms and would not soften. It moistened the coal dust so that, shortly, the water was black. He washed his face a little and then dried himself with a piece of sacking.

He went back to the market. The eggs were a windfall: he had to sell them. But he had his mind set on a shilling: a shilling or nothing. "How much y' give me for these 'ere duck eggs, missus?" he said to a woman on a poultry stall.

"Don't you missus me," she said.

"How much you give me?" he said. "Eight eggs."

"A penny apiece. Eightpence."

"Shillin' I want."

"Want on," she said. "That's all."

He walked off. A shilling or nothing. He found a woman sitting with her egg-baskets by herself, away from the market, on the edge of the street.

"A shillin' for these 'ere eggs," he said.

She looked up at him, with large shrewd eyes. "You'd look better," she said, "if you washed yourself once in a while."

"I jist washed," he said, astounded.

"It musta bin a lick an' a promise."

"I jist washed, I tell y'," he said.

"What with? A hund'ed o' coal?"

He stared at her, solidly. "Coal?" he said. "You don' wanna a hund'ed o' coal, do you?"

"What else do you sell?" she said. "Pigeon milk?"

"I gotta hund'ed o' coal I could sell y'."

"Where? In y' wescit pocket?"

He told her about it: how it was in a sack, in the cart, how he would bring it. She said, "How much?" still derisive.

"A shillin'."

"What?"

"That's cheap," he said, stubborn.

She could only stare at him, in wonder at coal so cheap. "A shillin?" she cried, after a moment.

"A shillin' for the coal. Shillin' for th' eggs."

"There ain' no difference, is there?" she said. "A hund' ed o' coal and eight duck eggs. There ain' no difference. A shillin'."

"I never said nothing about difference. I said a shillin'."

Astonished, she bought. He was to bring the duck eggs to her there, in the market. He was to take the coal to an address she gave. The house would be locked but there was a woman, next door, who would let him in to the cellar. He was to ask for Mrs. White. She was a widow.

"You come in here every week?" the egg-woman said.

"Yeh."

"You bring me a hund'ed o' coal at that price every week?"

"Yeh. I'll bring it."

"All right. You bring it."

She gave him a florin. He looked at it. "What's this?" he said. "This ain't two shillin'."

"What ain't? That's a two-shillin' bit."

He looked at it vaguely, at the Queen's head, shining silver. It meant nothing to him. It was one coin. Somehow he had fixed in his mind that he must have two. Two shillings, two coins. He gave it back to the woman. "Take it back," he said. "Give me the proper money."

"Proper?"

"I want two shillin's."

"That's two shillings, ain't it?"

"I want a shillin' for the coal and a shillin' for th' eggs. A shillin' for each."

In despair, she gave up. She took back the florin and gave him two shillings, separately. He was satisfied. He moved to go. "And while you're down there," she said, "go into my copper-house and find a mite o' soap and git some o' your muck off. And wash your eyes out."

He found the address: a two-storied house in a plain smoke-bricked row. He swung the coal out of the cart on his back and dumped it against the wall while he knocked at the widow's house for the key next door. He waited a moment and then the woman came and he was slightly astonished. She was a woman of less than forty. She was decent, with pinned-up brown hair and a clean sprigged pinafore. She was nice to look at, a real town woman, easy and just a little flash, with the blue cameo brooch on her neck and her polished button-boots.

He told her about the coal and the key. She went into the house to fetch the key then unlocked the next door and took him through the passage and the kitchen to the coal-house behind. He dumped the coal and then he told her about the wash-house. "She said I could wash. But I got another hund'ed o' coal to git rid of, and it don't seem worth it."

"In the cart?" she said.

"Ah," he said, "A shillin' a hund'ed."

"A what?"

He said it again. She, too, like the woman in the market, could not believe it. "An' good coal," he said, as though she needed encouragement.

"Bring it in," she said. "Bring it in through my place. I'll have it."

So he took the coal through her passage and dumped it, as before, into the coal-house, in the back yard. The woman said, "Come in, while I find the money. Step on the mat." He stood in the small, neat whitewashed kitchen, on the doormat, while she found her money. The money was in a green teapot, in a cupboard. The woman gave him a florin. It still did not mean anything to him and he put it in his pocket.

"Here," she said.

"What?"

"The two shillin'. The change. You said a shillin'."

He took the florin out of his pocket. "Yeh. A shillin'. That's right." He was vaguely aware of something wrong, but he did not understand what.

"I want a shilling change," she said.

He took the two separate shillings out of his pocket and held them in his hand. The woman took one. He let her take it, dumb, not understanding. She said, "How often are you going to have this coal?"

"I can git it every week," he said.

"Well, you bring me a hundred every week until the winter's over."

"Yeh. I will."

"Every Wednesday?"

"Yeh. Every Wednesday."

"You can come and wash in my kitchen," she said, "if you like. Wash at the sink."

She set a bucket of water for him in the sink, and a lump of soap. He put his hands in the water and lathered the soap a little. She said, "Have a strip wash. Take your coat off."

Slowly he took his coat off. There was something here that he had not met before. He did not understand it: the fact of the woman asking him in, asking him to wash, to take his coat off. His conception of life did not include it.

Then, as he took off his coat, the woman gave a small cry of horror. It was directed against his shirt. The shirt was an old one of his father's. It hung on him like a rag, sleeves ripped up, back torn up from the tail. He had an old pair of leather braces on, fixed to his trouser-tops with nails, and where the leather had crossed the shirt sweat and rain had brought out a stain the colour of cow-dung.

"This the best shirt you've got?" she said.

"Yeh."

"You don't mean it's the only one you've got?"

"Yeh."

"Take it off," she said.

He undid his braces and drew the shirt over his head. He had a body of mature thickness, the hair black and thick already on his chest and armpits and navel, and the woman, having had up to that moment the notion that he was a boy, seemed surprised by it. "Now git washed," she said, quickly.

She went out of the kitchen and he heard her feet above him, upstairs. She came down with a blue and white flannel shirt in her hand.

"How old are you?" she said.

"Twenty."

"You're more than twenty," she said.

"No."

She looked at his thick body, its black hairiness, the dirty rivulets of old sweat across the neck and arms. She stood as though slightly fascinated by the ugliness of it. She said: "Ah, go on. You're more than twenty."

"Twenty-one this year. This October."

"Ah, well!" He was telling the truth and it was clear she did not believe him. "How you come to be coal-hawking?"

"Well, it's my old man's trade, by rights. We git coal down in big lots, down the river. Then hawk it. This is the fust time I ever bin here."

She believed him. Though it was unnecessary, he covered up the lie with a slice of truth, quickly. "I just lost my mother. Things ain't very grand." That explained the shirt.

It also reminded her of the other shirt. She held it out. "It's a shirt of my husband's," she said. "I got no more use for it." She stood holding it; then she saw that, because of his wet hands, he could not take it. So she put it down on a chair, hanging it over the back, so that the empty arms hung loose. It looked like the limp ghost of the man who had worn it. Bruno struggled to soap his neck, and, as she finished laying out the shirt, she saw his difficulty.

"Here, let me do that," she said. "It wouldn't be the first time I'd done it for a man."

She took the soap from him and got a piece of soft flannel and rubbed the soap on it. She began to rub his neck and back, and he was conscious of the pleasure of an altogether new sensation; it came from the soft rubbing of her hands on him, her proximity, the unexpected intimacy of the situation. He rested his hands on the sink, bending his back. She drew the flannel down his spine, down to the lip of his trousers. His mental response to it was slow, a little uncomprehending. His physical response was abrupt: so abrupt that it produced in him a sudden anxious and yet weak rigidity of all his muscles. His stomach turned over. He clenched his hands in the sink while his body went through phases of passion and weakness and his mind through a dull revolution of thought in an effort to understand what was happening.

"Turn round," the woman said. "While I've got the flannel in my hands I may as well soap the front as well as the back. Make a good job of it."

"Ah."

"Your face'll look a lot prettier after a mite o' soap and water. I used to say that to my chap. He used to come home like this."

"What did he do?"

"He was a furnace-worker. Iron furnaces. He got killed there. His clothes were burnt right off of his body."

She spoke quietly and he was sorry for her. She had clear blue eyes and they were still young. She got the towel and began to dry him, with deliberate gentleness. She said, "I got trousers and suits of his. Nice suits. He earned good money. He was particular. No pop-shop stuff for him." She felt the tops of his dirty too-short corduroys.

"You're growing out of your trousers," she said. "You

38

finish drying yourself. I'll see if I can find you a better pair upstairs."

Two minutes later she called him. She told him to come up, that it was all right. Never mind his boots.

He went upstairs as he was, in his trousers, naked above them. He felt curiously fresh, vigorous. She had some clothes spread out on the patchwork counterpane of the bed. "I thought you could fit a pair on," she said. "I'd give you a pair and be glad to if they'd fit."

She took a pair of trousers and hung them down from his waist. She touched him. She took another pair and hung them down and she touched him again. Suddenly he felt an explosion of passion inside himself: a terrific ejection of something blowing him sky-high. He seized hold of her with strength that surprised himself. She put up no resistance and they lay together on the bed. Even when it was all over, he felt victorious. His conquest of her, the first woman he had ever known, smashed something inside himself to bits and yet left him extraordinarily strong, ready for new worlds. The woman with her gifts of clothes and her gentleness and her still young eyes meant for some reason very little to him. It was a symbolical conquest: woman. He felt himself hurled, like some white-hot trajectory, into manhood.

He remained in that house, with the woman, almost all morning, eating her food, talking. She gave him a meal of steaming boiled beef, with carrots and bread and potatoes, and large cups of cheap black coffee. While he was eating she cleaned his boots for him with spit-blacking, until they shone dully, like lead. He changed into the new trousers: they were of heavy tough broadcloth, and she was delighted because he looked so smart. He ate as much of the boiled beef as he could cram into himself. She laughed because he ate so well. "As though," she said, "you never had a mite in your life." She laughed with her eyes, with delight that was genuine, and with fire. But it was not her laugh, or her eyes, or the delight she felt that impressed him, but the meal, the beef, the hot vegetables, the coffee, the fact that she had given it him, the fact that she had been prepared to pay, and had paid generously, for that experience in the bedroom, and the fact, that, on top of it all, she begged him to go back, the following week, and take what she offered again.

And that night, as he drove back to Castor in the mizzling winter rain, with the lamps shining dull orange on the back of the horse, he brought reason to bear for the first time on the actions of his life, of that day in particular. Baffled, he tried to sort out the happenings of the day as a man sorts out dominoes, trying to make them fit. Money, profit, the act of washing, the boiled beef, the bedroom, the sweet smell of the counterpane, the undressed woman, the act of love: somehow they were mixed up into a disorder that he felt would, if he could think long enough, give up a meaning. He thought about it solidly, with the old immobile deliberation, but stubbornly, trying hard to find, as it were, the numbers that would fit. For a long time he felt no solution. He knew that somehow the money, the food, the pleasure and the woman were bound up together, that they were, perhaps, responsible for each other, but he could not see how. Then suddenly he saw it from another angle. The whole of the happenings of that day had been brought about by women. Up to that time he had not thought about women. Now suddenly he saw that they might be the key to a new kind of life: a life of pleasure, boiled beef, hot steaming vegetables, money, free clothes, passion itself. Why had that woman done so much for him? How was it she would not believe him when he told the truth and yet believed him when he told her a lie? Would another woman be like that? Would any woman take that amount of interest in him, be so generous, lift her breasts up to him with that same ease of passion and generosity, give him boiled beef and the invitation to come again? Had all of life, the life of woman, that perplexity and simplicity? He felt the clean broadcloth of his new trousers, remembered the taste of the beef, the feeling of the woman's body, and wondered.

All this was to assume a great importance in his life. Meanwhile what was most important of all was that now, for the first time, he had money. It had already occurred to him that coal meant warmth, but it was now proved that coal meant money. He saw that money and women were the predominant features of that day, but he felt also that somehow they were bound up with each other. They were the complementary parts of a new power. Somehow it might be possible to use that power: quite how, he did not know. His notions of money were amazingly limited. The day had yielded three shillings. If every day yielded as much he knew that, in a week, he would have money worth having; but exactly, how much he did not know.

He told Maria of the duck eggs; he told her he had got the trousers, second-hand, for a shilling. Maria had obtained day-work at a farmhouse in Castor. She got out of bed just after three o'clock every morning, walked in the darkness down to Castor and there proceeded to prepare bread-and-milk for thirteen men. She then worked all day, from one darkness to another, scouring dairy pans, scrubbing floors, peeling potatoes, washing, ironing, emptying the slops. For that she got her food and four shillings. Every three or four days she brought home a basin of beef or pork dripping which the children and Bruno lapped up like dogs. Sometimes she saved a little milk from going to the pigs and brought it home in a beer bottle. She was a hard-working, docile, lovable girl, honest like her mother, and thought it good, decent work with decent wages. Soon after Mrs. Shadbolt's death she came home and said that if Else was willing she too could have work at the farm: the same hours, same work, same food, but, since Else was only thirteen, for one-and-sixpence a week. Else took the job. That brought the wages of the Shadbolt household up to five-and-six, plus Bruno. The first week of the new round Bruno earned nine-and-six. He worked three days, not counting the two evenings he slid up to Spella Ho for coal. So that, working half the time, half as hard, he earned almost twice as much as the two girls together. And where, before his mother's death, he would not have noticed such a fact at all, he was now profoundly impressed by it. Either women were fools, or he himself was lucky. It did not occur to him that half the money was dishonest; it only occurred to him that it was easy. He had been brought up to think along the iron lines of his mother's doctrine; poor but proud, proud but humble, but somehow the freer ideas of his father threw him out of line. He had been brought up by his mother to believe that it was the duty of the poor, like themselves, to work, sleep, eat if they could and say nothing; but against that he had the example of his father, who got drunk three times a week, slid things up his sleeve whenever he got the chance, and kept another woman. His father had enjoyed life. Bruno saw that now. His mother had died, as he now saw it, of an incurable cancer of honesty. Another thing he had been brought up to believe was that work and money were as component as night and day; that there was and could be no money without work, though there might be, and often was, work without money. But was it true? If it was true, how was it that the Colworths had, at Spella Ho, lived a life of fatness and sweetness, with twenty or thirty or even more servants, without one of them ever lifting a finger? Had money, for them, dropped out of the sky? If it was true that there was no money without work, it was also true, as he saw by Spella Ho, that there was such a thing as luxury without work. The luxury of Spella Ho was imprinted firmly on his mind by reason of two things: the splendour of the staircase, with the great picture of the cherubim and seraphim and the naked women painted on the ceiling above, a picture that was to impress him as long as ever he lived; and by an earlier experience, the fetching of free soup from the back door of the house and of seeing that soup, rich with a golden swim of grease and lumps of meat, doled and slopped out by two kitchen-maids, with iron ladles, from a forty-gallon copper, as though it were no better than pig-swill.

He saw in Spella Ho an unattainable ideal, a miracle that had been worked without sweat. It fascinated him. For several weeks he continued to go up, under cover of darkness, to steal two or three hundred weights of coal, always in secret, selling the coal later, in Northampton, at the old absurd price of a shilling with the addition in the case of the widow, of a meal of hot meat and the pleasure of the bedroom. The house never failed to fascinate him: the enormity of it, the emptiness, the bareness of the gardens, the strange air of faded luxury. Occasionally he would go up just before darkness fell, and walk round it, and look in at the windows, and hear the starlings flocking explosively in the silence of the cedars and down the long avenues of limes, and feel inside himself some inexplicable, not fully alive notion of envy; and once he climbed inside again, walking from room to room in the falling darkness, staring at the staircase and feeling the apple-polish of the great upward bow of the mahogany balustrade, until envy turned to mystification, and he was led to try and straighten it all out for himself: the problem of work and women, work and money, luxury and poverty, of the things that were beginning and were to go on shaping his life for a long time.

Then, in the early spring of 1873, he had a narrow escape.

CHAPTER IV

HE was visiting Spella Ho, at that time, three or four evenings each week, fetching the coal. It did not occur to him that it was a crazy undertaking, that it was wrong, or that he might be found out. The days were lengthening and the evenings getting lighter and colder and often it was six or seven o'clock before he dare attempt anything. Then, one evening, he went up earlier than usual and suddenly, as he crouched there on his knees filling the sack with coal, a man walked into the courtyard.

Bruno lay flat on the coal, his heart going fast. The man came and stood in the centre of the yard and stared about him. He was well-dressed. He stared about him for a moment and then pulled a book and pencil out of his pocket and wrote something down. Then he stood back and looked at the house and then wrote again. Then he looked at the coal. Bruno lay stiff, face hidden, in a corner under the wall. He heard the man walk round the other side of the coal-heap and then stop. Bruno put his hand on a piece of coal about the size of a potato, and clenched it, ready to throw. The man stood still for a long time. He was continually coughing. Then slowly he began to walk away. He stood in the courtyard and coughed into his hand once or twice and then stooped through the gate into the garden, and disappeared.

That was the last time Bruno ever went to Spella Ho for coal. It was a severe blow. Coal was money; money was everything. He was puzzled as to what to do. Then, three days later, something else happened.

He used to stop at Orlingford, five miles from Castor, and pick up parcels at a small general stores by the post office. One morning, just as he was jerking the reins to go, a small fiery man ran out of the post office, waving an umbrella.

"Hey! Northampton?"

"Whoa. Yeh."

"Then why the hell don't you have it up on the cart? Give us a hand."

The small man got up into the driving seat. As he climbed up something dropped out of his mouth.

"Hey, wait a minute."

He climbed down out of the cart. In the mud lay a cough-drop, smooth-sucked. He picked it up. He rubbed it on his sleeve and put it into his mouth.

He got up into the cart and Bruno drove on.

"What say your name is?"

"Shadbolt."

"Shadbolt. Whyn't you have it painted up?"

"I can't write."

"You can't what? You can't *what?*"

The little man snapped and chattered in wonder. He kept baring his small yellow teeth like a ferret. He could not believe it.

"You mean to tell me you can't write? How the hell do ye expect to do business if you can't write?"

Business? A new word. Bruno did not answer.

"You want your name painted up. Shadbolt. Big letters. 'Shadbolt: Carrier from —' Where d'ye carry from?"

"Castor."

" 'Carrier from Castor to Northampton.' Big letters. Both sides the van. Bigger the better."

"All very well for you to talk, mister."

"Talk? I'm not talking. I'm telling you. What the hell's the use o' travelling with a turn-out like this, with nothing on it? How d'ye expect folks to know where you're going? You're in business. You gotta be fly."

Bruno sat silent, arrested. What was this business? Why should his name mean so much?

"How many people you reckon to take every week?"

"Two or three."

"There y'are. Two or three. Terrible. How many's this cart hold? A dozen? What I thought. Then why don't you have a dozen? Folks don't know, that's why. You ain't told 'em."

"I told everybody in Castor."

"How? Word o' mouth? Advertisement?"

Advertisement? Another word he did not know. Bruno sat puzzled.

"You never had nothing printed? No bills?"

"Printed?"

"There y'are! What I thought." Triumphantly; with a great air of mystification. "What I thought. You ain't awake. You ain't *born.*"

All through the journey the little man elaborated that theme: how Bruno was not yet awake, not born; how he ought to be aware, now, that he was in business; how he ought to expand that business, advertise, make folks travel; how he ought to have the name Shadbolt on the lips of the public. How else was he to get known, to do anything, to make money? The little man got worked up, ecstatic, bouncing about on the seat. Money. That was it. Money.

"Yeh," Bruno said, "that's it. Money."

"You mean that's your trouble? No money?"

"Well —"

"I know. I know. You're a little man. You got no capital. You're making a start." Then suddenly: "How much d'you want?"

"Me?"

"Yes, you. You want money, don't you? You want your name painted up, bills printed. How much d'you want? Name your figure. Same interest on all amounts."

Business, advertisement, capital, and now interest. They were terms which to Bruno meant nothing at all. What was this? A trick? The pulley operating his brain seemed to stick, so that suddenly he could not think. The little man rattled on:

"Will a couple o' pounds do you? Repay monthly. Shilling in the pound interest. You'll eat that. Won't know you're paying it. In a couple o' weeks you'll be carrying twenty or thirty people backwards and forwards. Easy. What d'you charge? Shilling? There's twenty or thirty shillings afore you can wink. In six months you'll be so smart you won't know yourself. New horse. Smart van. Look at that nag now. Look at it. Terrible. How the hell you think folks are going to travel behind a nag like that? Nothing but bone and guts."

The question of money settled, it came to a question of the printing. He, the little man, whose name was Coutts, knew of a place there, in Northampton, where printing was good and cheap. He had influence there. He could get a discount. He took a pencil from his pocket and a small rentcollector's notebook. "You want something like this." He wrote: "Shadbolt *the* Carrier. Castor - Orlingford - Northampton. And return. Twice weekly. Wednesdays and

Saturdays. Single 1/-, Return 1/9. All classes of goods carried. Personal supervision. Prompt attention. Cheap rates. Leave 'The Green Dragon', Castor, 8 a. m." He read it aloud.

Bruno was impressed, but at the same time slightly dubious. He tried to say something, but Coutts rattled on:

"I know what you're thinking. You want to know where the money is, don't you? If it's all above board? Eh? That it? Ah! I know. Well, listen. Where d'you eat? Midday? Anywhere? Never mind. You come along with me, to-day, and have some dinner at Porter's eating house, just behind the market there. Half-past twelve. All you got to do is sign a paper."

So he went along to Porter's eating house, at half-past twelve, and there Coutts was sitting at a scrubbed deal table, eating fried onions. He ordered fried onions for Bruno. "Fourpence," he said. "But I get 'em for three-pence. I'm a regular. I'll get 'em same price for you."

The brown delicious fried onions came on a thick white plate. Bruno shovelled them up and into his mouth with a knife. Coutts, almost finished, wiped his plate with a piece of bread.

"Good?" he said. "Ah, give me fried onions afore anything. Ease the bowels, free the kidneys, break the wind." He belched. "Manners."

He took a sheet of paper from his pocket. "Well, here you are. All you got to do is sign this. You better just read it first. Never put your name to anything without reading it." He gave the paper to Bruno.

"I can't read," Bruno said.

"Eh? Ah! I forgot. Clean forgot. Well, I'll read it." He put on a pair of steel-rimmed spectacles, held the paper out. "All it says is this — it's just to cover you — it says, 'I, Bruno Shadbolt, hereby agree to pay the sum of two shillings per month interest on the sum of two pounds loaned to me by Amos Coutts until such time as capital sum is repaid, delivered under my hand: pro. tem.' All you got to do is sign," Coutts said.

"When do I git the dough?"

"Now! No waiting. That's what it says. Pro. tem. On time. No waiting. All you got to do is sign."

Coutts had pen and ink on the table. Bruno picked up the pen and made a cross at the foot of the paper. Coutts wrote B. Shadbolt by the side of the cross. Then he blew on the paper and put it in his pocket.

"Well, that's that. Another plate o' fried onions? Then we'll go to see the printer."

Bruno had another plate of fried onions, under the impression, for some reason, that Coutts would be paying for it. But towards the end of the meal Coutts pulled some money out of his pocket, counted it and gave Bruno a sovereign, and then nineteen-and-fourpence in silver and coppers. "That's the money," he said. "I've taken the onions out."

Bruno wiped his plate with his bread and then put the money in his pocket. Coutts called the waiter and paid for the onions.

"Three plates, ninepence," the waiter said. Coutts gave him the ninepence.

They went out. As they walked along to see the printer Coutts said: "I'll give you a bit of advice. Never pay what folks ask. See? Take the printer. He'll ask for a pound. Sure to. Leave it to me and I'll get it done for eighteen shillings. Never pay what folks ask. That's a mug's game."

All that Coutts said, owing to his habit of repeating almost everything, was deeply impressed on Bruno. He never forgot that first meeting with Coutts: the money, the signing of the paper, the fried onions and later the dingy little printing-house, with its presses and inks and ink-smells, where they arranged for the leaflets to be printed. He never even forgot its details: how much the onions cost, how much the printing was to cost.

At first the printing was to cost twenty-five shillings. Coutts protested. He and the printer held a small argument. Then Coutts suggested that things could be better

48

settled perhaps, in private, and they went into a small office, leaving Bruno outside. When they came out, Coutts said, "It's like this. The printer don't know you. If you can put the money down he'll do it for twenty-two and six. Five hundred leaflets."

Bruno took some money out of his pocket. He made a pretence of counting it, but the florins and half crowns and shillings had no meaning for him at all. Suddenly Coutts saw this. "Let me count it. You're all fingers and thumbs," he said. He counted out twenty-five shillings and gave the printer twenty-two and six. The printer promised the leaflets for Saturday morning. Coutts and Bruno went out into the street.

Bruno was impressed but puzzled by Coutts. What was Coutts? What did he do for a living?

"Me?" Coutts said. "I got property. I speculate. I got interests all over the country."

Property? Speculation? The words had only the vaguest meaning for him. There was something here, in Coutts, in Coutts's manner of getting a living, that he could not bottom. He tried to look as if he understood. Coutts shook hands.

"Well, I shall see you. I'm always about. I'll see you once a month at least. And don't forget to get your name painted up."

He began to jog away on little frisky legs. Suddenly he turned back.

"Half a minute. Something else. I been looking at you. You'd go a lot farther if you smartened up a bit. Get yourself a shave or else grow a beard, one or the other. You'll get a shave for twopence at Wilson's, round the corner. I go there. He does me for a penny. You tell him you know me."

In the barber's chair Bruno sat thinking it out. Interest, speculation, capital, discount, property: the words stood up before him, making the structure of a new world. It was a world to which he felt drawn, suddenly, by a growing power not yet fully realized. He felt that he had to know more about that world, that there were things in it which he had to conquer and get straight.

"Tuppence," the barber said.

One of those things was money. "I know a man named Coutts," Bruno said. "He told me to say so and you'd do it for a penny."

"Coutts?" the barber said. "Ever heard of the forty thieves? Never mind what Coutts says. Tuppence."

He gave the barber sixpence and then stood in thought, turning over his words in his mind. The barber gave him three pennies and two halfpennies change.

"How much is this?"

The barber explained, counting the coins. "Don't you understand the value of money?" he said.

"Not altogether."

"Then it's damn near time you did."

He did not answer. He went out of the barber's shop and up the street, in thought. First the woman, the coal, the boiled beef, the bedroom. Now Coutts. Coutts, money, business, discount, interest, speculation. He rubbed his finger in preoccupied perplexity across his strangely smooth chin. What did it mean? Where did it lead to? It was time he knew. The boundaries of his world were growing. It was time he understood.

CHAPTER V

SPELLA HO was opened again in the summer of 1874. Bruno woke, one July morning, to see smoke suspended above it in small brown-grey clouds. He climbed the hay-stack in the Shadbolt yard in order to see it better. Even then he felt he could not believe it.

He had to go down into Castor that morning to fetch up a load of hides from the wharf and he stopped at "The Bell" for a drink, and the whole town was full of it: how the house was being opened again, by a family named Lanchester, how the bailiff and the first servants had already come. Then he went on with the hides to the small back-street tannery behind the pub and the men in the yard were full of it there. And listening, he felt that he caught an accent of reverence. The Lanchesters had money. Out of money sprang reverence. It was something else which he had not felt that money could command. Then as he went with an empty cart from the tannery back through High Street, making for home, a man named Fortescue hailed him from a shop. Fortescue was the classiest grocer in Castor. Bruno stopped the cart and got down and went across the street.

"You going anywhere near Spella?" Fortescue said.

"Going there now."

"Just the man I want. Draw over. I got about a couple o' hundred weight o' stuff to go up."

He drew across the street and Fortescue loaded him up with sides of bacon, baskets of eggs, cheeses, canisters of tea and coffee, bladders of lard, packages of spice, until the back of the cart was almost full.

"And for God's sake go careful. Mind them eggs."

And again Bruno caught the accent of reverence, really fear, inspired not by people but by money. Impressed but not awed he said:

"When do I git paid for this?"

"They'll pay you at Spella. Soon as they come. They'll pay all right, they'll pay. I've arranged that. You'll be all right."

"They got money?"

"Plenty. Pots."

"Everybody's making a hell of a fuss about them. What sort of family are they?"

"Oh! I don't know what sort of family they are. I don't know nothing about that. I only know they got money, that's all."

Bruno drove off, Fortescue looking after him with something like anxiety, calling:

"For God's sake be careful."

Bruno drove round under avenues of elm and oak, by

the wall of the park, to the front entrance of Spella Ho. For the first time for almost a year the gate was unlocked. He saw the greenish-gold dribbles of new oil on the hinges as he pushed them back. He drove up the long and now summer-dark avenue of limes and round to the back of the house, where the coal stood and where he had so often stood himself. It seemed strange to be there, to see the change brought about by habitation: servants clattering about inside the house, gardeners with green baize aprons digging over the flower beds, shearing the hedges of box and yew, tying the vines and peaches in the great glasshouses. He had so long connected the place with emptiness and silence, and now only the coal remained as he had always known it, the enormous black tomb of his first endeavours to make a start in life.

Servants came and helped him unload the groceries. When they had finished he asked about his money. He had in mind the sum he would ask, the sum for which he determined, even then, nothing should make him depart.

"You see the bailiff," the servants said.

The bailiff could not help. He was a tall streaky man with a lipless mouth who seemed to have gone beyond reverence into fear of something: "I got no way of paying you until Mrs. Lanchester comes," he said. "And she won't be here until Monday. Can't you send an account?"

"What's an account? I want the money."

"Sorry. No means of having your money until Mrs. Lanchester comes. When she comes she'll pay you, if she thinks fit. If she don't, she won't."

"I'll call Tuesday," Bruno said. "She won't eat me, will she?"

"Might do that."

Away from Spella, he pondered on that brief conversation, on the extraordinary reverence he had seen inspired by money and the still more extraordinary reverence inspired by a woman. It seemed to confirm his vague suspicions that money and women were the most powerful things on earth, that with an alliance of them it might be possible to accomplish anything. He was curious to see Mrs. Lanchester. He had now something approaching contempt for women; he thought of them as subservient, without subtlety. He had begun to conceive of them as a means of pleasant progression to a material end. As he had progressed by means of one woman to meals of boiled beef, he felt he might progress by others to different and higher things. With preconceived contempt, he felt he might progress by means of Mrs. Lanchester towards money. He did not know. He only knew that she was the first woman with money he had had the chance of meeting. He had no idea what she was like and he did not care.

So when he went up to Spella Ho on the following Wednesday he took with him some of his handbills. He reasoned that, with so large a house, many things would have to be carried up from Castor. He reasoned that there was here a chance not to be missed. He walked to Spella Ho through the fields, feeling neither awe nor reverence. Awe for the house was something he had already got over; reverence was an emotion he never felt himself and did not understand in other people.

The bailiff told him to wait and he waited in the yard. He waited for an hour. Though he saw servant-girls working in the rooms of the house and though gardeners were continually hurrying in and out of the gardens, no one spoke to him. He understood that later.

Then the bailiff came to fetch him. It struck him suddenly, then, that it was all unusual, that there was a great fuss, here, about something. He did not understand why the bailiff did not pay him, why there was this long-winded necessity of seeing Mrs. Lanchester herself.

The bailiff took him into the house by a side door and down the passages and on beyond the great staircase, where he had so often been. He knocked at the door of a room and a voice grunted something and Bruno found himself inside the room. It was the small room with the bullocks horn candlesticks and he remembered it well.

The room had been turned into a kind of office, with a

long mahogany writing table. The table was strewn with papers kept down by silver paperweights and a vast silver inkstand with wells of cut glass like wine decanters. At the table sat Mrs. Lanchester and a young girl. He was never shocked or surprised by the sight of a woman again as he was shocked and surprised at that moment by his first sight of Mrs. Lanchester. He saw before him a woman uglier than himself; an old small woman with a face like some distorted lump of clay, the skin having the same olive iron-blue colour and the same shining drawn-smooth texture as a fresh-cut lump of clay. He stared straight at her and she stared back, with small eyes as hard and round as nail-heads and with some kind of spiteful surprise, as though disagreeably astonished at seeing someone so young and yet so ugly. She was wearing a large absurd ecclesiastical sort of hat of black straw and it gave her face the appearance of looking out from a cavern. After looking at him for about forty seconds she turned and gave a great fiercely conceived gob into the stone spittoon on the floor at her side. It was a gesture of power, accuracy and contempt. It seemed to indicate, he felt, that she thought him so much muck. There was something victorious and monarchical about it: the gesture of a woman used not only to spitting in spittoons but to spitting on people.

He faced her. He felt a great desire to look at the girl, but the magnetism of the old lady held him. In turn something about himself seemed to hold her. Her eyes nailed him down, but his own also fascinated her.

"Shadbolt?" she said.

It was as though she had shot at him with a verbal popgun. She sucked in her already hollow cheeks, drew slightly back, and then ejected the word like a shot of spittle. He nodded. She shot again:

"Got your bill?"

"No."

"Well, you should have! You should have a bill. Always. How much is it?"

"Ten shillings."

He had fixed his mind on that sum, purposefully, unshakably. Nothing was going to shake him from it. He had ideas, at last, of what ten shillings meant, what he could do with it. He had not reckoned on the old lady. The moment he spoke he saw in her face a reflection, as it were, of all his own concrete determinations. She meant to pay him less and she was going to pay him less. Nothing was going to shake her from it.

Without saying anything to him she turned to the girl. She said: "Louise, pay this man five shillings and write a bill." The girl wrote; she wrote stiffly and laboriously, as though her great grey puff sleeves were made of iron. She kept her head bent at an angle of subservience. She had a great frothing mass of small-curled black hair, so that, as she bent her head, she looked almost like some silky spaniel. She wrote without speaking or looking up, with religious deliberation, in obedience to commands that had been spoken too often to need repeating now.

All the time the old woman stared at Bruno. He did not move. He was determined on one thing, inflexibly. She saw the determination in his face and it merely increased her own, and she sat with eyes that never once flickered away from the arrow straightness of long-practised contempt.

At last the girl had the bill written. She passed it across the mahogany to the old lady. She counted out five shillings from a chamois bag and passed that also to the old lady. The old lady read the bill; then counted the money; then she fixed money and bill together by a finger and thumb and slapped them down across the table; finally she sucked in her cheeks and shot out at him:

"Receipt that."

He did not move. Thanks largely to Coutts he knew, now, what a receipt was. He knew what money was; he was beginning to know what it meant and what it could do. He could count.

"I said ten shillings," he said.

"You'll take five and be glad of it and get out!" she shot at him. "Receipt that."

"No!"

"Receipt it."

He did not trouble to speak.

"Receipt that bill and get out of this room! Before I have you kicked out!"

"No!" he said.

Now, for a moment, she did not speak. She stared at him with swollen, screwed-up eyes, wonder lessening the contempt in them. When she spoke again it was more slowly, but also more viciously, and with if anything still greater determination.

"You may as well know now that five shillings is all I mean to pay and all I am going to pay. If I had my rights I shouldn't pay you anything. Fortescue should pay you, and next time, by God, he shall pay you."

"I don't care about next time," he said.

"Very wise of you. There'll be no next time. Now receipt that bill."

"No."

"Receipt it!"

"I'll receipt it for ten shillings and nothing less."

He stood stocky and imperturbable at the table, opposite her, unawed and unshaken. He felt, quite consciously, that to get that ten shillings was an important thing in his life. It was a test. If he could get ten shillings from her he could get anything from anybody. And he remembered for the rest of his life that moment: how he stood there unmoved, teeth clenched, how she sat there in a sort of controlled frenzy of angry determination, waiting for him to break down, and how the girl sat erect and beautiful and in some way negative at the table, like a beautiful quiet dog with clear black eyes set in a stare down at the table, as though seeing something precious hidden among the complicated white scatter of papers; and how, at last, the old lady made her decision, shooting it at him with the accuracy and spite of triumph.

"All right. Ten shillings. But you wait till next Lady Day."

As she spoke, he remembered Coutts. Coutts had put him up to many things.

He said at once:

"All right. Take ten years if you like. I'll charge you interest."

"You'll what?" she said.

It was her first display of surprise; it was noticeable in a slight slowing down of her speech, in a drawing-in of her wet thin tongue over her lips.

"I'll charge you five per cent," he said.

He was not sure of the means of charging her five per cent; and saying the words he had a momentary doubt about their accuracy. But he remembered some saying of Coutts: "Talk big and folks'll believe you."

But he saw at once that the old lady did not believe him. Momentarily impressed, she was now filled with the old contempt.

"Don't talk out of the back of your neck!" she said. "Most people are only too glad to get their money in a year, without charging interest."

"I don't see why," he said, "I should lend you ten shillings for a year for nothing."

"Five shillings."

"Ten," he said. "I said ten and I mean ten."

And again for a second time, she was impressed. She stared at him as though fascinated equally by his temerity and his physical ugliness.

"Who put you up to this?" she said. "Somebody put you up to this. Somebody told you I had money to throw about."

He did not speak.

"Well, you may tell whoever put you up to it that I have no money to throw about. I'm an old woman and what money I have I want. I've worked for it. Money has never grown on trees for me."

Again he did not speak.

"Where do you live?" she said. "On the estate?"

He told her, with a show of independent reluctance that impressed her.

"What do you do for a living?"

That was his chance. He took one of his bills out of his pocket and passed it over the table to her. She took it, with a special show of grimness. She read it without spectacles, with fiercely focused eyes and slightly side to side motions of her head.

"Who composed this?" she said. "You?"

"Yes."

"What's this about cheap rates? What's it mean? Cheap for those who can't pay more?"

"I'm the only carrier in Castor," he said.

She put the bill on the table. She smoothed it with her hands. Her hands had until then been hidden somewhere in the black folds of her dress under the table. Now he saw that they were extraordinarily crabbed and bent, the hands of someone really very old. They moved to and fro across the bill like two tired crabs of pale cheese-white shell.

"Do you want a job?" she said.

"I don't know," he said. "What is it?"

"I'm raising my rents on the estate. I want someone to collect them. You're about the stubbornest person I've met for years."

"What do I get?" he said.

"Commission," she said, just to see how he would take it.

"No," he said.

"All right, you can have it which way you like. Wages or commission. It's the same thing in the end."

"I want wages and commission," he said.

"You what?"

"It's dirty work. It ought to be worth paying for."

Her hands stopped smoothing the paper. She sat there in complete blank incredulity, motionless. She sat for almost a minute, speechless, looking at him and beyond him, in anger turning to a sort of acid respect. When she spoke again it was to announce a decision. By the very calmness with which she spoke he knew, at once, that it was a decision against which there was no appeal.

"I will pay you," she said, "five shillings a week and a commission of five per cent on all the increases you collect."

"You think I can't collect them?"

"Never mind what I think. Do you accept that?"

"Yes," he said.

"Get yourself a hard hat and a decent necktie and a dicky bit," she said. "You start next week, after the notices of the increases are out. You bring all monies to me. Don't take any notice of anybody. Bring it to me. Miss Williamson here will give you a list of tenants. You must see her. You'll know the people."

Suddenly she stood up, rather regally, her locket and chain rattling against the table as it fell into its great loose loop. It was an indication that it was time for him to go. She looked rather like the pictures of Queen Victoria. He was not impressed.

"What about my ten shillings?" he said.

For one moment she hesitated. Then she relented. It flashed across her mind that she could, anyway, get it out of him again, and she turned to the girl.

"Louise. Alter the bill to ten shillings."

The girl came to life, taking the bill and altering it, counting out another five shillings. Finally the old lady seized the bill and pushed it across the table with the money.

"Receipt that."

Bruno put the money into his pocket. Then he took up the pen. It was a momentous occasion in his life. He had already seen the effect on people of the fact that he could not write, and he knew it would be disastrous now. He had also seen Coutts's signature: a black splutter of ink like the trail of an angry spider, a flourish that no one could read. And suddenly he took up the pen, dipped it, and importantly wrote his first signature, a jumble of ink-scrawls heavily underlined. It was a signature that meant nothing and yet, to him, meant everything and was to go on meaning everything.

The old lady took the receipt, gave a glance at it and passed it to the girl. Then she said:

"I expect you here at eight o'clock next Monday morning."

He agreed, said good-evening and went out. As he went out of that room, with its still shut up odours of damp and sunlight, he looked back at the table: not at the woman but at the girl. She was still sitting there, like a black spaniel, head down, like some soft tired dog waiting to be taken for a run, and he knew that he wanted to see her again.

CHAPTER VI

HE did see her again, but not for some time. When he went up to the house on the following Monday, looking slightly absurd in white dicky front and paper collar and hard black hat and crêpe tie, it was the bailiff and not the girl who was waiting with the pony and trap and the list of tenants. The bailiff was also wearing a hard hat and white collar and front, so that they looked together like some semi-comic pair of ill-doers in disguise, Bruno monkey-like and grim, the bailiff tall and bony, like some starved stork. Bruno had wondered about the job and why the old lady had given it him and now he saw why. It was because she did not trust the bailiff. It was to be part of his duty, though she had not said so, to keep an eye on the bailiff, just as it was part of the bailiff's duty to keep an eye on him. They greeted each other and drove off and continued to drive, for some time, in an atmosphere of grim and acute suspicion. The bailiff had in his right-hand pocket the list of tenants and he had memorized the first half-dozen names on the list, so that he did not need to speak much. He also drove the cart and as they set off into a countryside that had slipped into the parched silence of August, a corn-yellow, corn-scented country of quiet distances and white dust scattered like bloom on the deep hedges of haw and sloe, he might have been a man driving to his own doom. As he sat there, with the obstinacy of a man in sorrow, staring over the horse's head into space, it was clear that he was eaten up with grievances.

They were grievances, it seemed, mainly about Mrs. Lanchester, but Bruno did not hear them until later. Now it was obvious only that he thought the job beneath him, that he resented the implication of dishonesty, above all that he resented Bruno. So they drove about the estate from house to house, collecting rents, in silent distrust of each other, hardly speaking. To Bruno it was the easiest job, the easiest money, of his life. But it was something else. He saw it as the beginning of an immense opportunity. He saw also that the bailiff and the girl were parts of the mechanism of that opportunity. He felt that he had to see the girl not so much for herself as for the chance she might give him. She had looked so oppressed and abject sitting there, like a curled kept dog, and yet he did not pity her. His predominant thought was to see her again, to know more about her.

He began to know more about her when, at midday, he and the bailiff stopped to eat a dinner of bread and cheese at a small pub just beyond the boundaries of the estate. The bailiff, bored and angry about things, began to drink gin. He got talkative, and gradually boredom gave way to reminiscence and anger to self-pity, and things began to come out: how he was hellishly dissatisfied with being stuck up there, at Spella, miles from anywhere, miles from London, penned-in, no excitement, no life, everybody suspicious of everybody else, no women, might as well be dead.

"What about that girl?" Bruno said.

"Who? Oh, the girl. Her. Cold pork, Shadbolt, cold

pork. Dead. Wouldn't let you look at her. Keep off it. London's the place for women. Whistle 'em like dogs."

"What's she do? What is she?"

"Don't know. Can't make out. She's a sort of companion-clerk—God knows what. Keeps the books. Got her fingers right in the pie."

"I got to see her. When can I do that?"

"Evening time."

"After we git back?"

"After we're bleeding well back, worse luck. I wish to hell I was never going back. What a shop. No life. No women. Ah, don't talk about it. Terrible. Drink up. What a shop."

Bruno drank porter. The bailiff ordered himself more gin. They talked until mid-afternoon, or rather the bailiff talked. Bruno had only to listen.

And listening, he heard a lot that he had not expected to hear: how Mrs. Lanchester had made her money, why she had come to Spella Ho. "Sprung from nothing," the bailiff said. "Made money by twisting people. Never did a minute's work in her life. No education, no breeding. Crafty as hell. Never pays a cent out without getting it back double or treble. Gets all her work done cheap—look at me. I was a clerk in a tea-broker's office and then something happened and I was down and out. So she gets me cheap. That girl—she comes out of an orphanage. So she gets her cheap. Now look at you. You don't look as if you're the Emperor of China. So she gets you cheap." Three parts drunk, resting on the pub-table with tired indiarubber elbows, the bailiff went beyond reminiscence into confidences. "Don't tell nobody, don't breathe a word, will you? She taken this place, down here, out o' the way, because it's quiet. Twig it? She ain't known here. And where she is known things is getting too hot for her. Twig it?"

Then, as they drove home, the bailiff, sobering up a little, was frightened. "By God, don't you say nothing. Don't you say nothing. Don't mutter a syllable to that

62

lump of cold pork, for God's sake. I'm supposed to be on the wagon. I promised."

Then, driving in the hot sun, he was suddenly sick and lay down in the roadside-grass for a little while, to get over it, while Bruno washed the gin-spew off the trap wheel with water from a pond. Then, as they drove on, the after-taste of sickness swinging him over to another extreme, he was full of sorrow and apology, faith and promises.

"Never told you my name, did I? Finch. Ezekiel Finch. What a name." He clasped Bruno by the shoulders. "By God you're a smart chap, Shadbolt. I heard what you said to the old girl, by God. Mustard. And anything you want—ask me. I'll do it."

"I want to see Miss Williamson, that's all. I got to see her about something."

"Ah, the cold pork, eh?"

After he had spoken the bailiff paused, stared and was convulsed.

"Mustard on the cold pork, eh? Ha! That's good. By God that's—mustard on the—Ha!"

They drove home to Spella Ho in better humour. When they arrived Finch took Bruno into the house, by various back entrances, to see Miss Williamson. She occupied a small sitting-room in the servants' quarters, a room of about ten feet square furnished with one cane chair, a deal table and a bamboo jardiniere. At the window hung coarse wallflower-red curtains which kept out a good deal of light. The girl was sitting at the window, with her hands on the ledge and her head on her hands, and he thought she looked, once again, with her mass of spaniel-curly hair, exactly like some forlorn tame dog waiting to be taken out.

That was the last of his early impressions of her ever to be repeated. All the rest that he had thought of her was blown suddenly into space. When she stood up she was about his own height. She looked rather pale; it was the sort of fashionable semi-refined, semi-starved pallor of the period and it gave her a look of intense and almost painful delicacy. She had very large dark brown eyes which seemed heavy with something: sleep or sleeplessness or emotion or the lack of it. Although it was a hot day she was wearing some impossible neck-buttoned brown dress that compressed her breast to the tight smoothness of an egg. She looked uncomfortable and unhappy, and when he came in she only stared up at him with large, surprised eyes, not knowing what to do or say.

He was not sure what to do or say himself. Then he said something about the rents being safely collected, and added, lying: "Finch said I better report that to you."

"Did Finch get drunk?" she said.

He was too flabbergasted to speak.

"He always gets drunk the first chance he gets after the first day of the month. He's paid then. Are you sure he didn't get drunk?"

He stood in momentary confusion. She on the other hand had a fine calmness. He remembered Finch's injunctions and stood silent.

"You can tell me," she said.

He looked at her, much as he had looked at the old lady, straight and with a determination not to be ruffled, and yet it was not the same. He felt some unspeakable quality of excitement when he looked at her. And after a moment, as though she saw it, she released, much as the old lady had released her words, an extraordinary smile. It struck him flat by its amused frankness.

"I know Finch," she said.

He still was not saying anything.

"You weren't frightened of Mrs. Lanchester," she said. "Surely you're not frightened of me?"

"Finch'll get into trouble," he said.

"No, he won't."

"Anyway," he said, "why should you trouble about old Finch?"

She looked at him with extraordinarily penetrating quietness. "Because," she said, "I don't want you to feel you've got to tell me lies."

Though they astonished him, the words took him much nearer to her. Then she said something else which surprised him.

"We're all in the same boat here," she said.

"Cheap labour?"

"If you like. Did Finch tell you?"

"Yes."

"What did you come to see me for?" she said. "You know you're not supposed to come and see me. There'll be trouble if Mrs. Lanchester finds out."

"This is your room, ain't it?" he said.

"It's where I'm put," she said.

He looked round the room. He had been in it before, several times. He remembered it as one of those rooms where he just held the door ajar and had stuck his head in to see a pile of forgotten croquet sticks and a litter of light-yellowed papers.

"This was nothing but a rubbish room," he said.

"I know. I cleaned it out myself."

He looked round the room again. He saw that it had no fireplace. Where the fireplace might have been two large white-doored cupboards had been built in. Then something occurred to the girl.

"How did you know?" she said.

"I worked at Spella once," he said quietly.

He knew she did not believe him. But this time she did not say so. She expressed her disbelief by another smile. He did not know what to say. He had wanted to say so much, to find out so much, and he was knocked flat by her astonishing candour.

"You're like most men. You think it rather nice to tell lies to women."

The value of truth had not struck him. He had not even considered truth. Truth was something you told when there was no excuse, no profit, in telling anything else. It was a movable quality. You could engineer it according to need. He had engineered it very often.

Then something happened. He caught the sound of

footsteps in the corridor outside. They were slow slipper-shuffling footsteps and, looking up, he saw for the first time fear in the girl's face. She looked at him helplessly. And that second of helplessness and fear rushed the two of them closer together than he knew they would have got in a month of talking.

She pushed him into the cupboard without saying anything and he lay hunched up, in darkness, among a stale litter of papers and dust and disused articles of croquet. He lay there and heard Mrs. Lanchester come in. He heard them talking. He felt the springing up in himself of some irresponsible excitement, as though he did not care a damn. He had, as he lay there, only one thought in his mind: to see the girl and to see her as often as reason and time would let him. It was not that simply he liked her. It was as if his life had turned a crazy somersault and he was no longer himself.

If he remembered for ever being in that cupboard, he remembered far better getting out of it. He almost fell out. The girl opened the door suddenly, in an anxiety to get him out of the place quickly, and he fell forward on the carpetless floor on his hands, hat squashed hard down on his ears, his dicky a smokey mass of cobweb dust. She brushed him down hastily, with her hands, taking off his hat and brushing that with her sleeve. She was horrified at the state of his dicky.

These little things were like nails driven into the plank of their intimacy. "You shouldn't have come here," she said. "She's a tyrant, that woman. She's everywhere."

"I don't care for her or anybody else," he said.

"I can see that. But I do. You've got to get out of the house."

"Well, I can git out. I've got out of it before."

He went over to the window and unfastened the catch. As he stood there she was horrified again by the sight of his dicky. "Take it off," she said, "and I'll get it washed and ironed in the kitchen. That'll save your mother the trouble."

"It will," he said.

He took the dicky off and gave it to her. Then all of a sudden she gave it back. "No, I daren't do it. She's got eyes in the back of her head, and I daren't. You'll have to take it."

He took it back. He got out of the window. Standing on the turf he turned to say something about seeing her again, but she shut the window. He gesticulated, moving his lips. She stood there shaking her head and he saw the large brown eyes imprisoned behind the glass, while he himself stood there like some helpless monkey in a cage.

CHAPTER VII

MRS. LANCHESTER and the girl played chess evening after evening in a large and almost empty room at the top of the house. There, from four windows, Mrs. Lanchester could see whatever happened across the park. Bruno learned this from Finch. "What an existence," Finch complained. "What a shop. Hopeless." To Bruno it began to appear hopeless too.

Then, when he went up to Spella Ho on the following Monday morning to begin work with Finch, he saw, without being told, that something had happened. Servants were running to and fro in dumb panic, the trap was not harnessed, Finch was not to be seen, and he had the impression of the old lady sitting there, somewhere in the house, like some tyrannical bomb ready to explode.

It was not until Miss Williamson came down to find him in the stables that he knew that Finch had packed his box in the night and had gone. "Everybody knows it," the girl said, "except Mrs. Lanchester. He told us all he was going. Now nobody dare tell her. I've tried to tell her, but she won't listen. She wants to talk to him about the rents. Now she's shouting about for you."

"Me?"

"Yes. You've got to go up."

So, in surprise, he followed her into the house and upstairs, past the great ceiling-painting he had often stared at and admired, and into Mrs. Lanchester's bedroom.

Mrs. Lanchester was still in her bed, a large mahogany four-poster with red drapings, and the tassel of her white nightcap was bobbing about in fury.

"Where's Finch?" she bawled at him. "Have you seen Finch?"

"No."

"Then what's happened to him?"

He stood at the foot of the bed and stared at her with deliberation. "Finch has packed his box and gone."

"What?"

He knew that she had heard and he did not trouble to answer. His indifference heightened her fury, which she turned suddenly on the girl.

"Why didn't you tell me that?"

"She did tell you," Bruno said.

"Where has Finch gone?" she shouted. "Get a conveyance and go after him! Do something. He can't get a train for miles from here. Do as I tell you. Do something, for God's sake!"

He stood where he was. She raved at him. Immovable, he stood like some grim and emotionless monkey, waiting for her to finish.

Then, as she saw how little effect she had on him, she calmed a little. Still angry, but quieter, she said:

"Why should Finch do this? He owed everything to me. If it hadn't been for me he'd have been in prison. He'd been in trouble. Why should he do it?"

He kept his eyes on that aged and amazingly virile face and said in a voice of no expression at all:

"For one thing, you didn't pay him enough."

She sprang into a fresh frenzy, so that her nightcap was partly dislodged, showing the bald putty-coloured head beneath. She began to shout at him. She had not spoken a dozen words before he turned and began to walk out of the room.

She called him back. "Come here! Stand here by the bed! Closer, closer. Here, by the table."

He stood by the bedside table. He saw her daytime wig lying on the mahogany, upturned, like some grey horse-hair bird's nest. He showed, and felt, no excitement at all.

"Don't you dare go out of that door," she said.

There seemed no need to speak.

"Now," she said.

He continued to look at her, as though to say "And now what?"

But what she said surprised him. "I want somebody to take Finch's place," she said. "I want you."

As though a little surprised by what she had said her-self, she added: "If you think you can do it? Can you?"

"What'll you pay me?" he said.

He spoke slowly, with completely unemotional hard-ness, knowing how hard she could be herself.

"I'll pay you what I paid Finch," she said.

"You won't!"

"That was a good wage!" she shouted.

He put his derision for that remark into another at-tempt to walk out of the bedroom. Again she called him back. Again he came and stood by the bed without awe or emotion.

"I don't know what people are coming to!" she said pettishly.

"You want somebody you can trust," he said, "don't you?"

"Of course I do. But that's no reason why I should pay you any more than—"

"I want double what you paid Finch," he said.

"Money! Money!" she shouted at him. "That's all you want! Money! That's all you think about! Money."

"You've put the rents up," he said.

The words were like a trap, which snapped over her. She seemed to realize, suddenly, that she was caught, that he saw through her and that she could do nothing. Even then she tried to wriggle out of it.

"I paid Finch five shillings," she said.

"And his keep."

"You can have your keep."

"No," he said. "I want a sovereign a week and my keep."

"You damned daylight robber!" she said.

Indifferent, he turned again to walk out. She let him get as far as the door. Deliberately he put his hand on the white glazed knob and turned it. At the last she made some impotent noise of pained acceptance, recalling him.

"All right," she said. "A pound a week and your keep. You wouldn't get a job like it in London."

"Put it on paper," he said.

At that she raved again, clenching her fist at him, shouting, clawing the absurd nightcap off her head with furious fingers, reviling him until a fit of coughing hit her like a blow and laid her back on the pillow. "Can't you trust me?" she whispered, "Can't you trust me?"

"Do you trust me?" he said. "Did you trust Finch? That was the trouble."

She had no answer immediately but a small wave of a bone-white hand, a tired and in some way pathetic signal moving feebly against the dark background of bed-curtains, dismissing him. Then she revived to say: "Get on with the rents. Take somebody with you. You'll be carrying money. Take Miss Williamson. She's got the books." And then a last spark of spite: "She ought to be safe with you."

When he left the bedroom the girl followed him out and they went downstairs together. All down the long spacious wine-carpeted staircase they had nothing to say to each other. Many things, as she afterwards said, were troubling her, but only one thing was, and had been for some time, worrying him.

And at the foot of the stairs he told the astonished Louise Williamson what it was.

"I can't read or write," he said.

BOOK TWO

LOUISE

CHAPTER I

HE sold his horse and cart and, having assets of eight pounds seventeen shillings, went to work and eat at Spella Ho. He tied the money in an old chicken meal bag and kept it sewn in the sackcloth mattress in his bedroom at the Shadbolt place, where he came back every night to sleep. In two days he felt that he was working for a lunatic.

All this, as he afterwards liked to recall, was a turn of luck for him. No one except a lunatic would have given him such a job; nothing except such a job, offering the chance to learn not only something about money and figures but about letters too, could have given him the opportunities he wanted. And at that time he felt that he wanted very little. Knowing that it was the key to so much, he wanted to learn to read and write. Above all, he wanted to be near Louise Williamson.

He saw the old lady every morning at half-past eight. He got to know the way up the magnificent staircase better than he had ever dreamed he could know it. He took orders, catapulted at him in rage or despair or semi-lunatic tears between great spits at the large white chamber-pot standing by the bedside, and kept up the illusion that he knew more than he did. From the first Mrs. Lanchester liked him. His presence often comforted her. She seemed to see in him, as it were, a kindred spirit of stubbornness, resource and also of ugliness. She admired in him the beginnings of a certain ruthlessness: she had been too often ruthless herself not to notice it.

His duties were so simple as to be almost crazy too. Mrs. Lanchester, hating all animals, kept no stock within the hundred and fifty acres of park, across which the sun-faded grass, never cut for two summers, rippled and shook its plumey seeds like corn. Everywhere grass and weeds and trees and hedges were allowed to stand uncut, to form a great protective barrier of greenness for the small fanatical creature hiding behind the still more solid barricade of the great house. On the hot late August afternoons the sunblinds, pale as parchment, were pulled down over all the windows on the south side, so that it looked like a house of the dead. In the park every gate was kept locked and it was Bruno's duty every morning, before the first interview with Mrs. Lanchester, to see that they were still locked. With a bunch of keys like a jailer's in his hand he did a two-hour walk round the grass-choked boundaries, ending at the main gate at the end of the avenue of limes, which he unlocked for the day. On Mondays, he collected, with Louise Williamson, the rents of thirty cottages. For the rest, he had nothing to do but to report his tour of the gates in the evenings and to be ready to respond, like a bell, to some lunatic and lightning call from the room with the silver candlesticks, where Mrs. Lanchester worked all mornings and most of the early evening over ledgers dating back to the 'forties.

All this gave him much spare time; and in that spare time Louise Williamson, a little scared of the position in which he found himself, offered to teach him to read and write. Mrs. Lanchester slept behind drawn blinds every afternoon and it was in the afternoons that they mostly worked. "You've got to learn," she said. "Because if she ever finds out, you're done." He saw that himself. And wanting to learn, he learned quickly. He employed the old emotionless method of, as it were, taking a double picture of everything. Having once learned, he never forgot anything. So that by the end of September he could read words of two syllables and could copy set sentences on double ruled pages. Emotion never interfered with this. It never seemed to him romantic to be shut away, secretly, in Louise Williamson's small room at the back of the house, or under some tree in the park, where they escaped on fine autumn afternoons. Emotion was there, but he kept it rigidly at the back of his mind, like a fruit not ripe enough to eat. It was as though he wanted to eat, when he did eat, with the lusciousness of certainty.

To him Louise Williamson seemed a girl of considerable refinement. She spoke well, with a slight London accent, and after a time he began to speak with a sort of stiff refinement himself. She was a girl who had always suffered from an excess of confinement: first at the orphanage, later over Mrs. Lanchester's books. For a time she had travelled with Mrs. Lanchester: Cheltenham, Tunbridge Wells, Droitwich, Brighton, and then Italy. "Where's Italy?" Bruno said. She told him about Italy: Naples, the canals of Venice, Milan, the cathedrals. His interest was expressed in a question. "That must have taken a lot o' money?" She replied by telling him how she was sick of money, and why: how in the Lanchester household they ate money, drank it, slept with it. "You can taste money on every slice of bread and butter. If you have a glass of water it tastes of money." She told him how she felt as if her life was slowly being confined by the iron bars of investments, debentures, stocks, shares, profit and more profit. "Money for the love of money," she said.

Listening to her, he was fascinated by two things: by the talk of money, which fired his imagination, and by the tender beautiful sideways expression of her small-curled head, always so like a tired spaniel resting and waiting. He had never known, and afterwards knew he never would know, anyone like her. And slowly, in his mind, the fruit of his emotion about her ripened. They would escape to lie under the limes of the park, in the heavy-coloured honey afternoons of middle autumn, in a world still untouched by frost, and he would feel his emotion for her turning over and colouring and filling with the juices of adoration. And yet, for a long time, he made no effort to touch it. Reading and writing first; love afterwards. He knew that his emotion would keep. It did not occur to him to think of her own.

She in turn was attracted by several things about him: by his initiative where money was concerned, by his immobile intentness whenever she spoke of it, and most of all by the extraordinary dreaminess that went with his ugliness. She was also troubled by something. Having been brought up religiously, in fear, she was slightly horrified that he did not know the difference between lying and truth.

"What about it?" he said.

"It's wrong. Don't you see?" she said. "It's *wrong*."

"You mean if you were in trouble and I told a lie to get you out of it that would be wrong?"

"That's a white lie," she said.

"All right," he said. "I'm a white liar."

"Don't you see?" she said. "It's terrible, it's wrong."

And she went on to try to explain it: how one thing was truth, the other not truth. He defended himself.

"I never told you a lie," he said.

"Yes," she said, "you did. You said you once worked at Spella and it isn't true."

So he told her about the coal. "That's what I mean about telling lies and being honest," he said. "We wanted that coal. But my mother was too honest."

"That coal wouldn't have saved her life," she said.

"How do you know?" he said. "How can anyone tell?"

One day she was more than usually upset by this and tried to make him promise always, as long as he lived, to tell the truth.

"As long as I live might be a long time," he said.

"Promise all the same."

"What good will it do you?"

"It won't do me any good. It'll do you good."

"I'll tell the truth when there's no use telling anything else," he said.

"No. Promise."

"You mean if I saw the chance of making a hundred pounds and I could do it by telling a clacker I wouldn't have to do it?"

"Yes."

"That's a tall order."

"Promise, all the same."

"It's daft," he said.

"It's not. It's right. Promise," she said, "for me."

"No!"

"Oh! Bruno."

He knew, suddenly, that it was the moment he had waited for. The way she said his name, affectionately, with some implication of dispair, suddenly broke through his emotion. They were sitting in long unmown and now almost whiteheaded grass in the park and he put his arms round her and kissed her twice, once briefly and tenderly, once at length, with passion. She lay back for a moment, as though to consider it, her thick curly black hair almost lost in the tall grass, and then, smiling, put her arms up to him. It was a gesture of complete happiness, of almost but not quite complete surrender.

After that she would talk of only one kind of promise. "Promise," she would say, "to love me as long as you live."

"As long as I live," he would tease her, "might be a long time."

CHAPTER II

THEY began to live a life of increasing intimacy. The days shortened and grew colder, and presently the afternoons in the park were finished. For a short time Mrs. Lanchester was ill, then recovered, then came downstairs to insist that Louise should work all day, over accounts, in the room with the candlesticks. In the early evenings, until Mrs.

Lanchester went to bed at eight, she and Louise played silent and apparently interminable games of chess in the large drawing-room, on a card-table lit by a single tallow candle in a brass holder. "You don't need light to play chess," Mrs. Lanchester would say, "you play chess with the mind."

So they were forced to meet in secrecy, at night. They met in Louise's small sitting-room, without a candle, for safety, and if footsteps approached she hid him in the cupboard. He began to see through her eyes into regions of unsuspected tenderness. She took off her clumsy tight-fitting dresses and breathed relief and he held her white-skirted body in the darkness. He ruffled his thick broad hands in her hair, curling the spaniel ringlets round his fingers. Afraid to talk much, they slipped down together into vague streams of unexpressed thought. Her passion for him was milky and quiet; she loved him naturally and sweetly, with beautiful generosity.

Just as secrecy had driven them into intimacy, intimacy very shortly itself began to drive them into the thought of something else: escape. This was, in the very first place, Bruno's idea. It was an expression of ambition. He longed to be moving. He felt that with Louise, with her education, her gift for figures, they could get away, to a large town, to London perhaps, and start life together. But Louise held back. Rightly she felt that they must have money. How were they going to live? How could they hope to make money?"

"How did Mrs. Lanchester make her money?" he said. "She swears she began from nothing."

"That's different."

"She made money by speculation," he said. "You know she did. Why shouldn't we do it?"

"That's just wild talk."

"How? What that crazy old tit can do, I can do."

"She's very shrewd and she hasn't always been crazy."

"All right," he said. "Take Coutts."

"Who is this Coutts you talk about?" she said.

He told her; he told her about the agreement. "I should like to look at that agreement," she said.

"Coutts has got it."

She looked at him in astonishment. "You mean to say you signed an agreement without being able to read it, and then didn't have a copy?"

Then he saw what a fool he had been.

"You'll probably go on paying interest on that loan for the rest of your life." She teased him gently. "And that might be a very long time." He looked despondent, angry at his own stupidity. "Luckily it's probably an agreement that doesn't hold water."

"Anyway," he said, "that's one mistake I shall never make again."

He had at that time not paid the September and October instalments to Coutts. Discussing what to do, they reasoned that it could not be long before Coutts turned up, looking for his money.

They were right. Coutts turned up at Spella Ho on a sultry afternoon in late October, having travelled by London North Eastern as far as Orlingford, walking the rest. He was sweating and in a temper. He had brought the agreement with him, prepared to brandish it like a sword. Seeing him sweating across the park, Bruno found Louise and they met him together at the gate coming in from the park. Coutts began to say what the hell did Bruno mean by not paying his interest and so on? He clenched the agreement in his hands and waggled it in Bruno's face. Louise then asked if she might read the agreement; read it; and finally gave it back to Coutts with the remark that it wasn't worth the paper it was written on. It wasn't legal, it wasn't witnessed and so on. Coutts went very white. He stood silent, slowly whitening, for about twenty seconds. Then rage exploded into blasphemy and he swore in hot fury at two people who if they thought they were going to cheat an honest man they were very much mistaken. He lost control of himself. Bruno snatched the agreement out of his hands, tore it up and threw the pieces in his face. He then seized Coutts by coat and breeches, and amazed at his own strength, dropped him over the five-foot iron fence into the park. Coutts stood for about ten seconds, weeping tears of rage, and then ran.

He ran straight down into Castor; and there, first in "The Bell" and later in "The Dragon", began the story that Bruno had beaten him up over some trivial matter of money. "He bent my arms back until they cracked and then kneed me in the guts and then threw me against a bloody great iron fence." A man said: "He'll come it once too often. He damn near got fighting over some rent over at Alf Bailey's last week."

"Rent?" Coutts immediately seized on this, a matter of money, as something in his own line. "What rent?" Then he heard, in exchange for his own story, the story of Bruno as it was then common gossip in Castor: how he had bitten off more than he could chew over the carrier's business; how he had nosed his way into the job at Spella Ho: how, as soon as he began to collect them, the rents had gone up. It was a story inspired primarily by jealousy; Coutts fed it with anger. "You say that old woman's dotty," he said. "What's to prevent him putting the rents up without her knowing and pocketing the difference himself?"

"You may depend that's what he bloody well does do," a man said.

That night the two stories, feeding each other, ran all over Castor. Mixed with liquor, they became fantastic. Inspired by jealousy, they began to be heard with hatred. Bruno had half-killed a man that afternoon up at Spella by bashing his head against an iron fence. "You know, that bloody great iron fence that runs round the park. Smashed his head against it." Bruno had put up the rents of the cottages, rents that had never been touched for years, and was pocketing the difference. There arose the picture of Bruno as some upstart autocratic giant, stamping on people. It became a public matter, and Bruno himself, for the first time in his life, a public figure.

A young man named Rufus Chamberlain was in "The

Bell". He was a head taller than Bruno, a smart fellow, with flashy black eyebrows and beautiful moustaches, who smoked cigars and reckoned himself the best-dressed man in Castor. He was a man who liked sport and it was he who first suggested that they should go up to Spella Ho, in a gang, get Bruno out, and give him something to remember. "It'll be sport if it's nothing else," Chamberlain said. "In any case who's going to be bossed about by a nit like Shadbolt?"

Late the following afternoon, Saturday, Chamberlain and about fifty men from Castor, all in beer, with half a dozen scrag-haired women, marched up the avenue at Spella Ho and stood on the terrace in the front of the house and chanted for Bruno. "Who put the rents up?" they chanted. "Come on, Shadbolt, show your ugly mug. Who put the rents up? Who put the rents up?" They stood there for about ten minutes, whistling and shouting and catcalling, before anything happened. Beer-warmed, they stood closely grouped about the front door, swaying about, hawking and spitting on the stone terrace steps and rubbing out the spit with derisive boots. Suddenly a second floor window was flung up, and out of it, as though in answer and almost as though to show them how, there fell a colossal gob like a wet white bird-dropping. It smacked on the terrace and the crowd upturned its face to see, a moment later, the descent of a colossal chamber-pot, like a falling white moon. Hurling down, it struck a man on the shoulder spun him on his back like a kitten, and smashed on the stone flags. The anger of the crowd shot up like an explosion.

"Shadbolt! The mucky sod!"

They set up a roar at the windows, elbowing about, booing, the women screeching like bony parrots. A man picked up a stone and threw it at the house. It was like a signal for a bombardment. The crowd surged down from the terrace to the flower-beds below, searching for stones, then began, at first in frenzy, then more systematically, the smashing of every window on the south side of the house. They threw in competition at the top windows of the attics. All the time they shouted for Bruno. They had in their minds the image of Bruno as they threw: the man who had not only put up the rents and beaten up Coutts but also had now spat on them in actuality and contempt and had thrown down on them a contemptuous missile that had almost killed a man. Men who had come up to Spella for fun now felt fired by a terrific frenzy of injustice. Their hatreds poured out of a new outlet. They yelled in anger for a man some of them had never seen.

All the time Bruno was not there. He was sitting at home in the Shadbolt kitchen, in nothing but his trousers, waiting for his only shirt to be washed and dried. Maria had been saying to him: "It's time you got another shirt. You're getting on in the world and you ought to have two." The slate-blue shirt, darned at neck and cuffs, was hanging out in the sun to dry. Bruno said that now he wore the dicky you couldn't tell but what he had got a new shirt, but Maria insisted: "You could get some stuff down at Beamer's and I could make you two. With plenty to tuck in."

They were still discussing the shirt, which was still not dry, when an under-gardener from Spella Ho came tearing across the fields in panic:

"They're smashing every window in Spella!"

Bruno put on his jacket, unexcitedly, without waiting for his shirt. He had only one thought: Louise. Not a good runner, he took his time across the fields to the house, saving his strength, nursing a slow but terrific accumulation of anger. He walked, almost marched, with the fixed determination of a man who knew, to a pin-point, where he was going.

He walked out of the park into the yard at the back of the house just as the crowd, having broken every window in the front of the house, was surging round to begin breaking those in the back. When they saw him they stopped. It struck them instantly that there had been a mistake. Bruno came straight on. He looked rather like some squat clock-work monkey made of iron.

The crowd for a moment did not know what to do. They had been angry, for about an hour, and with violence, with a man who had never been in the house. They felt momentarily ridiculous. Then suddenly anger surged back in them: anger not because he was to blame for the spitting and the chamber-pot but because he was not to blame. He had cheated them and they were doubly furious. Chamberlain shouted:

"Here the sod comes!" Bruno's jacket flapped open, showing his bare trunk, so that he looked like a man who had just hastily dressed. "Looks as if he's been sleeping with the old woman."

Bruno went straight on, without hesitation, and as though it had all been steadfastly preconceived, hit Chamberlain a terrific blow in the throat. He seemed as though not quite tall enough to hit him in the face, and the blow struck Chamberlain in the windpipe. He staggered back into the crowd and the crowd held him up. For more than a minute he fought for breath, while the crowd held him up and took off his coat and gave him advice, milling angrily and excitedly about him. Then at last he came on.

Bruno had also taken off his coat. He stood bare down to the waist, very hairy, and with a queer stocky muscularity that held the crowd fascinated. Chamberlain had long fancied himself as a sportsman and he took up a series of attitudes, classy, very quiet, threatening. In one of these attitudes Bruno went in and tried a repetition of his first blow. Chamberlain ducked and the blow hit him on the left ear like a lump of stone.

Chamberlain went mad. He came in and hit Bruno all over the place. He hit him three times in the face, knocking him down, and twice round the back of the neck, with a hook. He slit his left eyebrow as though with the cross-slash of a thin knife and then hit him with terrific power under the heart. Bruno went down three times and came up again.

He came up again as though automatically. The blows

had no effect at all on his determination. He got up and Chamberlain hit him; he fell down and got up and Chamberlain hit him again. He got up the third time with blood like a livid splash of ripe fruit all over his face.

Then he hit Chamberlain. It was a blow that, afterwards, was remembered and talked about for longer than the cause of the fight. He went in and hit Chamberlain, off his balance, a moderate blow in the chest. As Chamberlain staggered Bruno brought his fists together and smashed them down into Chamberlain's eyes. It was like a double hammer blow. It smashed down as though to squash out the pupils like jelly. It had in it all the concentrated force of his peculiar determination. It was murderous and without pity.

The crowd were thrilled and shocked. Chamberlain was down and they got him to his feet. They pushed him into the fight again. Chamberlain staggered about half-blinded, his head in Bruno's belly, Bruno down, the fight itself moving in circles and then diagonally across the yard toward the wall of coal in the corner, blood and spit and the shouting and bawling of the crowd and the beer-spew of a woman clotting about it in a thick pandemonium of excitement.

Finally the men could no longer stand on their feet. They began to hit each other, blinded by blood, in attitudes of falling. Chamberlain fell back in the coal, Bruno with him. They got up and raked the air with despairing semi-circles, launching at each other attacks of bloody and almost comic weakness. Finally Chamberlain sprawled forward on his face and could not get up again.

Bruno stood for a moment stolidly looking at him, for the first time indeterminate. A man broke out of the crowd swinging him round by the shoulder:

"You bastard, you throwed that pot at me!"

Bruno hit him automatically, almost with indifference. The man staggered back into the crowd, absorbed by faces. Those faces, as Bruno stared at them, waiting for an aggressive motion, seemed for some reason to be swimming in blood. They receded and swayed forward and yet remained. They moved and yet nothing happened. And after about a minute he knew that it was the end.

CHAPTER III

IT was also a beginning. The day was responsible for two things: a hardening of his determination to go away and the establishment, in Castor and in towns for fifteen miles round, of his reputation as a man of terrific fighting qualities. It was a day that, as time went on, was to become fabulous. For thirty and even forty years men were to discuss the fight between himself and Rufus Chamberlain at Spella Ho. They were to elaborate its fury, give him a reputation that, inspired first by jealousy and then fed by pure wonder, had no affection behind it. He was to become a man held by the public in awe and fear and even esteem, but never in affection.

At the time he had no notion of how tremendous the effect of that fight was. He had only one concern: Louise. That evening he heard how she and Mrs. Lanchester, alone upstairs, had heard the smashing of every window in the south aspect, the old lady stalking up and down the room in fury, stabbing her silver-headed walking stick into the carpet, spitting, swearing, and calling at intervals for a gun; then how they had from the windows of another room seen the fight, the old lady again beside herself, this time with a kind of blood-thirsty joy; how finally Louise, unable to stand such excitement in a period of tight-lacing, had fainted on the bed and had come round again before the old lady knew what had happened.

So that evening, Louise pale and ill, he himself sick and thick-eyed and thick-lipped, they sat in her small sitting-room and discussed how and when, if possible, they could get away. He wanted to go to London. Louise had told him much about it; he had a natural desire to see it for himself. Where he had once been driven by a single ambition, he was now pulled by three. He wanted Louise; wanted money; wanted to see London. He was going to strike out for himself. What he was going to do in London, how he was going to make money, was not clear. He felt he relied on the obscure revolutions of fate. It was this that dissatisfied Louise. She also had struggled. She knew London. She felt that she knew just what chances he stood there.

She had another reason. For some time it had been clear that the old lady would leave her money. "It might be a lot of money. It might not be very much. I don't know," she said. "But it would be foolish to lose the chance of it."

"You mean she'd cut you out of the will if you went now?"

"You know she would."

That impressed him.

"Supposing it's only a hundred pounds," Louise said. "We could do a lot with that."

That also impressed him. A little patience—and how much he might possibly do. On the other hand, affection for Louise together with the fight with Chamberlain had taken him up to the crest of a wave. He wanted to go over with it. He wanted to go over into a new existence. He felt it to be an opportunity. It seemed to resolve itself into a conflict between patience and courage.

In the end, rather to the surprise of Louise, he gave in to patience. They would wait. When he had said so, she gave him a new and better reason for having said it: the old lady. She also had been impressed by the fight, felt he had done a magnificent thing.

"You can't tell," she said, "what she might do for you some day."

She had hardly said this when a message came in from Mrs. Lanchester. It was time to play chess and would Shadbolt come in too? So Louise went and he followed after an interval of five minutes. Mrs. Lanchester was in the great drawing-room, looking more than ever like some small irate mummified caricature of the reigning queen. She was sitting at the chess-table and for some

84

reason four candles had been lighted and, as a further act of generosity, the butler brought in a decanter of madeira and another of port and some thin biscuits. For more than two hours he sat there watching Louise and Mrs. Lanchester move the Chinese chessmen, making small manœuvres of cherry-colour and ivory in the smoky-gold candlelight. "Fill up your glass, Shadbolt, don't wait for us," the old lady kept saying, and he obeyed. It was his first taste of good wine and perhaps because of it the beauty of the girl, smiling at him across the candlelight with deep and fascinating caution, struck him very deeply. He felt mere longing for her rise up into an anguish that was beautiful itself. Then, below both anguish and longing, he felt the quickening of some other and as yet only latent impulse: something fierce, devilish and potentially irresponsible. Stirred by wine, it grumbled warmly in him like a volcano. It was like the dull pricking of something inflamed. Dull-headed himself, he did not and in fact had no reason to pause and examine it. But whenever, in later years, he felt it again and knew what it was and obeyed it, his mind went back to the game of chess that he sat watching Louise and the old lady play that evening: to the candle-warm silver, the wine in the glass that looked like silver itself, the great elephantine shadows and the crusted ceiling above, the keen spittle-bright eyes of the old lady, and Louise telegraphing, with eyes so beautiful by contrast, her messages of devotion.

When the game was over, just before ten o'clock, the old lady stood up and, hands clasped about each other like grey crabs, ejected the nearest thing to a speech Bruno ever heard her make. She said: "Shadbolt, you did a magnificent thing this afternoon. If it hadn't been for you we might have been seriously hurt or smoked out or something. I don't know. Anyway, I don't feel safe any more. I want you to come and live here completely. Sleep here and everything. Well?" It was all shot out at him with generous and yet emotionless rapidity.

He saw no reason to refuse and, in fact, many reasons to accept.

"Good," she said. "Can you sleep here to-night?"

"There's my sister," he said. "She'll wonder about me She's upset enough as it is."

"Go home," she said, "and tell her and come back again. I'll have a room got ready for you while you're gone."

Louise and he walked across the park and the fields, in the sultry October darkness, to tell Maria and fetch his things. Coming back, wandering off the paths, they walked as it were in a sea of dew. He walked with his arms round her. In the anxiety of love, he suddenly wanted to lie down with her. She said tenderly: "It's so wet. Wait."

"Which room do you sleep in?" he said.

She told him: a small white-pannelled room, high up, with a mirror on the wall.

"Shall I be near it?"

"You'll find your way," she said.

They stood together, leaning against the wall of the house, before going in. She undid the neck of her dress for him and he put his hands on her breasts. And as he stood there, with the great mass of Spella Ho itself like a bulwark behind him and the extreme tenderness of her young breasts before him, he was conscious of an abrupt retreat and fading of all ambition. Where he had wanted to go, he wanted suddenly to remain. He felt he wanted to stay with her without the minutest change in the constancy of whatever she felt for him, for a longer stretch of time than he could measure: not merely for ever but, he thought, beyond even that.

CHAPTER IV

Two days later he went down into Castor to buy himself some shirts and, unprecedented thing, a nightshirt. It was no use, Maria had urged, putting it off any longer. Impossible to go on living at Spella Ho with only one shirt to

86

his back. Moreover, it seemed that men in only slightly superior walks of life had a separate shirt for sleeping. It took him some time to believe this.

There were two drapers in Castor, Faulkner's in High Street, Beamer's in the Square. He looked into Faulkner's and then went on to Beamer's and it was like looking into a mirror. He saw in Beamer's window the reflected arrangement of Faulkner's: the same rolls of winter flannel, the same fly-blown dickies, the same cat as it were asleep on the same rolls of dust-flecked calico. Hardly anyone in Castor bought shirts ready made and there were no shirts in the windows. He did not know what to do.

Turning away from Beamer's, he ran straight into Chamberlain. The two men knocked against each other and there was a moment of silence. Chamberlain's left hand was bandaged and he held it resting between the front buttons of his jacket and his eyes were a smoky plum colour. The slash across Bruno's eye had not healed and his hands were swollen. The two men stared at each other as though not believing the things they had inflicted on each other. They were men who had been through something together and suddenly it was as though the experience had taken them very close together.

Suddenly, showing very handsome white teeth under his bruise-thickened lips, Chamberlain grinned. He put out his hand and Bruno took it. Bruno tried to say something, but the pulley in his mind jammed and refused to work and he could only grin too. "The next time you want to fight," Chamberlain said, "for Christ's sake have a go at yourself. Your mug can stand it."

Bruno grinned again but could not speak and Chamberlain said, "Have a drink?"

They went into "The Bell". They sat there for more than two hours, drinking, always at Chamberlain's expense and in spite of Bruno's protests, first porter and then whisky. It was an occasion that caused, afterwards, almost as much a sensation as the fight itself. They talked chiefly about shirts. Chamberlain was horrified that any man should buy a shirt in Castor. The shirts in Castor had less style than the nightgowns of old ladies. He himself was well and rather flashily dressed but without dandyism, wearing a sort of grey derby hat and a suit of small draught-board checks and a black-and-white silk cravat. His black hair, greased with macassar oil, looked polished. He wore his jacket open and displayed a gold snake watch-chain and a claret seal. He was a man who travelled about and he was the only man in Castor who bought his clothes in London. He told Bruno about this and Bruno listened in a state of stupefied enchantment. "If you must get your clothes locally," Chamberlain said, "get 'em in Bedford. There's a good shop there and I often get the nag out and drive up. You don't want to wear a bloody old nightgown from Beamer's." And gradually as they sat there, in the pub, softened by porter and then fired by whisky, they began to be slightly fascinated by each other. They had already great respect for each other and now, Bruno so squat and ugly, Chamberlain so flashily dressed and good looking, it was as though they began to see in each other a counterpart. It was an attraction of opposites, and time and liquor increased it. That morning, also, each was much impressed by one thing about the other: Bruno by the fact that Chamberlain had money, Chamberlain by the fact that Bruno could drink. "That's what I like," Chamberlain said. "Head like a rock, by God." In time he himself grew slightly excited, and he painted a picture for Bruno of life in London, of gin-palaces, music-halls, women in skin-tights and even of women in nothing at all. "By God, Shadbolt," he said, "we must go to London." He put into the picture the touches of a man who knew his subject. "I know a woman in a pub off the Waterloo Road with a union jack on her drawers. It's half a dollar to salute the flag." He clasped Bruno's shoulders as they came out of the pub, swaggering, thick-talking, spitting in emphasis of fabulous truths. "Even in Bedford I know a tart who for next to nothing—"

Bruno was fired also by a spirit of devilry. By God, they would go to Bedford. "Next Saturday," Chamberlain said. "First the shirts. Then—" He looked at Bruno. "And a new hat." He took off Bruno's hat and looked at it as though it were a lump of horse-dung. "How the hell d'ye expect a woman to look at you in a hat like that?"

CHAPTER V

Whenever he came out of the house, in the mornings, he would find Louise on the edge of the park, feeding the chickens that had been let out from the disused pheasant-pens under the sycamore trees. It was a job that, as a sort of recreation, she had taken out of the hands of the garden-boy. That Saturday morning he could not see her there.

He went into the house. She had not been into the park, and for some reason no one could remember seeing her. He went to her sitting-room but it was empty, and at last he went along to the small room with the candlesticks, the room which Mrs. Lanchester then called her office.

There Louise sat at the table, motionless, as though she had given up whatever it was she had been trying to do. She was very white and in a moment he knew that she was in pain.

"What is it?" he said. "What's up?"

"I had a pain down my side in the night and I couldn't sleep and now it's come again."

"Whereabouts is it? What sort of pain?"

She tried to tell him. It was no use. "I sat on the edge of the bed, trembling all over," she said.

"Go and lie down," he said.

"No. It seems worse if I lie down. I'll walk about a bit. I'll feed the chickens."

He went with her into the park. He held the corn-bowl for her while she tossed corn and maize to the chickens. She moved gently, with a caution brought about by weakness.

They went back into the house. She was very pale. He was not scared, but something told him it was not right. He kept urging her to lie down. He wanted to fetch her something to eat or drink. "Some hot milk."

"No. It's all right."

"Tell me how it feels."

"It's all right."

"Is it something you've had before?"

"No, I've never had it." She thought of something and smiled. "Perhaps I've been lacing too tight. Perhaps it's that."

He got her to sit down in her room. He went down into the kitchen, bringing back hot milk in a glass. "The cook says if it's no better soon she'll put poultices on. They'll draw it out." He gave her the milk. She burnt her hand on the glass as she took it.

"It's too hot, I can't hold it."

"I'll get a basin," he said. "I'll get a basin and spoon. You'll drink it better."

He went to the door. She protested a little and he, thinking of something, stopped. "Have you taken your stays off?"

"Not yet. It's—"

"Take them off. Perhaps it's them that's doing it."

"I'll try while you've gone."

When he came back again she had taken off her high, impossible stays. Released, she breathed easily. "I feel better, much better. You go out and do your work. You're going out. You're going to Bedford."

He watched her drink the milk. "Not if you're no better."

"I want you to. I want you to buy some things. I want you to."

"What things? You made that up."

"No. I mean it."

"What things then?"

She hesitated. "For you. For you, if you must know."

"For me?"

"For your birthday. You're twenty-one. I didn't want you to know. Now I've told you."

He felt curiously touched. "How did you know?"

"Oh! I found out."

He bent down and, for a moment or two, put his arms about her. Without the stays, she was lovely to hold, soft and delicate, her body all tenderness. Holding her, he could not bear to think of anything happening to her.

He went out, leaving her to rest. Two glaziers had come up that morning from Castor to mend the broken windows. He gave directions, walking up and down the terrace with them. They regarded him, though he was too preoccupied to notice it, with detached respect. Suddenly he thought of something. "You see that window? The one next to the end?" The two men looked up, following his finger as it pointed to Louise's room. "Get that done first. Quick."

He could not work. In his phlegmatic mind concern would not resolve itself into fear. His emotion was not centralized. Now and then he felt within himself an indication of something larger than fear.

But it was not conscious. It did not resolve itself and it was some curious grumbling of premonition that took him suddenly into the house about eleven o'clock.

Louise, in her room, was kneeling down by the chair, pressing herself against it, in agony. He lifted her up. She stiffened out in pain, muttering a little, not speaking. He ran upstairs with her, calling as he went for Mrs. Lanchester.

He laid Louise on her bed upstairs. Mrs. Lanchester came up after him, stumping her stick on the carpets, grousing. She took one look at Louise. "Is there a doctor in Castor?"

"Yes. Dr. Black."

"Get him. Get the phaeton out and drive yourself down. Fast."

"Yes."

"Make him come." He saw Louise roll on the bed and stiffen out her legs in agony. He went out.

He got out the old dark-green and still high-polished phaeton, harnessed up and drove into Castor. He caught the doctor in the street. "Doctor! A girl at Spella Ho. She's in great pain."

"I'll come after dinner."

"No. Now."

"I'm off to another patient. What name is it?"

"Miss Williamson. Mine's Shadbolt."

Suddenly the doctor looked at him. It was as though he had suddenly remembered something. Bruno stared back at him with immobility, his face hammered out by concern and determination into a passivity which was itself threatening. Suddenly the doctor got up into the phaeton. The significance of this incident did not, at the time, strike Bruno.

Later, much later, he remembered it. Then, as he drove back to Spella Ho, only one thing had any significance at all. Thinking of it, he did not speak to the doctor. The doctor, who also did not speak, was a young man but, with a large brown beard already resting like a fox-tail on his collar, he looked somewhere between forty and fifty. He had an indeterminate manner, keeping his eyes on the distance, and it was clear that his reason for not speaking was a social one.

Up in the room, from which Bruno was excluded, the doctor pressed his hands on Louise's right side. "You feel it here?" She flinched. "Not much?" He pressed his hands higher up, and then lower. "Here?" She shot out her legs and drew them up again and lay still, paralysed with pain. The doctor went to the window and looked out. The two glaziers were climbing up the ladder, carrying glass and putty. Impelled by a sense of decency, he drew the curtains. Then he went back to the bed. He looked at Louise and then at Mrs. Lanchester, indeterminately. "I don't think it's serious. I don't think you need worry," he said. It was clear that he was talking for talking's sake.

"Can't you give her something?" Mrs. Lanchester said. He seemed frightened by the alert spit of her voice.

"Oh yes, I can give her something. If Mr. Shadbolt will come down he can bring it back." He seemed glad of the chance to get away.

Bruno drove back with the doctor to Castor. When they drove up to the house, a large beautiful cream-plastered house on the square, the doctor disappeared into the house and did not come out again. After twenty minutes an old woman emerged, to give Bruno a medicine bottle. The medicine, still unsettled, looked like milk.

As he drove back, the medicine settled, throwing its white deposit, leaving the liquid clear and not quite colourless. Curious, Bruno pulled the cork and smelled it. He smelled peppermint. Then he put his tongue on the bottle and let a little of the medicine run on to it. It seemed to him that underneath the peppermint he could taste Epsom salts.

Something about the whole thing, the doctor's indecision, the medicine, seemed to him unsatisfactory. He had no faith in what was being done. He took the medicine upstairs. He knocked on the door and the cook came out. "You can't come in. We're putting poultices on her." He gave her the medicine. "I'll give you the wink when you can come up." She hesitated. "I tell you what I'll do. I'll pull the curtains back across the window."

He went downstairs again, trying to measure his fear. It eluded him. He went out on to the terrace and talked to the glaziers, who were packing up. It was almost noon, and at noon he heard the bell ring for Mrs. Lanchester's midday meal and he knew that with luck she would be coming down. He stood on the terrace, looking up at Louise's window. Suddenly the curtains were drawn back.

He went upstairs. She was alone. To his relief she

looked much better. "I'm all right. I want you to go," she said.

"No." He could not rid himself of his lack of faith. "I got work to do here."

"I want you to go. I want the things."

"I don't want the things."

His meaning was not clear. He meant to convey that, since it was a question of remaining with her or having the things, he would prefer to remain with her. She did not understand this. She started to cry. He stood helpless, with a feeling of compassion and stupidity. He tried to explain himself. Her tears started to fall on the bed.

"I'll go. I'll go," he said.

"Don't go just for my sake."

"No. I'll go. I want to go. He can drive me straight back."

She dabbed her eyes on the sheet. Crying had given her face colour, so that he felt for a moment reassured about her.

"I wanted you to get yourself a watch and chain."

He was staggered. A watch and chain had always been beyond his scheme of material things. It was too much. "You can't afford it," he said.

"I can. I want to." She told him where she kept her money: in the top small drawer of the chest, in a glove-box. "Take two sovereigns."

"No. I—"

"Please."

Impressed, in a conflict of misery and doubt, he at last got out the glove-box. Then, as he held it in his hands, it seemed a very personal thing and he could not open it. "No," he said. "You do it."

She took it and opened it. "Look," she said. "That's all my money. Fourteen pounds. And then you say I can't afford a watch and chain."

"You can't either."

In answer she gave him the two sovereigns. She pressed them into his palm softly and firmly, with her thumb, in a way that recalled for him some game with buttons he had played with Maria as a child. "Get the watch and chain and then get your shirts and your hat and come straight back."

"All right."

"You'll look so smart," she said.

He hated leaving her, so small and, with her hair down, more than ever like some frightened little dog on the great pillows of the bed. "I'll be back by five." He suddenly leaned across the bed and kissed her, more out of fear than tenderness. "Smart Bruno, with his watch and chain," she said. "I shall think about you. Now go and get ready."

"You don't feel that pain now?"

"No. Not now."

"You don't want anything?"

"No."

"You're sure?"

"No. Yes."

That small confusion and the smile which followed it reassured him. He went out at last. The two sovereigns seemed to stick to his hands like warm lozenges.

At one-thirty Chamberlain picked him up at the gates of Spella Ho. He drove a dandy little trap of bottle green with chrome-yellow wheels, with a black high-stepping mare. In a suit of real check tweed and a gold pin in his white cravat and looking very dashing with waxed moustaches, Chamberlain talked with generosity and friendliness, as though feeling that he had something to make up to Bruno. He talked with colour, drawing for Bruno pictures of various ladies. "By God, Shadbolt, it's my ambition to run a little lady in town. You know, properly. Keep her. Set her up in a house, so as you know where to find her. Some day I shall do it."

They spanked out at a fast pace into Bedford.

"What about a drink first?"

"I got to get a watch and chain."

"A watch and chain? What the hell for?"

"It's a present from somebody. It's my birthday."

"Birthday? You never said. Well, that calls for a drink."

They stabled at a smart hotel by the river. "The hottest shop," Chamberlain said, "in town. It don't look it. But you wait. Wait till to-night."

"I got to be back by five."

"You what?"

"I meant to tell you. It's the old lady. She's cranky about being left after dark since the windows were busted."

"Christ, that don't give us time to get fizzed up."

"I can't help it."

"Well, don't let's waste any more time, that's all. Waiter! Two more gins."

Bruno drank quickly. He felt that he needed it. Drink might straighten out in time the complexities of fear and faith. His mind seemed loose. He wanted to tighten it up.

When they came out into the street, almost an hour later, Chamberlain was already a man fired with large ideas. "I'll get you the best bloody hat and the best bloody shirts and the best bloody watch and chain in town. Come on."

"I got to get that watch and chain first."

"All right."

At the jeweller's Chamberlain revealed himself as a man of luxurious taste. "Have this hunter. It strikes. Listen. What's the price of this hunter?"

"Twelve pounds."

Bruno picked up a small Swiss-made watch. It was smooth as a mirror, without engraving. "Thirty shillings," the jeweller said. "See your face in it."

"I'll take it."

The jeweller wound it up. "I'll set it right for you," he said. "Twenty minutes to four."

Suddenly Bruno felt anxious. "Show me a chain," he said. "Quick." He envied Chamberlain's snake chain and in the end he bought one like it, in supposed silver, for fifteen shillings. He felt suddenly very proud as he walked out of the shop and, opening his jacket, he walked with his thumbs in his arm-holes.

Chamberlain was slightly disappointed. "You should have had that hunter. You could have knocked 'em flat with that. Get'em listening to a hunter striking and you can do anything."

At one outfitters which from time to time Chamberlain patronized—"when I can't get up to London"—they bought shirts and a high-crowned squarish grey hat. It made Bruno look slightly taller. He had to buy collars and a necktie for the new shirts, and the whole purchase landed him for a sovereign more than he could afford. "Hell, what's a quid?" Chamberlain said. "Pay me when you like." He put down a sovereign. "You just put a new shirt and collar on while I hop round the corner. I got to get some cigars."

Cigar in mouth, Chamberlain met him five minutes later. "Have one?"

"It's damn near four. I got to get back."

"That don't prevent you having a cigar, does it?"

Bruno took a cigar, chewed the end off and stuffed it into his mouth. Chamberlain lit it and Bruno blew large clouds of smoke. "Suits you," Chamberlain said. "Makes you look somebody. But take the band off."

They went back to the hotel. Bruno was uneasy. Looking out at the river, he thought of Louise.

"It's no use. I got to get back."

"Just one drink. It's your birthday."

They had large gins, twice. Chamberlain was stimulated to greats ideas, to a great scheme whereby they should go back to Spella and then return about eleven that night. "That's the time here. Enough to burn your whiskers off."

A woman came and stood in the doorway as they talked. She looked first at Chamberlain, then, more slowly, at Bruno. She was dressed to kill, with a curiously saucy white hat that perched on the front of her head like a scallop shell, and large white ruffs to her flouncy black dress. The dress was loose on her figure, but somehow, by leaning on the doorpost, she managed to accentuate the line of her hips. She wore white pear-drop ear-rings and she had, Bruno noticed, a mole about the size of a lady-bird low down on her left cheek. After about a minute, she went out.

By her arrival and still more by her departure, Chamberlain was put into a state of eager excitement. He passed his tongue once or twice over his lips, like a man confronted with a large portion of steak. Suddenly, and before Bruno could protest, he got up and went out too.

Bruno drank his gin and waited. After ten minutes Chamberlain had not come back. Bruno took out his watch: it was almost half-past four. He finished his drink, his cigar going out in his hand. Then suddenly he had a premonition that Chamberlain was not coming back. He pushed the dead cigar into his mouth and went out into the hotel yard. An ostler cleaning the wheels of a carriage was the only person there. "See a gentleman go out just now? Wearing a check suit?"

"No." Then, suddenly seeing the cigar: "No sir. No sir. I ain't sir. No sir."

"Or a lady?"

"No sir, no sir. I ain't sir. No sir, I ain't sir."

Bruno went back into the hotel; then into the smoke-room, from there into the dining-room; then out into the yard again. Nobody had seen Chamberlain. It was almost five o'clock.

Suddenly he had an immense and very powerful premonition about Louise. He had to go, he had to get home. Something was happening. He seemed to see her, in the bed in her room at Spella Ho, shooting out her legs in pain.

He went straight out of the hotel and, not stopping, began to walk out of the town. It was ten miles. Walking steadily, he could do it in something over two hours. As he walked he kept taking the dead cigar out of his mouth and putting it back, chewing its end. This, and the continual glances at his watch, were his only signs of emotion. He had gone almost four miles before he realized that the cigar was not burning.

It was then getting dark. Suddenly he heard behind him the sound of wheels and turning, saw Chamberlain coming, driving hard.

"What's up? Why did you run off like that?"

Up in the trap, Bruno told him about Louise, how he felt that something was wrong.

"Christ, why didn't you say?"

"I felt it was all right. Then all of a sudden I knew something was up."

They drove in silence, fast. After a time Chamberlain said: "That pain, is it down the right side? If it is it sounds like an aunt of mine. They called that a stoppage."

Bruno did not know what to say. He had a continual impression, increasing as they drove, that he was watching the course of something inevitable and that nothing he could do would stop it. He wanted to change the subject.

"Who was that woman," he said, "at the hotel?"

"Her? Now you're talking. Sophie. And by God would she keep you warm on a cold day?"

Bruno felt he had to talk about the woman, about anything. "Was that mark on her cheek a mole or is it a patch just stuck on?"

"It's a mole. And I'll tell you something else. She's got a mole somewhere else, if you know where to look for it."

Suddenly he did not want to talk. He did not want to hear about women, about a woman. He felt that no other woman would interest him again. The concentration of his whole life was now on Louise, on that small bedroom at Spella Ho.

Chamberlain drove him through the gates and up the avenue, through great drifts of fallen lime leaves that were brushed by the horse's feet with a sound of sea-waves in the darkness. It was a sound he was to hear again, but never with the same sea-like ghostliness. He was driven by that sound into his first phase of actual fear.

Chamberlain drove him to the door. "Shall I wait? Do you want me to get the doctor?"

"No. It's all right. I'll get in."

"I'd like to come round in the morning," Chamberlain said.

The drive had sobered them; they felt close together. "You still got your cigar in your mouth," Chamberlain said. He began to drive off and then turned to call: "You know where I live if you want me."

Bruno did not know. But it was all the same. It did not matter. He went into the house. In the kitchen the cook met him, her face white. "She's worse. It's no use denying it, either. She's bad. She got worse after that medicine." She looked hard at him. "Your cigar's out."

"Can I go up?" At last he threw the cigar away, into the kitchen grate.

In the bedroom Louise lay stupefied by a long recurrence of pain. Her face was like the peel of an unripe lemon in the candlelight. He put his hands on hers: they were hot, and yet her arms were rough with goose-skin. "Are you all right?" he said.

"Did you get your watch?"

"Yes. How you feeling?"

"I feel as if something's going to burst inside me. Have you got your watch on?"

"Yes."

"Show it me." He showed it her. She rubbed it against her hand, quietly.

"And the chain. That's nice. Like a snake."

He held the watch against her ear and she heard it ticking, her eyes far away. "And is that your new hat?"

He had put his hat on the bed. "Yes."

"It's nice. Put it on." He put it on. "You look a swank in it." She was smiling.

Suddenly she clutched him, fearfully, very hard, like someone sinking into an abyss. Pain destroyed her smile like a puff of air putting out a candle. She stared up at him out of a darkness of agony.

While she lay there in pain he thought of something.

"Stay with her," he said to the cook. "Stay here with her while I go down to Mrs. Lanchester. Where is she?"

"In the big drawing-room."

He went downstairs. In the drawing-room Mrs. Lanchester was reading, by the aid of a large pair of silver lorgnettes, some cumbersome treatise on medicine and anatomy. She was concentrated, when he entered, on a large anatomical diagram of the female form. She was in a state of outrage, brought on by what was, to Bruno, an astonishing display of affection for Louise and by contempt for Dr. Black. "That medicine was nothing more than Epsom salts flavoured with peppermint. The poor creature was fifty times worse less than an hour after she took it. It's my belief she may have an internal abscess. That being so, a physic could only aggravate it."

She spoke with impressive vigour and sanity. What she said confirmed, in detail for which he could not help feeling a great respect, his own fears. He told her what was on his mind.

"Let me take her to the infirmary."

"How? How far is it?"

"About fifteen miles. I could drive her in the phaeton. We could shut it up."

She sat considering it. Suddenly, as he stood there, immobile against the mahogany table, his coat undone, she saw his watch and chain.

"Where'd you get that watch?" she said.

"She bought it me. Louise."

As soon as complete understanding of the situation came to her she did not hesitate. "Get the phaeton out," she said. "Tell them to get blankets ready. And see that you've got good candles in the lamps."

Half an hour later, when he carried Louise downstairs wrapped like some small dark Eskimo in blankets, Mrs. Lanchester met him in the large hall. "You'll want money. They'll do anything for money." His hands being full, she put into his pocket what he later discovered to be ten pounds, in sovereigns. "Go on, now. Good-bye."

He carried Louise out into the darkness and packed her into the back of the phaeton and in a few minutes drove away.

He drove slowly, at very little above walking pace, the reins tight. The night was very dark, but not cold, with a promise of rain. He could hear things from a great distance. The sound of lime-leaves rustling up again in the avenue seemed to pursue him for a long time.

He spoke to Louise in the back of the phaeton. "Are you all right? Am I driving too fast?" She did not protest. He drove for long intervals without speaking. Then, because she was so silent, he was afraid she must be lonely, thinking of things. So he began to talk again. He began to tell her about the infirmary, how he had been there. Making it funny, he described the old woman, how, except for the business of the duck-eggs, he might never have done all that he had done. "You might see that old tit. She might still be there. If she is and you see her you tell her about me. Ask her if she remembers the duck-eggs." He laughed a little. He spoke with unaccustomed garrulity, trying to be light-hearted. All the time he felt inside himself a great lump of fear.

Then she began to speak. "What will they do to me?"

"Do to you?" He tried to make light of that too. "Give you a new set of works." But he knew that it was a poor attempt. He knew that whatever fear she had was not dispelled so easily. Again, at odd intervals, he knew that he was afraid himself. What would they do to her?

He drove so slowly, in the mild soft darkness hardly pricked by lights, that it was almost eleven o'clock before he drove up to the infirmary. He carried Louise into the waiting room and set her down on a wooden form and left her there while he went to look for someone. He walked up and down several stone corridors. It was all shadowy, ill-lit by oil-lamps, and there were stale diffused odours of carbolic acid. There were many doors and he did not know what to do.

He was coming back to Louise when a woman accosted

him. "What are you tramping up and down here for? How do you suppose patients can sleep?"

He told her. "She's in great pain. I must see someone."

"You ought to make proper application at the proper time."

"It's an emergency."

"See the night-sister on duty at the women's ward. Ward No. 7."

He turned to go. A man in a dingy black top-hat went past, carrying a patent leather bag. Bruno clutched him. "Are you a doctor?"

"What do you want?"

"Are you a doctor?"

"Yes, I am a doctor."

"There's a woman, a girl." He told the doctor about it too. The doctor listened with the air of a man who was thinking of something quite different. Like Black, he had a large beard, which he kept stroking. It seemed like a gesture of both vanity and indifference.

"See the night sister on duty at the women's ward. At this hour —"

He walked away, down the corridor. Suddenly, watching him go, Bruno remembered something. He strode after him. He gripped the lapels of his coat and stopped him. "Does it make any difference if I have the money?"

The doctor seemed affronted. He opened his mouth, then paused, as though framing an angry reply. Then, before he had time to speak, Bruno put into his hands Mrs. Lanchester's money. "For Christ's sake do something. I brought her all this way in a phaeton. Fifteen miles. For Christ's sake."

"In a phaeton?" The doctor stared at Bruno, at the money, and it seemed as though the aspect of things was at once altered. "Where is this lady?"

Back in the waiting-room, the doctor put his hand on Louise's forehead. He stood with watch in hand and took her pulse. "The sister will take you and find you a bed."

"Can I go with her?"

"No. She may not be out for some time. It would be better if you went now and came back later."

He did not know what to do or say. He stood indecisively looking at Louise, who seemed suddenly very small, helpless and alone. He felt that she was going from him for a long time and that it was essential he should do something. His mind all at once went blank. Then he saw the doctor putting his watch back into his pocket, and it reminded him of his own. He suddenly took it out and gave it, with the chain, to Louise.

"You'll be able to look at the time in the night. It won't seem so long."

She did not want to take it.

"Yes," he said. "It'll help you. It won't seem so lonely. You have it."

Suddenly she took it. She stood nursing it in her hands. "If I don't come out of here again," she said, "you're to have my things."

He could not bear to speak, and suddenly the nurse lifted her into her arms and carried her out of the room.

He went out of the hospital and walked up and down in the dark street. His mind felt like a piece of worn elastic. Spiritless, it could not stretch out to either hope or despondency. He was kept by it in a state of extreme loneliness. He walked up and down for half an hour outside the hospital and then finally went back and sat in the phaeton. It was beginning to rain slightly and it was much colder. He saw before him the constant image of Louise with the watch in her hands, until it was lost at last in the dark swim of his own weariness.

He went to sleep. When he woke up, about seven o'clock, the carriage lamps were out and it was raining fast. The horse stood with lowered head, in misery. He climbed out of the phaeton and went into the hospital. It seemed an extraordinarily empty place, without life. He sat down in the waiting-room. He could not think and he sat watching the rain slide down the high hospital windows.

Not properly awake and afraid of falling asleep again, he went out into the rain. He let it fall on his face. Then he wiped it off with his sleeve, feeling a little fresher. Then he got into the phaeton and once more stared at the rain.

Almost an hour later he heard someone calling him. He got out of the phaeton and went across to the door of the waiting-room and it was the night sister. She was holding something in her hands.

"Is this your watch?"

He held out his hand without speaking. The watch was cold and the chain fell on his hand like a small cold snake. He stood looking at the watch. He stood for quite a minute, looking at it, in complete silence. Then it occurred to him, suddenly, that it had come back from the dead.

BOOK THREE

GERDA

CHAPTER I

HE struggled out of his ignorance very slowly, stupefied
by the death of Louise. Time and existence did not matter,
and it was the year 1879 before anything of importance
happened to him.

In the late autumn of that year the Chamberlains invited him to supper. They owned the third largest house
in Castor, a once six-roomed house to which, year by year,
Charles Walker Chamberlain had added bays, cupolas and
turrets in the manner of French châteaux. Mr. Chamberlain was a muscular Christian: a small man with powerfully
short thick arms and a face like ruckled bark. With the
doctrines of the Church he managed also to mix the
doctrines of the Spartans. Winter and summer, indoors
and out, he wore a straw hat. Bought in 1865 and worn
continually ever since, this hat had ceased to be a hat and
had become an emblem. Tilted slightly back on a pad
of gingerish hair, it stood for something more than Sparta
in the modern world. It combined Sparta and Christ,
stood as a denunciation of the sin of pride. "Accuse me,"
Mr. Chamberlain would say, "of what you like — the sin
of unbelief, the sin of covetousness, almost any sin you
like to name. But not the sin of pride." During supper he
got up from the table and put first one foot and then
another on the red plush upholstery of an armchair. He
was wearing the too-large kip-leather boots of a labourer,
thick with the old and fresh mud of weeks. The boots left

wet imprints on the fine expressive plush. "Honest mud. God's mud. You see what I mean? I am not too proud to walk in it. I am not too proud for it to go on my chairs." He wiped the mud off with his hand. "Or on my body." He wiped his hands on his trousers and sat down, incongruous and fiery in his straw hat. "Or my clothes. Or anywhere. What was good enough for God to put here is good enough for me."

"And you, Mr. Shadbolt." He looked at Bruno, who had just finished sucking gravy off his knife and mopping lumps of bread over his plate and had now turned the bread-cleaned plate upside down, ready for the pudding. "You Mr. Shadbolt. I see you're not too proud. Good. I like that. Turning your plate over for the pudding. I like that. An action like that would have stood for something in Sparta."

After supper Bruno went with Rufus and Mr. and Mrs. Chamberlain into a room built into one of the new turrets. It was a round room, completely windowless. It was filled with books. Except for the library at Spella Ho, Bruno had not seen so many books. They went round him in huge sombre circles. "Yes," Mr. Chamberlain said, "they encompass me about. The windows? Another idea of mine." He began to take his jacket off and then sat down in his shirt sleeves, resting his muddy boots on the arm of another chair. "A room for books don't need windows. Books are windows. Take your coat off. Make yourself at home. Put your feet up if you want to."

"You read 'em all?" Bruno said.

"The books? Every one. Every one. Every one bought by me and read by me." He jumped up. "You read much? Ever read this?" He pounced at the bookshelves, clasping a large book in his hands like an eager red squirrel. He thrust it into Bruno's hands and snatched it away and was up at the shelves again. He began to call down titles. "Like to borrow it? You read, don't you?" He began to pile books on a side table. "Rufus, fetch string. Mr. Shadbolt, I'll give you a copy of my pamphlet."

He pounced to the other end of the room. All this time Mrs. Chamberlain sat by the fire in silence and as though nothing were happening: a woman in grey upholstery, soft, negative, her large amber and jade necklaces the only sign of a slight inward extravagance of spirit.

Mr. Chamberlain pounced back at Bruno. "My pamphlet on the meaning, justification and necessity for Spartanism to-day, one penny. Yes, I charge you for it. If I didn't charge you it would be too easy for you. That's not Spartan."

Bruno felt in his pockets.

"I got no money with me."

"No money? Good. That's the wisest thing you could ever say, think or do. If you never carry any money you never spend it. I never carry a cent myself. Never. You'll give me the penny some other time?"

He pounced off to the bookshelves, pausing to make a note in his pocket diary. "Of a thousand pamphlets I have now sold two hundred and sixty-three. I calculate that in two or three years I shall show a slight profit. In ten years fifty-four per cent."

Bruno watched him mount the book-ladder, red hair fiery against the mouse-dull books.

"Some time," he said, "I'd like to get hold of some book on money-making."

"Eh?" Chamberlain appeared ready to pounce. "What's that? Making money? No such book, no such book. Mr. Shadbolt, that's the one book I never read. Any such book would be pure theory, Mr. Shadbolt, pure theory. I'm not interested in theory. Practice, practice, practice —that's what I'm interested in." He half turned on the ladder. "I started my business on a capital of three pounds, Mr. Shadbolt. Leather-dressing. Try to imagine what that means. Three pounds. And I lost it all in the first year. A terrible affair, Mr. Shadbolt, terrible. It struck me down. And why? Pride, the old story. The sin of pride—too high and mighty for this, too high and mighty for that. What did I do? I found out about the

Spartans, Mr. Shadbolt, and then I went round to every leather-tanning town in this county and bought up every inch of the dirtiest offal I could find. All the filth, the muck, the throw-out stuff that nobody wanted. I walked miles, everywhere, carrying that stuff on my back That taught me. I never lost a penny from that day, Mr. Shadbolt, not a penny. Pride shows no profit, Mr. Shadbolt, that's the only rule I got. Pride shows no profit. Didn't you ever hear the story of the man who made a fortune out of shovelling up the dog-dirts in the street?"

Bruno said nothing and in a moment Mr. Chamberlain came down the ladder. At the foot, turning sharply, he almost knocked off his straw hat. He caught it with wild hands and turned to Bruno the face of a man suddenly taut with fear and avarice. "Nearly, nearly, nearly. Never have another if I lost that. Never afford another."

This incident of the hat seemed to subdue him a little. In half an hour Bruno left, taking with him a parcel of fifteen books tied up with scraps of bootlace and string.

CHAPTER II

AT Spella Ho, during the winter of 1880, bitterly oppressed by loneliness, he made slow, painful attempts to read these and other books. They forced him more and more into himself. On the fly-leaves of the books Mr. Chamberlain had written his name, the dates of purchase, the prices: "This book belongs to Charles Walker Chamberlain, Purchased October 4, 1874. Price paid, 2d. Present value 4d." Bruno chanced to say something about this, to ask where books could be bought. Mr. Chamberlain said that books could be bought at Orlingford market, Saturday nights, where he had himself bought books for twenty-five years. He was proud of his Spartan courage in having walked to this market, wet or fine, rain or snow, always in his straw hat, in order to satisfy twenty-five years' passionate interest in literature. "And I shall walk there for another twenty-five. I shall walk. Even if the railway comes and picks me up and sets me down at my front door I shall still walk. And the railway will come. I know it will come. One of the days I am waiting for, Mr. Shadbolt, is the day when the railway will link up Castor with the outside world."

"Why?"

"Why? Never mind that, Mr. Shadbolt, never mind that. I have reasons. This town needs a railway. I shall never use it, mark you, but we need it just the same."

"Where will the railway come if it does come? Where will it come from?"

"Mr. Shadbolt," Mr. Chamberlain said, "I am not a prophet. I don't need to be a prophet. It is obvious where the railway will come and where it will come from. It will come from London and it will skirt the south side of the town and go on to Derby and the north."

"What makes you think that?"

"Think? Think? I don't think, Mr. Shadbolt. I know."

On a March Saturday night Bruno walked down to Orlingford market. He stood in a wild wind and looked with inexhaustible patience at many books. A man with the tired sunken face of a starved dog stood behind the paraffin-flare and blew constantly into his thin red hands and stamped his feet on the cold cobbles.

"What sort o' books you lookin' for, mister?"

"Eh? Just books."

As he stood there a woman also came to look at the books. She stood and looked at book after book with the same tireless patience as himself. She had very fair hair coiled into a magnificent thick bunch that rested heavily on her neck. She had large soft blonde hands. He stood and stared at her hands.

He heard her ask for German books. The bookseller said yes, he had the poems of Goethe. He got the book out for her and blew on it and she took it and looked at it. "No," she said, "no. In German. Please in German."

"In German? No, you got me beat."

"Please?"

"I say you got me beat. Ain't had a German book for donkeys years."

"Please? You might have something another week?"

"Might do. Must it be in German? Can't you read in English?"

"I am German," she said.

She went away and Bruno stayed to buy Brock's *Treatise on Agriculture* for threepence, not wanting it.

A week later he was there again and after a time she came too, asking again for books in German. As she turned over the books, as though not wanting to go without buying something, Bruno stood again fascinated by her large soft blonde hands. With methodical patience he turned over books himself, and once, reaching out for a book, he knocked his hand against hers and hers was as warm as new bread. Blowing on cold fingers, the bookseller watched them.

She did not buy anything that week and Bruno did not buy anything. The next week she was there again and as before he stood fascinated by her large and in some way beautifully comforting hands. They turned over the books together for almost an hour, not buying anything, until at last the bookseller was tired of it.

"Ain't you two licked the steam off for long enough?"

"Please?"

"He says if we don't want no books we better go."

She turned away almost before he had spoken and automatically he went with her. They walked out of the market without speaking. In the street they stopped and he looked at her. In looking at her he felt a great sense of familiarity and comfort. He saw in the deep placidity of her face an expression of something deep and tender.

"I could get you German books," he said.

"Please, but where?"

"Up at Spella."

"Please?"

He told her about Spella Ho, how he felt that there were German books in the library there.

"But they don't belong to you."

"That don't matter. I could borrow 'em for you and take 'em back and she'd never know."

"She?"

"The old lady. Mrs. Lanchester. Haven't you ever heard of her? Where do you live?"

"In Castor."

He could not believe it. He stood in astonished silence.

"Yes, in Castor," she said. "I'm the wife of Dr. Black. I came back from Germany with him at Christmas last."

Thinking of Louise, he could not speak. He felt crushed back into stupidity and apathy. He felt that there was nothing he could do, that there was nothing now that was worth doing.

Suddenly she was telling him how much she wanted books, above all books in her own language. There were no German books in the doctor's house; she had exhausted those she had brought from Germany. "It means so much to read in your own language. It means so much." And he knew without her saying any more that she was homesick and like himself lonely.

He said suddenly that he would try to bring her books on the following week. Something made him say that he would bring them there, to the market, and not to the house, in Castor. She heard distinctly and did not protest. She said that she drove to Orlingford with her mother-in-law every Saturday evening, visiting relatives, and that they excused her for an hour while she looked for books. "It's better if you bring the books here. Yes! If I go back so many times without books they must begin to think it strange." He asked her to write down for him the names of the books she would like if he could get them. "I'll write just the authors' names," she said, and in her level German hand she pencilled on a piece of paper the names of Goethe, Schiller, and others.

"Anything by them. Anything," she said. "I've nothing

to do with myself all day." He asked her what he should do if it rained, not thinking she would come. She looked at him with large eyes from which her former placidity had been burned out by excitement. "I shall come in any case," she said.

He struggled down to Orlingford on the following Saturday with a dozen books tied up in a sack. He was excited, a little perturbed that they were not the right books. He had put on his best suit and was wearing the watch Louise had given him. He stood in the doorway of a shop and kept looking at the watch. It was a fine night, with a hard March breeze. He stood there for an hour and nothing happened.

Agitated, he at last put the books on his back and went into the market, and there she was, waiting by the book-stall. He could see that she was agitated too. They had not understood each other about the meeting place; they had each been afraid of being fooled. When she saw him she threw up her hands in a sudden gesture of surprise and delight, laughing because he had brought the books in a sack. They went out of the market and into a back street and stood outside the window of a ham-and-beef shop and he opened the sack so that she could see the books by the light. She took the first book in her hands and looked at it but said nothing; then she took the others. She looked at all of them in the same way: at first excitedly, then without excitement, suddenly depressed. He saw her face flattened by despondency.

"Is anything up?" he said.

"Please?"

"Haven't I done right?" he said. "They're the names you put down for me."

"Yes," she said, "but they're in French, not German. They are translations from the German."

"Eh?" he said. "I thought French and German were the same."

She loved that, and very shortly they were laughing again. He had made a mistake; it could be put right. "You could come up to Spella," he said, "and I'd give you all the books in the library until you did get what you want."

"You mean I should call?" she said. "In the afternoon? In the proper English way?"

It was his turn to laugh, and they stood laughing together. He saw her despondency replaced by elation, eyes lit up, white teeth shining in her broad mouth. He wanted to go on talking to her, to prolong the pure pleasure of hearing her laugh. He put the books back into the bag and they stood together and looked into the ham-and-beef shop: fresh sausages, cured ham, warm faggots, snow-rippled basins of lard, spiced beef.

"Makes you feel hungry don't it?" he said.

"Yes," she said, "I am hungry."

He caught the odour of faggots. "What about a faggot?" he said. "I could eat a bullock."

"Please?"

"A faggot." He pointed into the window. "See 'em? The brown things. Hot."

"Yes."

"You want one?"

"Yes, please yes."

He went into the shop and came out with the faggots in a basin. "She let me have a spoon and a basin. Only I got to take 'em back," he said. "You git yours down you while it's hot."

"Please?"

"Eat it. With the spoon. While it's hot. Go on."

"You?"

"When you've done."

"No," she said. "Now. With me. It's better."

They began to eat. She would take a spoonful and then he. Sharing the spoon with her he felt a sharpening sense of intimacy. He felt the friendliness between them solidify into something concrete and yet warm and secret.

"Good?" he said.

"Yes, good. Very good."

"You can't get 'em in Castor. Dead alive hole." He gave her the spoon. "You like living there?"

"No."

He was startled. It came out so suddenly. He did not know what to make of her and could not speak.

"I like Germany," she said. "Only Germany."

She had finished the last of the faggots and stood holding the empty basin. He took it from her. Instinct, the hardborn instinct of the days when he had never had enough to eat, made him lick the spoon and basin until they were bone-white. She stood watching him, amused and yet, somehow, knowing why he did it.

"That was good," she said.

"Yes," he said. "The last mite's the best." He looked at the empty shining basin, and suddenly he saw the funny side of it all himself. "Well, that's one dish she won't have to wipe up."

He looked up to see the woman in the shop watching them from behind the lamp in the window. He went back into the shop with the basin. The woman looked at him queerly, suspicious. He had some vague impression that her face was familiar, but he could not place it. He went out and again she looked at him as he stood in the street.

"She's looking at us," he said. "She thought we were going to nick the basin."

"Nick?"

"Pinch."

"Pinch?"

"Bone it, nab it."

"Please."

"Steal it."

They began to walk down the street, out of the shop light into darkness.

"Are they good words?"

"Yes. What's wrong with 'em?"

"I never heard them, that's all. It's nice to hear new words. Different words. It's nice to meet different people."

"Like me?" He was mocking a little.

"Yes," she said. "Like you."

The moment of candour held him in suspense. They stood in the street. She was going and he knew there was only one chance of seeing her again.

"When'll you come to Spella for the books?"

"What is to-day?" she said.

"Saturday."

"It couldn't be to-morrow. Not Sunday. It could be Monday."

"I collect the rents Monday. It'll have to be after dark. I don't get back till six."

"Then it must be after dark."

They arranged he should meet her at the gates. She said good-night and walked across the street.

Suddenly she was back again.

"No. That would not be right. I couldn't come. Not to the house."

"No?"

"No. You could come down to Castor? If you come to the corner of the street I will send out a maid for the books."

She seemed suddenly frightened.

"All right," he said. "I'll come down."

After darkness on Monday he went down to Castor with two volumes of Goethe, in marble boards, wrapped up into a brown paper parcel. It was raining. He stood outside the back carriage gates of the doctor's house and waited. He could see lamplight splitting the curtains of the windows that looked on to the street. He waited for the maid to come, walking a dozen paces one way and then the other, not daring to go away. He held the books under his coat. After a time it began to rain so fast that he could feel the wetness coming through his coat. He walked up and down. His action had in it the pig-headed determination of a man who has something to do and must do it and will do it. He walked up and down for almost three hours. Nobody came.

HE did not see the doctor's wife again for six weeks. During these six weeks something happened. He received an offer of business. It came through Rufus Chamberlain. A man named Stokes had set up in business as a dealer in leather. Stokes had fifteen years' experience of leather and a small workshop in a back-yard in Castor; the business needed money. Bruno could be a sleeping partner, putting in capital for ten pounds. He hesitated.

While he hesitated Chamberlain pointed out something which had only vaguely occurred to him before. "When the old lady pegs out," he said, "where are you?" He talked of the business as an insurance against the uncertainty of the future. "There's no risk, no work. Stokes is a good man. There's money in it." Impressed by Chamberlain's enthusiasm and by the thought that he was the son of a man who had also risen from nothing, Bruno decided to accept. To the surprise of both Chamberlain and Stokes he insisted on a deed of partnership.

Stokes was indignant. " Ain't my word good enough?"

"No."

He insisted on the drawing up of an amazing document. Chiefly he bargained for fifty per cent of the profits and an option, exerciseable at the end of three years, to purchase the business outright if, up to that time, Stokes had not increased the capital by an amount equal to or above his original sum. He stipulated for the power to decide in all matters of finance and for a return of five percent on his money. These proposals staggered both Stokes and Chamberlain and the lawyer laughed at them. Bruno walked out of the office. Two minutes later Stokes was running down the street after him, begging him to go back. He went back and to Stokes's dismay added a proposal insisting on a yearly balance sheet. Stokes signed the agreement, thoroughly frightened.

Bruno was not impressed by Stokes. He was a small pale-faced man with a high squeaky pig-voice of protest and shifty hands. His workshop was a disused loft above a stable in the backyard of an empty house. Half a dozen sacks of scrap leather were piled up in one corner. "What do you do with it?" Bruno said. Stokes then showed him how the leather was sorted and graded. "Where do you send it?"

"Where Chamberlain used to send his. I never worked five year for Chamberlain for nothing."

"I never knew you worked for Chamberlain. Where does he send it?"

"Two firms in London. One in Manchester. And there's others."

"All right. Book everything down."

"What?"

"Book everything down. Every ha'penny, every bit and scrap that goes out and in. I'll come in every Friday and look at the weeks' accounts."

"Anything else?"

"Yes. What screw are you taking out?"

"A quid. That's what I thought."

"You take fifteen bob for a week or two and be satisfied."

"That ain't much. That ain't—"

"Whose money is it?" Bruno said. "Yours or mine?"

He felt momentarily elated: business, partnership, profits, money. He felt himself swinging out to a new circle of experience. He was a big man, things were great, times were moving. In this mood of cocksureness he went down to "The Bell" to find Chamberlain.

"Hey, Rufus, there y' are. Have a gin, man, and drink to the business."

They drank. "Here's to Stokes and Shadbolt!" Chamberlain said.

"Shadbolt and Stokes, damn you. And don't forget it."

"Shadbolt and Stokes! All right. Shadbolt and Stokes. Luck!"

"Your old man started on three pounds. I'm starting on ten. Next year we'll buy him up!"

Then as they ordered more gin, drinking to a business of

already mythical proportions, Bruno remembered something.

"You never mentioned that Stokes worked for your old man for five years."

"Christ, not so loud. You want everybody to hear?"

"Why didn't you tell me?"

Chamberlain did not speak.

"Come on, what's at the bottom of it? Why did he leave? What was it?"

"The old man sacked him."

"What for?"

Chamberlain was quiet again.

"Come on, what for?"

"Boozing. You know he's dead against it."

"That all?"

"Yes."

"Where do I come in?"

Chamberlain ordered another gin. For a moment he did not touch it. "I got his daughter in the family way. He found it out just after he got the sack. Said he'd tell the old man if I didn't do something for him."

"And all you could think of was for me to cough up ten pounds."

"No. No."

"What then?"

"I was going to cough up. Then I couldn't raise it. Every now and then the old man hears I've been on the loose and stops every ha'penny."

Bruno stood with his hands tight together, the glass between them. The thought of business suddenly meant nothing. Elation was ironed out; the flat plane of things dead. He felt he had said good-bye to his ten pounds, that the whole affair was a swindle.

That suddenly infuriated him. He slammed down his glass on the bar and cracked it. In the bar nobody said a word except himself. "Where's he hang out?" he said to Chamberlain. "Stokes."

"You'll find him in "The Swan"."

Bruno walked out of the bar without another word and across the square and down into High Street, head slightly down and forward, long arms loose, body rolling like that of an angry baboon. He reached "The Swan" in about five minutes. He went straight into the bar. Stokes was sitting on a wall-bench, three-parts drunk, his eyes smoke-hazy. Bruno went to him, dragged him up and out of the bar and, on the causeway outside, hit him in the face. Stokes rose to his feet like a man coming to the surface of water, arms paddling. Bruno hit him again. Stokes fell back against the wall of the pub and stood staring and Bruno got ready to hit him again. Stokes did not move. Bruno lifted his arm. "Get up off that street and back to the shop."

Stokes walked dully up the street and Bruno followed him to the workshop. There Stokes sat on the pile of leather scrap and nursed his face.

"You're in business with me," Bruno said, "and don't forget it."

"What's the bloody game?"

"You're in business with me," Bruno said. "That's the bloody game."

Stokes did not answer.

"How many hours a day did you work for Chamberlain?"

"Twelve."

"That's a damn lie. You worked fourteen."

"Have it your own way. Fourteen."

"All right. You work fourteen here."

"Who said so?"

"I said so."

Stokes nursed his face.

"All right. You're the boss."

"Yes," said Bruno, "I'm the boss."

After that he called every evening at the workshop. He lumbered heavily up the outside wooden stairs and into the upstairs room where Stokes would still be working by the light of a tin oil-lamp hung on the white-washed wall. He would take off his jacket, revealing the immensely thick ugly arms bare almost to elbows, and begin to work himself. He would work on for two, three and sometimes four hours, poring chiefly over the small accounts, adding up simple columns of figures with agonized concentration, straightening out the muddle of Stokes's arrangements, slowly and painfully but at last triumphantly evolving for himself some crude system of book-keeping. At Spella Ho he found, in the disused stable, a high desk, with attached stool, left there by some former owner. He carried it down to Castor under cover of darkness and installed it in the workshop. He bought a flat lock-up tin cash-box and in it put all the capital the firm possessed, keeping both keys for himself. Soon afterwards he came across a partition of matchwood and a door knocked down at some period of renovation at Spella Ho, and now discarded among empty pheasant-coops outside. Thick varnish had partially kept out the rain. He dried the wood in the sun and revarnished it and then carried door and partition down to Castor under cover of darkness. With this door and this partition he built up, in the corner of the workshop, a small office. He bought a second cheap oil lamp and hung it on the wall. Beside it he hung a calendar. In this small secluded cubbyhole he assumed an entirely new position. He was elevated to a position of importance; a man of figures, books, a man only to be got at through the closed door of an office. At night he locked the office. It remained locked until he appeared on the following evening. In it, with painful but defeatless concentration, he examined letters, checked bills and, most painful business of all, wrote letters. He wrote with semi-illiteracy, composing letters by some system of jig-saw puzzling, word crudely matched to word, his name signed with small capitals.

It was a strange arrangement and it seemed, very soon, as if it could not last. In the first two months the business succeeded in earning just enough to pay Stokes weekly wages. Then suddenly there was a small boom. Orders began to come in with great rapidity. To Bruno's dismay it was not possible to meet them. Their small stock was exhausted. They stood in an empty workshop. In a few days the business was standing still.

From the first Bruno had not liked the business. Its potentialities were small. Scrap leather was something despised; it fetched despised prices. The Chamberlains had long since gone beyond this and now tanned leather. Thinking of the great extent of the Chamberlain business he was restless. Then his stocks began to be increased again and things moved slowly on. Yet he was still dissatisfied.

He worked every evening. He knew, somehow, that he was getting nowhere. There was no trust between himself and Stokes. He tried to evolve new schemes. He felt the lack of some kind of inspiring force. He thought of Louise, seeing her now as the lost mainspring of his ambition. Without her, ambition was a stopped watch.

Every evening, after locking up cash-box and office and finally workshop, he walked out of the back streets into High Street and so up into the Square. He would stand outside the doctor's house and watch the split of light in the dark curtains. He would stand and think of the German Mrs. Black, and the soft blonde hands as they had lain on the dark books. He wondered why she had not come or sent for the books. Then, for three weeks, he walked down to Orlingford on Saturday night and stood by the bookstall and hoped he would see her there. She never came.

He did not see her for six weeks. Just before this happened Mrs. Lanchester fell ill. She sent for him on the Saturday before Whitsuntide: a close day of oppressive sunlight, Spella Ho itself white in the sun above the surrounding may-coloured park. She lay in the too-warm south bedroom. She had not been up since morning. "Shadbolt," she said, "I've a feeling I shall never see Whitsuntide." He said he would get a doctor. "I don't want a doctor," she said. She spoke quite strongly; there was nothing in her of the dying woman. He asked if he could get her anything: some brandy, a glass of milk, some camomile.

"Get me the Bible," she said.

He went downstairs to the library and after a long search found a Bible. He had never before heard her speak of God, religion, Bible or church. She had remained aloof from these matters, like a hermit, as she had remained aloof from the rest of the world.

She took the Bible eagerly. "Oh! Shadbolt, I need the comfort of the word of God."

He did not say anything.

"I'm a wicked sinner, Shadbolt."

"Yes mum," he said.

Shortly afterwards she begged him to leave her. He left her propped up on the feather pillows with the Bible open on the coverlet. He took not the slightest notice of what had passed. He had long known her to be a little crazy. A little craziness more or less meant nothing.

Towards evening she pulled frantically at the bell-rope, and he went up, the bell clanging all over the house as he mounted the stairs. He found her caught up in an orgy of self-chastisement, beating her hands on the coverlet and her head on the pillows. "I'm a wicked woman, Shadbolt, I'm a wicked woman. I've been a wicked woman." He quietened her impassively.

"Have some tea, mum," he said. "Some camomile."

He made as if to go.

"Don't leave me, Shadbolt! Don't leave me."

"What you want is a good clear out," he said.

He went out and downstairs, to the kitchen. She screamed and clanged the bell for him to come back. He came back at his own pace and in his own time, bringing the cup of steeped camomile. She was furious and exhausted.

"Here," he said, "you drink this. It'll cool your blood and open you out." He moved the plush covered mahogany commode nearer the bed. "Ring the bell if you want me."

She drank the camomile, muttering about religion, God, wickedness, the Bible. "I'm a wicked sinner. I've been wicked. I've forgotten God, Shadbolt."

He went out. She did not ring for him and when, at

half-past nine, he looked into her bedroom she was asleep and he considered it already as all over.

The bell clanged in the night. He put on his trousers over his nightshirt and tucked in the shirt tails as he went along the main landing. The bell ceased clanging as he stopped on the landing at a chest to get a candle and light it. Going into the bedroom he saw Mrs. Lanchester lying on the floor. She had been out to the commode and could not get back. He lifted her back into bed. "I'm going, Shadbolt," she said. "I'm going."

He sat with her for the rest of the night. She breathed as though trying to break a hard crust of something in her throat: great laboured frustrated breaths of crackling pain. In the morning, as soon as it was light, he called one of the maids and got out the one horse from the decaying stables and rode down to Castor for Dr. Black. Before he went Mrs. Lanchester revived enough to hurl at him threats of damnation if he ever brought Black into the house again. "Black's gone away," he lied. "There's a new man named Mackenzie now."

In the stable yard of Black's house he could smell coffee. It was not quite five o'clock, dead still, a little misty, the sun not really up. He knocked at the kitchen door and Mrs. Black opened it.

He stood quite still. She did not say anything. Fair, startled, with her broad un-English face, she looked remote and at the same time intimate. He felt a momentary breaking up of self-confidence, a split inside himself, a sudden baring of the idea that he wanted her. Then he spoke. He told her about Mrs. Lanchester, asked if the doctor would come. She asked him into the kitchen and he went in and stood there, smelling the hot strong coffee heating on the stove, while she went upstairs to call her husband. Before she went he told her how, on no account, must the doctor call himself Black, how he must introduce himself as Mackenzie. She went upstairs and came back again in about five minutes, saying the doctor was going. She reached down two cups from the dresser and he followed the line of her upstretched body: fair arms, bodice pursed outward by the full breasts, the rather heavy blonde neck. "You have some coffee?" she said. He could not answer, but only nodded, and she poured it out, black and strong, with just a dash of milk. "I was just going to have mine as you knocked. I wondered who it was. And it's you, of all people." He sipped his coffee, looking at her. It had been winter when he had seen her last, and muffled up, behind fur collar and muff, with a large heavy brown hat, she had looked older. Now he was shocked to see her so young. He felt that she looked ten years younger than Black, that perhaps she was ten years younger. As he drank his coffee he kept his eyes fixed on her, more unconsciously than not, and for a time she was unaware of it. Then suddenly she was aware of it. She looked at him with the realization of it, steadfastly, very quietly, as though she had partly expected it and partly wanted it. Afterwards she told him how inwardly startled and frightened she was by this. "You looked as if you could eat me," she said. And he said: "I could."

As they stood there drinking the coffee he heard the doctor drive off from the yard outside. Mrs. Black stood with head up, listening. There was an expression of restrained relief on her face. "He's in a bad temper. Didn't come in to say good-bye." She turned and reached for the coffee-pot from the range. Without asking she filled up both cups, adding the dash of milk.

"Real coffee," Bruno said.

"Real good German coffee," she said.

"We used to have coffee made of parsnips. All we got."

"Please?"

"Parsnips. You know." He explained to her. "We baked them and then scraped them and poured water on them and that made coffee. All we ever got."

Apart from that his beginnings, his poverty, were not mentioned between them. But he was aware, instantly, of a feeling of understanding, of acceptance. He felt that they stood on the same ground.

In a moment she laughed. "Always when we are together we talk about things to eat."

"Why didn't you send for the books?" he said.

She looked out of the window. The sun was coming up, and he saw the golden shininess of her very fair eyebrows quiver slightly, and he knew quite well why she had not sent.

"They're still there," he said.

"Yes?"

"Yes."

"I couldn't come."

"Why not?"

"How could I?"

"Some people ride up in dog-carts," he said. It was his only way of expressing the tensity he felt, obliquely, talking in small fine riddles. She understood and said: "I haven't read a German book for five weeks."

"None at the bookstall?"

"I gave up going."

"I went," he said, "once or twice."

She looked at him, straight, inescapably direct. He looked back, the point of intimacy explosive. He felt as if they had gone slap into each other. As though to escape it she said, "What a nice day it's going to be. All the trees out, so warm. Very nice. But you should see spring in Germany."

She drank her coffee. "Cherry trees. Birches. Oh! so much cherry-blossom."

He was taking no notice, only fascinated by her voice and the reverberation, inside himself, of the moment of explosive contact between them. Then suddenly she said:

"I'm going back to Germany."

"When?"

"I don't know. Some day."

"This year?"

"I don't know. I don't know when."

"You want to go back?" he said.

"Yes."

He looked at her hands, fascinated by the pure sun-blonde flesh.

"Don't you like England?"

"Yes."

"What is it then? The people?"

"Some people. You have some more coffee?"

"No," he said. "No thanks. Which people?"

She smiled. "What makes you ask such questions?" she said.

"I want to know about you," he said.

For a moment she did not answer. He drained his coffee. Then: "You go," she said, "now. It's better." They were back at the point of intimacy and he said he would go.

"You'll come for the books?" he said. "Some time."

"Yes," she said. "Some time."

As he rode back to Spella Ho he felt himself permeated by the idea of her, like sun beginning to soak into his flesh. The sun was already a little warm and he could smell the May-odours of haw and chestnut-bloom coming faintly off the half-misty park. At the entrance to the avenue he met the doctor.

"She seems to want to die," he said. He spoke as though his task began and ended with the reluctance of Mrs. Lanchester to live. "I've bolstered her up with a draught."

"You're coming back?"

"I'll come this afternoon."

Mrs. Lanchester slept till midday. At twelve-fifteen she sent for Bruno and he went up to her. She seemed fresher and she began to tell him about her life. "I was born in the last year of last century," she said. "I had a rough time. A bad time. That's why I took to you. That's why I took to Louise." She rambled on, talking of her life with alternate clarity and incoherence. She had begun to be persecuted by her religious shortcomings, by the notion that her soul was not clean before God. She talked of property, money. "I own a great deal of property in London, Shadbolt. Very handsome property." She was struck cold by momentary fears for her salvation. "Shadbolt, I'm a wicked woman.

I've sinned in the sight of God, and He knows. And there's no escaping His eye." She rambled on, lost in a maze of incoherent clap-trap on godliness. She returned to talk about her life, sanely, with brief bitterness. "Ever read *Oliver Twist*, Shadbolt? That's how I was brought up. Charity, workhouse. Come from nothing, nobody. Now I own property in London. Handsome property, Shadbolt, nice property." She would seem momentarily happy in the thought of achievement; then religion shook her again. She suffered torments at the thought of soul-damnation. Then sanity made her say: "Shadbolt, it's been my wish to leave you something. Which would you rather? — money or property."

"I leave it to you," he said.

"Property *is* money," she said.

"All right," he said. "Property."

"Well, we'll see," she said. "We'll see."

She rambled on until the middle of the sultry, May-drowsy afternoon. She was convincing him of the necessity of dying with her soul washed to the cleanness of the soul of a child, rambling wildly, when a maid came up to say that the doctor had come. "Dr. Mackenzie has come back," he said and he went out of the room, passing Black on the stairs. Black, who was in white flannel trousers, did not speak and Bruno went downstairs and opened the big front doors, to let in some air. He opened the doors and then went out on to the terrace. At the end of the terrace, on the drive, he could see the doctor's dog-cart. Mrs. Black was sitting in it.

He went slowly along the terrace in the warm sunshine. He went to speak to her and he felt that she had come so that he could speak to her. She was wearing a white summer dress. She carried the correct white sunshade, silk-tasselled, and was wearing white kid boots. He stood by the dog-cart and looked up at her. She did not speak. He did not know what to say either, and before either of them could think of anything to say Black himself came out of the house and in thirty seconds the dog cart was being driven away. He stood looking after it, in a state of furious inertia, angry at having done nothing and at the same time knowing nothing could be done.

Back in the house he went up to Mrs. Lanchester. "Sit with me, Shadbolt. Sit and talk to me." She was tired, weary from the thick May-heat, beyond patience with the doctor. "Up here and down in a second. No time for me. Must go and play at cricket. Mackenzie! Scotsman. Just as bad as Black."

"Mackenzie's a good man," he said.

"Oh! I feel a woman and a half when he's gone and you're with me."

They talked. She said: "Shadbolt, when I'm gone you're done for a job. What are you going to do?"

He decided to tell her about Stokes. "I was a fool, but now I'm in it and perhaps we can make something of it."

"Don't sound very lively to me."

"No," he said, "it don't sound very lively."

"You'd make a good bailiff," she said, "to somebody. I'll see you get references."

"No," he said, "I'm done with bailiffing."

"Want to make money? That it?"

"Yes. That's it."

"Go in for property, Shadbolt," she said. "When you save a little money buy a little property. Draw your rents, save a bit more, buy a bit more property. No reason why you shouldn't own Castor some day."

"Go on," he said, "tell me I'll own London."

He talked with her for an hour. She seemed stronger, much livelier. When he left her to lock up the gates of Spella Ho for the evening she spent an hour and a half writing letters. About seven o'clock he walked down to Castor to post these letters and to pick up pills and medicine for her from Black's surgery. Instead of going to the surgery he went round to the kitchen. The door was opened not by Mrs. Black but by a servant girl. "Medicine? Side door please, and remember next time!" He got the medicine but deliberately left the pills on the shelf by the surgery trap door and then walked slowly across the Square to "The Bell". He went in and had two glasses of beer. The bar was crowded, the air stifling. He took his second glass and stood outside with it in the cool entry. He asked a man what time the cricket finished. "Seven. It's that now." Two minutes later he put his empty glass on the bar and walked back to the doctor's house and rang the surgery bell. "I must have left the pills." "Leave your head next." He said: "It's a good thing I did. Mrs. Lanchester's worse. We want the doctor to come up as soon as he can." "Who's worse?" the girl said, and he said "Mrs. Lanchester. Up at Spella Ho." She opened her mouth. "Up at Spella Ho? Why'nt you say so?" He turned away, taking grim revenge. "I did," he said, "but some folk never seem to wash their ears out."

In this mood of grim obsession, his mind permeated only by one idea, he went back to Spella Ho. Mrs. Lanchester was sleeping. He walked about in the park, in the May dusk, thinking solely of Mrs. Black. In the still warm. chestnut-scented air he listened for the approach of wheels in the avenue. When they came, towards nine o'clock, he went back to the terrace. The dog-cart was standing there as it had stood there in the afternoon, but it was empty. He walked along the terrace, stood under the first trees of the avenue, and listened. Someone was moving on the grass, under the trees. He knew instinctively who it was and he waited for her to come nearer. She must have known he was there too. She came on and finally they stood together, each waiting for the other to say something. And once again, as in the afternoon, they could think of nothing to say. It was still very warm; she was still in her white dress and she had long white gloves on her hands. He noticed these things vaguely, but he must have stared at the gloves, for suddenly she said: "I must wear them. It's correct. I have to wear them." "Take them off," he said, and she began to take them off. He saw the whiteness of gloves replaced by the living colourness of her hands. "Feel," she said. She put out the gloves and he touched them. They were moist with sweat. "Feel my hands." Her hands were warm and clammy. She let her fingers fall out of his. "I wear them since two o'clock." He did not say anything; could only look at her. In the imprisonment of her hands by the white gloves he saw the imprisonment of herself by the conventions of Black's life, and he knew that that was what she meant him to see. He knew why she had come up to Spella Ho, and he knew, for some reason, that she meant him to see that too. By the very fact of doing nothing and saying very little he felt himself drifting towards an immense intimacy with her. Conventions, some sort of fear only, were keeping him back, and he saw it as only a question of time before they were washed out.

He knew why she had come up. Now he wanted to know only when she was coming again. He asked her.

"To-morrow."

She answered with a promptitude of which the assured quietness staggered him. It seemed suddenly as if she had it all worked out: like someone who knows the answer to all riddles before they are asked.

She looked towards the house. "She is very ill?"

"I don't know. It's old age."

"How long is she going to live? Not long?"

"Not long."

"I'll come every day until it's finished," she said.

They walked back towards the trap, listening for Black's footsteps on the terrace. The park, its trees, grass, air, everything, was very still on all sides of them. She looked up again towards the house, an obscure mass of colourless stone with here and there a daub of lamplight. "It's so big," she said. "Very nice. Very English."

"Yes."

"I want to see inside it."

"When?"

"One day. I'll tell you when."

They stood in silence again. A few moments later Black came out of the house. Bruno walked along and stood under the tree and saw the trap drive down the avenue.

On Sunday Mrs. Lanchester was the same, agitated by eternal fits of religious misgiving, bouts of semi-hysteria, talk of God and damnation, with small periods of sanity. He lifted her in and out of bed, attended her bodily needs, made her comfortable.

He could not rest. He felt completely permeated by the idea of Mrs. Black: saw her over and over again in the white dress, with the sweat-soaked white gloves; saw the deep blonde hands which fascinated him so much. He expected her that morning, with Black, about eleven. When he heard Black's trap arrive he went downstairs. He met Black in the hall. Black said. "You're the bailiff, aren't you? I want a word with you before you go," and he went upstairs.

Bruno went out on to the terrace. The trap was empty. He walked round the house, came back. She was not there and he could not believe it.

As he stood there Black came out of the house.

"Shadbolt?"

"Yes."

"My wife is very interested in English architecture. She would very much appreciate it if you would show her over Spella Ho."

"Yes, doctor."

"She suggests Tuesday afternoon. That suit you?"

"Yes, doctor."

Black pulled on his Sunday gloves: white gloves, with guides of black. "And about Mrs. Lanchester."

"Yes."

"Mrs. Lanchester is sleeping in a feather bed. Change it."

"Why?"

"Do as I say. She'll never die in a feather bed."

He got up into the trap and drove off. Bruno went into the house. He did not change the feather bed. He had no intention of changing it. He thought dismally, with determination and obsession, of Mrs. Black, knew now that he could not see her till Tuesday.

On Tuesday morning a Mr. Carmichael, solicitor, arrived from London with his clerk. They spent the two hours from eleven to one o'clock with Mrs. Lanchester. Shortly after one o'clock the bell clanged and Bruno went up to Mrs. Lanchester's bedroom. She was in a state of exceptional coherence, quite calm, not the old shrewd, downright, calmly rapacious self, but ineffably calm as though she had put herself through the fire of self-chastisement. "We need witnesses to some documents," the solicitor said. "Bring the cook and a maid. Ask if they can write their names." Five minutes later Bruno stood at the bedside while the two servants witnessed with laborious scratchings various sheets of what he knew must be the will. At the conclusion of it all the old lady made a grand gesture. "Now I can die in peace." Bruno kept her down to reality: "Never mind about dying in peace. You haven't been out on the commode for twenty-four hours and you'd better see what you can do." An hour later, the solicitor gone, the house quiet in the May sunlight, she lay back in bed and folded her hands: the gesture of one splendidly ready to die. "Leave me in peace, Shadbolt," she said.

He left her and went downstairs and, in the hall, found Mrs. Black waiting. "I walked up," she said. "Across the fields." In her hands she had a bunch of cowslips. As he led her across the passages, into rooms, up stairs, he could smell the golden scent, the wine warmness of the flowers. In a voice that did not mean anything he told her about the rooms, bits of history, showed her dates carved in the stone above doors and fireplaces. They moved quietly. She did not speak much. He knew by now that the house meant nothing to her: only the silence, the secure seclusion of it. In the sun-fusty rooms they stood and looked out over the park, on the solid partition of green lying like a thick leaf mattress between themselves and earth. "As if," she said, "you could jump down and bounce on it." They stood quiet, at the very top of the house, held in momentary elation, waiting for something to happen.

He knew quite well this was the moment she had come for. He stood and faced her and without a word she put her arms round his neck. He stood in silence, feeling her soft beautifully full arms. The necessity for quietness, for dead secrecy, made the moment in some way painful, and he felt the bursting of relief in himself when she spoke. "Nobody can come?" He shook his head. Then he asked her the thing that was troubling him. "Your other name. I don't know it."

"Gerda," she said.

"Gerda." He repeated it. "How do you spell it?"

She spelt it. He thought about it for a moment.

"You don't like it?" she said.

"Yes," he said, "I like it."

That was almost all that happened that day. On the following day she came up to Spella Ho again: the secrecy, the silence of the warm afternoon were repeated. From empty rooms in which nobody had lived and nothing had happened for a long time they looked down on the park. She put her arms round his neck and they stood still. He felt that all of it had the drawn tensity of a spider's web. It was something that could not last. During the next day and the next this feeling increased. He felt he could not go on: it was too delicate, he longed for a moment of concreteness, a rock of consummation on which something would split. He knew, at the same time, that it had not come to that.

Mrs. Lanchester lived out the week. She continued to experience grave periods of self-absolution, of deep penultimate content, in splendid readiness for death. The next morning she was fretful again, able to get out of bed, as far from dying as ever. Between the two women, the old woman trying hard to die, the young one just finding something for which to live, he had the hardest week of his life. He felt that he was on the verge of something catastrophic. His nerves set themselves on edge like soured teeth. He tried, without success, to see beyond the death of the old lady: where he should go, what would happen.

"You're worried," Gerda said. "You shouldn't worry. It's all right."

"It's the old lady. What happens to me when she's gone?"

"You shouldn't worry about that."

Taking her over the house had made him realize something: how much the house now meant to him. He had begun to feel his life built round the place. It was an immense axis of endeavour. He had begun to be aware in it of an enormous friendliness.

"Is it far to the sea?" Gerda said one afternoon.

"The sea?" he said. "Why?"

"I was just thinking."

"It's ninety miles or more."

"Not far."

He had grown up to think of it, as he had grown up to think of London, as being beyond the ends of the earth. Why was she thinking of the sea? Suddenly he knew quite well.

"You're not going back? Not to Germany?"

"It's not right to stop here. Living like this."

"Oh! for Christ's sake don't talk about it," he said.

He knew then, without any doubt, that if it came to a choice between herself and the house he would have no choice.

Mrs. Lanchester lived over the week-end. He did not see Gerda on Sunday, a day of grim sacredness at the Black household, with Scottish prayers and bleak Scottish self-denial, nor on Monday, when from eight to six he collected the rents. Then as he drove back to the house on Monday evening he knew that something was happening. As he drove in to the stable yard the cook came out to tell him how the doctor had called that afternoon and had ordered the changing of the bed. They had changed the bed and Mrs. Lanchester was dying.

He left the horse in harness and went up to Mrs. Lanchester. She put out a resigned, age-skinny hand on the counterpane "Shadbolt." He sat with her. She shut her eyes. "Shadbolt," she said again. For half an hour she lay silent, only moving her lips as though trying to frame some difficult sentence that she wanted to say to him. Finally she succeeded. She roused herself to say "Shadbolt, you're ugly, but you're all right," and died, very quietly, her mouth still open, just after seven.

He drove down to Castor to inform the doctor. Black was out. "Is Mrs. Black in?" he said. He waited and in a moment she came out and they stood together in the big stone porch. She shut the door and kept her hand on the knob. He told her that Mrs. Lanchester was dead.

"I feel somehow as if everything is finished," he said.

For about a minute she did not say anything. She put out her free hand and he took it and held it. "How do you know it is not just beginning?" she said.

CHAPTER IV

Six weeks later he ran away with Mrs. Black, using a horse and trap he had bought at the four-day sale at Spella Ho. They drove away after darkness on the night of July 12th, making east, towards the coast. She had a small valise, about forty pounds in money, some cold coffee in a wine-bottle and some cold beef and bread. He had all his money, about fifteen pounds, and the clothes he stood up in. They aimed to take three, perhaps four days on the journey. Gerda was full of what was to him a strange determination, showing no hysteria, not even excitement. That night they drove about thirty miles. From three to five o'clock in the morning they had a sort of half-sleep under a haystack, giving the horse a feed of hay, and at five o'clock they got up and had a meal of coffee and bread and meat and then drove on. They did not stop to wash and Gerda combed her hair as they went along, an immense thick mass of polished yellow which she plaited unto two ropes, holding one plait in her mouth while she finished the other. They drove on into

Cambridge and straight through it, not stopping. Then, beyond it, about nine o'clock, they had another meal, the bread and meat and cold coffee, as before. They found a pond surrounded by sloe-bushes and while Bruno watered the horse Gerda took off her dress and washed. Bending over the water, cooling her wrists, with arms and face magnificently strong and brown in the hot sunlight, she looked very much like a beautiful mare herself: solid, dependable, patient, not at all the sort of woman to be running away with. They drove on all morning into strange flat country, potato fields, green-yellow fields of corn, lines of willow with shining leaves rippling over grey and grey-green in a perpendicular sun. At midday they stopped and spent their first money. He fetched beer and bread and cheese from a pub. They drank the beer outside the pub, giving the horse ten minutes' rest, and then drove on again, to rest again all afternoon by a brook, under willows, where they ate the bread and cheese and had a short sleep. About four o'clock Bruno woke up to find Gerda washing her feet. She dried them in the sun. Strong, flat, beautifully solid, they had the same look of utter dependability as her brown arms and face. They were the sort of feet that might have gone on, in the same way, doing the same things, for ever. And gradually he began to feel that this was exactly what Gerda and himself were doing: going on, from village to village, in a succession of rests and journeys that must gradually pile up into infinite distance.

They were then about fifty miles from home.

The horse was already tired and they decided to put up for the night. They stopped about six o'clock at a small pub that was also a farm: a small low house of terra-cotta wash, with tarred outbuildings, a pond, a coop for hens.

"Beds for the night?" The woman clumped up the wooden stairs in front of them, a big, panting, asthmatical woman. "Been a warm day, ain't it? Well, this is it. Ain't been used jes lately and I'm ashamed on it. But I'll put clean sheets on and it'll be all right. One room or two?"

"One room," Gerda said.

"Like to take it?"

"Yes," Gerda said, "we would like to take it."

They went to bed early and lay together between the almost cold clean sheets in the wooden bed. The act of sleeping with her was a consummation of all the happenings of the summer. He felt incredibly far away from things of the past, transplanted to a new and in some way much more dependable world. Lying there, in the strange bed, his hand on her body, sleepy, he felt that she and himself and their affection were the least ephemeral things in the world.

"You think she knows we're not married?"

"I don't know," he said, "and I don't care."

"She seems nice, like a real fat German woman."

"Asthmatical." He was almost asleep.

They lay in silence. He was on the verge of sleep when she said, "How far is it now to Harwich?"

He did not answer the question, but when he woke, next morning, about five o'clock, it was as though she had only just asked it. He sat up in bed. Harwich, the sea, boats, Germany. He knew, then, why she had asked, why in fact they had come. He got up and put on his trousers and went downstairs, without waking her. In the yard, under a hovel, the man, Mitchell, was milking his one cow, and Bruno asked him for a pair of pincers. "In the nail-box in the stable," Mitchell said. "Anything wrong?" "I got a tracing buckle bent a bit," Bruno said. "I thought I'd straighten it." He went into the stable and found the pincers. What he was going to do had an almost unconscious spontaneity about it, as though the idea had been evolved in his sleep. He got the pincers and took out three nails from the left fore shoe of the horse, loosening it, so that it clipped. Then he went back to the hovel and for about half an hour talked to Mitchell. Mitchell told him how he had a long day ahead of him, lifting early potatoes, pea-picking, turning a small meadow of hay. "Things git a-top on you," Mitchell said.

"I'm short-handed in the bargain. I got to git down to Stortford market to-morrow an' all." His voice, pleasant, unaggressive, had the quiet sibilant hiss of the milk flowing into the bucket. "I know how it is," Bruno said.

At seven o'clock he and Gerda had breakfast in the pub parlour. Sun was turning the slight summer mist to orange, dispersing it. She did not speak about Harwich, but she seemed happy. After breakfast he went out and fetched the horse, leading it into the yard, half-harnessed, as she herself came out of the house. The yard was cobbled with brown egg-pebbles and the clip of the loose shoe was sharp, the horse slightly lamed by it. He stood and regarded horse and shoe with a great show of annoyance, surprise and disappointment. "Just our luck." He fetched Mitchell. "Blacksmith?" Mitchell said. "About four miles on down the road. Lovell, name is. If you went now you'd get back in time to make a start afore dinner. Where you going?"

"Harwich," Gerda said. "Haven't you a horse you could lend us?"

"I got one," Mitchell said, "but things are all on top on me here and I got to get down to Stortford market to-morrow. I couldn't do it."

"I'll get straight down to the blacksmith's," Bruno said.

He borrowed Mitchell's pincers again and drew out the rest of the nails from the loosened shoe, taking it off. "I'll come with you," Gerda said. "No," he said, "stay and rest." He took the horse and led it down the road, keeping it on the grass verge. He did not hurry. At the blacksmith's a carter with a team of four chestnut punches had arrived just before him and he sat for more than two hours under an apple tree in the yard, eating small sourish early apples, waiting for the punches and his own horse to be finished. It was past noon when he got back to Mitchell's. Gerda was not in the yard. He tied the horse to a hovel-post and went into the front parlour, to look for her. "Here!" It came from the kitchen. He went down the passage and into the back kitchen. Gerda was standing at a small bread-trough, sleeves rolled above her elbows, kneading dough. The immediate impression of her warm, happy face, sweat-dewed, sprinkled here and there with a dusting of white flour, filled him with relief. "You see, I had to do something," she said. "We thought you were never coming." Fascinated, he watched her fine strong hands attacking the dough. She began to cut up the dough, batching it. He sensed a change in her; she said nothing about the horse, about going. Mitchell's wife began to take the dough and transfer it to the oven. Gerda had a little dough left over, not enough for a loaf, and she began to shape it into figures, four small dough dolls with skewer-pricked eyes and buttons. "Mrs. Mitchell, Mr. Mitchell, Gerda, and you." She was very happy, laughing; Mrs. Mitchell wheezed asthmatically; and soon the dolls were in the oven, laid side by side. "You move up Mitchell. Move up, Gerda. You want all the bed?" And then the three of them were laughing so that they could not stop and it seemed, momentarily, as though they had always been there, Gerda, himself and Mitchell's asthmatical wife, friendly and laughing, fixed figures in an uncomplicated world of bread and bread-dolls and the good smell of bread on the summer air.

"When are we going?" he said.

"We?" She stood flour-faced, happy. "Oh! don't ask me at least until the bread is done."

He did not say anything. Mrs. Mitchell squeaked asthmatically. "Look at the time. Past twelve a'ready and we reckon t'eat at ha'past."

"She knows about us," Gerda said. "I told her."

"Some folks'd look down their noses," he said.

"I aint' got time to look down my nose at folks," Mrs. Mitchell said. "We slave enough now for the little we git, let alone looking gift horses in the mouth. I slept with Mitchell afore we were married and I ain't found out what difference it made to me yet."

"I'll set the dinner-table," Gerda said.

Twenty minutes later Mitchell came in from the potato-field and they sat down to eat at the same table. There was suet dumpling, the marks of string and bag imprinted on it, and after it cold pork and bread. They ate dumpling on the upturned plate, pork on the right side, in the way Bruno was used to, and he was happy. And after dinner it was again as though they had lived there for a long time: Gerda drying the dishes, Mitchell getting up to serve the bar, the desultory voices of men breaking the heavy summer silence, the familiar rising smell of bread. It was a life fixed in tranquil permanence. There was no cause to change it, no need to go on.

He went out to the potato field that afternoon, with Mitchell, as though it were something he had always done. The heat of the day had reached its height; the dark earth rose in small grey clouds from the fork. Potatoes lay like rows of sun-yellow eggs and the afternoon unrolled with slow somnolence, hot, apparently infinite, the division of time not marked off, time itself something which had ceased to matter. Somewhere between four and five he looked up to see Gerda coming across the field with tin tea-cans and Mrs. Mitchell, some distance behind, with a basket. He and Mitchell knocked off and sat down where they were and Gerda and Mrs. Mitchell sat down with them and all four drank tea and, more in silence than not, ate thick buttered slices of the new bread of Gerda's making. The day was suddenly thick with the smell of tea and sun-warmed butter, sweat and potatoes. After tea the women stayed on, picking up the potatoes, he and Mitchell sacking them. "I'll get the nag and the cart," Mitchell said. "So's we can load up here." "What's wrong with carrying 'em?" Bruno said, and Mitchell said, "That's where I'm done. I wear a truss."

"Give us hold," Bruno said.

One by one he lifted the sacks of potatoes to his back and carried them from the field to the yard, a hundred-weight and a half at a time, a distance of about three furlongs, without trouble. He felt an enormous contentment arise out of the use of strength. He felt excitement solidify into a permanence that was a new experience. When he looked forward to the future he saw it not in terms of Harwich, the sea, Germany, doubts, a complication of fears, but in terms of Mitchell's potatoes. "How far is it to Stortford?" he said, as though his going there, with Mitchell and the potatoes, were already an accepted thing. Mitchell told him it was ten miles. "Like to git a start about six or just after," he said.

In the morning he drove down in Mitchell's cart, with Mitchell, to take the potatoes to market. The day moved slowly, tireless. They arrived back in mid-afternoon. When they came back he had heard the beginning and end of Mitchell's life and philosophy. "We git through," Mitchell said, "and as long as we git through I don't bother."

The words, saturated with contentment, began to impress themselves, unnoticeably, on his own life and Gerda's. The anxiety to go on diminished; almost died completely. Gerda helped in the kitchen, made beds, hung the beds from the windows, German fashion, and baked bread. Morning and afternoon he went into one of the three small fields with Mitchell, pea-picking, digging potatoes, cocking and carrying the last of the hay. July moved on towards its end and all through the month there was a strange sea-washed loftiness over the flat land, a pure candescence of white cloud above white roads and whitening patches of barley. On the last day of the month Mitchell's oats were ready, and the four of them, the Mitchells, Gerda and himself, were up at daybreak, Mitchell mowing, the women making bonds, he bonding and setting the shocks. Wheat followed oats and they worked on, in the same way, until the middle of August, going from wheat to barley. Every week Gerda paid Mrs. Mitchell ten shillings each for bed and board and every night they lay in the large double wooden bed and scratched sleepily at the day's harvest-bumps and the itch of barley beards on sweat-tired skin. They slept heavily and in the morning were up at daybreak, working on through the day as before, happy, finding in physical effort a satisfaction neither had ever found before: a depthless and almost mindless content, complete in itself, self-sufficient, generating no other desire but the desire for each other. By the end of August Gerda's face had a shining German brown-goldness, her hair bleached almost white. September came in with rain and the days suddenly shortened noticeably, but they still worked on, morning to evening, between the rains, carrying Mitchell's corn, dragging the stubbles, with the old self-sufficient energy and content, as though corn and land were their own.

The pause after harvest brought a change. Gerda grew restless. The days were less full; there were empty spaces in which the mind was made aware of itself. Bruno spoke to Mitchell: "Mitchell, what I should like is a place round here, a place like yours. Field or two. Just mullock along. Cow, bit o'wheat or barley."

"Well, that ain't much t'ask for."

"Know of a place?"

"I got a brother," Mitchell said, "down at Ongar. Got a place down there, little house, about seven acres. Alla time talks about giving up."

"You think he'd sell?"

"I ain't sure. No harm in going down to see."

He spoke to Gerda, telling her about the house: how they could perhaps rent it, make it pay, save money. He was again bitten suddenly by the idea of money, the expression of his own released restlessness. He saw Gerda and himself living as man and wife, setting up a new life in a new district, unmolested, making headway. "Wha' you say?" he said. "Let's go and see it."

"No," she said.

"Why?"

"I don't want to go."

"You want to stay here?"

"No."

"What then?"

She did not speak. He was filled with an immediate

sense of foreboding. He had an impression that something between them was about to break. He said: "What is it? What's eating you?"

"Please?"

He saw her turn away her face. She was crying. He did not do anything. He saw that it was not something between them that was breaking, but something within herself. It was not only the first time he had seen her cry but the first time he had seen in her a sign of weakness. He had grown so completely used to the beautiful solidity of her nature, the feeling that she was in complete mastery of herself that now, seeing her momentarily broken up, he felt a sudden crack in his own security. He spoke with automatic and clumsy words of comfort. "Come up to the bedroom. Have it out there." They went up to the bedroom. It was early evening, damp, the room slightly chilly. She sat down on the bed. For a long time she did not speak. She sat still and cried and did not trouble to dry the tears as they fell. He was embarrassed and did not know what to do. He stood for a time at the window and looked out: rather like some imperturbable monkey looking out of a cage, pondering on the thought of escape. The evening darkened rapidly as he stood there. He stood until the individual edges of the land were no longer visible. Then he went back to her. "You don't want to stop here," he said. "Where do you want to go?" He sat down with her, touching her, putting one large clumsy hand on her head, moving his hand backwards and forwards in the thick hair. She did not answer at once. And suddenly, because she was so quiet, he had a moment of panic, seeing himself deprived of her, life turned into a vacuum, seeing her as life, more important than ambition, money, Spella Ho. In the anxiety of the moment he put his hands on her breasts, feeling love for her thicken within himself like a thundery curdling of the blood, realizing for a moment the agony of being without her. "Where do you want to go? Back to Castor? Where? Gerda."

"I want to go back to Germany," she said.

THREE days later they packed what few things they had, harnessed horse and trap and set off to do, by easy stages, the rest of the journey to Harwich. He knew that it was the end. In saying good-bye to the Mitchells, Gerda wept again and now and then throughout the journey he would again see her crying silently, whether from despair or relief or happiness he never knew. They stayed one night on the journey, at a small roadside pub kept by a friend of Mitchell's, and went on the next day after breakfast, getting to Harwich in the late afternoon. It had begun to rain soon after midday and it was blowing a half-gale as they came into Harwich, the sea ugly, the sun setting behind wild bars of crimson and iron-purple cloud. They got lodgings near the harbour: a grey bay-windowed house, the word Lodgings written on a card hanging in the window, a woman with a face like a pale potato to take them up to a second floor room overlooking the sea, a candle flagging in the draught as they went upstairs. "You married? I hope so." Gerda, tired, sat on the edge of the bed. "Yes, we're married." The woman banged the candle on the marble washstand. "Very like you sit on beds where you come from. But I don't." Gerda stood up. "That'll be ten shillings the two of you if you like it. Blowing up for a gale, ain't it?" Bruno got ready to speak, but Gerda interrupted. "You mean we pay now?" she said. "Yes," the woman said, "You pay now. I've been had afore to-day." Gerda paid with half a sovereign. "Ain't you got no luggage, only that valise?" Gerda did not answer and in a minute, reluctantly, the woman went. "The bell don't work. You'll have to come down if you want anything."

In this atmosphere of suspicion they went to bed early and lay listening to the gale rising beyond the harbour, to sounds of wind and sea smashing and tearing with increased violence as the night went on. For a long time they could not sleep. The strange room, a feeling of narrowness pressing in on them, the notion that the woman was listening somewhere just beyond the door kept them awake and silent. The gale came in long minor shrieks down the chimney, flapping the painted cardboard grate-screen. Long after midnight they were still awake and Gerda began talking. He listened vaguely; she was talking about Germany. She had an aunt in a village near Coblenz, a long way from Dresden, her home; and she began to tell him about this aunt: how they could go to her, stay for a little while on the pretence of having come for a holiday, then tell her the truth. The aunt had a small farm. As she described it, oxen pulling the low frame-carts, vine-yards, a few acres of potatoes and rye, it sounded as un-ambitious, peaceful and satisfying as the Mitchells' farm. "She is a good soul. She would be upset for a time, but she would get over it." He still listened vaguely. Suddenly he came to his full senses. He understood in a flash what she was talking about. We, us. He saw that she meant the two of them. He said stupidly, "You mean we should both go?" And she said, "Yes, of course, why not?"

Why not? He could not answer. He only knew, without conscious reason, that it was impossible, that he was not going. Some kind of intuition, partly suspicion, held him back.

"Why have you got to go?" he said. "Why can't we stay here, in England?"

"I don't know. I just want to go home to Germany, that's all. "

"Why?"

"I don't know. It's just a feeling, inside."

"Stop here," he begged. He searched his mind for some convincing idea, a reason for her to stay. "We'll start an eating-place. Dining-rooms. You could cook. I'd serve. Think of the foreign sailors that come in here—they'd go for a place like that."

"No," she said, "I shan't be happy until I can hear people speaking German again."

They lay awake half the night, listening to the gale, trying to thrash things out. In the morning the gale had almost blown itself out, there was a hard wild sun, and things seemed better. They went out and down to the sea. It was coming in with curdled dirty turbulence, white-crested beyond the sea-wall. A few smacks, a lugger or two, were lying in shelter. A mass of invading white cloud was blowing wildly in from beyond the sun.

Gerda stood looking at it with distant, slightly troubled eyes. "Perhaps it will be better when we go over."

"We? I'm not coming," he said.

"Bruno."

"No," he said.

"Please? Not for me?"

"No," he said.

They walked dully back into the town. She was curious to go to the shipping-office, just to find out how often there were sailings. He stood outside in the street while she went into the little office. Something inside himself had massed into a block of bitterness, impregnably hard. He was losing her and, victim of his own stubbornness, was doing nothing about it. He was bitter against himself and the colossal intuitive stupidity that forced him to act as he did. He saw that he ought to have given in, making a sacrifice, and yet had no notion of doing so. His mind moved along a metal track, steel-fixed, impelled by some sort of fatalism as though towards predestined ends. He had the strange, incontrovertible feeling that it was settled for him to act as he did.

Gerda came out of the shipping office. "There's a boat to-night. Then another on Friday."

"What's to-day?" he said. "I've lost count."

"Tuesday."

"That's three days if you stop till Friday."

She knew what he meant. "I'll stop," she said.

Towards midday they walked back to their lodgings, arm in arm, feeling very much like lovers again, happy but anxious, looking ahead to the moment of security in the bedroom, the moment when passion could be satisfied. They climbed upstairs and Gerda opened the bedroom door and there, in the bedroom, the woman of the house had Gerda's valise open on the bed. "What are you doing?" Gerda said. "Please, what are you doing?"

"Jes finding out things."

"What things? You have no right to touch this room."

"What things? You ain't married. That's what things."

"What the hell's it to do with you?" Bruno shouted. Gerda stood speechless.

"You mind your manners when you speak to a lady, mister!"

"What lady?" His mouth spewed out the old derisive speech before he knew what had happened. "Shut your chops afore I shut 'em for you!"

"Bruno!"

"Let's get out o' here, quick."

"Yes, and you better!" the woman shouted. "First you ain't married and now bad language on top on it. I'll git the police."

"You call the police and I'll strangle you," he said.

Gerda was frightened. He pushed the woman outside the door, slamming it. "Come on, let's hop it."

She hastily packed the valise, really frightened, her face sick. He had no notion of fear and stormed downstairs, livid, banging feet, hardly knowing what he did. At the foot of the stairs the woman came out of the glass-doored, peep-hole sitting-room, shouting again, "My husband's aboard ship and lucky for you he is. He'd knock y' into next week."

He lifted his free arm. She dived back into the sitting-room, slamming the door, jangling curtain rod, key falling out of lock. "Ain't fit to be wi' decent folks. Dirty-minded way o' carrying on! Living on tack!"

Gerda and Bruno went out into the street. The door slammed and he walked away quickly, in a frenzy, not caring where he went or what happened. She followed, frightened, not speaking. Then, just before turning the street-corner, they heard the door of the house slam again and turned to see the woman running away down the street, apron over head, shoes slopping.

"We're done," he said.

He felt a momentary spasm of fear himself; police, bad language, threats, Gerda and himself living together, respectability. Things were against them: strangers in the town, not married, Gerda a foreigner. They had stabled the horse at a pub, two streets away. His first instinct was to go there, harness up, and get out of the town. Then he calmed a little, thought better of it. "We'd be better out of sight." He remembered the woman searching the valise, saw that for them it was a strong point. With reason his calm returned.

But Gerda remained frightened. They walked back to the town, found a dining-room and ordered a meal of boiled mutton and onions. The gale was dying a little, the white clouds kinder and slower. Gerda sat quiet, not eating much.

"Don't worry about it," he said.

"I am worried," she said.

"Don't you see?—the valise," he said. "It's all right."

"Yes. But it would be better if I went to-night."

He knew then that her mind, like his own, was in reality already made up. That afternoon she went back to the shipping office and paid her passage in a boat leaving that evening at six o'clock.

Just before the boat left he went on board with her and down to her small cabin. The boat was going not to Germany but to Rotterdam, and Gerda was sharing the cabin with a Dutchwoman, who lay on her bunk, ready to be sea-sick. They said good-bye in the presence of the Dutchwoman, kissing each other again in the passage outside, and then went back on deck. The gale had almost died but the sky was darker again, the light falling rapidly, and suddenly as they stood there he wondered why he hadn't the sense to be sailing too, and could not understand the queer force of feeling, stronger than himself, that kept him back.

Soon after six o'clock he stood on the quay and lifted his hand. On deck Gerda's head stood out magnificently, a heavy mass of gold against a sky of blue storminess lying out to east. She lifted her hand too, waved it. She was not crying. She stood statuesque, except for the moving arm, as though unutterably calm.

Just before the boat made the open sea he saw her name scrolled on the stern: *The Northern Belle*. He read it, fixing it in his mind, and a moment later Gerda held her hand still in the air, not waving it, for the last time.

That same evening, two hours after the boat had sailed, he set out for London.

BOOK FOUR

ITALIAN JENNY

CHAPTER I

Ash Wilmer, Brakes and Wagonettes, Landaus for Hire, Funeral Arrangements, was where he came to on the following afternoon, a mile out of Stratford. He had been looking for some kind of place all day, hoping to sell the horse and trap.

"Whaddee think we are?" Wilmer said. "Knackers?"

"It's a good horse."

"When was it? I don't see no good horse about it. Another thing, we ain't got no use for nothing only blacks. Owing to the funerals like."

"Dye it."

"Eh?" The joke filtered slowly down through the fat layers of the man's mind. He was a bony man with perpetually open mouth, as though suffering from some aggravated form of adenoids. He took the joke seriously. "Wouldn't do in the London trade. No, sorry, couldn't make you no offer."

"All right. I'll get on."

"Tell you what," Wilmer said. "You like to leave it here, I'll do what I can for you. If we don't sell it we'll use it for wagonette work. Make it earn its keep if nothing else."

"All right."

"Goin' be in London long?"

"I don't know," Bruno said, "that I don't know."

He left the horse and trap and walked on through Stratford, Bow and Whitechapel in the darkening afternoon. He had a little over eight pounds in his pocket. He walked slowly, stolidly, as though going with deliberation to a given point. His mind had the dead lumpishness of cheese. About six o'clock he felt violently hungry and went into the first eating-place he saw and a Jew cut him a plate of spiced beef, serving it with bread sprinkled with caraway. He shovelled it into his mouth with his knife, elbows on the marble-topped table; ordered a second plateful, eating it in the same way. He walked on, completely lost, the names of streets meaning nothing, his mind grasping dully at bright, confused impressions: lights, streets, cabs, top-hats, women, soldiers, eating-places, horse-buses, lights, different impressions evoking in him the same dumb effect. About eight o'clock he had wandered as far as Clerkenwell. He had begun then to look into shops, stopping often, resting his feet. He had hardly begun to think about sleeping. Slightly hungry again, he looked into the windows of eating-places, pubs, dining-rooms, reading bills of fare; steak, trotters, hot peas, cuts from the joint, tripe, fried fish. He stood looking at a plateglass window steamed from within by the frying of fish dipped in pans of batter. He stood fascinated by the golden-fried bits of fish, the good smell, the slick hands of the man frying. Fish: something he had never eaten. Fried fish, chips, both things he had never tasted. He went into the shop. "In your 'and?" He came out with fish wrapped in newspaper, warm against his hand, the grease dripping through. He ate the fish as he walked along, attacking it like a dog, batter grease on his face. Good, rich. He sucked in hot chips, burning his mouth. Rich. Perhaps too rich. He felt the stirring of some kind of sick offence in his stomach. He walked on, still eating, but now gradually without pleasure, until the sickness in his stomach rose suddenly and filled his throat and blinded him. He stood in a back entry and spewed himself to relief and weakness. He had not shaved for two days and suddenly he could feel the stubble of his face stand out from the drawn sweat-cold skin. He walked slowly on. And when, a little later, he saw a barber's shop he went in and sat in the chair and shut his eyes, letting himself be shaved in a world of relief and darkness. As he sat there he began to think about sleeping. He had money; it was all right. He came out of the barber's feeling better, but still vacant, Then as he walked round in a circle and came into Gray's Inn Road a woman picked up with him. Forty or forty-five, she walked along with him, mincing her bottom, talking la-di-da. He did not speak a word. She lost patience. "Egging a gel on and then don't bloody well open your mouth!" He did not speak and abruptly she took herself away, mincing high horse across the road, swearing good riddance to him. Then a little later he stood and looked into a small bookshop, reading the titles under the sizzling gas-lights, fascinated a little, coming slowly out of the stupor produced by sickness, strange surroundings and the shock of Gerda's departure. He looked into the bookshop for a quarter of an hour and then decided to go in. "What sorta books you want? You want books on philosophy, religion? Summink like that?" The bookseller, a tall grey haired Jew with thick glasses, peered him up and down. Bruno did not know what to say. He looked round, stared at the bookshelves as though they were piles of bricks, and felt briefly helpless. He thought suddenly of Gerda, the small bookstall in the market, the German books. If she were with me, he thought, it would be all right.

He stayed looking at the books for half an hour. "You decided on anything? Because if you ain't I wanta shut up shop."

Suddenly he decided to tell the bookseller how he was fixed: his first time in London, not knowing where to sleep, everything.

"You wanta a room? That it? You don't mind what sorta room?"

"No."

"Ah. I dunno I'm sure, I dunno I'm sure. Can I trust you?"

"Yes."

"I gotta room just offa Rosebery Avenue. Ain't much. No bed, just a couch. I just keep my surplus stock there."

"I don't mind what it is."

"All right. You can walk with me that way and I show you what it's like."

He walked through the streets with the bookseller, who took him up three flights of stairs in a house off Rosebery Avenue. The room was about twelve feet square and lined on all sides with books, with an old leather couch in one corner. "You think you can manage?"

"Yes, I'll manage. Thanks. It's all right."

"You mind if I lock you in?"

"No."

"I'll let you out at eight o'clock in the morning. If I ain't here on time you read some books, eh? Do yourself a bit o' good."

He listened to the bookseller go clumping down the bare wooden stairs, hearing the clang of the street door at the bottom. He lay down on the couch without undressing. In the dead silence of the room padded by so many books his thoughts sprang up and marched up and down across the waste, tired spaces of his mind. Gerda, Spella Ho, Harwich, the Mitchells' farm, happiness, thoughts of the recurrent fatuity of things. After a time he dozed a little and then woke. He could hear the sound of rain spilling and hissing off roofs and gutters, and for a long time he lay listening to it: London rain, strange rain falling on what was for him a strange place, the rain, perhaps, he thought, of a new life?

CHAPTER II

"THERE'S a place where you can eat, round the corner there, see? About work I dunno I'm sure I dunno I'm sure. We'll see after breakfast."

He went round the corner from the bookshop to the

eating-house recommended by the bookseller: a dark little place, bare wooden tables, mustard spilled and dried on the cruet. He had lumpy porridge and a mug of tea, a tin spoon to eat and stir with. Eating, he looked out on the opposite wall of the alley: sun on grey windows, grey Nottingham curtains, finger writing on the dust-bloom of the glass. So this was it: London. The porridge was semi-cold, thickening like glue. London. What was he going to do? He tried to straighten out the confusion of his thoughts, his intentions. Outside, down the alleys, into streets and squares beyond, coal-men were yorping coal. He listened, chawling the dreary porridge round his mouth, swallowing it hard, thinking of coal. He could hawk coal. He knew something about coal. Winter was coming on. That was one job. Another? He called for a second mug of tea, drinking it hot, his self-confidence returning a little. Impress people, act as if he were somebody. He went on from the idea of coal to the idea of something bigger, conceiving large vague ideas of business. He was going to get through, do something, make his way. The revolution from confusion to confidence was like the turning of an immense cumbersome wheel. The wheel went forward over what had seemed difficulties, crushing them. He had eight pounds; he reasoned that it might last him sixteen weeks. He could live rough, poor, used to it. In sixteen weeks he could walk all over London.

In this mood of confidence he went back to the book-shop. "Work? I don't know I'm sure. What kinda work?"

"I been in business."

"Where? What kinda business?"

"Leather."

The bookseller thought a minute. "Well, there's a man in Bermondsey, a factor. What he don't sell ain't worth selling. Israel Kahn. Sells everything. Leather, linen, thread, nails, eyelets, all the things what go in boots. You go down there, say 'Mr. Kahn I come from Mr. Paul Oppenheim and what can you do for me?' Mind, I ain't saying there'll be something and I ain't saying there'll be nothing."

"Where's Bermondsey?"

"I forgot you don' know." He gave directions. "You jus' keep asking your way. Where you goin' to sleep to-night? You want the room?"

"Can I have it?"

"You be here at nine."

He walked to Bermondsey, losing his way, asking it again, feeling himself in an iron prison of streets, the sky slit into grey rectangles above endless grey roofs, the mist lifting reluctantly off the river, the air sulphur-sour, tiring his eyes. Towards noon he found the warehouse of I. Kahn and Co, entrance like a tunnel, a crane suspended over two upstairs street doors, bales of belly-leather lying outside on the pavement, a queer smell of dog-turds and darkness.

In the warehouse he saw a small spectacled Jew with pencil and paper, checking more bales of beilies. "Mr. Kahn?"

"No. In the office. Upstairs. Knock and wait."

He went upstairs to the first floor warehouse, walls stacked with illimitable boxes, bales of lining, bundles of hessian, and knocked at the door of the partitioned office, very like the office he had put up for himself in Castor. After three or four minutes a voice made a sort of bubbling bellow beyond the glass. He went in. "Mr. Kahn? I come from Mr. Paul Oppenheim." A big egg-bald Jew sat on a high round stool, squabbing over.

"Vad Mr. Paul Oppenheim? Dere must be a million Paul Oppenheims."

Bruno told him, explained why he had come.

"Ah, de bookseller? Vy'nt you say so?" He looked half through, half over thick bulbous spectacles. "Vell, I don' know vad you can do but can you do it?"

"I been in this business. In leather."

"Vhere?"

He told him.

156

"I never heard of it." He looked suspicious. "Still it ain't vhere you been it's vhat you know. Come here. Come outside." Kahn waddled out into the warehouse, padding on rubber slippers. "Vad you know about leather?" He pulled the pink tapes of rolls of upper leather, brown and black. "Show us." He fingered with large soapy hands a skin of russet calf. "Vad is 'is?"

"Willow."

"An' vad is 'is?" Small skins of goat.

"Glacé."

"An' vad is 'is?" Rolls of kip, greasy.

"Army."

Kahn suddenly exploded. "Army! Willow! Glacé! Git out! Git out afore I don't do something!" Kahn raised balled white hands, dithering, his eyes jellied with anger. "For my mother's sake get out afore I don't do something I am sorry for! Go on! Get out!" He flopped his hands in a last effect of despaired protestation. "Get out!"

Bruno went down and into the street without a word. Defeated, he walked out into Bermondsey, riverwards, pointlessly, his chance gone. He walked slowly, not thinking. Suddenly meaningless, the day began to go past him in a panorama of dead brick and stone, noises, wheels, automatic and meaningless movement. He went as far as the river and from the end of London Bridge stood and looked down stream, towards the sea. The sea, Gerda, Germany. He groped about for confidence. Why had certain things happened, why was he here? Much more, where was he going? He walked across the river. Thin autumn sun lay like silver oil-film on the water. The river moved thickly, with sleepy-muscled current. His mind reacted to the sight of it, felt just so heavy, moving without direction, laboriously impelled by sombre forces. Over the river he found a place to eat. Hot sausage, bread, potatoes, gravy into which he mopped the bread. Food again aroused a feeling of confidence, not strong, but living. What now? His mind found a bulwark in the thought of money. Money, so long as he had money he was all right, must be all right. Money made a difference: he had seen that. It was power. Five minutes later he saw it proved again. His small change gone, he paid for his dinner with a sovereign, saw the man behind the counter look at it, stare, blimey a thick'un, lucky John Hobbs, bite it and put it in the till, handing over the change as on the large white plate of a smile. The change heavy in his pocket, Bruno went out into the street, his confidence tangible again, courage slowly solidifying into the old indomitable mass of strength.

He went on like this for another three or four days, then for another three or four weeks: up and down, courage ebbing and flowing according to the food he ate or according to the prospects of the moment. Each day he pared off a thin shaving of his money, as a man pares off the rind of cheese. He began to know London, yet he remained lost, trying to find himself. He tried to get work, burrowing in the back-ways of city alleys, warehouse cellars, shops, factories, anywhere. Ponderous, ugly, over-determined, he created a feeling of resentment wherever he went. Other things went against him: he did not know anything, had no experience. His great assets of determination and strength could not be written on paper, added up to figures. "Any references? No? Your chances would be improved by references," or "How the 'ell you expect to get a job wivvaht references and a dial like that?" or even "We will keep the job open for you until you bring your references." So he got the bookseller to write him a reference, genuine as far as it went. "I have known Bruno Shadbolt for some time and can testify..." He took the reference along to the offices of the firm of Lancashire cotton manufacturers in Cannon Street, but the job had gone. He had odd jobs, lasting a day, half a day; once sandwich boarding, Rescue The Heathen! God's Mission to Darkest Africa! Meeting To-night; once hand-bills tramping all day through Walworth, down to Camberwell, pushing bills under doors and in letter boxes, Progress or Poverty? Capital or Labour? Socialism or Starvation?

walking through thin sooty November rain until he could feel rain seeping down to his chest, the bills masses of pink blotting pulp in his hands, the fiery message extinguished. Standing in queues, turning away at their breaking up, eating in back-alley eating-houses, he heard about him the growl of discontent, a rumour to cut wages by an eighth or a half, anger, discontent, the rumble of empty bellies. He had come to London to feel the sting of the flipped tail of a trade depression and did not know it. He stopped at street corners, occasionally, to listen to the harangue of new politics, socialism, new religion, the Hallelujah Band, new thought, Women's Suffrage, the Spiritualists. They seemed to have no relation to his personal problems, gave him no hope. They were the beating of fists and voices and tambourines in a void outside him.

It was now November and his money dropped below the five-pound mark by the end of the month. He saw the bookseller getting restless. He had so far paid nothing for the room, had done nothing. Kindness had gone as far as it could, farther than he had reason to expect. On the last day of November the bookseller explained how things were, how he would need the room for more books, but there was no need for this evasive, kindly method of eviction. Bruno understood and on the first of the next month was out in the street. He spent all that day on the south side of the river, looking for rooms, up and down squalid stairs to the attics and basements of Walworth. He reasoned that in a cheap district he could find cheap rooms, but independence, an aggressive solid independence which seemed now to thrive on adversity, made him determined to find a room for himself. No lodging-houses, he thought, no rotten doss-house. A room to myself. I can eat there. Bread and cheese, anything. Cheaper than eating-houses. What I save on eating I can spend on the room. I can do it. I'm going to do it.

By evening he was on the verge of defeat, rooms dearer than he had expected. He had set himself a price, five shillings, less if he could get it. He tried bargaining. Landladies squawked him out, until one said: "You ain't thought about sharing a room? I got a room you could share for three-and-six. Ain't got no gas, that's all."

"Gas don't matter," he said, and followed her up dark feet-splintered stairs to see, on the top floor, the room about which she spoke. The door was open. "The catch ain't very good," she said. "It shuts if you bang it proper." He walked in holding the candle she had brought. What struck him first was that the room had no window, only a small thick-glassed skylight. He saw a low iron bed, a chair, a chamber on the bare boards, caught the dust-foetid odour of a room into which even the street air had never penetrated. "Where's the other bed?" he said. "Well," the landlady said, "I gotta get that up from downstairs. My daughter's been sleeping on it. It's all right, it's a good bed, only I ain't got nobody to help me up with it until Bandy comes in." "Who's Bandy?" he said, and she said "Bandy? He's the bloke what'll share the room with you if you take it."

"I'll take it," he said.

He went out again. He bought a loaf and a quarter of cheese and then after about half an hour went back to the room. He wanted to eat, think if he could, sleep. As the street door clanged and he began to climb the stairs, feet hollow-thumping the rotten boards, the landlady shot out her head from a downstairs door. "Oh! it's you. Thought it was Bandy." He stopped on the stairs. "I can help you up with the bed if you like," he said. She lifted her hands in surprise, thanks. "You're a bleeding Christian," she said.

"Which," she said, as they carried up the bed in sections, iron slats flapping and rattling together and on the bare stairs, "is more than Bandy is. He's a bleeding Atheist."

"What's that?"

"Don't believe in God."

They slotted and screwed the bed together, she spreading

the one bed-stained, iron-moulded blanket. Going, she put her head back round the door: "And keep your mince-pies open."

"Eh?"

"Your mince-pies. Your eye-pies. Peepers. Keep 'em skinned. Your optics."

"It's like that, is it?" he said.

"It's like that," she said.

Taking off his boots, he lay on the bed. The room was cold. He lay and ate about a quarter of the loaf and the cheese. It was quite dark. He had forgotten to buy a candle. Must remember it, he thought. After he had eaten he got up off the bed and groped about for a place in which to keep the bread and cheese. He could find nothing, no cupboard, and finally he put it in its news-paper under the bed. Then he lay down again, this time covering himself with the blanket, not undressing, turning over to try to sleep as he was. He lay thinking, trying to straighten things out, make decisions, salvage confidence from the wreckage of wild ideas, disappointments, be-wilderment; his mind went back to Castor, to the too-easy, swaggering days, when the composition of life had been, by contrast, as uncomplicated and neat as the lines drawn in a child's exercise book. His mind swam back into half-dreams of Spella Ho, sinking away.

He woke a long time later, to know that someone was in the room. A candle had been lighted. He saw a man taking off his waistcoat. The man turned, full into the candlelight. He saw a narrow, spectacled face, hair thin-ning at the temples, a studless shirt revealing a neck that seemed to have undergone some persistent pressure of iron. In his hand the man was holding collar, tie and dicky bit. "Ullo," he said, "you're awake."

"How do," Bruno said. "My name's Shadbolt."

"Bandy," the other said. "Mine. Clerk to Portslade and Wimbush, city. Ever hear of 'em?"

"No."

"God help you if you do."

"I thought," Bruno said, "you didn't believe in God."

"Who said so?"

"Her downstairs. She let it slip."

"As a figure of speech, yes. As an entity, no. That's all."

Bruno lay silent, trying to figure it out. "What time is it?" he said at last.

"Two. Just after."

"Where you been?"

"Stocktaking," the clerk said. "Past twelve last night. Past one to-night. What do you do?"

"Nothing."

"A capitalist."

They laughed, the clerk tired, bitter.

"Like a chance at Portslade and Wimbush? Fourteen hours a day. Fourteen bob a week. Pen-pushing. A bloody collar round your neck all day as if you were a chained dog. Nice firm. Old established. Woollen goods. They'd shave the hair off your chest and sell that if they got half a chance."

Bruno lay silent.

The clerk went on talking, undressing, haranguing Bruno as though glad of a long-delayed chance of oratory: prolonged and involved talk of theoretical socialism, trade unions, co-operative movements, the desire, the necessity for socializing the state of violence, talk of a man named Marx, another named Hyndman. He lay down on the bed, eyes on the ceiling, tired face rejuvenated by passion and the possession of an audience. He talked of plans and, getting up, pulled from under his bed a large tin trunk, which he opened. He set the candle on the lid and from a mass of books and papers began to take out rolled sheets tied with pink office tape. He opened them briefly, letting them snap back like roller-blinds. "Plans. Diagrams. Plans of every important vantage-point, every important building in London." He spoke with a slight fanaticism, with the inspired incoherence of a man who has taken an excessive stimulant. "They are the plans to smash the exciting system of chaos. Chaos, yes, capitalistic chaos, chaos, chaos."

"What are you?" said Bruno.

"I'm an anarchist," he said.

He folded up his papers, put out the candle and lay talking for a long time, not tired now, telling Bruno of meetings, secrecy, drumming out the theory of anarchy against chaos like a man playing the same hysterical tune over and over again on the keys of a piano slightly out of tune. In occasional bars of coherence, he spoke of a meeting that week. "The night after next. You must come. In a church off the Waterloo Road. It'll be held like a church-meeting, so that there can't be trouble. We have to guard against that. Suppression of meetings and so forth. You'll hear all the best speakers."

He had gone when, about eight o'clock next morning, Bruno woke; but he had left the candle-end. Bruno lit it and, stupefied from sleeping brokenly in the small airless room, groped under the bed for the bread and cheese. He could not find it. He went down on his hands and knees to look for it, bringing the candle closer. Then he saw a piece of bread, then another, and picked them up; and then saw how, in the night, rats had torn his loaf to pieces, carrying away the cheese altogether, gnawing paper to shreds.

He put on his boots and coat and went downstairs and out into the street. It was raining. The tops of tenements had the dull shininess of lead sepulchres. He felt courage sink and curdle into a mass of sour dejection; thought become nullified.

CHAPTER III

Bruno went to a meeting of the Workers Democratic Federation two nights later, sitting at the back of a small square pillared Russian orthodox church lighted by hanging oil-lamps. In an atmosphere of suppressed fervour and stale odours of incense and oil he listened for two hours to speeches he did not understand, his mind inattentive, forced back to the bitter preoccupation of his own case. As speaker after speaker rose and talked of plans for the anarchical reform of the world's social and industrial evils he felt himself turned more and more into himself, thinking, "It's no good to me. I don't get no forrader. It don't stop the rats eating the bread", the words of many bearded, fist-waving orators gradually forming themselves into a vast vaporous murmur of protest that gave him a slight, queer feeling of light-headedness. It was as though the incense had intoxicated him. Towards the end of the meeting he was no longer listening and it seemed as though the voices of the speakers boomed up from some interminable tunnel beyond the altar.

This feeling persisted after the meeting had broken up and he and Bandy were walking together in the street. Bandy, fired to a point of semi-hysterical fanaticism by the speeches, talked excitedly, waving thin white-cuffed hands, dramatizing himself, but it seemed to Bruno, at intervals, as though he were on the far side of the street. This feeling of distance was responsible for another strange feeling that his arms were of inordinate length, that he could reach out across the street and touch Bandy and pull him back to his side. All this time he felt an increase of physical depression and his head had begun to ache a little at the back. He was also thirsty. "Let's get a gin," he said.

"I can't afford it," Bandy said.

"I'll pay, it's on me," he said, and then for a moment it seemed as if he had not said it and he repeated it. "I'll pay, it's on me. I'll pay," he said.

In the gin palace he took out his purse, fumbling for silver, feeling that there was no co-ordination between his brain and hands. It was as though he were partially drunk. Suddenly the purse slipped out of his hands and fell down between the counter and the brass foot-rail, not spilling anything. He moved to pick it up, but Bandy had already

164

stooped. Bandy looked at the amount in the purse and said, "You're almost a capitalist after all. You want to take care of it."

Bruno drank three gins, breaking a purely economical resolution not to drink, and after them felt a temporary spasm of relief. His head was still being bumped continually by regular throbs at the back. Bright mirrors shot out a wild reflection of himself. He got up without warning, knocking over his stool, and elbowed Bandy into the street again. "Come on, let's go somewhere." It seemed as if his head, now, out in the air, were a volcano, that it must erupt, bursting itself. "Go? Go where?" Bandy said. Bruno put out his hands and grasped Bandy by the coat and again it was as though he had pulled Bandy over from the other side of the street. "Anywhere. Music-hall. Ain't there a music-hall? I'll pay, I'll pay."

And then he was in the music-hall, not knowing how he got there, not remembering anything. He and Bandy were standing up, at the back, in darkness. He clutched the promenade railing, felt behind and about him a crush of other people, men, tarts waiting for the lights to go up. Impressions began to assail him in waves, thundering in from the back of his head: dimmed gas-lights, the red lights of exits, faces of women averted to look at him, long dusty scent-waves of powder and cheap perfumes; then men spitting, scrape of boots on floor, noises, laughter, cat-calling, pressure of soft legs easing along the promenade railing, pressing his own, "Dearie, Honey", he himself not listening, taking no notice, eyes fixed on the stage. Then a second barrage of impressions: the stage, white footlights, a street of pink bricks, a comic singing, wide check trousers, ginger mop, shirt tail hanging out, the audience happy, whistling. Then others, a dud, patter, the stuff flat, the crowd restless, hissing at last, the curtain coming down, thud of oranges hitting the cardboard wings. Then in the interval he knew vaguely that he was ill, that he had never in his life felt like this. He clung to the railing, the pressure of the tart's legs insistent now, meaning

165

nothing. A girl was on the stage, frilled skirts lifted to show soft pink thighs among frizzed swans-feather whiteness. She was very dark, slim for music-hall taste, bare white arms picking up the skirts with easy devilry. He watched her and had the sudden feeling as in the street, that he could reach out and touch her. He lifted his hands from the railing and felt the world go round, the girl swinging away down a revolving slope of light and blackness. He clutched the rail again, felt the pressure of thighs on his, a voice: "Easy, honey, I got you." On the stage the girl was singing, the light strong voice easily hitting the gods. He watched her with an eagerness that was slightly light-headed. The girl, the dark face, the swan-white skirt, the pink thighs on the stage and the heavy seductive thighs pressing his began to be inseparable parts of the same confusion, a nightmare. Then he got into his head that, somewhere, at some odd moment of time, he had seen the girl on the stage before. The sense of familiarity, frustrated, became a secondary pain. He struggled to get at the reason for her familiarity. It eluded him and in a few minutes she also had gone, the curtain down, up again, the white arms upstretched, accepting applause, the dark face, with its passionate air of familiarity, at last disappearing. Then he was pushing his way out, the tart close to him in the crowd, honeying him, he himself trying to catch sight of the girl's name on the programme bill. He saw it at last outside, under the green-white gas-light. "Italian Nightingale." The name meant nothing to him.

After that he did not know what happened. He knew that he was ill. He wanted to lie down. His head was on the verge of explosion. Then after a long time he was lying down, vaguely conscious that there had been some trouble, the tart not wanting to let him go, a sort of scuffle, dirty names, Bandy struggling to get him upstairs, taking off his coat and trousers. "You drank the gins too quick." He lay fighting with the explosive waves of pain in his head, knowing it was not the gin, until pain and the tart and the girl on the stage were again complicated into hideous nightmare.

When he roused in the morning Bandy had gone. He did not try to get up. He could hear rain pouring on the skylight. He had the occasional impression that there was no skylight, that the rain was pouring in on him, pricking his skin. He knew he must do something about this, call for someone to shut the skylight. Then he put one hand on another and felt the rain pouring off him. It was warm sticky rain, but he himself was cold. Then suddenly he knew that it was sweat.

He lay there all day, alone, far-off feet bumping in the tenement below him but no one ever coming. It continued to rain and he continued to have the impression that the rain was falling down in small sharp drops on his face and hands. Towards evening he raised himself up in bed and groped over to the box where Bandy kept his candle. He made three attempts to light the candle, all unsuccessful. Then he made a great effort and succeeded. Pale warm yellow light fell on his hands, momentarily comforting him.

Then he had a shock. It seemed as if the impression of rain falling on his hands must have a basis in reality. His hands were covered with spots. He opened the neck of his shirt and saw the same rash covering his chest. He lay down again in the sweat-moist bed, passing his hands over his face and over each other, feeling the spots, now only waiting for Bandy to come, so that something could be done.

He waited what he knew to be hours. Then Bandy was in the room, standing over him, lighting a new candle from the old stump.

"By God," Bandy said, "it's what the landlady's kid had."

"What? What is it?"

Bandy looked scared, mouth open in the candlelight. "Scarlet fever. The kid died."

He lay silent, his thoughts diminished to the smallness

of bullets which fear shot through his consciousness. The bed, fever, the girl dying. He knew now that it was serious, that at last he was up against something.

Bandy began to undress, giving way to fear. "Mean my job. If I get it. How do you feel? How did it start?" Then the candle went out, but it still seemed, for a long time, as though Bandy were walking about the room. Bruno's coat and trousers were hung on a nail on the wall and once during the night it seemed as if they fell down and that Bandy was there, picking them up. He tossed and turned about in the wet bed all night, not caring, taking no notice of even the rats under the bed.

Then, in the morning, he woke to find Bandy lying fully dressed on his bed. "I got as far as Elephant and Castle and couldn't go no farther. My head's banging like hell. Mean my job. Mean the sack if I can't get there s'afternoon."

They lay there all day together, Bandy never attempting to get up. Bruno felt desperately weak, but calmer. All day he was puzzled by something about his trousers and coat. Whereas he had been sure that at first the coat had hung over the trousers, the trousers were now hanging over the coat.

Towards evening he struggled up on the bed and got down the coat and trousers. Lying down again, he went through his pockets. He could not find his money. Hammers banged in his mind: fear, desperation, weakness. Then he went through his pockets again. The money was not there and he lay trying to reason it out, going back over his movements: the gin-palace, the streets, the music hall, the struggle with the tart. The details of all that had happened were lost in mist.

Twice that evening he went through his pockets again. Then he would lie down and the loss of the money would seem momentarily part of sickness and nightmare. In this way he had periods of false security and in one of them he fell asleep.

He woke to hear Bandy groaning, light-headed, now

very ill. It was almost morning. The rain had ceased on the skylight. He waited about an hour and then crawled out of bed and dragged himself to the door. He called down for the landlady and in about ten minutes she came upstairs. He was then back in bed and now, in the light, he could see Bandy's face covered with bright pink spots.

"Get a doctor," he said. "We both want a doctor."

"Can you pay for a doctor?" she said. "Because I know *he* can't."

"Do something."

"You can't do nothing," she said, "but let it take its course."

"Undress Bandy anyway," he said. "He's sleeping in his kit."

So she undressed Bandy. "Clothes are wringing wet," she said, and suddenly as she flung coat and trousers over her arm he heard the chink of money in the pockets and he knew by some extraordinary flash of intuition whose money it was. He remembered Bandy walking about in the night, the coat and trousers falling down. He tried to say something in explanation and protest, but in a moment the landlady had gone. "You lay quiet, I'll try and dry his things by the fire."

That day he felt he struggled through all the possible conflicts of fear and bitterness, his soul prostrate at the bottom of a pit. He was conscious enough to hear Bandy groaning, to think: "Sooner or later I can get up. I can go down. I can get it back." Bandy was obsessed by delirious terror. "No, Mr. Portslade. Yessir, yessir, yessir. Mr. Portslade it's a mistake I assure you a mistake never happen again I assure very good I know I have it in mind Mr. Portslade yessir I'm coming back sir, yessir, yessir." During the day the landlady came up twice, but she did not bring Bandy's clothes and gradually he conceived the idea of going down, under cover of night, and getting them back. But then, by the time night came, he was too weak and fell down when he got out of bed and could hardly drag himself back.

Two mornings later he woke and turned over to call Bandy. He felt better for the first time and had slept well. "Bandy," he said. Bandy did not move or answer. "Bandy," he began again. Then he saw the mouth of Bandy lying open, the lip stiff over the brown teeth.

Later in the day the landlady came up with an old walnut-faced woman wearing a large worn Inverness cape and a cockney bonnet and between them they laid out the worn under-nourished body of the clerk-anarchist. In death Bandy did not look like a man who could blow the world to bits. They covered him with the sheet and throughout the day Bruno lay there with him, under-taker's men lumping up the stairs in the late afternoon to uncover the body again and measure it.

Too weak to move, he lay there with Bandy for another night. He woke later, feeling still another stage better, to hear the bump of Bandy's coffin being set down on the small landing outside. As the men opened the door and brought in the coffin and whipped the sheet off Bandy's body he could bear it no longer. He pulled on his trousers and holding them up with his hands went down to find the landlady.

"Money?" she said. "I ain't seen no money."

"In a purse," he said. "Bandy took it. He took it the night I was taken so bad, the night before he was bad."

"That's a funny thing to say if you can't prove it."

"I could prove it," he said ,"if I could see the purse."

"You can look through his pockets," she said, showing him Bandy's trousers and coat hanging on the airing line above the stove, "but I ain't found no purse. Wish I had."

He looked through Bandy's pockets, out of pure formal-ity, finding nothing.

"As soon as I can get out I'll tell the police."

Before he could speak again she laid the purse on the table. "Don't fall over yourself," she said. "How can you prove it's yours?"

He took the purse and opened the flap. His initials, "B.S." had been pokered on the inside.

"He could never keep his flappers off anything," she said.

He began to count his money. It was not all there. Where there had been almost five pounds there was now less than forty shillings. "Depend he spent it," she said, and he knew he could never prove it otherwise. But something made him look at her. "And don't look at me," she said, "either. It's a bloody cake-walk for me, ain't it? Him owing three weeks rent. Somebody ought to pay that."

"Somebody?" he said and knew what she meant. "Not me," he said.

Bandy was buried on the following day and Bruno stayed in the room for another week, feeling strength return in slow hesitant cycles. At the end of the week he paid the rent he owed, a whole week and a broken week at half-rent, a whole week at full rent, a total of fifteen shillings.

He came out of the house with a little over a pound in his pocket. As he walked along, peeling off the old dead skin from his hands, he did not know what to do, where he was going.

CHAPTER IV

HE struggled through December, into January: doss-houses, sleeping out, days with the sandwich-boards, his shoes like paper, his money slowly but inevitably dwindling, days when he could have eaten cat's meat. He existed by an indomitable and almost mindless sort of courage. He went on; was going on. At the back of his mind he kept, like a final piece of bread he did not want to touch, the thought of his horse and trap, left in Stratford. For this horse and trap he had paid twenty-five pounds at the sale at Spella Ho. The thing that kept him going was the thought that he could sell the horse and trap, buy himself food and boots and then walk back to

Castor; or he could sell the trap and ride back to Castor. He would sell the outfit for anything, ten pounds, whatever he could get. But he would do it only in some insurmountable extremity. He felt this extremity on January 17th of the New Year.

Nothing happened to make the day worse than others; but suddenly he could stand it no longer. He walked slowly, by painful stages, down to Stratford. It was bitterly cold. He did not notice it. His defeat was concentrated into the pain of the sole of his left foot. He walked with it cringed up in the almost soleless boot, the flesh blistered like a scorch-mark, so that he was almost lame. He had fifteen pence in his pocket and he got down to Ash Wilmer's coach and undertaker's stables about two o'clock in the afternoon.

"Mr. Ash Wilmer about?"

"Ash Wilmer?" The stable hand was shovelling muck. "Yeh."

"Well," the stable-hand said, "he's about, if you call it about. About somewhere. He's been dead about three weeks."

Bruno stood dead still. He did not say anything.

"Took sudden. Always had that asthma. Used to say the horses give it him. Took bad in the night, couldn't get his breath and were gone afore morning."

"Anybody I can see?"

"About a job? I know th'ain't no jobs if that's what you're looking for."

"Not a job. Business."

Five minutes later he stood talking to a man he knew to be Ash Wilmer's son. He told him about the horse and trap, the arrangement, everything. He felt, as he spoke, that he was speaking to a brick wall. "'Av you proof of this?" the man said. "Papers or summat?"

"No, I took his word."

"I ain't seen no trap. No horse either, as I know on." He stood red-faced, hostile.

"I could pick the horse out."

"You better pick your feet up and git out."

The man stood solid, dangerous. And suddenly, even in anger, Bruno saw how it must look to him: an odd arrangement, he himself turning up almost without boots on his feet, no proof of anything, only his own miserable rotten rags proof that he was down and out, a man no more likely to have a horse and trap than a gold watch and chain. He was too weary to struggle against defeat.

"Come on," the man said, "bloody well git off while your shoes are good."

He turned and went slowly out of the yard. As he reached the stables he saw the stable-hand still shovelling muck. The stable-hand spoke. Bruno stopped, and something made him say: "Ain't got a mite o' leather I could tack on this sole?"

"Leather?"

"Harness leather. A strap or something like that. Anything."

The man went into stables and came out after a few minutes with a leather strap and buckle. "How's this?"

Bruno took it. He wound the strap twice round his boot and buckled it over his instep. From the sudden thick tightness of the leather he gained momentary comfort. The buckle kept his blistered foot off the ground. Leather, he thought. Better if I stopped in Castor with Stokes and sold leather. Better if I'd got a job with Chamberlain. He walked out of the stable-yard, his foot slightly better. Castor, he thought. Castor's where I should have stopped. Where I ought to go. Where I can go.

He began to make his way, slowly, slightly less painfully, up through Hackney and Holloway, out towards Highgate. Although his body moved, his mind remained completely static, not calculating distances, not considering or analysing the bitter loss of the trap. It remained fixed in a void. This void generated a kind of courage that would not have been possible from conscious thought. It drove him on past the calculated limits of endurance, nullifying pain. Some long time after darkness he was going on towards Colney Hatch. He stopped to spend a penny on bread and cheese, going to the back door of a small pub. There he had a piece of luck. "Don't want no sticks chopping? No wood or anything?" he said. And the woman said: "I don't know's we don't. It damn well blows cold enough." She gave him an axe and a candle and he chopped a pile of kindling for her in a small out-house, working for more than an hour. Back in the pub kitchen she gave him bread and cheese and a glass of stout. "Want anything else?" he said. "I'll clean the privy out. Empty the bucket. Anything." So she let him do that, surprised that he should ask to do it, surprised enough to say, when he asked if he could sleep in the wood-shed: "Yes, I don't know's you can't. Only it's a funny place to want to sleep."

"I can sleep anywhere," he said, and she said: "Well, you're welcome. It's cold enough indoors, let alone out. Cold enough for snow."

He slept that night in the woodshed, covering himself with sacks, lying down on a mass of sawdust, bark, shavings. There was a sack that rats had chewn beyond usefulness. He ripped it to single lengths and tied it round his boots. During the night his feet were almost warm and when he set out, on the following morning, it was as though he walked on cushions.

The morning was bitterly cold, the wind east, the sky a driven mass of snow-cloud. He walked steadily on, northward, less mindlessly than on the previous day, but still as though his mind were set in a void. About nine o'clock it began to snow. He did not mind it. The light fast-driven flakes gave him the illusion that he was moving fast. For a time it snowed thinly, with reluctance, the flakes hard, not settling. Then as he went on he looked up to see a mass of snow advancing out of the east and north, blotting out distance. He walked into it and it covered him, the fury of snow-heavy wind holding him momentarily still. Then he struggled out of it and went on, his chest and face and thighs gradually covered with solidifying snow. He kept his eyes fixed mostly on the ground. Once or twice when he lifted them it was not possible to see. All the time he had the impression, vaguely comforting, that such snow could not last, that the wind must inevitably drive it over. This notion kept him walking on. He walked on for more than an hour. Wind and snow had never lessened and now he was part of a world already snow-buried, his sack-bandaged feet like lead, the solid mass of snow falling off his chest in great crusts, his eyes wind-watered. Now and then he went momentarily blind and once he fell down, his already numbed hands hitting the snow flat and hard, so that he felt blood spring up into his nails in a pin-pricking agony of pain. He got up and went on and in a short time he fell down again. Later the same thing happened, and then the same thing again, and then it became automatic, almost a relief to fall down and lie for a second or two in the thick mass of snow, already six or seven inches deep.

He walked on for a space of time which snow and his own blindness made it impossible to measure. During this time he did not stop to rest and the snow did not stop. He rammed mouthfuls of bread and cheese into his mouth as he walked along. He was driven by the same mindless forces as before. Thought had the repetitive quality of some inward pain. He knew that if he stopped there was some possibility that he would never go on again.

He stopped about four o'clock in the afternoon. He saw a pub, red-brick walls white-crusted with snow, a row of empty barrels lying in the yard outside buried to the pure white shape of a switchback, and he went inside without thought or hesitation, as though he had been making for the place since morning. It was still snowing and he could still see the white wall of it advancing out of the now darkening northern sky.

"By crikey," the landlord said. "You know you're the first man in here since ten o'clock this morning?"

"Eh?"

"You ain't come fur?"

"Colney Hatch."

"Christ!" the landlord said. He stood with fat, open mouth. He could not believe it. He stood looking at Bruno, at the fantastic snow-covered bandaged boots. "In them baffs?" It was a joke. It did not reach Bruno. "You better take 'em off," but Bruno did not do anything. He sat staring at the landlord, his mind snow-blank, on the verge of dumb craziness. "Git'em off and git warm," the landlord said. Bruno stared and did not move.

When finally he did move it was to put money on the table: a shilling. "All I got," he said. "Something t'eat. You let me sleep in the wood-shed? I can sleep anywhere. It's all I got."

"You git summat hot down you," the landlord said, "and we'll talk about money."

His wife came in, a robust, reddle-necked woman, kind-eyed. Bruno sat staring while she looked at him.

"From Colney Hatch," the landlord marvelled. "Walked it. In them baffs. In this lot."

She too marvelled, voice soft, to Bruno soft and also far off. "You must be daft," she said, "daft to do it. You better get your boots off. Quick!"

He did not speak. He felt daft: dumb and daft, like a man lying half over the edge of sanity. He tried to bend down to his boots. He then felt that if he did bend down he would immediately go over this edge of conscious sanity. I got to sit still, he thought. All right if I sit still. Got to sit boots all right if I sit untie boots all right still if I sit still, he thought. Then, even as he thought this, he painfully lifted one boot and rested it on the other knee. His hands went to the knots in the sacking. He touched them, made an immense effort to grapple with them. Where there should have been some point of contact there was nothing. His hands were frozen beyond feeling and he began groping about like a child.

He saw the landlord's wife stoop down and begin to untie the rough snow-sodden knots in the sacking. "Arth," she said, "you rub his hands. He ain't got no feeling nor nothing. That right? Can't feel nothing, can you!"

Yes, he thought, that's right. Whatever she said was right. He sat dumb, no feeling, helpless, she untying his boots, the landlord chafing his hands.

Then abruptly his feelings broke. He began suddenly to cry. He knew that he was crying for nothing, for the mere sight of two people doing two simple acts of kindness that he could not do himself. Tears were the dumb expression of his weakness and gratitude. He went on crying. The woman cut away the knots and the sacking with a carving knife and he could feel his feet. And then suddenly it was as though fire were being poured through the blood of his hands. Pain became real, maddening. He pressed his hands together, did not know what to do with them, his tears turning to tears of agony.

"Hot-ache," the landlord said. "I know'd you git it. Bloody cruel. Hold on. I got y'. I got y', mate, I got y'."

The landlord held his hands sandwiched between his own, as though between lumps of warm meat. His wife went out, returned. "Ask me, it'll snow all night. Think yourself lucky you got in when you did." Bruno sat still, listening, his mind working. Agony slid slowly back into pain, pain itself into an ache of understanding.

CHAPTER V

HE stayed that night with Arth and Emma Watford, sleeping in a bed, food inside him: his first turn of luck for weeks. The names of the man and woman fixed themselves in his mind, imprinted by gratitude and pain. In the morning the snow, ceased now, lay to a depth of three feet, in places drifted to six or seven feet. Huge smooth crescents had blown far up the windows on the north side and all over the land lay a strange diagram of hedges, buried and raised up, the wind whipping up the snow in brief bitter storms like driven salt.

All that day he and Arth Watford and sometimes the woman worked at the job of shovelling the snow from the house. He worked strongly, not tired, only his eyes weak sometimes in the freezing wind. The sky remained sunless. "Lick me if we don't git some more," Watford said. "Them boots all right?" Watford had given him boots, good russet brown boots, rather on the light side, which he had again covered with sacking. "Had 'em ten year now, and now they ain't easy. Corn on every bloody toe. That's what it is." By afternoon they had cleared deep channels running from the doors of the pub, but the sky had not cleared. "Damn the snow," Watford said, "that's why I say. Nobody in all day and ain't likely to git nobody. You see if we don't git more to-night. You'll be lucky if you ain't here a week."

He was there four days. On the fourth the wind turned and he could feel the warmth in it. Snow began to come down from the roof of the pub in sudden avalanches and over the land the diagram of hedges broke black through the flat white distances. People had also begun to move and there was a man, a packman with a wicker basket of stockings, card-buttons, boot-laces and odd drapery, who came in an hour or so before Bruno set out again.

They talked. "Well, there's a living in it," the packman said, "if you call it a living. What's your line?"

"Nothing."

"If you're going far," the man said, "it's no trouble to sell a thing or two while you're going. Take laces. Everybody wears boots."

"If they're lucky."

"Well, say so for argument's sake. Everybody wears boots. Two boots, a pair of laces. One family, three or four pair of boots."

"Fat profit on laces."

"Sixty per cent. If you're going far why don't you take something like that? I'll sell you laces at three-pence a dozen. You sell 'em at sixpence. Take three or four dozen, you'd sell that in a day. Shilling profit. That'll keep you going."

When he said goodbye to the Watfords, an hour later, he had two dozen ladies' bootlaces in his pocket. "Ladies are what you want. First the men ain't at home and second you can talk to the ladies." The Watfords gave him food, a loaf, a cut of boiled bacon, some cheese. He felt as though he were starting a new life. "Some day I'll come and see you again," he said. He was oppressed by an overwhelming sense of gratitude.

That day he walked another ten miles. Calling at houses on the road-side, he sold three pairs of laces. In the afternoon it began to freeze bitterly, but he did not mind it. He felt that he had started a new phase, that his luck had turned. The next day he walked almost twenty miles, working his way up through Bedfordshire. Everywhere the land was iron-frozen now under broken islands of snow, and men were not working. At midday that day he got into a barn to eat, and to his surprise, as he sat there, three labouring men came in. He told them who he was. "Peddling a bit. Can't sell you a pair o' laces for the women?" One, the youngest, said: "That's jis what I want. I bust my missus' high-legged 'uns last Sunday, lacing 'em up." They all laughed. "How high do they lace up?" They went on for a time pulling the young one's leg. He was eating his dinner out of a sheet of newspaper and when they left, half an hour later, he left the paper lying on the snow. Bruno picked it up. It was an old newspaper, bacon-stained, slightly yellow. He sat there for some minutes, reading it.

Suddenly he was not reading any longer. He sat staring. Then he looked at the date of the newspaper: November. Then he was reading again what he had already read. "It is now learnt that in the gale off the East Coast of Friday night last the packet *The Northern Belle*, bound for Holland out of Harwich, foundered with all hands."

He got up and walked out of the barn. He was flung back into the old mindless state, the void in which he moved mechanically. He was not conscious of a sense of loss. He felt oppressed by a sense of fatalism: that it had to happen, Gerda going, he not going, exactly as it had happened, everything. All his bitterness returned.

He was advancing into Bedfordshire. Names on signposts began to have vague meaning for him. Late that day he sold the last of his laces to a woman in Cotton End. "Busted me last pair this morning, pullin' too nation hard on 'em. Allus doing it. You better gimme three pair."

She looked hard at him.

"Ain't seen you afore as I know on. New round here?"

"Yeh."

"What's your name? I allus like to know folk's names."

"Shadbolt."

She stared at him in wonder. "No kin to him at Castor?"

"Yeh," he said, guarded, "I got kin at Castor."

"Well," she said, "if all I hear's right you needn't be traipsing about wi' laces no more."

"How?" he said. "How's that?"

"Oh!" she said. "I ain't saying nothing. You don't catch me gossiping. It's only what I hear."

Going on, he forgot, in time, what she had said. He came into Castor on the following afternoon. It was bitterly cold, the road ribbed with bars of ice. On his left foot the old blister, opened again, was stinging as if with salt. He walked with a slight limp, head unconsciously down in the wind, the stubble black and frowsy on his face, his eyes wind-bleary.

As he went down High Street and through the Square he saw people he knew. He would look at them, as though to speak, but they had no recognition. Then suddenly, a second later, when he had gone, they knew him. He turned then to see people looking after him, and once a woman slipped and slithered across the ice, running to tell another across the street, the two heads joined excitedly, looking after him, jawing long after he had gone. And once he heard a voice from the open door of a shop: "Shadbolt's back. I seen him. God struth jes now," and turned to see a knot of people gaping down-street after him.

He walked on in the same slow painful fashion as ever,

not stopping, not even looking from side to side. He felt the bitterness of things to be complete. "As if I ain't had enough," he thought, "but they must come out and look at me, as if I were a monkey on a stick."

CHAPTER VI

"GAPIN' at you? I should think they was gapin' at you. Folks everywhere talking about you. Everybody looking for you high and low for months. Mr. Carmichael got notices in the papers about you."

"Mr. Carmichael?" He was talking to Maria, back at the old Shadbolt place. Maria had got married, her husband an ex-soldier, a tall handlebar-moustached man who loafed about in carpet slippers tied on with bits of string. "Mr. Carmichael? What Carmichael?"

"You forgot that too? Mr. Carmichael the London man. The solicitor. Her solicitor."

"Her?" He was a man trying to pick up the too-fine threads of the old life, his mind too numbed and coarsened to feel them.

"Her. Yes, her. The old lady. Her at Spella."

"What about her?" he said.

"She's left you money. Two or three thousand pounds and property in London," Maria said.

He could not say anything.

"I heard," the soldier said, "it were fifteen thousand and a row of houses in London and some land at Spella."

It was still beyond him to speak.

"You got to get in touch with Mr. Carmichael," Maria said.

"How? In touch, how?"

"Through Mason and Freebody. On the Square. They been here times. Said they were acting for you."

"Acting?"

"Gettin' the dough," the soldier said.

Bruno, grasping things with painful slowness, suddenly

understood the situation in terms of the room in which he sat. He looked about it. Something had happened. He remembered the broken windows stopped up with board and sacking, the boxes for chairs, the broken floor covered with old coal-bags and sacking. Now the windows were filled up; he saw fresh putty marks on the new glass. On the floor, scrubbed now, were strips of matting; he saw a square kitchen table, with plush green cloth, a whatnot in the corner, with a teapot, "A present from Yarmouth", and a likeness of Maria and the soldier, just married. He saw the whole situation resolve itself, but he still could not speak.

"Got 'em on strap," the soldier said. "Till you come back. Natty, ain't they?"

"The place was so bad," Maria said.

"Yes," he said. "Yes."

"We coulda got any mortal blamed thing," the soldier said. "Furniture, grub, beer, anything. Only gotta mention your name and we coulda got it."

He had nothing to say. He felt that nothing could excite him now. He had been down to the bottom of things, had lost Gerda, had known what it was to lie at the bottom of a pit. From starvation to a fortune in one leap was something belonging to the realm of the ironic. He appreciated it, but his mind, still sick, weary and baffled, had no other response.

He went to see Mason and Freebody on the following day. They spoke to him, treated him as a man who had come back from the dead. They called him "Mr. Shadbolt" and once Mr. Amos Mason's clerk called him. "Mr. Shadbolt, sir."

In another two days he was talking to Mr. Carmichael, again in the office of Mason and Freebody. "But Mr. Shadbolt, where have you been?"

"London," he said.

"London, London? Where in London? Where did you stay in London?"

Trying to make an answer, he could think only of the bookseller. "Near Grays Inn Road," he said.

"Well," Mr. Carmichael said. "Well. Did you ever! I was just round the corner."

He tried to show interest in this extraordinary coincidence. Mr. Carmichael went on talking. Bruno listened, registered understanding through a series of impressions: papers taken from Mr. Carmichael's pocket, seals, a reading of extracts from the papers, figures, the sum of £250, more figures, the name of a piece of land, Anchor's Quick, connected with Spella Ho, more figures, then talk of property in London. "You are very fortunate Mr. Shadbolt, very fortunate." Impressions grew stronger; he began to accept them more consciously. He began to understand how he had become the owner of a block of six houses in London. "Camden Town. Perhaps you know it? The houses are not of the best residential class, Mr. Shadbolt, but the gross rental is not to be sneezed at. Certainly not to be sneezed at!" Then more figures, more explanations. Finally a proposition from Mr. Carmichael, in terms of advice: "If you will take our advice, Mr. Shadbolt. The land now, Anchor's Quick, here in Castor. To you, as land, useless. Sell it. Benefit yourself to the extent of another fifty pounds. Then the houses, in London. To you, here, in the country, more bother than they are worth—as houses. Repairs, rates, trouble with tenants, a source of endless worry. Sell them too. We could get you, say for the sake of argument, another £750. Give you a thousand pounds in all, Mr. Shadbolt. Make you a rich man, Mr. Shadbolt, a rich man."

"I daresay," he said.

He sat thinking. Houses in London, Bandy, the room in the tenement house. For one room he and Bandy had paid seven-and-six, a room without windows, with no air except by the broken door and the skylight. In that house he knew there were ten other rooms. On the basis of seven-and-six a room he tried to calculate the value of the house in rents. He did not pause to consider the difference between letting and subletting. He put the rental value at a round seventy shillings and then tried, in his slow, crude way, to multiply in his head seventy by the fifty-two weeks of the year. He knew it must come to somewhere between £ 150 and £ 200 when Mr. Carmichael spoke again.

"I may tell you," he said, "for what it's worth, that the rates in London are bound shortly to go up. There is an agitation for raising wages. Trade unions, labour agitators, hot headed fellows everywhere. If wages go up rates are bound to go up."

"If wages go up," Bruno said, "rents can go up."

Mr. Carmichael went on talking, trying in a slightly aggrieved voice to induce him to sell the property in London. All the time he was not listening. Reckoning his age to be now almost thirty, he was trying to calculate how much would come to him, in rents, if he should live to be sixty. By crude, laborious mental calculation he got a figure of between four and five thousand pounds. Then he remembered that this was for one house, that he must multiply the figure by six. He remembered then that Mr. Carmichael had said nothing about rents, that it was possible that rents might be higher or lower than he himself had imagined.

"What are the rents?" he said.

"On these six properties? Well, that would have to be gone into, Mr. Shadbolt, have to be gone into."

"Gone into be damned!" He was suddenly out of patience, on the verge of anger. "You've been solicitor to Mrs. Lanchester for God knows how many years and yet you don't know the rents and prices of her property?"

"Well—"

"Well, well! What the hell's the use of a well without water? If you don't know the rents, give me a rough idea."

Mr. Carmichael turned over his papers, found the figures, gave them out at last. "The gross rental is £ 954 11 s. 3 d. per annum."

"Means a year?"

"Yes Mr. Shadbolt."

He made his decision. "I keep the property," he said "I want rents collected weekly and forwarded here every week, less your commission. Mason and Freebody'll act for me here."

"You would want to come up to see the property, perhaps?" Mr. Carmichael said.

"No," he said. "I'm done with London."

He stayed to arrange affairs and sign papers, going over every syllable of every paper with deliberate and careful determination, until almost five o'clock that afternoon. Coming out of the office and going across the Square, he met Stokes. Stokes appeared to have changed. He looked alert, more in command of himself. He began to tell Bruno about it as they walked together to the workshop. "I got converted." He was a man being tossed on the waves of religious fervour. "Happened while you was away. Come on me all of a pop. I got the blues one night and went into the Plymouth Brethren and suddenly it got me. I see God. See him as plain as daylight. I never bin the same since, Shadbolt. I see Him. I feel His Presence. I know He's with me. It made a big difference, Shadbolt. You see if it ain't made a big difference."

They went together to the workshop, and no sooner was the door opened than Bruno saw the difference. The shop had been fitted with benches, and four men, shoemakers, were standing at them, working over lasts. The place was alive with hammering, dancing of tacks and sprigs, the smell of hot-wax, leather, warmed heel-ball. "As soon as this thing come over me," Stokes said, "I went to old Abel Sanders and told him how it was. He said 'I thank the Good God, Stokes. And if you can get the men I'll give you the work.'" Even as he spoke three small boys, sweaters, came in with sacks of uppers, struggling up the wooden steps outside. "Yes," Stokes said, "I got sweaters too." He seemed very proud of the sweaters. "Four men and three sweaters. That's a move since you were here, ain't it?"

"What made you give the leather up?"

"I ain't give it up," Stokes said. "Still keep it on. Side line. Do a deal now and then." He again grew fervent. "Oh! Shadbolt, if you knew the difference. Work, honest clean work. God watching you, with you, all the time. And prayer, Shadbolt, prayer. I kneel and pray sometimes until I can't bend my joints back."

"What profit are you making?"

"That's all right, don't worry about it." He took Bruno into the office. "Every week since this happened your fifty per cent has been put aside just as if you was here." He took a cash-box from a drawer, unlocked it. "Some weeks a couple o' pounds. Some weeks only twenty-five bob. One or two weeks nearly three pounds. It's all here. God has given me strength and guidance on everything, Shadbolt."

"You want me to come in and work?"

"What, now? With this money the old lady left you?"

"There ain't no money. It's all in bricks and mortar."

Stokes looked immediately depressed. "Pity, pity. What we want is money, Shadbolt, if we had money we could build a business. See? Trade's coming on. If we had the cash we could get big orders and employ gals and women for the closing and give the work out instead of having to get it out. We could knock Jolly and Lawrence out of business. They're rocky. I know. Lawrence is old and they don't turn out half the stuff they used to. See what I mean? All we want is money."

"How much?"

"We could start on a hundred and fifty. I bin thinking we could take Matson's old shop. Abe Sanders is bunged out with stuff. He give us a start. If we could get price right and quality right we'd be made."

He felt suddenly impressed, deeply influenced by Stokes's way of speaking. "How much?" he said. "A hundred and fifty?"

"A hundred and fifty."

"I'll find it," he said.

And when, an hour later, he came out of Stokes's workshop he felt as though he were walking upside down. It was as though the world had been turned upside down. The old ideas of money and profit, ambition and progress, had the effect on his starved mind exactly that of a sudden meal on a starved body. Intoxicating ideas of money, property, business, profits drove him into a state where, momentarily, he did not know what he was doing. His mind went through a period of brief but complete blankness. When this blankness had gone he found himself walking up the avenue to Spella Ho, as though the old lady had never died and he had never gone away. He did not know quite how he had got there. He walked along under the bare trees and went up on to the terrace and stood looking at the house.

It was empty. It seemed to stand with a greater effect of hugeness and solidity than before. He stood very impressed, for a moment almost touched, by this effect of solid and empty grandeur. The house seemed part of his life, a central force about which his life revolved. He stood there looking at it for a long time, the white stone outlined against the winter sky, and then he walked slowly round it, his head slightly down, unconsciously, like a man who had come back to look for something lost.

CHAPTER VII

FROM this moment he began to get on: not solidly and slowly, with the old blundering determination of a man advancing in darkness, but suddenly, shot up like a rocket. Where other men, successful, felt themselves to be on their feet, he felt during the next seven or eight years as though he were flying through space. During all this time the wind of luck blew him continually one way. In the summer of 1882 he and Stokes moved their premises, taking the empty factory Stokes had suggested, the partnership under new agreement, Bruno putting up £ 150, Stokes £ 50. These sums seemed to him colossal. Colossal days, colossal sums of money, but who knew, perhaps, colossal profits? At first he and Stokes employed only six girls on the sewing-machines and about a dozen men in the making and clicking rooms. By the end of 1883 they employed twenty girls and about forty-five men. Profits rose too: a bare £85 on the first year's working, a good £300 on the second. "All due," Stokes would say, "to God watching over us." Bruno knew nothing about leather, less about making boots. He never learned. It was his job to interview commercial travellers, hard working and often weary men who walked the five miles from Orlingford Station with large leather bags of samples, thread, eyelets, linen, buckram, grindery: men who did not like Castor, a dead-alive town without a railway or a hotel or even, in these days, a decent place to eat. He found it easy to intimidate these tired men, who hated the town but hated still more the thought of walking another five miles without an order in their pockets. It was his system to set himself a figure as far below their figure as he dared and then browbeat them down to it. He interviewed travellers at the top of the stairs, never in the office. There, on the match-boarding partitions, were tacked printed notices of Stokes's invention or selection. "The Lord is my Shepherd I shall not Want." "To whomsoever it may concern: There Are Many Roads in Life, the Rough and the Smooth, the Narrow and the Straight. Take Rough and Narrow rather than Smooth and Straight, for Straight is the way and Narrow is the gate that leadeth to Salvation." And in larger letters than the rest: *"You have Come To Show Us Your Samples. Remember There Also Cometh A Day When You Must Lay Out Your Samples Before Him."* Under these notices Bruno browbeat dozens of sun-weary or half-famished travellers, adamant to a farthing or an eighth or even a sixteenth of a penny. In this way, hard, unsentimental, consistently relentless, he felt that he gained a revenge on a world that had been for so long hard and relentless towards him. He gained something else. As far as the gossip of travellers could extend at the time of day, for a radius of twenty or thirty miles, he gained the reputation of being a hated man.

In a few years the form of ambition had crystallized, become unchangeable. Money: he thought of it as with capital letters. He was now past the middle thirties. People still talked, with envy, wonder, but mostly malice, of young Shadbolt. Self-centred, he did not know of any such public reaction to himself. Every week Mason and Freebody received from London the rents of his property and once a month he called at the small gauze-windowed bank that opened one day a week in a private front room on the Square and called for his pass-book. He did not touch this money. It grew with the steadiness and inevitability of one day adding itself to another. This inevitability fascinated him. To know that it could go on and on, never diminishing by a farthing, always increasing, seemed to him not only a fascinating thing but a beautiful, powerful thing. He knew that money made money; and where, to Stokes, money was linked with a creed that was itself beautiful and powerful, to him money was a creed, unconscious but wonderful, a force that inspired and obsessed him. It was inevitable that he should be driven by this force to try, as time went on, to make more money.

During this time he was very friendly with Rufus Chamberlain. He began to dress like Chamberlain: the latest in swank hats and collars, oiled hair, pointed shoes, an inclination towards dandyism in canes and coloured waistcoats. In Chamberlain, handsome, dapper, red-haired, it was a natural taste; in him it seemed like an expression of something grotesque. He never wore a yellow-and-purple waistcoat or a pair of lavender trousers without looking as though he had stepped out of the pages of a comic paper. When he smoked cigars, always with the band on, it was as though he were doing it for the first time. He never got himself a pair of patent leather boots without they squeaked, from the first moment to the last, as though he were a verger in a church-aisle. Flashy clothes sat on him with an air of discomfort and a slightly ludicrous depravity, accentuating his ugliness, the tight coats bringing out the long arms, the light-coloured shoes making the great feet seem larger and flatter, the high choker collars raising up the huge head, with the protuberant determined eyes, as though it had been barbarously cooked and served up in a basin too small for it.

He was never aware of this. It made him conspicuous wherever he and Chamberlain went, and throughout the 'eighties they began to be known in every pub and hotel and ball-room and penny-gaff and travelling vaudeville all over the county. Using Chamberlain's turn-out, they went wherever women and drink and fights were cheap. In both there was a streak of miserliness, an inward conscience that protested against waste: the streak that, in Chamberlain's father, made the expense of a new straw hat a crime. For the sake of fights they showed an interest in politics, breaking up political meetings everywhere: Liberal against Tory even though they did not know a word of one creed or another, rioting on election nights, fighting drunk, and in between times fathering easy bastards for miles down and up the river. In these affairs Bruno did not distinguish one woman from another and passion began to assume a fundamental, everyday necessity, taken like so much bread. All the time the legend of notoriety, begun by the fight at Spella Ho and the gossip of the inheritance from Mrs. Lanchester, grew up about him steadily and fantastically. He became a man regarded not only with hatred by tired commercial travellers whom he outwitted on farthings, but with jealousy by almost everyone who knew anything of his history: jealousy because he had money and was now trying to make more money, the jealousy of prudery because he had neither religion nor conscience in matters of bastardy, the gigantic, insuperable jealousy of a small Victorian town resenting behaviour that it was itself too slow or frightened or horrified to commit.

He saw much not only of Rufus Chamberlain but of

Charles Walker Chamberlain, too. The older man now had something like reverence for the younger. A man who could not only make money, but who could walk from London to Castor, facing a blizzard, after almost dying of fever in a rotten East End tenement, was a man after his own heart. Chamberlain, with almost more reason for jealousy than any man in Castor, felt no jealousy at all. He looked forward to times when they could eat together, coats and collars off, plates upturned for the pudding that was eaten first, and then they could talk together, dirty boots propped up on the expensive plush of the library chairs. They found a dozen questions which argument could never settle. Bruno had been powerfully impressed, in London, by the new incandescent gas-lighting. "I shan't be satisfied until the streets of Castor are lit like that." But Chamberlain could not bear the notion. "God gave us the darkness for a reason. And he gave us the moon and the stars to light up the darkness. That's sufficient reason for not lighting the streets of Castor with stinking gas-light." They talked of the old, vexed and now much more pressing question of the railway. Chamberlain held that a long new main-line would come, starting from Bedford, going on through Castor and the north. It would come through the south and south-west sides of the town. "You only think that," Bruno said, "because you own half the damn land there." Chamberlain agreed. "Of course I do. I shouldn't have bought the land there in the first place if I hadn't thought that. You're so cocky, where do you think it'll come?" Bruno said: "I don't know. But not from Bedford. That's certain. There's no place between here and Bedford that's worth a passenger a week to a railway company." They would argue with unrelenting stubbornness on these questions until the early hours of the morning. They were agreed only on one thing: that Castor was not, and could never be, a town of any importance until the railway did come. "Even if it's only a damn single line," Bruno said.

One evening in the year 1888 he stayed very late arguing

the railway question with Chamberlain. Just before twelve o'clock Chamberlain felt hungry and they sat and argued for another hour with hunks of bread and cheese under their thumbs. Going home, Bruno had a vivid and terrifying dream. He was standing in his field, Anchor's Quick. He had lately let the field for bullock-grazing and now, at one end of it, a herd of bullocks were massed ready to stampede. Suddenly they moved towards him at a great pace, in one immense roaring mass of flesh, and he tried to run. In his sleep he could not run at all. He could only turn round. When he did turn round he saw that it was not a herd of bullocks that was pursuing him, but a railway train. He saw it with terrible clarity coming down a single track. As it roared and shrieked behind him he flung himself with a great effort off the track, falling just in time to see the small-tendered engine and half a dozen coaches go rumbling past. A second later, waking up, he found himself lying on the floor, his body oily with cold sweat.

In the morning the dream remained with him. He went to the factory, but he could not forget it. That afternoon he walked up to Anchor's Quick. The bullocks were there, grazing quietly, and he climbed over the gate, standing in the field much as he had stood in it in the dream. Anchor's Quick was on the east side of the town, below but separated by a road from Spella Ho itself. He went back to the factory and got down a district map from the wall of the office. He laid a ruler along the east side of Castor; the line made by the ruler ran down to Orlingford. From that moment he felt there was no doubt that the railway, when it came, would come from Orlingford. It would be a little branch line, on a single track, and it would go through Anchor's Quick.

From that time he began to go about with almost nothing else in his mind but this inspired idea of the railway. He went again and again to look at Anchor's Quick and the fields stretching away on a straight line on either side of it. Who owned this land? Was there a chance of buying it? He went to see Mason and Freebody. "Parker owns about a hundred and fifty acres of it," they said. "Candlestick Parker." Then he remembered Parker, an old man now, a man who for forty years had gone about with the legend of patent candlestick clinging to him like a comic story. This strange invention, highly complex, impossibly economic, had been built by a brain that saw a fortune in an arrangement that would save mankind the trouble of striking matches. His machine kept a succession of candles perpetually alight. Bruno decided to go and see him. He found Parker alone in a large house of sienna-coloured ironstone which Parker had himself built in the 'forties. He had told Parker that he had come because he was interested in inventions, and the old man, feeble, a little weak-minded and egg-bald under the plum-coloured smoking-cap, took him upstairs to a large room, empty except for a plain mahogany table, on which stood the famous candlestick. Up to that moment Bruno had imagined a candlestick of normal height, shape and size. Parker's invention, built of solid brass, stood almost four feet. It looked like some complex and silent chronometer: an affair of dials and weights, a hopeless, polished intricacy of beautiful and insane mechanism. "It works," Parker said, and he touched a spring. The wheels revolved, a small blue flame on a methylated taper blobbed up and lighted the wick of candle. "If you have enough candles," Parker said, "it can go on for ever and you never need be without light. You like it?"

"Yes."

"You do? I had a gentleman here from Hammersmith in 1852. He liked it and he was going to buy it, but I never heard from him again. You're not from him? He didn't send you?"

"No, but everybody talks about your candlestick."

"Yes? All it needs is putting on the market. Someone to finance it."

"You'd need factories," Bruno said, "foundries, to build a thing like that."

"Naturally, naturally. I know, I know. I have it worked out."

"I thought it was smaller," Bruno said. "A thing I could do in a small way. It's so big."

"Oh no! If you compare the size of it with the size of the benefit it confers on humanity it's nothing."

They went downstairs. The house was full of other inventions, patent bells, trap-doors, blinds, windows, doorstops, clocks, kettles, all the insane paraphernalia of a kinked mind. "If you sold it," Bruno said, "what would you want for it?"

"The gentleman from Hammersmith talked of giving me two thousand."

"Too much."

"You don't think it's any good now? You said you liked it."

"I think it's a knock-out. But how ever am I going to develop it? Two thousand to you, then I got to buy land and build a foundry. Then put it on the market."

He stayed talking for another two hours. Parker brought in an almost empty bottle and glasses. "Rum," he said. "You see, when I was a boy I went to sea for a time. It has always been my greatest ambition to make a boat that would not sink."

That night they did not even talk about the land. It was a subject that came to be approached gradually, over many weeks and over many bottles of rum, supplied as time went on by Bruno. When it came to be discussed at last it seemed that Parker also had ideas about the land. "It has been my idea to invent a new kind of steel. Steel that would not stain or rust. You see what it would mean? In engineering, in the house, on railways."

"Well, what's that got to do with the land?"

"There's iron there. Don't you know? Don't you ever look at the colour of the soil there?"

"That red colour? Is that iron?"

"Of course yes. Thirty years ago, I mined enough there to experiment on. You come with me. I mined enough to build this house."

He took Bruno into the back-yard of the house and

there, in an outhouse, showed him a small experimental workshop. Steel in many shapes and sizes and in degrees of colour from dull blue to silver was littered about the place. "I can't do it now. I haven't the strength. I got it so that it would not stain but it broke just like slate. Then I got it hard but it was a bad colour. Always something. I wanted twenty more years."

They would talk on about steel and land and Parker's schemes until the old man was feebly drunk. Then a strange change took place in him. Without drink, he talked quickly, sometimes inconsequently, a little mad. Slightly drunk, he spoke more slowly, with the morose regret of a man who knew he had failed. Behind the old whitish, drink-moist eyes Bruno could see the ghost of the Parker of other days, the young man who had wanted to revolutionize the world by the realized dream of new steel. One night, as they were drinking, he said:

"Well, if you can't sell the land, I can't buy the candlestick."

Parker began to cry. Tears of age and weakness and destroyed illusions seemed suddenly to condense in his eyes, without falling. He sat in silence and cried for some time, a man with a mind broken down to feebleness by the weight of its own fecundity, the brain driven to the edge of sanity without quite losing its reason. When he had ceased crying he said:

"What makes you so anxious to buy the land?"

"The candlestick. I got to develop it. You can't develop a thing like that on ten pole of ground."

Parker thought it over. "No," he said, "I want to keep the land."

"Because of the iron? The steel?"

"Yes."

"Look, Mr. Parker. I tell you what, I'll buy the candlestick and the land. But you can reserve the mineral rights in half the land as long as you live. Then they come back to me. How old are you now?"

"I'm almost seventy-five."

"Nothing! You got another twenty years."

"You think so?"

"Why not? Another thing. You keep on with steel experiments and some day you'll hit it. Then we'll go into partnership."

Looking into Parker's eyes he saw them illuminated by the light of slightly insane delight, and he knew that it was settled. He knew also that he had no more belief in the steel than in the candlestick, no more belief in either than in Parker himself.

CHAPTER VIII

I RISH'S Travelling Vaudeville Theatre came into Castor at the beginning of the second week of August, feast-week, in the same year. Bruno, with almost five thousand pounds invested in Parker's land, had entered a period of great cautiousness. Time alone could show whether he was right about the railway. The present alone could help him consolidate his position in case he was wrong. That Monday night he turned down Rufus Chamberlain's suggestion to go into Irish's and stayed working in the office, going over the books, until midnight. The next morning Chamberlain came round to the office before nine o'clock in a state of immense excitement.

"Irish's got the hottest bird I've ever set eyes on. God, you can burn your fingers on her from the back row."

"What's she do?"

"It's not what she does, man, it's what she looks like. She picks her skirts up above her knees and you can see her legs. No tights, nothing. Any road, if they're tights they're the tightest tights I ever seen. Everybody went barmy."

"Didn't get near her?"

"No bloody earthly. All we want to-night," he went on, "is a pair of field glasses."

They sat that night on the plank seats of Irish's Vaudeville Theatre, hearing about them outside the faint moan and crack of fair-organs and shooting-galleries, and waited for her to appear. All about them there was a state of suppressed tension. The crowd let up a roar when the girl came on. She was full-breasted but otherwise rather slightly built, with slim legs and very slender thighs. It was the thighs, covered with smooth flesh tights and suddenly revealed by uptossed scarlet skirts, that set the house roaring. Chamberlain fixed his eyes to a pair of large black field glasses like a man eagerly watching a race-horse and the girl was singing her last song, rolling large dark eyes, before Bruno could get the glasses from him.

When he first looked through the glasses the focus was wrong. He had the impression of looking at the girl through mist. Gradually he altered the focus and in a moment he could see her with a strange magnified proximity. He could see the slightly unreal painted expression on her face and it was as though he could reach out and touch her.

Then he knew, suddenly, where he had felt that odd emotion before. He was standing at the back of the music-hall with Bandy, ill, fainting down slopes of space, and he was looking at this same girl with the slim pink tights, his sick mind occupied with the impression that he could stretch out his arms and touch her. He looked hard through the glasses. There was something he recalled very vividly about her. She had white, slim arms. Then he saw that the girl on the stage also had white, slim arms and suddenly he knew that she was the same girl. He was overcome immediately with a tremendous, fatalistic sense of familiarity, the idea that at some moment of his existence, perhaps far back in time, he had known this girl before. In another moment she had finished singing and had disappeared. He went outside and looked up at the names of the artistes painted up on the paraffin-lighted boards above the platform entrance. She was there, slightly changed, but the same without any doubt at all: "Italian Jenny."

"What's up?" Chamberlain said. "God, she's good, isn't she?"

"I know her," Bruno said. "I met her in London."

"You what?"

He did not speak. He felt that he did know her. The sense of familiarity bred in him a sense of unshakable certainty.

"Well I'm damned," Chamberlain said. "Where do I come in?"

"I don't know," he said. "I don't know where I come in myself."

They went together to see her dancing and singing in Irish's hot cheap tent, two houses a night, for the next four nights. Bruno could not rest. He thought of her with the same insuperable determination as he thought about money. He was filled with the old crude, blundering anxiety to get something and to get it no matter what happened. On the fourth night he lost Chamberlain in a boxing-booth after the second performance at Irish's and went round, alone, to the back of the theatre. He could not see her. He saw Irish himself, a tremendous cask-shaped man with topper and white waistcoat, talking to some of his men, and from Irish, after a moment's reluctance on Irish's part, he got to know which was her travelling van. "Who are you?" Irish said, and something made him say, with natural promptitude, that he was a shoe-manufacturer. "She send for you?" Irish said, and he said yes, she had sent for him. "All right. In the yellow van," Irish said. He went up the steps of a long yellow living-van at the back of the tent and knocked on the door. He could see a lamp burning inside, and heard her voice: "Who is it?" He opened the door, his mind made up now as to his reason for coming. He stepped a foot or so inside the van. The van, shut up all day in the August sun, smelt hot and airless and he saw her lying down, in her red performing dress, on one of the bunks. She lay there and stared at him, hands clasped behind her head, the white arms branched together, showing the dark bare armpits. He could see the outline of the breasts drawn sharply and smoothly up by this attitude, and her face shining partly with perspiration, partly with grease, in the lamplight. "Who the hell and blazes are you?" she said.

He told her. As he spoke he looked straight at her, fascinated beyond himself by the small dark eyes shining with familiar indignation. "I saw your feet to-night through a pair of field-glasses. You'll kill yourself if you don't get some different shoes."

"What difference does it make to you if I do?"

"I thought we could make you some new shoes," he said. "Two or three pair."

"Shoemaker, are you?"

"Yes," he said.

"All dolled up an' all."

"You're a hot dancer," he said. "You want good shoes."

"Hot's about it." She dropped her arms, exhausted. "Well, I got no dough for new shoes. So that settles that."

"We shan't charge," he said. "Not a cent. Nothing."

"You don't mean you're giving shoes away?"

He had not once taken his eyes away from her. Now she looked at him, for the first time, with the same directness. He felt between them a momentary flash of contact. "We give shoes away to you," he said. She did not speak. Her face now had an expression of slight bewilderment, as though she were trying to clarify some obscure remembrance of something. It lasted about a minute. "Funny," she said. "I thought I'd seen you somewhere before. You know that funny feeling you get about some folks?"

"I seen you before," he said.

"What?" she said. She sat up, trying to straighten the stiff ruffles of the dress over her knees. They sprang up again from her hands, like scarlet springs. "How do you mean you seen me before?"

He told her: where it was, what year, the exact night as near as he could remember it. "That was you?" he said. "The Italian Nightingale."

"Yes," she said, "that was me."

He did not know what else to say. For the first time his eyes left her face and he looked instead at her feet. She was not wearing shoes. On the feet of the tights he could see dark sepia sweat-marks where the shoes had cut her and on the ball of each foot a small hole, cut by the friction of a thin shoe. She lifted her right foot and put it on her left knee, feeling the hole with her finger. "More holy than righteous. That's me all over."

"What shoes do you walk in?" he said.

"Slippers."

"They're no good," he said. "You want something to rest your feet and support 'em as well."

"Go on, tell me next I want crutches.'"

"Your feet hurt, don't they?"

"They hurt like hell and blazes," she said. "And you're a good man if you can do anything about it. I never had shoes to fit me yet."

He raised his eyes slowly from her feet, looking gradually up the legs and thighs and body to her face. "I'll make you a pair o' shoes that'll fit you like your tights do your legs," he said.

"That'll be close enough," she said.

They looked at each other in silence again for about half a minute, she drowsy and ironical, dark eyes tired but shining, he with the sense of familiarity, at intervals almost hypnotic. Finally she lay down on the bunk again. "When do I get these free shoes? With a pound of tea?"

"I'll come and measure you to-morrow," he said. "What time you like."

"Don't come before twelve," she said.

He went away, five minutes later, with a sense of elation that was more like a feeling of hot illumination than any emotion. He felt at once burning and dazzled, his mind like a lamp-glass, ready to crack with the heat inside it. In the morning he was in the office before six o'clock, turning out the few skins of fancy leather that Stokes and Shadbolt possessed. There was a skin of buckskin, pure white, but he knew that what she needed was scarlet. It would take time to get scarlet, but he knew that he would get it, that it was inevitable that he should get it.

He began to be oppressed, in time, by an increasing sense of inevitability. Soon after twelve o'clock he went round to the back of Irish's and knocked on the door of her travelling-van and heard her voice asking "Who is it?" again. He went in and she was lying on the bunk, in the same tired attitude as before, bare arms branched over her head, as though she had not moved since the previous night except to take off the red dress and the tights. Her legs were bare under a grey dressing-gown, and old red velvet slippers hung on her toes, showing bare heels and ankles. The heat of the August midday struck down through the wooden roof of the van and hung like a hot dust vapour. Her black hair was still down, in two pigtails, and she looked at him as though she had never seen him before.

"I come to measure you for the shoes," he said. He had paper and pencil and a skin of buckskin in his hands.

"Well, knock me down!" she said. "I thought it was a joke."

"No," he said.

"You mean you'll just give me a pair of shoes? Like that? I thought you were boozed when you said that."

"No."

"You'll just give me a pair of shoes and it's not a joke?"

"Yes," he said. "I got a piece of buckskin here. It'll be soft to your feet. I'll get a skin of special dyed calf— red or something. Yellow if you want it. Anything."

"What day of the week is it?" she said.

"Saturday."

"Am I barmy?" She lay back on the bunk, eyes closed. "I must be barmy."

"Stand up," he said.

"Eh?" Her eyes shot open, black splits of indignation. "First you kid me and then you order me about."

"Stand up." He unfolded a large sheet of drawing-paper. "I want to draw your feet."

She grinned then, and stood up. He spread the paper on the floor. "Stand on it," he said. "Both feet. Natural."

She stood on the paper, bare feet apart. "Thought you were kidding. I get hot-tempered all of a sudden if folks kid me."

He drew the pencil slowly round the shape of her right foot.

"Whatever you do for God's sake don't tickle me. Is this for dancing shoes?"

"No." He explained: "You got to have special lasts, special patterns. I don't think we could do it."

"Just ordinary shoes?"

"Yes."

"High-legged or just shoes?"

"Which you like."

"I always wanted a pair of high-legged buckskin, right up," she said. "White. With black laces and a bow and high heels."

"Just what you like," he said.

She went on talking of how she would love the high-legged buckskin boots. He drew the pencil round her other foot: a man moved by some inexplicable force, by something just beyond reason and emotion.

"How long to make them?" she said.

"Tuesday," he said.

"Tuesday? We go on to-morrow morning."

He already knew this. "Where to?"

"Peterborough."

"I'll come to Peterborough," he said.

He had finished the drawing of her feet and she stepped off the paper and he rolled it up. She moved to lie down on the bunk again. "Stand still," he said.

"You give your orders, don't you? Hell and blazes!"

"If you're going to have high-legged," he said, "I got to measure your legs."

"Me all over." She grinned. "Hot-tempered."

"Hold your dressing-gown up. How high do you want the legs?"

She held up the dressing-gown. "Right up. Real swanky, right up to the knees." He ran the tape measure up her white legs, to the small knees, hard and round, like apples. "Funny, you seeing me down the Waterloo Road there."

"Yes." He told her how he had been taken ill soon afterwards.

"Compliment to me. Stomach-ache?"

"I got scarlet fever. I got lodgings and there was an infected bed."

"No?" she said. "Go on? Just like me. I got lodgings and got a damp bed and got landed with congestion of the lungs. Pleurisy. Laid me flat and I lost my bookings. That's how I came to be landed with Irish."

He finished measuring her legs but she still stood looking down at him, holding up the dressing-gown, smiling. "A nice free look for you. Think yourself lucky."

"Why do they call you Italian?" he said, "Italian Jenny?"

"Simple. My name's Jenny and my mother was Italian."

As he listened to her telling him things about herself he felt himself drawn slowly and surely towards a central point of intimacy. In his mind he saw her in the white high buckskin boots. He saw her travelling in the van to places at immense and impossible distances away. He saw that there was some possibility of his never seeing her again. "Where do you go after Peterborough?" he said.

"Grantham," she said. "Then Lincoln. Oh! I don't know where then. Nottingham Goose Fair anyway in the autumn."

Outside someone began banging a spoon on a tin frying-pan and she got up off the bunk. "Cook house," she said. "You'd better go." He went out of the van and across the fair-ground like a man in a dream. She called after him: "I believe you about the boots when I see 'em!" laughing.

It was still in the same dream that he drove the thirty miles to Peterborough on the following Tuesday to take her the boots. He bought himself a neat spanking turn-out in black and green and a small black mare for the journey. The weather was still hot but thundery now, and over the corn land hung a kind of thick bruise-coloured haze of heat, stifling. He had damned and blasted clickers and makers and finishers all day on Monday in order to get the boots made in time. He saw her in the afternoon. She was asleep in the van when he arrived and got up, frowsy and sleep-muddled, her hair still in pig-tails, to ask who the hell and blazes it was? "Well, knock me down!" she said. "Come in." He went in and she tried on the boots, more excited than a child. She tugged at the laces and pulled them up, creasing the long white tongues. "Steady," he said. "You'll have no lace left to tie with. You want a big bow, don't you?" He took her leg and held her foot between his knees, pulling up the laces firm and tight with his finger tips. "How do they feel?" She was in a rapture. "Grand. Skin-tight. I feel as if I'd wore them months." Then when she had both boots on she strutted up and down the van, holding up her wrap, swinging her hips, looking over her shoulder to see how the boots looked. "Swanky," she kept on saying "terrible swanky." And then: "Are they fast?" "Yes," he said. She laughed and clicked her heels together. "Fast is just how I wanted them."

She flashed her arms up and down and then rested them on her hips, fingers spread fan-wise. He saw the shine of a wedding ring. He felt dismay. "I didn't know you were married."

"Married? Me? Don't make me laugh!"

"The wedding-ring," he said.

"Just a blind. Like barmaids. Must wear it or I'd never get any peace at all."

He was relieved, and said: "I'm getting you a pair o'red boots."

"Red? No!"

"Special stuff. It might be in this week. Perhaps next."

"You want to send me mad or something? First white, now red. You made of money? You do this to all the girls?"

They talked like this for about an hour. He told her how he would make her not only a pair of red boots, but a pair of black. "You want to spoil me?" she said.

"Yes."

"You're going the right way."

"I could bring the black over one day," he said. "Friday or Saturday. "

"We'll be here till Saturday," she said.

All the time, in the van, and again as he drove back through the stormy hot countryside to Castor, he could feel the thick moist heat of thunder increasing. That night the storms broke. He lay awake and heard the crack of thunder splitting over the mass of trees at Spella Ho, and Maria got up, in her nightgown, and came into his bedroom, frightened. "It looks just as if Spella'll be struck," she said. He looked out of his window and saw blue claws of lightning tearing the sky apart, revealing the great roof among the trees. He could hear the great roar of rain, itself blotted out by the intermittent bombardment of thunder. The storms kept on all that night and he got up to see a land flooded and steaming slightly in the sun. The air did not clear that day and storms began to gather up again in the late afternoon, breaking at dusk, lightning splitting over Spella Ho all night, with the same immense roar of rain.

On Friday he decided to go by train to Peterborough. He walked to Orlingford in the early morning and caught the first train out, at eight-fifteen, travelling all morning up the flat flooded valley, seeing corn floating, beached on the railway banks, the river in places blotted out. The train moved slowly, stopping at all stations, like a creature cautiously exploring a waste land. He did not arrive until after twelve o'clock and he went straight to the fair-ground, knowing that it would be a good time for her.

He stood looking at the empty fair-ground for almost

five minutes before realizing what had happened. He stared at the blank churned mud and listened to a voice of a man telling him all about it. "You should ha' seen 'em! Mud! Water! Looked like Noah's bloody ark."

"Where'd they go?"

"Grantham, they said."

Back at the railway station he found that there was no train to Grantham until nearly three o'clock. He went out of the station and had a meal of three boiled eggs and some tea. He did not think of going back. He knew that he could not get to Grantham before early evening and that it would be another day before he could get back to Castor.

He got to the fair-ground in Grantham just before six o'clock. It was trying to rain again and the girl, when he found her, was in a fit of depression. "Boots? You better make me a pair o' sea boots. I'm sick of it. Smashed the whole theatre down at Peterborough, one man killed by lightning, everybody flooded out. We pulled out of there at three o'clock in the morning. Haven't got over it yet."

She looked out of the window, pulling back the lace-curtain, and Bruno could see the rain steadily falling on the awnings of shut-up shows and roundabouts, the warm straight rain of the aftermath of days of thunder. "See that? Nice how de do again. Irish'll be happy."

"No performance?"

"Not likely. Still, I got to dress up and show up. That's Irish's rule, whether it snows cats."

"Want me out?"

"Go out and get me a bag o' buns from somewhere, there's a duck. I'll be ready when you get back. Haven't eaten a morsel since dinner."

He went out and bought a loaf and a pound of cheese and some Grantham cakes and four bottles of beer. When he came back she had gone. He arranged the beer and food on a table, and sat down to wait. She came in after about ten minutes, in her red dancing frock and tights, with a rain-cape over them. "Irish's tearing his hair out in lumps," she said. Then she saw the beer and the food on the table. Her dark eyes opened wide, in mock unbelief. "Oh! you're a duck," she said. "First you gave me a pair of boots, and now this."

"You want to try the boots on before we eat?" he said.

"No. Let's eat first." She began to cram cakes into her mouth. "Oh! you're a real duck."

By the time they had drunk half the beer and had eaten most of the food it was almost dark. At intervals between eating she lay back on the bunk, as he had first seen her, arms above her head, the favourite attitude, and he would see the white flesh merging to the dark armpits and the look of sleepy and waiting passion in the half-shut eyes. The springy ruffles of her dance dress stood up from the slim legs, like a mass of red foam, in a way that accentuated their strength and slenderness. He sat on the bed, all of a sudden, and put his hands on her bare arms. She did not say anything. He ran his hands up her arms to the shoulders and then down again, very slowly, looking at her. She continued to say nothing and she looked at him with some latent accumulation of passion or anger that made him wonder what she was going to do. He moved his hands along her arms again, slowly upward, and then suddenly she pulled him down.

Some long time afterwards she told him to get up and turn the key of the door. It was dark and when he moved back to her he put out his hands and touched the frills of her frock. "Take it off," he said.

Her voice was surprisingly quiet and remote: "You give your orders, don't you?"

"Take it off," he said. "Undress."

She lay in complete acquiescence, in a dead stillness that he knew afterwards to be a sign of immense passion. "You," she said, "You do it for me."

CHAPTER IX

HE stayed with her for two days, going back to Castor on Sunday. More and more he felt as though it were all the recurrence of something that happened before. He felt as though he were being driven, arms and hands tied, to some inevitable and preconceived point of time.

In Castor, Stokes was troubled. Stokes had built himself a new house, a house of clean red brick, with white stone sills to the bays, lattice work for roses, and a stone tablet: Rose Villa, 1890. He had become prominent among Plymouth Brethren, wore a semi-frock coat on Sundays, and battled hard for a religion of fire and blood, talking of a new Jerusalem. With a position to keep up, he was ashamed of a partner in business who treated morals with contempt and latitude and had never entered chapel or church in his life. For a long time he had been tolerant; now he felt obliged to speak. "This gadding about with women, Sundays an' all, I don't hold with it."

"Who asked you to?"

"You been away half the week with some woman or other."

"Who said it was a woman?"

"All right. I suppose you had white buckskin boots made for yourself?"

This position grew worse, Stokes suspicious, troubled by conflict between respectability and immorality. Gradually there arose a second point of difference between them. Stokes was for caution in all things. "Steady does it. Expand gradual." Bruno was for opening out, taking risks; he wanted to enlarge the existing factory, if possible build a new factory. Stokes would not hear of it. They stayed quarrelling in the office, at nights, after the rest of the factory was in darkness. "You built a new house," Bruno would say, "why the hell shouldn't we build a new factory?" "That's different, that's different." "How different?" "Oh! it's different, that's all, it's different." This conflict between ambition and negation went on for the rest of that year, iron grinding itself on stone, sharpening itself but gradually wearing stone down and away, until, towards the end of the year, Stokes surrendered. They would build a new factory. "The biggest factory in Castor," Bruno said. "We're going up, and don't forget it."

Building on the new factory started in the New Year. It began to rise in a huge raw rectangle of brick on the east side of the town. It did what Bruno knew it would do; it impressed and infuriated Castor. People would have been glad if it had fallen down in the night; it affronted taste and ideals and accepted methods of business and progress. It was the personification of a man who had no illusions of beauty; it took on the same solid, ugly, indomitable air. Going up quickly, it stood ready by midsummer, a barracks of brick with three tiers of thick opaque glass windows, without even the ornamentation of name or date, nothing to say what it was or why it was there. It was filled with a hundred and twenty workers by July.

It was a year in which he was hardly conscious of the progress of time. He was caught up by the fascination, almost the hypnoticism of two dreams: the factory and the woman, Italian Jenny. She moved about the country with Irish's Travelling Vaudeville from the August when he first met her on through the winter and spring of the following year, never staying more than a week in one place, and there were times when, momentarily, he lost touch with her. Yet her existence in his mind remained unshakably fixed. He never thought of her as being at a distance. From time to time he wrote short, painfully conceived letters to her and after an interval of a week or even a month he would get a reply, from as far north as Newcastle or as far west as Bristol: "Dear, Dear Bruno." Then suddenly she would move and come down to the Midlands, to Nottingham or Oxford, and he would get her hastily scrawled postcard, or even a telegram, urging him to meet her there. He would go and would again be held by the strange inevitability of it all, as though they were meant to meet, at exactly that moment and that place, by some remotely preconceived arrangement, for some equally preconceived end. After the show, if it were a big town, she would change her dress, and they would go into the town and have supper: steak and porter, tripe and onions, fish and chips, and then back through the almost dark fairground to the van. They came together out of an immense mutual longing for passion as natural and necesssary as breath. They had very little to say; only something huge and tenderly inarticulate to express by looks, silence and the act itself. In May that year she moved back from travelling vaudeville to music-hall. In this way he saw her more often. She was more in big towns, and he made slow roundabout railway journeys, twice and sometimes three times a month, to see her, leaving Castor on Friday and not coming back till Monday. There was one difference: she took lodgings and they would live for three days as man and wife, sleeping in cheap rose-papered rooms, laying late on Sunday mornings like a newly-married couple, luxurious sometimes in great brass bedsteads. Under the warm bedclothes he would tickle her and she would spring like some soft white eel, struggling and kicking until the bedclothes were thrown off and her body was half-naked, the white legs kicking up the nightgown, she herself very fierce and quiet in the final moment.

In the August of that year he went as far as Halifax, late on a Friday afternoon. When he got there she met him at the station and told him how, that morning, there had been a small fire at the theatre. "It wasn't much but it burnt the stage quite a lot and while they're at it the management are going to shut shop and put in a new stage altogether. It means a week off." She was excited, had made plans. "We'll go to Blackpool." They went on the following day and took lodgings for the whole week. He bought her a red silk dress and a red parasol to match her red boots and he smoked cigars while they drove in a landau along by the sea and out into the country. She was ecstatically happy, and he went back to Castor like a man who could not see straight.

When he arrived Stokes was furious. Bruno had not written a word of his whereabouts. Stokes argued: "Here we are with a brand new place, over heads enough to kill us, trade slack, and you go gadding off for ten days and don't say a word."

"Trade slack?"

"We had a gross in last week. A gross! A month like that and we'll go broke."

"Keep your hair on, for Christ's sake."

"Leave Christ out of it!"

"All right, leave Christ out of it. But don't horse-face at me!"

They quarrelled in the new office all that afternoon. In the morning, for Bruno, it was all over, a thing of the past, and he interviewed and browbeat a dozen commercial travellers as though nothing had happened. For Stokes it was different; he could not forget it. It seemed to him that there was some connection between the immorality of Bruno and the fall of trade. By the reasoning of his religion the one was fruit of the other. He began to go about obsessed by this idea. Women, immorality, loose living, bad trade, bankruptcy, one terrible thing producing another. It began gradually to bring the pressure of some malignant growth on Stokes's mind. Trade hung slack all through September and October, men standing off, rooms silent. Stokes saw it more and more as the fruit of Bruno's behaviour. His mind began to clamour with the shout of biblical parallels, confused, obsessed, without any reason; he saw the sin of whoremongering, adultery, incontinence producing the barren fruit of things wicked, the consuming fire of Divine wrath. By the end of October he was like a man suffering from some malignant pressure on the brain.

On the last Saturday in October Bruno set off for Nottingham. He came to the office dressed in his best clothes, but to Stokes it was as though he had come naked. The factory was not working and the huge silence of it closed on about the office like some depressing vacuum. Stokes could not bear it any longer. "We're losing money, but you can throw money about on women as if it growed on trees! I won't have it! It can't go on! I won't stand for it!"

Bruno remained calm. Stokes began to shout about sin and God, punishment and wickedness. "I was wicked, but not like this! Not like this! Not *this* wickedness." He continued to shout, his voice wild and righteous, and he was still shouting about sin and redemption and fire when a sweeper-up from downstairs came into the office to see what was the matter. "Fire! The eternal fire of eternal damnation! *That* fire! That's what you'll have to face."

The sweeper-up came in and asked if anything were the matter.

"Nothing's the matter!" Stokes shouted. "Get out." He slammed the door so that the key bounced out of the lock. He turned and continued shouting at Bruno.

To Bruno the way out was simple. He had a train to catch at Orlingford at twelve-five, and at eleven, with Stokes still raging in the office, he went to catch it.

For another hour Stokes remained in the office. The pressure on his mind seemed to increase. He sat with his head on the deal desk, trembling, like a man in a conflict of prayer. After a time he did pray. He prayed, with some inflammable combination of hatred and jealousy and despair and anger, not for Bruno but himself. He asked to be made strong, "Give me the Strength of Thine Own Hands. Fill me with Thine own Power that I may set him right before the fires of Thy Wrath consume us both." Towards midday he locked the office and went out. He felt weak and faint. He walked slowly into the centre of the town like a man coming out of a long illness. His hands were trembling and he did not know what to do. Then eventually, driven by sheer physical necessity, he did something he had not done for a long time. He walked into "The Swan" and had a glass of brandy. After it he felt better. The fire of fresh confidence began to burn out the weakness of his mind. He had a second brandy, and much later it seemed to him that this glass of brandy lasted longer than any glass he had ever known. It was then three o'clock. His mind was flaming again and he was obsessed altogether by the idea of fire : the fire of God, of his own mind, of hell and damnation, of an immense and bitter fire of hatred against Bruno. He sat drinking till four o'clock, more and more driven by self-pity towards the idea of taking some kind of revenge on Bruno.

Soon after four o'clock he went out of "The Swan" and back to the factory. He did not know what he was doing. He could not fit the key into the lock of the office door and as he stood there, fumbling, a man going by with a barrow-load of potatoes stopped and unlocked the door for him. Stokes went in and down to the making-rooms. He dragged a heap of scraps of kip leather together with his feet. He overbalanced and fell down and then stood up again, clinging to a bench. His obsession with fire had at last become a realization. He put a heap of newspapers and linen lining over the leather and then a half empty wax-pot on the paper. He then lit a match and dropped it on the heap. As the first flames sprang up he felt as if they were the consummation of all his confused anxiety for revenge. Crawling out of the factory, holding on to the benches, forgetting to turn the key in the door, he felt suddenly purified and frightened.

By six o'clock the whole of Castor and the surrounding countryside could see the furnace of Shadbolt and Stokes against the night sky. While it burned, Stokes sat in the dark front room of his new house, crying in the scared way of a child after nightmare.

CHAPTER X

BRUNO was arrested at Orlingford Station as he came off the two-forty-seven from Nottingham on the following Monday afternoon. He spent that night in the two-cell lock-up at Castor. He was brought up in the court-room, with Stokes, on the following morning, on a charge of conspiring with Stokes to set fire to the factory, maliciously in order to get the insurance money. Stokes, without the advice of a solicitor and in a fit of tears and remorse, pleaded guilty. He was persuaded to revise the plea, and both he and Bruno were committed for trial at the Quarter Sessions. From the first things went against them: the evidence of a sweeper-up hearing their quarrelling, Stokes shouting the word fire, on the morning of the day when the fire broke out; the evidence of the landlord of "The Swan," as to Stokes drinking until the late afternoon like a man trying to put courage into himself; the evidence of the man with the potatoes, letting Stokes into the factory because he was too drunk to put the key into the lock; the evidence of a courting couple just off for an evening walk who had seen Stokes, but whom Stokes had not seen, as he half crawled, half fell down the factory steps an hour before the alarm was given. This was not evidence against Bruno, but it began to build up against him, slowly, an atmosphere of prejudice. The evidence against him was indirect: the fall of trade, his going away on that afternoon. When he was asked why he had gone away that afternoon he did not answer. When the question was put again he said simply that he had gone to Nottingham to see a friend. What friend? A lady or a gentleman? Whichever it might be, why were they not here to give evidence? He did not answer that either. The court drew its conclusions. From the first he had it fixed in his mind that Jenny must be kept out of it. She was playing that week in Liverpool and Birkenhead. He did not want her to lose a minute or a penny because of him. Fixed in his mind also was the knowledge that he was innocent. Nothing could shake or alter that. Nothing, it seemed to him, was needed to prove or disprove that. It came as a terrific shock, like an explosion near his face, when Stokes was sentenced to two years and himself to six months.

He went into Northampton Gaol towards the end of that year. While he was there something important happened in Castor. On a mild February afternoon Dr. Black came

214

home from a meet of hounds; it was warm, he was hot with sweat, and he unbuttoned his coat. That night he took a chill. He lay very ill for five days, dying of pneumonia on the following Sunday. Long before this, even before Bruno had come back to Castor from London, Black had given it out that Gerda had gone home to Germany. "The climate never suited her and she didn't seem to get on with people. She is German and Germans are not English, you understand." From that time Black would go away from Castor five or six times a year, for three or four weeks at a time. He went to London, or to friends of his student days who had practices in the West of England, where stag-hunting was good, or even to Scotland; but ostensibly he went to Germany, and people would say, "Dr. Black has gone to Germany again, to see his wife. Nice to be some folks." When Black died a search was made for Gerda's German address. It could not be found. There was a letter from Gerda instead. She had written it on the night before she and Bruno had reached Harwich. It was a very simple letter. "Dear Alistair: I am running away from you. I am running away with a man named Bruno Shadbolt, who has been kind to me and has lent me German books. We are in love with each other and to-morrow we shall get a boat for Harwich, to go back to Germany. We have been staying on a little farm and I think we shall try to get a little farm in Germany. My Aunt Anna Maria has a little farm on the Rhine and perhaps we shall go there."

In two days it was all over the town; not merely that Bruno had run away with Gerda, but that he had come back without her; not simply the scandal of it, the immorality, but the treachery. "Take her away, then leave her stranded. By God, that gets me." The bitterness of opinion against him, already strong, went sour. It spewed itself up like some rank and acid sickness, stinking. It was licked up and spewed out again by a town for whom the worst of Shadbolt, now, was not bad enough. Not enough that he should go to prison, that he should run away with one woman and leave a dozen others, and perhaps her, with bastards, but he must be the author also of all the immorality and treachery and deceit that he had not done but which they would like him to have done. "You may depend he led Stokes on. Stokes ain't a man who'd do a thing like that. That's a sort of dirty trick Shadbolt would do." His reputation grew with the rank rapidity of fungus into some monstrous and stinking legend. "And that Spella affair. Funny, wadn't it? That old gal? You gonna tell me she left him that money for nothing? Used to be in the bedroom all hours of the day and night. You know what old gals are."

The stink of his reputation had not died down at all when he came out of gaol in the early summer of that year. When he came out he had the hope, very faint, but stimulated by sudden freedom after confinement and loneliness, that some one, perhaps Maria, just possibly Jenny, might be there to meet him. He came out into an empty street.

He began to walk along it, slowly, a little dazed, in the early morning sunlight. Suddenly, at the end of it, he saw the wave of an unmistakable straw hat.

"Shadbolt! Bruno!" Charles Walker Chamberlain shook hands enthusiastically. "I'm glad to see you, I'm glad, I'm glad. Don't say anything. Don't talk. You're a great man, Bruno, a great spartan. Don't say anything! I got things to tell you. Come and have something to eat. I got news for you."

Over a meal of coffee and bacon and eggs he listened to Chamberlain talking.

"What d'ye think happened? What d'ye think's *going* to happen?"

"I don't know. A hell of a lot of things have happened to me."

Chamberlain tilted his straw hat forward and put a hand over his mouth.

"The railway's coming."

"Eh?"

"It's coming. The railway. It's been settled."

Bruno felt his heart stand still. "Where? Where's it coming?"

Chamberlain put his thumbs in the armholes of his waistcoat. "Where d'ye think it's coming? Where's the only place it could come?" Bruno waited. "Where I've been saying for twenty years it would come! Where d'ye expect?"

Bruno could not believe it. "It's a rumour. A tale."

"No, Bruno. No. Not this time. They've been to see me. They've been to look at the land. They're making a valuation now."

Bruno could not speak. He drove home in almost complete silence in Chamberlain's trap. "What are you going to do?" Chamberlain said. "Make a fresh start? They tell me the creditors are whistling."

"You're a creditor."

"I know and I don't care. I'm not whistling. You're going to pay us. I know that."

"Yes," Bruno said, "I'm going to pay you."

"Good! Magnificent. That's what I like. That's Spartanism!"

He stayed to eat midday dinner with the Chamberlains, walking home in the afternoon. Going through the streets, round by the church and the east side of the town, he saw several people he knew. They did not speak to him. He walked on to the burnt-out factory. He stood and looked at its black-silked timbers, scorched walls, iron girders twisted by heat, for the first time since he had quarrelled with Stokes. He could smell the strange rank odour of old fire on the summer air. He walked on to his sister's. She was nursing a baby of three months and he felt somehow that he could not breath in the small house, with the crying baby and the rest of the family and the sourish smell of baby-clothes drying by the stove. He walked outside into the yard and found Maria's husband, the ex-soldier, nailing and sawing at a rabbit hutch. "Paying game, rabbits." He talked to the soldier for a moment or two, and then got over the fence, into the meadow that led up to Spella Ho. He had a sudden longing to go up to the house, to stand and look at something substantial and large and familiar, some immense bulwark against which his mind could rest.

"Here, where are you off?" the soldier said.

"Up to Spella."

"Not bloody likely. Look."

He looked up at the house. He could see then the smoke of its fires blowing in small dark clouds above the bank of summer trees. "Who is it?" he said.

"Hell of a big family. Arkwright. Twenty-three servants and about twenty horses and I don't know what. Much as you dare to look at the place."

Bruno climbed back over the fence and went into the house.

"A lot of things can happen in six months," Maria said. "You seem to think you can come out and find things just as they was when you went in."

"Any letters for me?" he said.

"They was some," she said. She searched behind the pier glass standing above the mantelpiece. "If I ain't lit the fire with 'em. They bin here weeks and months as it is until I got sick an' tired o' seeing 'em." She found four letters; gave them to him. He looked at them, seeing his own handwriting on two of them, the address to Italian Jenny crossed out and a new address written and then crossed out, and finally the pencilled "Return to sender". He looked at the others, at the post mark; they were from her, posted in January from Newcastle, in February from Manchester. "Dear, Dear Bruno." She wrote as he knew she would write: in distress, tenderly, wondering what had happened, why he had never written. In the letters she gave him addresses of places where she knew she would be. They were all out of date. She had gone beyond them, travelling about the country, and he knew suddenly that it was going to be difficult ever to find her. "Dear, Dear Bruno," she wrote in the second letter, "if you don't answer this I shall know you won't want to write." He felt suddenly blinded by a rush of anger, of inarticulate fury against the bitter futility of circumstances. He wished suddenly he had written to her, dragged her into it. In despair and rage against himself and Stokes and everything he tore up the letters and threw them into the empty fireplace.

Maria swooped down on him. "Ah, go on, litter up the place now you have come back."

"What's up?" he said. "What the hell have I done?"

"Littering up the place with paper." She was down on her knees, scratching up the torn paper. "What's the use me trying to keep it decent?"

"What have I done?" he said. "What have you got to horse-face about?"

"Done?" she said. "What you done?" She got up off her knees, her face flushed. "Things I never thought you'd do."

He was quiet. "What things?"

"Owing folk money, for one."

"I got money. Everybody's going to be paid."

"H'm."

"What else?" he said. "You'll tell me in a minute I've been in quod."

"Gaol's too good for you!" she cried.

"What?" he said. "What?"

"After the bits you done, the dirty bits you done to some folks, after the bits you done."

"What bits? What bits I done?"

"Make out you don' know! Make out you never run away with her, never had nothing to do with her. Now he's dead it's all come out, it's all come out."

"Now who's dead?"

"Black. Dr. Black."

He walked out of the room into the small back kitchen, where he had left his bag. He did not say anything. He picked up his bag. "Women! That's all you think about! Women, getting folks into trouble. Getting her in trouble.

Her, a doctor's wife. Runnin' away and then turnin' round and leavin' her. Women, that's all you think about!"

He let her shout, did not say anything. He opened the door and walked out, carrying his bag. She came to the door shouting after him, beside herself. "I'm ashamed on you if you ain't! Gittin' folks in trouble I'm ashamed on you, downright ashamed."

He walked down the road and back into the town. He felt as if he had come to a dead-end: no going forward, only a going back into past defeat and distress, Louise, Gerda, gaol, Jenny, the huge intangible atmosphere of ill-luck and calumny and hatred. His mind began to harden beyond a point to which he had felt it could not harden. He felt it push itself forward, defeatlessly, in a sense stupidly, against the dead-end of things. Even as he came up against the mass of it, the momentary blind end of everything, his mind paradoxically grasped at the notion of making, beyond it, a new start. As he went past houses, he began to look for lodgings, cards in windows. His mind revolted from respectability, with its white curtains, aspidistras, white door-steps, knowing that it would probably revolt against him. In the lower-end of Castor, by the river, there was a district nick-named the Rookery. He went down to it: rows of dog-kennel houses, broken windows nailed over with cardboard, fences broken and torn up for firewood, hop-scotch chalked on yards and pavements, a man playing a cornet in a bedroom, and there, some time later, he got lodgings with a family named Brand. "My chap ain't in yet. Gone a-ferretting, I reckon, or summat else fly. But it'll be all right. Any road I'll be glad to git a bit extra, chance it." She was a well-made, portly woman, apron pulled over bosom like a white balloon. She took him upstairs. The house was clean. His room, small, with iron bed and box for clothes, overlooked the valley. "It'll do," he said. "I like it." He set down his bag. "Sorry there ain't a chair," she said. "Perhaps I could borrow one." "I'll buy a chair," he said, and she said: "You don't mind eating with us? Saves bother," and he said no, he didn't mind anything. "There's a cup o' tea now if you want it," she said.

After he had some tea he went out to buy a chair and some candles. Forced in upon himself, he wanted to read. It was early evening and before buying the chair and the candles he went up to see Chamberlain. Rufus was away in London. "I'll be there myself to-morrow. Endless discussions." He stayed to have supper, crudely served and eaten in the beautiful dining-room on the beautiful round mahogany table. Afterwards, in the library, he looked for books, still not fully himself, unable to make a decision. "You better take the encyclopaedia," Chamberlain said. "That's got everything."

He took home Volume One of Chamberlain's encyclopaedia that night. It went up to the letter H, and for the next week he sat in his room reading it, solidly and systematically, with the iron attention of a man condemned to do something in penitence. He would read until late at night, sometimes after midnight, by candlelight, absorbing knowledge because he had been starved of it. In this way, his attention distracted, he unconsciously broke down the feeling that he had come to a dead-end. His mind marched over the immense obstacle of prejudice and bitterness, his courage more or less unconsciously triumphing.

One night he read for so long that his eyes ached. He had reached the letter G. Soon, after resting his eyes, he found himself reading about Gas. And suddenly he was struck by the enormous stupidity of the situation in which he found himself: here he was reading by candlelight when there was such a thing as gaslight. Incandescence, the white-green brilliant light—he remembered it in London. He got up, excited, and looked out of the window over the dark countryside. The railway, expansion, building, new houses, new works: they all needed light. He felt suddenly as though his mind had been illuminated. He wondered then what time it was. He went downstairs. It was not quite nine-thirty by the clock in the Brands' kitchen and he walked straight out of the house and up to Chamberlain's. Rufus was there and Bruno told both him and Charles Walker Chamberlain what he felt about gas. "Everything'll need gas. The railway, the station, factories, everything. Only a dead-alive place like this would have been without gas so long." They talked until three o'clock in the morning, Rufus and Bruno on one side, Chamberlain on the other. "I'll have nothing to do with it. Rufus may do what he likes. He has money of his own. But me—no. I'll sell you a piece of suitable land if you like. Near the railway. You'll need that."

A week later Bruno met the creditors of Shadbolt and Stokes in the offices of Mason and Freebody. He talked to them in an atmosphere of hostility and distrust. He and Rufus Chamberlain had raised, together, almost £ 2000 towards the formation of a gas-company. It was not enough. He told them how he would pay them in full on the old account, how he was about to form a new company, how he could give them, as business men of the town and locality, the first refusal of taking up part of the issue of shares.

"What company?" a man said. "What sort of company?"

"Gas."

The man put his hat on. "That's about all you do! Gas— and women!"

He and four other men got up and walked out. A sixth man, Larkin, head deacon at Castor Top Meeting Baptist, got up and delivered a small lecture. "Grateful though we are and conscious though we are." He talked with a kind of pitying melancholy, with a look-upon-this-poor-sinner attitude, locking and unlocking his hands. "We have had a fire," he concluded. "Let us not have an explosion."

The creditors left one by one. He stood alone in the room with Mason and Charles Walker Chamberlain. Hostility had hardened him, made him bitterly resolute.

"You can make a public issue of shares," Chamberlain said.

"And if there's no response?"

"There will be a response. But whether there's a response or not I'll stand as your guarantor at the bank. For ten thousand."

"I thought you didn't believe in it?"

"Who said I believed in it?" He tilted his absurd ancient straw hat back on his head, defiantly. "I believe in you."

So he gradually got it moving: the Castor Gas Light and Coke Company. The public response was slow, distrustful. He moved it forward by his own energy and determination, by a colossal, stoical refusal to be defeated. He worked late at night, not tiring, working over plans, schemes, finances, interviewing applicants for posts. From the North of England came a burly young man with yellow-white hair and hairy fingers, who looked as though some inner fire burned just beneath the skin of his face. He was a chemist, had come through a University, and was named Preston. He understood what was still, to Castor, the new miracle of gas, was eager and ready to rip up every cobble in any pavement, cherished dreams of gasometers, retorts, wholesale illuminations. Gas seemed to burn with candescent white energy in his own heart. He talked to Bruno of a town illuminated from end to end. Bruno liked him, felt his own energy revivified by the white heat of this young man with fired face and correct stiff white collar. He influenced his appointment and from that moment the Castor Gas Light and Coke Company seemed to be made. All the time the railway itself was approaching, a huge furrow of clay ploughed by river-diggers and men across the bare countryside from the south, past the little outlying villages, through flat acres of grass and corn. There began to spring up in Castor and on the fringe of it box-like workers' dwellings, in long rows. Run up fast, they were like red scabs on the face of the land. He saw the urgent need for such houses and began, in the spring of the following year, to build them himself. He bought land from Chamberlain, cheap land now, lying on either side of the raw railway cutting, and put up on it rows of flat-faced speculative houses that backed down close to the line, cheap, shoddily-built, monotonous houses, but to him good houses, clean, decent, with water on tap and soon gas also on tap. Looking at these houses he thought of his mother, the house in which he and Maria and the rest had been born; he remembered the tenement in London. By comparison he felt he was putting up palaces. Then, as though to support the idea, he went to live in one of them himself, an end house, from the windows of which he saw a permanent and to him almost beautiful picture of gasometers, red-lead colour in the sun, the new raw houses, the white steel railway track running in its bank almost level with the upstairs windows of the houses. He could see at night the white or orange glow of house windows, lit by gas; he felt in a way that they were lit by his own energy, by his own bitter and irrepressible determination to get on. He knew now that he would get on. Nothing can stop me, he thought, if I want to do it. Nothing can stop me. Nothing is going to stop me.

That year he used Chamberlain's influence to try to get the town itself lit by gas, the streets, the few old-fashioned public buildings. Instantly it was as though he had come up against the old solid wall of prejudice. "I don't know which stinks the worst," a councillor said, "the gas or Shadbolt. We can git on without either on 'em." He found himself facing the massed forces of conservatism, religion, convention, morality, stupidity. He knew quite well that time could and must break them down, but he was furious. He saw the need for a miracle, some realistic revolution that would make a staggering impression: a wholesale display of illumination, an advertisement in light. With Preston he tried to evolve some scheme, knowing it must be outside the range of official prejudice. It did not come to him until Preston said: "Some big building, some big house —if we could light that," and he was caught up instantly by the fascination of a new dream: to illuminate Spella Ho.

Almost blindly, the scheme not fully developed in his mind, he went up to the house. He had not met the Arkwrights; he thought of them only as living behind a guard of livery and horses, held aloof by an impenetrable network of class. In his mind he conceived the Arkwrights as stuffed birds, old, fat, pouch-eyed; drink-ridden perhaps. He was surprised to find Julius Arkwright a young man, with no interest in the world except, apparently, water. The lake at Spella Ho had been drained and cleaned and now Arkwright was planning a complicated system of weirs and fountains, arrangements by which he could raise and lower the level of water. He had introduced a pumping system, a costly steam-driven plant housed in a converted summer house on the edge of the lake; it was his aim to take the water by pipe to Spella Ho, lay it to the kitchens and stables and even perhaps the garden. He was a man so caught up and blinded by the passion of an idea that he saw Bruno and talked to him for an hour without knowing who he was or inquiring who he was, taking him for a foreman of the gang of labourers already cutting the first trench across the park, walking up and down the lake edge with him, arguing, waving his small fine hands or brushing them against his thick aristocratic moustache, laying out before Bruno, in elaborate language, all the details of a marvellous scheme for laying water to the house.

"I come about another scheme," Bruno said.

"Eh? I beg your pardon?"

"My name's Shadbolt."

"You mean to inform me you're not the foreman?"

"No."

"Fatuous of me. Most fatuous. A mental aberration on my part. Don't you know that's a damned remarkable neck-tie you're wearing?"

Arkwright was dressed like a labourer: corduroys, string round the legs, a black muffler, thick flannel shirt. Bruno did not know whether to like or dislike a man so much the poseur and so much the idealist at the same time. Uncertain, he began to talk of his scheme for lighting Spella Ho: how a great house could be improved, beautified, and made safer by gas, how the company would undertake the laying of the main without charge, how it could be done artistically, with as little inconvenience as possible, how the value of the property must go up in consequence, what a magnificent thing it could be.

"Yes, yes, magnificent." Arkwright agreed with everything, effusively, with elaborate aristocratic politeness. "I agree, magnificent. A noble scheme. But perhaps later. When I have finished my water scheme."

"Yes? When would that be?"

"Impossible to forecast. A year, two years. Five years."

"As long as that?"

"Why not? Why not longer?" Arkwright said. "I'm young. I bought Spella Ho with the specific purpose of reconstructing the lake and the water arrangements. I can wait twenty years. I've nothing else to do."

Bruno went back to Castor not depressed by Arkwright's remarks, but fired. He called a meeting of his three directors that afternoon; told them what had happened, how they could never hope for another chance like it in the history of the company or the house. "He's opening a trench a mile long. If we're quick we could use it. It would save time, money, everything."

Opposition came from Rufus Chamberlain: "A big expense, waste of money."

"It's investment. When Castor sees Spella illuminated inside and out by gas everybody in the town will want gas. The corporation will want gas. I tell you there'll never be a chance like it again. Get Preston."

Preston came in after a moment or two, with fired face and high spirited Northern speech. "What's oop?"

Bruno told him. "It's about two miles from here to Spella, going by road as far as the lake and then using the cut Arkwright's making. Get a town-map and see if you can work out the cost of piping, the number of houses passed on the way, and roughly the cost of piping the house. Get me some paper and I'll draw you a rough plan of the house."

All that afternoon he bullied the three directors, with Preston supporting him, as he had once bullied tired commercial travellers on the stairs of Shadbolt and Stokes. After they had gone, unconvinced but bullied at least into temporary acquiescence, he stayed on in the office with Preston, preparing plans, roughing out estimates. Just before eight o'clock he went home, washed, changed his clothes, putting on a spotted black-and-white cravat, and then drove up to Spella Ho. "Name please?" the butler said and he answered with a half savage feeling of resentment, "Shadbolt. And tell him it's about the waterworks." After a few moments he went straight in. Arkwright was in the library, playing chess with a woman. They were both in evening dress, the woman in a long, tightwaisted grey-blue gown, silk, low at the neck. He looked at her, arrested. She was very fair, with pure Nordic skin and ice-blue eyes, with magnificent shoulders. "My wife," Arkwright said, and she shook hands. He felt an immediate emotional response, a slight start of sickness. She spoke with full heavily round voice. "Don't tell me it's about the water again. We'll all have water on the brain."

He then told them, speaking to her rather than to Arkwright, why he had come. He became aware of a recurrent sensation of magnetism when he looked at the woman. He felt words drawn out of him with unexpected readiness. With Arkwright, in the morning, he had felt a suppression of his own enthusiasm. It arose from the fact that he could not make up his mind about Arkwright. From the first moment he knew what he felt about the woman. He knew that whatever he felt was prompted, in a sense, by what she felt about him. He felt slightly shaken.

"Yes, an interesting scheme, Mr. Shadbolt," Arkwright said, "but hopelessly uneconomic."

"Uneconomic!" she said. "You to talk about uneconomic!"

"Now, my dearest—"

"Hark to him talking about uneconomic, Mr. Shadbolt. He with a water-works scheme that's economic from first to last."

"Now, my dearest, you know how—"

"Am I teasing?" she said. "Well, I can only say that a gaslight would be very useful at the head of the stairs. Where the two extra steps go up. Before I break my neck."

"Yes, it's bad there," Bruno said.

They looked at him, astonished. "How do you know?"

He told them how he knew, how every inch of the house was as familiar to him as his own hand. "Well, that's wonderful," they said.

"I know how much this house needs light," he said.

"We had gas in the town house in London before I was married," Mrs. Arkwright said. "It was great fun. We liked it. My sister blew the ceiling out of the music-room. An explosion."

"I have no sort of doubt," Arkwright said, "that that is what would happen here. Water at least can't explode."

"It wasn't the gas," she said, "and you know it. It was Virginia. She'd explode anything by looking at it."

"Virginia is mad," he said.

"Oh, certainly," she mocked. "But that doesn't alter the fact that I should like gas in the house. Lovely to have real light, real illuminations!"

"That's what we plan," Bruno said.

"Illuminations?"

"We would give you free illuminations for a week—as much light as you liked. Fairy lights, displays, illuminations inside and out. You could illuminate everything. Trees, windows, everything. I've got the best man in England. He could illuminate the bottom of the sea."

Suddenly Arkwright stood up. He stood up as though startled and began to walk round and round the room like a man with some form of mental toothache, clenching and unclenching his hands. He walked round the room five or six times. "The sea. Water. We could illuminate the water. The lake. We could illuminate the water!"

He continued to walk round and round. All the time Bruno and the woman stood looking at each other, detached, faintly ironic, not saying anything, as though there were things between them that did not need to be said.

BOOK FIVE

LADY VIRGINIA

CHAPTER I

ON a midsummer night of that same year, 1896, he saw Spella Ho illuminated as he had wanted to see it: fairy lights in blue, crimson and gold piped along the terrace and on the flat stone face of the house; inside the house an elaborate brass system of chandeliers and brackets, on the stairs a great blaze of uprights, like candles, lighting up magnificently the dim cherubim and seraphim on the ceiling above. The house and gardens and park were thrown open to the public and were crowded; the lake like some miniature sea on a Bank Holiday: fairy lights piped among the embroidery of trees along the water-edge, the water oar-rippled and rainbow coloured, shining as oil. And all the time, a background to the noise of voices, a quiet hissing of gas, drowned finally by the string-band on the terrace, the Strauss waltzes, the laughter, the shuffle and swish of feet and skirts dancing on lawn and stone. He stood on the terrace and made a speech, his crude strong voice like a tear in the plush fabric of the evening, and felt it to be the supreme moment of his life: the gas, the crowds, the toffs, himself rubbing elbows with people of class, talking to them, explaining things, moving among them at last as a man to be reckoned with. It was a triumph for himself and Preston, who alone knew what it had cost in energy, time, money and courage. He walked about rather like the manager of some elaborate vaudeville show, wearing his first top hat with an ordinary suit, his cuffs slipping down, his huge body mocking the slight dandyism of tight white waistcoat and steep collar. He looked and felt immensely proud of himself walking about there in the glow of his own gaslight, like some large ape that had learned to do its tricks at last.

On the following Monday morning he sat in his office with the slightly lost, dead feeling of a man who has completed a piece of creative work and does not know how to go on. He knew that all Castor was talking about him, about what had happened. He felt about him the tangible atmosphere of prestige, not complete, but growing. It seemed like a proof of all his earliest crude reasoning: money and success commanding respect, a top-hat increasing stature. He had had money, but never success, never a top-hat. And here he was, at last, with all three: successful, monied, top-hatted, a man reaching middle life, a man just beginning to feel the strength produced by almost twenty years of reverses, defeat, bitterness, conflict.

About eleven o'clock that morning his office boy came into the dark, pitch-pine, slightly gas-odoured office to say that a lady was waiting to see him.

"Who is it?" he said.

"It looks like the lady from Spella Ho," the boy said.

"Show her in," he said.

When she came in she was dressed as he had not seen her before, in a pure cream silk dress, with large cream hat and cream parasol to match. Her face had the same look of Nordic candour about it, the eyes blue and aristocratic but with something more vivacious in them than he remembered seeing before. He got up to shake hands with her. "Lady Caroline," he said.

"No," she said.

He stood looking at her, dumb for a moment. Then he knew she was fooling him. "You were last time I saw you," he said, "and that was Saturday."

"No," she said. "No. I wasn't, all the same." She was smiling. All the time there was something about her he could not get quite straight in his mind.

Finally he gave it up. "If you're not Lady Caroline you're her twin sister."

"I am her twin sister," she said.

He stood dumbfounded. He still felt as if he were being fooled, like a boxer being taunted by a better man. She stood teasing him by the everlasting wide lovely smile and he did not know what to do. He could only say what she had said. "Her twin sister?"

"Lady Virginia," she said.

"You?"

"Yes, me."

He sat down in his office chair, baffled, then remembered himself and got up again.

"You talked to me long enough on Saturday," she said. "You knew me then."

"I was talking to Lady Caroline," he said.

"You were talking to me. You were talking to me down there by the lake."

"Down there? By the lake? That was you?"

"Down there by the lake."

She was still smiling. He could not speak. He could only look at her again and see the extraordinary resemblance between the two women, with the slight difference only of the eyes, a difference between two shades of light, between ice and water. He walked away and looked at her from another angle. "It beats me. I can't get it. I can't believe it," he said.

"On Saturday," she said, with the slow ironical smile, "you weren't so slow, Mr. Shadbolt."

"Saturday," he said. "Saturday was different."

"You were talking to me. "

"It was a fraud. I didn't know."

"Squeezing my waist."

"I didn't know," he said. "I thought it was somebody else."

"Makes it worse," she said.

"It does now."

"It did then," she said. "I kept thinking of poor Caroline. Awful for her. Having her waist squeezed. Her earrings tickled in her neck. And all the rest. All in the dark. Awful for her."

"So you came to explain things."

"If you're going to tickle women, Mr. Shadbolt, you ought to know one from the other."

"It's a bad habit I got," he said.

He grinned and she widened her beautiful ironical smile and they stood looking at each other exactly as he and her sister had first stood looking at each other, amused, in instant contact, the point of intimacy pre-established. After about a minute she put her parasol on the desk and sat down, kicking her skirts away from her legs. "Thank God you don't have to wear skirts, Mr. Shadbolt."

"Well," he said, "you know the alternative to that."

"Yes?"

"Wear trousers."

"I do," she said.

Even he was slightly flabbergasted.

"For my bicycle," she said. "Meanwhile, ten yards of material so that you shan't know I've got legs."

"I know you've got legs."

"You mean you know my sister has got legs."

"Same thing."

"It's a good thing I'm a New Woman. Mr. Shadbolt," she said.

She stayed in the office for almost another hour, talking, bantering, leading him on to an ironic exchange of views on bicycles, Freedom for Women, Women's Suffrage, the New Woman, herself. She began to excite him and after a time it was clear to him that she knew she was exciting him, that she might even have come with the express purpose of exciting him. She looked lovely, cream hat and dress accentuating the pure sun-colour of the Nordic face, the eyes at once tender and mocking.

It ended by her asking him to dinner at Spella Ho. That, she said, was what she had come for. She would be there for the rest of the summer. "We want you to come to-morrow night. I'll wear a pale blue dress, and I think Caroline may wear pink. That'll teach you the difference."

"Between what?"

"Between one set of ankles," she said, "and another."

When she had gone he knew he had never been so excited by a woman, or so happy. It was the quality of happiness and light about the affair that took him off his feet. With her there was no feeling of depth or inevitability, the strange powerful idea that he was being driven by incomprehensible forces to a fixed and perhaps tragic point in time.

On the following night he went to dinner at Spella Ho in the same incongruous vaudeville rig-out as he had worn four days earlier, top-hat, ordinary suit, white dicky, white waistcoat, pale brown shoes. They were clothes which brought out in him some curious quality of strength and attraction, making the ugliness itself fascinating. All through dinner—the plates whisked away before he could decide whether to turn them over or not—he sat looking at the two women, with their clear cream-white flesh as alike as two statues made from the same cast, only the emotional response of the blue eyes different. In return they would look at him, smiling, both knowing the joke now of his mistake with their identity. "Even Julius," they told him, "does not know now whether he married the right one or not."

"Visible evidence is not everything," Arkwright said.

He stayed at the house until after midnight, talking, laughing, bantering, lifted off his feet by a remarkable sensation of light happiness. He was talking for the first time in his life with people who had been born with money, to whom the problem of the struggle for existence meant nothing and had always meant nothing, people who had been born ringing a bell for someone to bring them something they were too tired or lazy or bored or weak to fetch for themselves. He had seen money and lived with money in the same house in which they themselves were now living, but he knew now that it was different; there was money and money, the money made, as Mrs. Lanchester's money had been made, and as his own money was being made, by astuteness and care and courage and hard work and even dishonesty, and the money that was not made and did not need to be made but was drawn in by the mouths of one generation from the breasts of another. He saw this monied quality in the Arkwrights and Lady Virginia, a something which shone out of them, a kind of radiance. He felt it colour and illuminate the way they spoke and walked and behaved, what they spoke about, how they lived. It awed and fascinated him. It was romantic. Born in the extreme bitter poverty of a house only a stone's throw from the very room in which he now sat drinking Arkwright's brandy, he felt dazzled, as though suddenly brought from a cellar into a blaze of his own gaslight. All the time he was dazzled also, but physically, by the sight of those two lovely creatures, products of a world which was to him still almost a legend, so alike that he was still not sure of the difference between them. They looked at him all evening with candidly teasing blue eyes, with brief moments of fixity when they appeared to have been suddenly fascinated by him. In this way, between the two women and the brandy and the feeling of dazzled contact at long last with class, his state of light happiness passed into a sort of intoxication. Like a man who, looking at one thing, sees two of it, he began to feel that he was looking only at one woman but that he saw her, by a miracle, twice. Then, just as he saw her as two, he began to see himself as double: double in everything, in size, importance, money, power, prospects, achievement, fascination, the big man of Castor, the little King of a new era of light, the moving force behind the gas-works, a man who could and would do anything. He was not now merely going somewhere, he had got somewhere. He was among people who were people. These are the people, he thought, I ought to have met donkeys years ago. Who kept me back? Not these people. My own people. They kept me back; talk, gossip, spying and jealousy, rotten miserable spying and jealousy. Not these people. They never kept me back. The minute they saw me they helped me. You wouldn't catch Castor folk doing that in a thousand years. They helped me, these people. They put me where I am, know a man when they see one. Good people, real people. He felt that they understood, and he went on boasting all the way home in that warm happy frame of mind: a man of achievement now, a man of new ambition, seeing himself as the potential builder of a new Castor.

CHAPTER II

THAT was it: the builder of a new Castor. Suddenly, even in his sanest and most phlegmatic moments, he began to toy with that not quite crazy idea. It was at first quite nebulous, a coloured cloud, real but remote, pleasant to contemplate. He did not yet think of it as even possibly concrete.

During that summer he was always at Spella Ho. They liked him there; their word for him was unconventional. Arkwright, apeing the working man with his string-tied corduroys and neck muffler, a devotee of Tolstoyan philosophy, slightly ahead of his time in England as a socialist aristocrat, saw and admired in Bruno all the raw virtues of the self-made man. As the purest sort of product of his own class he had come to the point when he did not believe in class. He had picked up from Tolstoy, believing it to be new, something very old: that all men are equal and free, the gospel that under another name was already two thousand years old. Work, he would say, that's the thing; we must work, all of us, not only the poor but the rich. If I'm born so rich that I don't need to work then I must make work; drain the lake, devise a new water system, cultivate land, help to do it with my own bare hands. Break down the barriers, he would say. Not Death the Leveller, but Work the Leveller. Work—the great new idea, great fun. And he, who had never known what it was in his life to work a twelve-hour factory day or a ninety-hour labourer's week, entered with extravagant zest into that new, well-meaning but more than slightly snobbish doctrine. He accepted Bruno eagerly and with a warmth that was partially genuine, when, at that moment, ten thousand of his own upper class could not have touched a self-made man with a barge pole. In that sense he was more unconventional than Bruno had ever dreamed of being as he aped the dandyism of Rufus Chamberlain.

The two sisters were unconventional too, but differently. It was an unconventionality that sprang from natural rebelliousness of spirit. They had that curious god-like gift of twins, a double-dose of divine devilry. They were not thirty-five, an age when, in Castor, women still began to think of black and the long staid years beyond the forties, their spirits caged in corsets of a terrific convention. In Castor no one had heard of the New Woman. Those two lovely creatures, who looked nearer twenty-five than thirty-five, were the New Women. Castor had already seen emancipated women, tough creatures who wore mannish skirts and carried riding crops and trilby hats and who talked of standing up for the rights of women while in fact aching, consciously or unconsciously, to have been born men. They were slightly despised, a little laughed at, by both sexes. When the twins appeared at Spella Ho they were adored by everybody. They flew into the crow-black small-town Castor world like two bright humming-birds. Castor tried to peck them for a bit: swift, dazzling, outrageous creatures. Did you ever, I never would, I'd never be seen out like it I wouldn't not for love or money I wouldn't. But it could not go on pecking for ever two creatures who for every fault had some lovely virtue. And gradually it saw that it could never pin anything on Lady Caroline Arkwright or Lady Virginia, that they were beyond the labels or indictments or price-cards of Victorian convention. If they rode bicycles in knicker-bockers or in skirts that showed those other knickers that were not meant to be seen, they came to church on Sunday, beautifully dressed, like two quiet alabaster angels; or if they appeared at dances with their magnificent golden shoulders bare almost to the upper breasts they were rich, and the rich could do things, even with their bodies, that the poor could never do, and anyway it was nice of them to come at all, and they were the only gentry that did come to the dead, waltz-sleepy Assembly Room dances held in Castor half a dozen times a year to the music of two fiddles and a piano. And so finally Castor took them to its hearts rather as the public takes an actress, as an ideal, as something lovely and romantic that they themselves might have been if things had been different.

At Spella Ho Bruno saw them, almost always, together. Dressed differently, so that even Julius Arkwright should know them, they still baffled him. So alike, perfectly matched in their appearance of golden aristocratic bloom, they were at first slightly mystical to him. When he got over this mystical bewilderment they had something else to baffle him: behaviour and conversation. If they saw him as unconventional he saw them as female revolutionaries. They loved talking, and they talked, in long heated discussions over the dinner-table or the after-dinner brandy at Spella Ho, as he had never heard women talk: anarchy, social equality, William Morris, divorce, Votes for Women, Education for Women, the virtues of bloomers, Fabianism, Sport, Free Love. They talked terrifically, logically, with heat and passion and sound sense. He had been used to women behaving like ostriches, burying their heads in the sand of modesty or ignorance; or with the pure passion he loved, giving their bodies simply, whole-heartedly, and suffering the consequences. Here were women who talked of love between the sexes as a kind of crazy arithmetic: Free Love, putting two and two together, consciously and logically preventing the old answer. They slightly intimidated him, making him sometimes a court of appeal. "You think so, Mr. Shadbolt, don't you? You agree, Mr. Shadbolt, don't you? You've got sense, Mr. Shadbolt." Then they ceased calling him Mr. Shadbolt. "We like

Bruno best. It suits you. Besides it's less formal. And if there's one thing we're against it's formality." And suddenly, hearing the familiarity of his name on their lips, he felt as if he had known them for years.

On a hot afternoon in August of that year he drove up to Spella Ho and saw them coming down the slight incline of the lime avenue on a bicycle, Lady Virginia steering and pedalling but not sitting, her sister sitting with legs wide out. They were not dressed for cycling and when they saw him coming Virginia, in a panic, steered into the grass. He saw them go over with legs and skirts flying high, giving him a vision of pink drawers such as he had not seen in public before. As he came up they lay flat on the grass in hysterics, laughing so much that they forgot about the pink drawers and he standing there looking at them, in natural fascination. At last they sat up. "Oh! great heavens, here's Bruno looking at all we've got. I hope you like them, Bruno. They're the latest in fast colours."

That set them laughing again. He got down out of the trap to look at the bent front fork of the bicycle. Seeing it too, Caroline was sorrowful. "First she tries to make a water bicycle out of her own and sinks it. And now she must ride tandem on mine and bust that."

"Put the bike in the trap and I'll drive it back," he said.

She held the handlebars and worked the front wheel. It responded. "No, I'll ride back," she said. She felt her waist with one hand, grinning, "Something's gone in the underwear department. If anything's coming down I'd rather it came down on the bicycle."

She rode back up the avenue, magnificent even on the absurd seat of a bent bicycle, waving her hand as she went out of sight.

"You'd be safer in the trap," he said to Virginia, "than on that thing."

"Safe!" Terrifically scornful. "Who wants to be safe?"

"Take you for a drive," he said.

"If you drive fast, yes," she said.

"Fast as you like."

"All right," she said. "Fast as Hell."

A dazzling, revolutionary conversation: he remembered it many years later, in an age when women swore as well as men and wore skirts up to their necks and often nothing between skirt and body, and when bloomers and Free Love were laughed at or forgotten.

But that day he was fired by such a woman and such a conversation, such hot unconventionality. They drove off out of the great gates of Spella Ho like a couple of eloping lunatics, at something under fifteen miles an hour, and off along white August-dusted roads towards woods and cornfields in the east. He had just time to think of another drive along the same road, also in summer, also with a woman: the serious, solemn face of Gerda leaving her husband, his own fixed determination to help her escape, to see it through. He was not conscious of happiness then; now he knew it was there but had not time to be conscious of it. He drove at a furious pace, Virginia bouncing up and down on the seat, the horse lathering. He cut a corner and they bounced up and down in the air like two acrobats falling down into the safety-net. They drove later under an avenue of low beech, and he felt more than ever as if he were doing tricks in a circus. "We'll break our damn necks," he said. "Right," she said. "Good. If I'm going to break my damn neck I'll damn well break my damn neck driving with you."

They shot out into the open and she made him drive on the verge, a wheel prancing on the ruts, the horse slightly frightened. It was all very terrific. He had known women: but not like this. "Drive over the stones," she shrieked. He drove over a heap of roadside stones. The world went drunk on its axis and they looked for a second over the edge. He did it again and saw ahead of him a long white chain of stone heaps. "We'll bust the damn trap," he said. "Good. Bust it. Over! Bust it." Woods again, and the piles of stones lying in shadow. He was caught suddenly between two hazards: stones and branches, and the trap went over, the horse rearing in air like the rampant figure on a crazy coat of arms.

He lay still among summer-flattened leaves of bluebell, feeling his bones, and then knew it was all right. He got up to look for Virginia. She was sitting on the verge, between tears and laughter. "All right. I fell where all nice ladies ought to fall. Accidents will happen." He looked at the trap, heeled over, the horse still struggling. Between them they righted it. "A cracked shaft," he said. He bound it up with string and a strap. "Well, we must walk it."

"Need we? Must we all at once? Let's stay a bit."

"Quiet then. It's hot."

"Lady-like," she said. "Let's walk through the wood and see what's at the other end."

At the far end of the wood cornfields opened out and ran away, almost white, the farthest tented with shadowy shocks, down a small hillside. Woodland and white-eared standing corn met in a sharp line of contrast, dead dark green against white-gold, the faint damp smell of closed woodland against the warm wheat smell. She wanted to sit and rest. They walked along the small gap between corn and trees and sat down and then she lay down, looking up, strong fair face almost the colour of the wheat. "Lie down," she said, "and look at the sky." He lay down and looked up and then, after about five minutes he came to himself: knew suddenly that women did not lie in cornfields simply to look at the sky, and put his arms round her quite quietly, wondering how she would take it. She took it as he had not expected she would take it, without a sign of craziness one way or the other, without passion or temper at all; but with extraordinary serious quietness, just smiling. He suddenly felt as if all the unconventionality and craziness were just show; that she was really the quietest creature on earth. He wondered momentarily about all the talk of Free Love. What about that? Did that change too? He put his hand on one of her breasts and could feel underneath the dress a tremendous beat. "You want me?" she said. He nodded, fired with anxiety. She looked at him, conveying something more powerfully than by words. "Promise it'll be all right?" she said. "It'll be all right," he said, and he saw a small look of fear beat itself into anxiety and then out again.

They stayed there, between the high corn and the sunless woodland, until most of the light had gone, talking things out. With other women it had never been necessary to talk things out. Passion spent itself, was renewed, petered out, there was an end. He had played with most women, Gerda, Louise and Italian Jenny excepted, but there was less playing here than ever before. Now he found himself up against an affection that to him was like silk, something rare and delicate and almost in a way untouchable. He got to know, later, that she felt it all as something very sacred; touchable all right, but rare in sublimity and complete seriousness. Underneath all the craziness and mad acrobatics she was a creature of principles: earnest, a little high-souled, a woman of great but very sweet character.

Her effect on him was quiet but very powerful. She softened his character, brought out something in it that had never been even remotely touched before. "Bruno, Darling." That was the sort of endearment he was not used to. Less tender, but more aristocratic than Jenny's "Dear, Dear Bruno," it made him slightly self-conscious. For the first time in his life he felt himself making love with something more than his body and his senses. He was happy, but it was the conscious and controlled happiness of the mind. He rose to a new plane.

She in turn was the first complete woman he had ever met. She satisfied mind, senses, body, ambition, everything: in every way a lovely creature to whom the idea of stinting herself on him in matters of body and soul would have been unthinkable. This generosity was responsible for something else: she could not bear secrecy. She could not bear the idea of hushing up the thing that had happened to them. It must come out into the light. She wanted to share it with the world on the principle that the food

you share has a finer taste. "We must tell Caroline."
She was drawn back to her sister as if they were tied
together by some invisible natal thread. "We must tell her.
I can't bear not to tell her."

So they told her on the following day, simply, with
formality. "We're engaged." She immediately began to
cry. "Oh! darling, darling." She put her arms round Virginia and they cried and laughed together for about five
minutes. Such expression of emotion did not belong to his
world, was new to him. The idea of engagement was new to
him. In Castor people got married hastily, out of necessity,
or phlegmatically, without fuss, or with respectable decency, but almost always on a wage that could not afford engagements. The idea of an engagement, queer at first,
elevated him. Here was something new, a notch above.
Something strange. Sometime afterwards Arkwright
shook hands with him and Caroline said, "Oh! Bruno, I'm
glad. I'm happy. I could kiss you."

"Kiss him." Virginia said.

So Caroline kissed him, and it was almost like being
kissed by Virginia. He felt that it was all like a baffling
dream, that he was being kissed by two creatures so alike
that they had been sent to torment him.

Then they had a small family conference. "We must
announce the engagement." It was Caroline speaking.
"Yes, but no fuss, please." It was Virginia, "We could wait
a little. Give an immense supper after harvest." It was
Arkwright. Bruno did not say anything. He felt he was
not expected to say anything. He felt that in any case it
did not matter, that no engagement or formality or discussion could increase what he felt or wanted. He knew
that he wanted to marry Virginia, that he wanted her as
often as she could give herself, that there was only one way
for that. He spoke at last. "These engagements. I don't
see that they do much good. Let's have a short one and
then get married. We're not kids in arms."

"That's logical," Arkwright said.

Caroline began to cry again. "Just nothing. Happiness,

that's all. The way he said kids in arms—that did it."
She was laughing and crying at the same time. They were
all laughing.

Finally Arkwright rang for the port and they stood,
five minutes later, looking up through the raised glasses,
all very happy, with the sentimental tearful happiness of
people who are happy for each other: the most romantic,
the only truly romantic moment of his life.

CHAPTER III

THE engagement was announced in September; they
would be married, it was hoped, in the autumn of the year
1897, the year of the second Jubilee. His stock went up in
Castor like the shot of a try-your-strength machine at a
fair, hitting at the top the biggest bell it was possible to
hit in Castor: respectability. At Spella Ho there was a great
engagement party for a hundred and fifty guests of all
classes from the town and the estate; a great display of
fairy lights again on lawn and terrace and lake; dancing
in the warm September evening that smelt of autumn
and women's scent and corn. The Chamberlains were
there, Rufus crazy-drunk, his father in muddy boots,
straw-hat, dirty dicky-bit, green-black coat, with the
simple reason for it all as hand-pat as ever: "A triumph for
Spartanism, my boy." Bruno walked about among the
guests, among people who had despised and envied and
distrusted and even hated him, with Virginia on his arm.
She had on a dress of sky-blue velvet, long in the skirt,
with parallel rings of dark blue swinging round the hem
and darker waist-bows and shoulder-bows and a bow on
the throat; it was low at the breast, and her shoulders,
naked to the tips, looked magnificent. The engagement
ring, diamond and turquoise, had cost him a hundred and
fifty pounds: more money, it crossed his mind, than his
mother had ever had to scrape up a rotten existence for
five years. And somehow the story of that engagement

244

ring had got about, travelling snowball fashion, becoming fantastic, so that all Castor and half the county knew how he had paid something between a hundred and a thousand pounds for it, an incredible story that was to become as fixed and less true but more powerful as legend than the story of his fight, twenty years before, with Rufus Chamberlain.

That engagement ring, slightly fabulous, did more than the engagement itself to swing round opinion behind him, for the first time in his life, instead of against him. You could fall in love with a woman, even a lady, for nothing, but a ring costing a hundred or three hundred or a thousand pounds, that spelt something. For Castor it spelt a number of things: respectability, progress, money, but above all success. No use denying it, the man's got on. Say what you like, he's got on. I don't like him, never have liked him, mind you, but he must have something in him, somehow, somewhere. You can argue, but a man sprung from nothing and getting on like that—you can't get over that very easy. He's got push. Mind you, I ain't saying I like him. Not I. So opinion swung round, solidified, blotting out contempt.

That night, walking round among the guests with Virginia on his arm, or by himself, he saw many people he did not know at all, and a man came up to him to speak.

"You wouldn't know me. You wouldn't remember me."

"Face seems familiar." He looked hard at the face: worn, scraggy, broken up under thin white hair.

"It ought to be," the man said. "I'm your dad."

Bruno stood impassive, not saying anything.

"Come over from St. Neots. Walked it. I heard all about you."

Bruno did not speak. He listened to the old voice, broken but still slick, easy. It took him back twenty-five years: the house with the canary, the woman, his father, his first conscious feeling of hatred against things.

"Heard all about you. You got on summat wonderful. A licker."

He still did not say anything. He remembered how he had reasoned, crudely, that something between his father and himself had to be straightened out, somehow, even if it took half a lifetime. It would happen sometime: this was it. He stood impassively still.

The man took off his cap, showed the white hair almost gone. "I'm sixty," he said. "Over."

Bruno spoke for the first time. "What d'ye expect me to do about it?"

"I'm done. Broke. I ain't got nothing."

Not speaking again, he stood hard, his hatred as complete and resolute after more than twenty years as at the beginning.

"Git us a job or summat," his father said. "You can git us a job. Handyman or summat, you could git us summat, summat like that."

"No."

"You could git us summat." It was as though he could not think of anything else to say. He began to cry, a man broken up, tired, asking for pity.

"No," Bruno said.

"You could git us, you could do—"

"I said No!" Bruno said. "Ain't twice enough? No!"

He walked away. He carried with him a short remembrance of his father standing there, crying, in the rainbow colours of the fairy lights. It did not touch him. The reversion to the old self, hard, relentless, almost brutal in its determination to carry out a resolution even after twenty years, was complete while it lasted. It lasted about twenty minutes. He stood with Virginia again, talking, hearing the lovely voice that had its profoundly softening effect on himself. And suddenly he had a bitter attack of remorse. He walked away from Virginia and went back to where he had seen his father, but his father had gone and though he walked about for almost an hour he never saw him again. For the first time in his life he felt bitterly and miserably ashamed. It was a thing that could never have happened except for her.

Between the autumn of that year and the summer of the next many more things happened that could not have happened except for her. In the November of 1897 he stood at the borough elections, getting a seat and third place in the poll. It was the beginning of something outside personal ambition; again something he would never have done except for her. She softened and broadened his ambition until it ceased to be a selfish thing, until its purpose was self-sacrificial. "You work for other people. The rest will come." She was an idealist. Because she had had the luck to be born to a personal Utopia she dreamed of an outer and much greater Utopia. Her ambition fused itself with his, and there emerged something that did not belong to politics and could not be accomplished by politics but which she began to feel more and more must be expressed by politics. Arkwright was a Liberal and that year he began to pull strings. Bruno, who had made one or two pugnacious speeches at municipal council meetings, began to appear on Liberal platforms. Virginia was always with him and once, roused by an insult, Bruno got down off the platform and took the man bodily off his seat, carried him out above his head and flung him out of the hall. Struggling, the man tore Bruno's coat, ripping out a sleeve. Back on the platform Bruno took off the coat, revealing the thick pugnacious arms, and the minds of people in the audience went back to the day when he had fought Rufus at Spella Ho. From that moment he was not only accepted, but feared. He continued to speak at other meetings with his coat off. People came to hear him because he took his coat off, and throughout the early part of 1897 he was in the thick of all the blood-boiling Liberal-Tory dog-fights of the day, fighting for social reform against reaction and stupidity and all the harsh or unjust conditions or conventions of the day. At home or at Spella Ho he read books again, not haphazardly now, but with some purpose. He read the first volumes of Booth's Survey of *The Life and Labour of the People in London*, remembered London as he had known it and knew the picture of misery and rottenness to be right. He could speak about that from his heart. He could demand better conditions for the poor, better wages, hours, everything. "Because I know, because I'm one of you and I've been through it"—forgetting that he had once employed sweaters at sixpence a week and had browbeaten tired and ill-paid commercial travellers down to a fraction of a farthing; not aware, either, that he was a slum landlord in Camden Town himself, never having once been to see that property, not aware until some big-mouthed political heckler threw it at him one night in Castor Public Hall.

He bluffed himself out of the accusation, but Virginia was upset. "It's a bad debt against us," she said. He protested, and truthfully, that he had never known that he owned a brick of slum property. "I own houses in London and that's all I know." Twice, on Carmichael's advice, he had put up those rents, and it was the rents alone, steady year after year, that had enabled him to consolidate himself in Castor. Out of the proceeds of a block of slums in London he had built, and was still building when he became engaged to Virginia, streets of jerry-built houses that were to become, in time, almost the slums of Castor. He never saw it like this. All his standards of living and housing were based on that miserable sack-windowed shack where his mother had struggled to keep respectable. Whenever he heard people talk or rant of better conditions and better food he remembered the condition of that house; anything was better than that, the misery, the bitter death-coldness of his mother's hands.

But Virginia was upset, seeing things differently. "If you've never seen the property I think you should see it." But he was against that. "I hate London. I went through enough there." "Then," she said, "I'll go and see it." She went, and came back with a report that made Lady Caroline and Arkwright sick. He had been drawing money for years from the living blood and sweat of the poor and did not know it. Virginia, too physically sensitive to a memory of cockroaches and stench and refuse-bins fermenting on dark rat-rotten stairs, was almost ill. She wanted him to sell the houses, implored him to wipe out and heal up such a hideous fester. Knowing what a way life had of coming up and hitting him in the face when he least expected it, he hesitated. That property, slum or not, was his only protection against bad luck. It had saved him already. He knew it might save him again.

While he fenced and hesitated, agreeing to a temporary scheme of repair for the houses, there took place in Castor the largest sale of land and property the town had ever known. The Fitzmaurice land, with thousands of inviolate acres and whole streets and blocks of Castor property, was to be split up and auctioned. It was a sale that lasted a week, and he knew it to be the greatest opportunity of his life. Virginia saw it too: knew that if they worked together he could, with luck, control almost half the town and its land. "Control it," she said, "and change it." And it was she who stood bond at the bank for him, to treble Chamberlain's earlier amount, doing it out of pure love and belief in him and out of the strength of an ideal that was already far too lofty. So he emerged, that spring, as the owner of more houses, a large section of High Street frontage on the north side, and some odd sections of land in and outside the town. He knew that all that would have been beyond dreams except for her, and it put him under a tender but powerful obligation to her that made him slightly uneasy.

Except for that it was a wonderful year. England celebrated the Diamond Jubilee, and Arkwright, the lake finished, bought himself a new toy, a motor-car. In this daring twelve-mile-an-hour vehicle Arkwright drove Bruno and Virginia and Caroline about the soft, honeysuckled summer-dusty countryside. Bruno sat between the two women on the high back seat, he in reversed check cap, they with mauve silk veils tied over fine blonde hair. He looked like some impressive gargoyle between a pair of duplicate goddesses. And everything was all right. Sitting on that high, aristocratic, slightly grotesque seat between two lovely and adoring women he felt that he was on top of the world. He felt that nothing could happen now.

CHAPTER IV

In London, on a hot August day of that year, Italian Jenny sat down to write a letter to Bruno. "Dear, Dear Bruno." It was as though nothing had happened.

She was living on a fourth floor back in Clerkenwell. She had not seen Bruno for five years. During that time, first in 1894 and again in 1897, she had been ill with bouts of pleurisy and now, outside, in the streets, the celebrations and flags and banners waving for a small old woman in Windsor had no meaning for her. The second bout of pleurisy had knocked her out. She was writing in bed. "It's no use, I'm down the course," she wrote. "I want help from somebody or I shan't get on and you're the only one I know. I keep writing, why don't you write? Why don't you write? It's funny. One week there we were all right and the next week you didn't come. Have I done something? What have I done?" During that five years she had written to Bruno, on an average, three or four times a year, perhaps fifteen or sixteen times in all. There had never been an answer and every time she felt the same. She would get very low and then angry and decide never to write again; and then she would write, and it would be the same again. "Dear, Dear Bruno." She felt a tenderness towards him that seemed infinite. She went on writing like someone presenting a petition. This time there was a change, not in the way she wrote, but in the way she addressed the envelope. She had addressed him continually at the old Shadbolt house. She suddenly felt that in five years he might have moved. She addressed the letter to Castor S.O., marking it "Please forward".

Just at that time it happened that there were other changes and developments in Castor besides the buying of property by Bruno, Arkwright's motor car, and the launching of the town's newspaper *The Castor Argus and Free Press*. Until that year Castor had never been more than a sub-post office, subordinate to Orlingford, and without a postmaster. Its three postmen still walked miles into the country after the one morning town delivery, and people put Castor S.O. on their letters. That year Castor ceased to be a sub-office and became a post office, with a post office building in the High Street and a postmaster, though people were to go on putting Castor S.O. on their letters for another twenty years.

When that letter came Bruno was staggered. "I keep writing, why don't you write? Why don't you write? Have I done something?" He could not believe it. It was like a reconstruction of a lost part of life. "I keep writing." What had happened to those letters?

He went down to see the new postmaster. If there had been letters for him where had they gone? He felt drawn by the old feeling of inevitability to find out. He felt as though he were the victim of some dirty trick played on his conscience. The postmaster questioned his postmen. There was a fat, old, sore-footed postman who did the once a-day delivery along the road by the Shadbolt place. Yes, he had taken letters there. How often? Well, every so often. Had they been letters for Mr. Shadbolt? They might have been. Yes, it was possible. How many letters? Couldn't he remember? No, he couldn't remember justly. One here and one there, once or twice a year. But why had he taken them there if they were addressed to Mr. Shadbolt? He had a good answer for that: he delivered by address and not name and anyway if they were wrong why hadn't someone told him? He blamed the sorters.

There was only one answer to that: Maria. Bruno went to see her. She stood on the doorstep, hostile, one arm elbowed against the lintel. "Letters? What letters? I ain't seen no letters."

He knew, because of the postman, that she was lying.

"Letters for me. They come here. The post office says so."

"Post office, post office," she said.

"They come here," he said.

"Well, an' if they did?"

"Where are they?" he said. "Come on, where are they?"

"Who're you talking to?" she said. "Ain't you got no better way o' talking to folks? First you turn on Dad and now you turn on me. Whatta we done?"

"You kept them letters."

"Kept 'em? Kept 'em? Who kept 'em? I never kept 'em a minute longer'n I could help. I never said I kept 'em. Burned 'em, tore 'em up. That's what I done. Burned 'em. I see who they were from. Burned 'em. That's what I done. "

She was white, the pent-up anger of years released at last. He could not say anything.

"We ain't y' Jim Muggins," she said, "we ain't. Keeping your letters. If we're good enough to keep your letters we're good enough to be spoke to. Good enough for them. Up there. You don't want us, that's the drift on it. Don't want your own kin. Your Dad. Turned on him. Turned on your own father."

"Who said that?" he said. "Who told you?"

"He did. Who d'ye expect did? I gotta look after him, ain't I? Somebody's gotta look after him. Keep him. Board him. After what you done."

"I never meant that," he said.

"Funny, ain't it?" she said. "You never meant it. Now the time's come you never meant it."

"I'll make it right," he said. He took out his purse, shook sovereigns and silver into his hand.

"We don't want no making right!" she said. "What you done ain't goin' be made right by money!"

"Here," he said. "Here's a couple o' quid. Take it. It'll help. Take it." He held the sovereigns out to her on the flat of his hand. "Go on, I—" He had not finished speaking before she slammed the door in his face.

He went back to Castor, furious, humiliated. He felt helpless. "I keep writing, why don't you write?" It was a dirty trick played on him by a combination of circumstances. If there was anything to do he did not know how to set about doing it. He could write a letter. He would try that. "Dear Jenny." He got no farther. He felt preoccupied, not with what he felt himself, but what she felt. "Dear, Dear Bruno." After all that had happened it was as though nothing had happened. The deep tenderness behind it all remained untouched, unaffected by anger or reproach or bewilderment. He stayed in the house all evening, trying to write a letter that would not only give an explanation but express some part at least of his own feelings. He never finished it. Towards nine o'clock he heard the flip of the letter box in the passage and went to see if someone had called. He opened the door and looked out and someone was hurrying away down the street in the twilight. Going back into the house, he stepped on an envelope.

"Bruno, if it's all the same to you and no offence could I have the two pound as you offered this afternoon as we are in a poor way Yours and oblige, Maria."

He tore up the note in anger. It seemed suddenly to settle his account with Maria, make him free. It seemed to clarify the situation, bring it down to the simplest and most irresistible terms. He knew that there was only one thing for him to do.

He took the first train to London on the following morning. For years he felt that he had hated London, that he had the bitterest of grievances against it. Now, going through hot, grey streets to find the Clerkenwell address, he felt that he hated it more. He felt the old magnetic inevitability that dragged him down.

The landlady had her hair in curling rings. "It's a nice time to call I must say and it'd surprise me if she was up." It was about ten-thirty. "Anyway I suppose you can go up. End door on the fourth."

He went upstairs and knocked on the door.

"Who is it?"

He could not speak. He opened the door. The bed was

behind the door and he could not see her. He went into the room.

"Bruno."

He did not move. She was lying in bed as he had first seen her and as he had so often seen her: hands clasped above her head. She looked the same, not older, only thinner. Her hair was down. She lay looking at him in an agony of surprise, without reproach. She tried to say something but nothing happened and he went and stood by the bed. "Bruno," she said. He wanted her to be angry with him but she was not angry. Anger would have simplified things, let him out. "Bruno." The emotional simplicity of that one word tied the whole of life into knots. He sat down on the edge of the bed. He sat down as though she had magnetized him and he had no resistance. She sat up in bed and put her arms round him and he felt that all that had happened for years had happened only as a preliminary to that moment. He felt himself driven and now held by inescapable forces.

He tried to say something, offer some explanation.

"It's all right, honey. You needn't say anything. I don't want you to say anything."

They sat together. She held his head, pressing her own against it. No anger, no reproach. Time, severed by accident, joined itself up, warmth and feeling flowing through it again, their own lives subject to the same fusion, the renewed feeling of indissolubility.

"Don't you want to kiss me?" she said.

"Yes," he said.

It was she who kissed him. "Something happened. I know. It must have done."

"I didn't get the letters," he said.

"You moved?"

"I was in quod. Then when I came out I moved."

"In quod? Bruno!"

He began to tell her about it. She stopped him. "Not now. I'll get dressed. We'll go out somewhere and have something to eat and drink."

She got out of bed, in her nightgown. She began to put on her clothes under her nightgown, stooping to pull on her stockings. As she stooped he could see her body, the small creamy breasts with sleep-smoothed nipples, and he felt a more violent emotion for her than he had ever felt for any other woman at all. It struck him like sickness. He put his arms round her and felt himself held by the great inescapable force of it. Her arms were imprisoned, sleeveless, under the nightgown, and she could only respond by immobility. But in that immobility he felt the force of affection and agony complete.

About an hour afterwards they went out and got a hansom and drove slowly westward. She looked sweet, in a tired thin way. The heat of the thick, horse-fusty air sucked up her energy. She lay back on the cushions of the hansom, told him how she had been ill, as much else of things as mattered. The past comforted her. "Remember that time you first saw me? Here? Know how old I was? Seventeen." She chattered a bit, hiding deeper emotion. He suddenly saw the gap between them as he had never seen it: he almost forty-five, she more than ten years younger. Before, with himself in the thirties and she in the twenties, it had not seemed to matter; now it did matter. It offered an excuse; age could cut him free.

They had lunch at Gatti's: cold beer and steaks. To her Gatti's was heaven; she suggested going there as a joke and when he agreed she could not believe it. Then he told her about things: how he had got on, the property he owned, the gas-works, the prospects he had. "You'll be telling me you're married with a family next," she said.

He did not speak. She was frightened.

"You're not married?" she said.

"No."

"Is there anybody you're going to marry?"

"No."

"Does anybody stand a chance?"

"Can you think of anybody?" he said.

They laughed, but he felt far from happy. He ordered

more beer and it came with great heads of foam. "I'm old," he said, "soon I'll have a beard like that froth. You don't want anybody as old as that. Not like me."

"I want you," she said.

"When you're forty," he said, "I shall be fifty-five."

"I don't care. I just want you," she said.

He looked up and she was crying: large tears of illogical, genuine happiness. In the shining spontaneous tears he saw fresh manifestation of the forces against him. There was no escape without hurting her and he felt that he could not hurt her.

"What's up? Why're you crying?" he said. "What's up?"

"I don't like you to talk like that," she said.

"It's true."

"Even if it's true I don't want you to talk like it."

"Let's get out," he said, "I'll buy you something."

"I don't want anything. You and this—that's all I want for one day."

"Some new clothes," he said. "Some glad rags. A new rig out."

She brightened up. "Know how long it is since I had any? Ages. Years. My underthings are more holy than righteous and the rest only fit where they touch, I've gone that much thinner."

They went out into hot bright streets, to walk on asphalt burnt by sun. She put her arm in his, locking it over, holding it down with the other. The thin bare arms had a kind of fierceness in them. "Now," she said, "now I feel as if I'd got you."

CHAPTER V

"Go to Brighton. Get yourself some nice lodgings somewhere and get on your feet again. Sea air. That's what you want."

"You'll come down to see me?"

"I don't know."

"Come to see me."

"I might. I'll see. I got business."

"You could come. You could come. Easy. They run trips. It's easy. You could come."

"All right," he said. "I'll come."

He stayed with her that night in London, going back to Castor and subsequently to Spella Ho on the following day. Before catching his own train he saw her down to Victoria, and on the platform she put her arms round his neck and kissed him. She had an ostrich feather hat and a deep mauve, almost violet-coloured dress with leg-o-mutton sleeves. She had made him choose it for her. "I only want what you want me to have. I only want the things you like." She looked very young, slim and attractive, dark eyes excited. Before the train went she kissed him again, with a sudden but deliberate burst of passion, as though wanting to impress on him something that he could never forget.

And going home he knew that he never would forget it. His train did not arrive until the middle of the afternoon and already, when he got to the house, there was a telegram. "Dearest arrived twelve-forty sweet little lodgings so happy love Italian." He put the wire in his pocket and went over to the office and tried to do some work. By a great effort of will he kept himself there until six o'clock. Shortly after six he went back to the house, made himself some tea and boiled a couple of eggs and tried to read the paper. He was expected at Spella Ho for dinner at eight o'clock. At seven-thirty he set out to walk. During every second of this time his mind was not free of her. He did not think of her in terms of anguish or impatience or despair or longing, but in physical terms. He saw her as she was, in a recurrent series of physical attitudes: the lovely way she lay in bed, arms branched up, the way she changed her clothes under the nightgown, the warm, excited but tired face, the slight swagger of the hips, expression of the actress in her, as she walked in the mauve dress. She was photographed indelibly on his mind, and his mind in turn was predominated by a single idea. He felt magnetized. He had wanted her to be angry and she was not angry. Now he wanted to escape and he knew there was no escape. He was held down and controlled by forces which he could not grasp.

Going to Spella Ho was like going back into another world. He gave reasons for his absence, talked, had dinner, talked again, drank. He was held in warm fascination by the beauty of the two women, held consciously, by clear, tangible emotions which he himself could grasp in turn. Here were things that were logical, that had reason. There was no reason why he should not go on talking to these people, in this way, for ever. Nothing can stop me, he thought. Nothing can stop me. It's all right. This is what I want, nothing can stop me.

They talked about the wedding. It was fixed now for late September. They would marry in London. It would be quiet and they would go to Naples afterwards. "Italy," Virginia said. "Lovely to hear Italian spoken again. Lovely to have everything Italian. Italian food, Italian opera. Everything Italian." The word bounced about in his mind like a celluloid ball in a shooting gallery, mocking him, irrepressibly bobbing up every time he thought it was gone. Then Arkwright talked. "A thousand pities you couldn't have been here during the week-end. We had Baumann here. Jew of course, but a great Liberal. He was most anxious to talk to you. He'd heard about you and said there was no reason at all why you shouldn't be considered for parliamentary candidature here in four or five years' time." Parliamentary candidature? Another step. More than a step, a flight. He saw himself as a political figure, top-hatted, frock-coated, taking the oath, addressing constituents, a man holding fresh power in his hands. "Then," Virginia said, "that would mean a town house." He saw the town house, the carriage waiting outside, he himself going to the House, his name bawled by newsboys. "Shadbolt's Fighting Speech Extra." It was a dream, but it was by the establishment of such dreams that he had worked himself up. "Tories Stand Condemned by Shadbolt." Why shouldn't it be? He would not be the first man in the House to have risen from nothing. He would not be the last. There was room for men who had risen from nothing. "The Governments of this country," he had once said, "have been composed too long of men who have been unable to raise their voices because of the silver spoons in their mouths." That was the sort of utterance, as Arkwright had told him, that would be better appreciated in Westminster than in Castor. "You're a fighter," Arkwright had also said. "What we want is a fighter."

He stayed at Spella Ho, talking with these three people who had done so much for him, until after midnight. Somewhere towards one in the morning he walked out into the park with Virginia. It was warm; he could smell the August odours of harvest, the heavy fragrance of tobacco-plants from the garden. The limes were over. He could hear the weir down on the lake. "In the middle of the night," Virginia said, "you get a feeling that Time stands still." They halted and listened to the weir falling in the night silence and it was exactly as she said. It was as though Time stood still. She stood close to him and he could feel the shape of her body, firm and beautiful, nourished by expensive care and expensive food, and it seemed to beautify and soften the whole of life. With her he felt that he had the prospect of a life without harshness or difficulty. Existence became a piece of aristocratic silk that wrapped itself round him and lay between him and the contact with things outside, insulating him. It was the sort of life he had never known; it fascinated him. It seemed romantic. It was based on beauty and adoration, on trust and nobility, the permanence of abstract things. It did not bind him by a sense of fatalism and did not need to be expressed, on her part, except in the simplest and deepest terms. "If anything happened now it would break my heart. I know it would break my heart."

CHAPTER VI

In the morning there was a picture post-card of the aquarium from Brighton, "Dear, Dear Bruno. I've got such nice lodgings. Thirty shillings a week. I've been strolling on the prom all morning and I'm tired but I feel better already. But I can't stay a fortnight unless you come. You must come on Saturday. You promised. I'm so lonely. You please will come?"

His mind was split in two, as though by a diabolically accurate stroke. The division of his affection was balanced with crazy accuracy. He wanted to be two men, in two places, at the same time. He was presented with an insoluble problem.

His only hope was in time. By not going to Brighton, by not seeing her, he hoped the force of her effect on him would gradually diminish. He hoped that the photographs of her in his mind would fade out. He wrote to her. "Can't come this Saturday. Will try next." Time, a fortnight, might simplify things. Two mornings later there was a letter. "Please, Bruno, you promised." It was a long letter, written partly in fear, partly from sheer loneliness. "Don't you want me? If you don't want me say so. You said you'd come. Now you won't come. Why is it? I'm so lonely and miserable here by myself." He did not know what to say. He did not answer. On Friday evening there was a wire. "Ill. Please come." He went by the first train on Saturday morning.

She was not ill. Mentally, perhaps, but not physically. He wired from London, "Arriving twelve-forty", and she met him at the station, thin and worried, but not ill. "I couldn't bear it, that's all. I just couldn't bear it. That's all. I thought you didn't want me."

She put her arm in his, locked it over, held him tight. "Now I've got you again I'm all right. I'm happy now." He walked in silence. "You're not angry? Don't be angry."

"No, I'm not angry," he said.

She took him straight to her lodgings: a neat, respectable little boarding-house with polished brass stair rods and bell and fern-pots. "I'd love to keep a boarding-house. It's my ambition," she said. The front door was open and they walked straight in and then, as they were going upstairs, the landlady came up out of the basement, thin locketed neck strained up.

"Oh! it's you, Mrs. Shadbolt. I just wondered."

"Yes, it's me," she said.

"So he did come all right?"

"Yes, he did come."

"How de do, Mr. Shadbolt. Mrs. Shadbolt told me about you. Make yourself at home, I'm sure."

"Thanks," he said and she stood watching them as they went upstairs.

"Mrs. Shadbolt?" He took hold of her shoulders in the bedroom. "What made you tell her that?"

"She saw my ring and asked me if I was married, and what could I say?"

"Why do you wear that ring?"

"I put it on when I was eighteen and now it won't come off." She sat down on the bed and stretched her arms up to him. "Now you have come don't be angry."

He did not move and she stood up and kissed him.

"Don't you want me?" she said.

"Yes."

"Say you want me."

"I want you."

"Say it again. Better this time."

"I want you."

"You don't mean it," she said. "You say it as though you didn't mean it."

She began crying. Partly Italian, she showed emotion readily. Her whole outlook on life itself was emotional. Emotion and passion governed, ultimately, all she did and said. She wept a little and he comforted her. "I felt I'd throw myself off the pier if you didn't come." And he felt certain for a moment that she meant it.

Later they went downstairs and had dinner in the

boarding-house dining-room, among little crowded tables of clerks and suburban business men and their wives and children. There was a clatter of knives and forks, a smell of roast beef and sea-air and linoleum polish. For a time Bruno was quiet, and then suddenly she pressed his foot under the table and squinted at him with bright dark eyes, mocking. "You feel very married?" she said, and suddenly he knew how much she meant to him and how much he loved her, with her full passionate dark eyes and her way of showing emotion and the feeling that she had some inner fiery adoration for him that was beyond suppression.

They walked on the promenade in the afternoon. "Remember the time we went to Blackpool?" He nodded. "We had a carriage," she said. He remembered it. "I wanted to have our likenesses taken and you wouldn't," she said. He laughed. "Break the camera." Photographic touts took off their hats and wheedled them as they walked the promenade. "Come on," she said. "Have it taken now." So at last they had it taken, standing on the sand, with their heads through the holes in the coloured canvas, hands that were not theirs permanently joined in earnest bliss. All the time, with her head through the opening, she shrieked with laughter, intensely happy. His own feeling, with his great head stuck in the hole that was only just large enough to admit it, was that of being caught in a trap. It was the old feeling of being inescapably bound to her, partly with pleasure, partly against his will, as though his hand was really locked with hers as permanently as the painting on the canvas.

That feeling continued all day, and throughout the next, and the next. It was his intention to go home on Monday. He did not go. The feeling of inescapability increased. On Thursday they lay late in bed, like a honeymoon couple. He tickled her and she kicked off the clothes and lay naked, and it ended as it had always ended in the days when he had followed her about on tour.

"Now say you don't love me?" she said.

"No."

"You mean you don't love me or you don't say it?"

"I don't say it."

"Say I don't love you nicely."

"No. Yes."

"That means yes."

"It means yes," he said.

"If we were married," she said, "I could love you whenever you wanted."

"We're married. Mr. and Mrs. Shadbolt. The landlady married us."

"I mean really."

"This is the same."

"No. I want something that can last for ever."

"This can."

"No it can't. I lost you once already. Do you want me to lose you again? Don't you want to marry me?"

In that way she gradually forced him, for his own peace of mind, into a decision. One way or the other he had to do something. There was no escape. He wanted to be in two places at once: two men, all his affection equally divided between two women. He had to perform a miracle and make a decision.

Walking along the promenade, late that night, after she had gone to bed, tarts accosting him, people strolling past him in the warm August darkness, he tried to work it out, failed, and about midnight went back to her.

They talked in bed. "What do you want to do?" she said.

"I'll do whatever you want to do."

Tired, he lay stretched flat out, listening to the sea, the promenade noises, the intermittent silences. He could not detect in his mind the most infinitesimal alternation in the balance of his affection. He felt suddenly mad, quite desperate. Get it over. Do something. Finish it. Finish it.

"What do you want to do?" he said.

"You know."

"Marry?"

"You know that."

"When?"

She lay against him, beginning to cry a little. "As soon as we can."

He lay silent. The strange room, the sound of sea and traffic, her arms across his chest: they all seemed suddenly oppressive, forces engineered against him, holding him down.

CHAPTER VII

On the following Tuesday he went back to Castor. She came with him as far as London: Mrs. Shadbolt. He had already telegraphed the office: Taking few days holiday back Thursday. That day he wrote to Virginia. He sat in the waiting-room at St. Pancras and wrote on two sheets of notepaper bought from the bookstall, writing in pencil. He did now know what to say. The truth. Easy to think it. Not so easy to say. it. He got it down, at last, by pain and sweat. "I am going to tell you something. I am going to tell you I was married last Saturday to a friend I have known for a long time."

He posted the letter in the station and caught a train to Castor about six o'clock. He arrived home about nine o'clock. It was dark. He was glad that it was dark. At the house there was a note from Virginia. Where had he been? What had happened?

This recurrent question obsessed him throughout the next day, Wednesday, and the next. Something terrific had happened and yet it was as if nothing at all had happened. He sat in his office, interviewed people, gave orders, had things brought to him: accounts, ledgers, letters, figures. They were real, had point; he grasped them in the notion that their solid reality would counteract the unreality of what he had done. He waited for something to happen: some sort of sign from Virginia, a letter, a visit, some expression of bitterness or outrage. Again he wanted to be the victim of anger. Nothing happened.

On Friday he felt he could not bear it. Silence, negation: it terrified him. He decided to go up to Spella Ho and see Virginia. They could talk; he heard in imagination her friendly quiet voice, reasonable, understanding. He remembered how she had said, once, that if they should break down in affection for each other they could always continue on a basis of platonism. "Reminds me of Chamberlain's Spartanism," he said. "For some people," she said, "it might be the same thing."

He went out of the office about half-past two, walking. He walked through back-streets, over the railway, intending to cut across the fields to the house. Newsboys came yelling down Park Street from the printing works of the *Castor Argus and Free Press*, waving the weekly edition of the new paper. He could not hear what they were shouting. "You never can," he thought. He walked on as far as the works and there stopped to look in the street window. The presses were still running. In the window there was a placard, ink-lettered: *"Terrible Tragedy at Spella Ho Latest."* The thunder of the presses bore him out, like waves, into terror.

He stood still. A boy came rushing out of the works-entrance with a pile of papers. Bruno grabbed the boy and paper. He began to turn the pages over and over, frantically, trying to find what had happened, eyes dazzled by sun-whiteness and the maze of print. He went all through the paper and could not see anything. He began to go through it again and then suddenly, on the back page, in the quarter-column stop-press, he found what he wanted.

He read it and stood still. He tried to walk on and then again stood still.

He stood against the wall, sick. Virginia had been drowned in the lake. Suddenly sunlight seemed to blacken him out; the thunder of presses to bear him farther and farther out on waves of terror.

BOOK SIX

MRS. SHADBOLT

CHAPTER I

HE had been hit by scandal before. What hit him in the autumn of 1897, and went on to be a force against him until and with many people past the turn of the century, was more like a disease. He had done something now which could not be washed out by money or politics or success or the buying of property. He was suddenly, to a town still under all the cast-iron rules of Victorian convention, a man dirty with a sort of moral leprosy.

Virginia, buried under young white poplars by the lake, had drowned herself for a reason that everyone felt they knew, and the combination of small circumstances coming out at the inquest built itself up against him: his letters to her, his long absence in London, her own final letter to him, and all were magnified and bloated by gossip and hatred as they had been swollen long before in the case of Gerda. But they were touched, at first, with a slight pity: pity for a man who had the force of things against him and could not altogether, perhaps, help it. At that time no one knew of Italian Jenny, Mrs. Shadbolt. No one knew of her until the beginning of 1898. During all that time she lived in London. Bruno had said to her: «Before you come to Castor I want to get a decent house there. While I'm looking out for something you stop here in London and pick up the furniture and things. The stuff you get in Castor's all ten years out o' date." He tried to speak in a matter-of-fact way, off-hand; but he was a man speaking in reality with desperation, trying, even before the death of Virginia, to keep her away from Castor as long as he could. From London she wrote to him every week: "Dear, Dear Bruno. Have you got the house? When can I come?" And then a long list of things she had bought, sofas, whatnots, curtains, beds, cutlery. Those lists of things built themselves up in his mind as more bitter forces of reproach than anything that was ever said or thought in Castor. At last he got the house: a heavy red brick villa standing in walled grounds shielded by pink chestnut-trees and laburnum and holly at the north end of the town. He had chosen even that with an eye to business. Its hundred and eighty feet of frontage could never deteriorate, must rise, in value. One day he could cut the garden in half and build shops there. He could build anything. He had suddenly lost interest in ideals; felt bitterness drive him back to the former level of speculation, money, hard fact unalleviated by dreams. Castor wondered why he had bought the house. It knew why he had bought it by the first week of 1898, a fortnight before Mrs. Shadbolt arrived.

That Christmas a man named Lichfield went with his wife to spend a holiday at Brighton. The woman had been ill with phlebitis and could not walk much and they spent most of their time in the drawing-room of the little brass-staired boarding-house where they were the only guests. At night, sometimes, the landlady came in and talked to them. They talked about illness. Mrs. Lichfield described the symptoms of phlebitis: went back in time to describe the symptoms of pleurisy. "That fetches you down," she said. "Yes," the landlady said, "I remember a young Mrs. Shadbolt here. How it fetched her down." Shadbolt was not a common name and the Lichfields were surprised to hear it. "Shadbolt? We know a man that name." "Don't suppose it's the same," the landlady said. "Biggish man. Ugly. She called him Bruno." Suddenly the Lichfields felt as excited as though they were on the verge of the solution of a detective mystery. "Yes, it's him. When was this?" they said. "When were they here?" The landlady told them. "August. Oh! it was his wife all right. I'm strict on that sort of thing. Besides I do know, because I used to have confidential and friendly little chats with her like, often. I got her photo too."

The Lichfields went back to Castor with a story that went through the town like an infection: how Shadbolt was not only married but had been married before Virginia had drowned herself. "And now we know," they said, "why she did drown herself." Here and there someone would ask the Lichfields how it was they were sure it was Shadbolt. "This Shadbolt. They might be other Shadbolts." "That's just it," the Lichfields said, "we see a photo. We see a photo of the two of 'em, standing arm in arm on the sands at Brighton. It was Shadbolt all right." "Even that don't prove nothing," someone said. "That might a bin took ten years ago. You know what Shadbolt is." "That's the funny thing," the Lichfields said. "The date was stamped on the back. It was August all right, last year."

A fortnight later Mrs. Shadbolt came to Castor. Bruno had given her two hundred and fifty pounds and with it she had bought not only the furniture but new clothes for herself; she came in a dashing black cape and coat edged and revered with scarlet, and a scarlet hat; the black cape blew out behind in the January wind and showed the lining of scarlet silk. It was louder than anything Castor had seen and it was as though she had put it on purely for swank or spite or out of devilry. There was a touch of theatricalism about it and Castor put her down as a common woman. That day, when she arrived, it was raining in gusts, but she did not mind it. She was tremendously excited, in a fever at being with Bruno at last, and though later she was to be depressed and bored by the rows and rows of working class streets and the huge dim factories and all the grim rawness of a new town eating its way out into the country-side, she was excited that day even by Castor. She liked the house, with the big garden and its espalier fruit-trees, and the high bay-windowed rooms, with the flowery-papered walls which later she was to hang with rows of early photographs of herself as a dancer in Irish's Travelling Vaudeville and in London music-halls and on tour. She said, "I shall be happy here. I know I shall be happy." It was all very much like a fresh part in a new play; she ran up and down the white-banistered stairs for the pure pleasure of it, stopping only to say, "Here I shall have the ottoman," or "I want red curtains at the landing window. Real red. So that they look hot and burning when the light shows through them." Fired by these things, she was like a flame running through the house herself, setting everything alight. Through her, Bruno caught a glimpse of a warmer, perhaps friendlier future.

This condition lasted for three weeks, while she worked hard to create the effects she wanted with red curtains and jade velvet and the pictures of Italian Jenny, by which the drawing-room gradually took on the air of a reformed stage dressing-room. She loved the liquid feeling of creation, pent up for so long, which now flowed out of her. It was the great age of formal calls, of card-leaving by ladies in middle afternoons, but during her first month no one called on her, though she was talked about in Castor more than any woman had been talked about, except Lady Virginia and the Queen, for many years, arousing more feeling than the Boer War itself was to arouse a year later. She did not mind this; did not expect callers and in a way did not want callers. Behind the thick barrier of trees and then still further behind the warm enclosure of the house itself, she was quite happy, living for the moment and in the moment, in a state of oblivious and almost delirious ecstasy.

Then in February she had a solitary caller. Rufus Chamberlain came, partly to see Bruno, partly out of curiosity to see what sort of woman he had married at last. In matters of women Rufus and Bruno had drifted apart. Bruno had stopped philandering; Rufus was still the arch-devil of half the county, unmarried, a man whom drink and women had oddly enough kept fresh, still the best-dressed man in Castor and looking perhaps ten years younger than Bruno, though they were almost the same age. Rufus called one evening just before supper. Bruno met him at the door and took him into the drawing-room and introduced him to Jenny. "Mrs. Shadbolt."

Rufus took one look at her and knew who she was. She had not changed at all and his mind went back to the week when there had been almost a minor riot to see her legs in Irish's Travelling Vaudeville. He had often thought about those legs, seen through the circles of a pair of field-glasses, and the terrific question of whether they had been naked or covered. There were very few women in Castor whose legs even he had seen at that time, and there were none at all whose legs could be seen, except by some sort of accident, in public. He thought of this as he shook hands with her. Somehow the question of legs seemed to reduce her to the level of public property. He felt that sanctity of marriage did not mean much with a woman who had been dancing in skin-tights for ten years, over half the country.

"I've seen you before," he said. He stood with a slight bow and smiled.

"You have?"

"I have," he said, and told her where. "Bruno and I almost scrapped to get a look at you."

"You did? Bruno never said a word!" She was in a happy, teasing mood, glad of company. "Bruno, you wicked creature. All the men in Castor rioting to see me and you never said anything."

"When I'm on a good thing," he said grinning, "I keep it to myself."

That was something that Rufus could not do, and never had done. For forty years he had been the antithesis of his father: very open and very generous, liking company and talking and gossip and free-and-easiness. The meeting with Mrs. Shadbolt staggered and excited him a little. When he left the house he walked back into the town and went into the new "Station Hotel", then one of the jokes of Castor, the word hotel having no relation to fact. He went in and ordered a whisky and said to a man, like a child with a secret it cannot keep: "I just dropped in on Shadbolt. Trust him to have something up his sleeve. You know who his wife is? She's that dancing kid out of Irish's Vaudeville. She hasn't changed a minute."

The next day it was all over Castor: "They say. They say. You know what I heard? You know what they got about?" Simply at first, then through gradual complexity to an impossible entanglement of spite and dirt and disgust, it went through the factories and shops and clubs and tap-rooms and private houses. "They say. They got it about. I know it's right because I heard it from whosit and they heard it straight from somebody as knows it's right." Lips leered over back fences. "They say. They got it about. You ever hear such bits?" They talked about her in bars and tap-rooms, not as a woman, but as Chamberlain had thought of her, as a piece of public property, a pair of legs. "You can argue, but I heard it. I know." She ended up as a caricature of herself, something spewed up by dirty mouths. "They say. They say. And you only got to look at her to see as it's right." Bruno had not only married a cheap music-hall dancing tart but someone as near to a prostitute as mattered.

A day after Rufus had called Jenny had another caller. She had wanted to call ever since she had sat in the boarding-house drawing-room and talked about her own phlebitis and young Mrs. Shadbolt's pleurisy. A week at Brighton had helped her a lot and now, on fine dry days, she could get out and walk a bit and take up again her collecting for Missions to the Heathen in Darkest Asia. Mrs. Lichfield went to the Shadbolt house with her subscription book and Jenny invited her in. She went into the drawing-room and Jenny, touched by her first caller, put down a subscription of half a crown. She fetched it from her purse upstairs and while she had gone Mrs. Lichfield had sat staring at the walls, with their rows of pictures of the young dancer, and the one particular picture of Jenny and Bruno clasping cardboard hands on the Brighton seashore. She went away and spoke about this picture. "Mind you, I'm not saying anything against her. She was very nice to me and she gave half a crown. But there it was. There they were the same as I saw them at Brighton."

The story went through the last phases of complexity and resolved itself at last to the simplest terms. It was as though the hot air evaporated and there was left a small distillation of dirt. Castor had been fond of Lady Virginia; had adored the gay affectionate nature so beautifully and perfectly reflected in Lady Caroline. It seemed suddenly clear to people why she had killed herself: that she had killed herself not merely because Bruno had married another woman, but because he had married that type of woman. That woman. Her. A cheap foreign-looking bit off the stage. For all you knew a cheap bit off the streets.

With him gossip had gone as far as it could. It ceased to touch him. With Mrs. Shadbolt gossip had only just begun. It could no longer hurt him directly, but only through her. Gradually opinion gathered like cloud and darkened and then seemed to freeze, shutting her out. She remained shut out. She lived through her first year in Castor without a single friend.

CHAPTER II

In the following year the Boer War began and while, during the next three years, people were preoccupied with the thought of Kruger and Mafeking and Ladysmith and of the Queen sending her own guards and her own chocolate to help a cause that seemed sometimes to be going the wrong way, Bruno was occupied with the thought of something else. He was thinking of the internal combustion engine, the power that could be harnessed to wheels, making a vehicle like Arkwright's automobile, at first ludicrous, now accepted, and for which he foresaw tremendous possibilities. He remembered his dream of running a carrier's passenger service; how he had actually begun it. This dream, never forgotten, had become another. Its realization was still far off. But he felt that some day, somehow, it would be possible to run another kind of passenger service, by omnibus, a service that could spread itself out beyond the point where the small short-sighted one-line railway had ended. He did not know how this could be done. Time would show. But if there was going to be a moment in Time when it could be done he wanted to be ready. Up to and beyond the turn of the century he watched very closely every development of the motor car. He bought himself a motor car, as though to bring himself a step nearer the realization of the dream.

He would sometimes speak to Jenny about this dream-plan for self-propelling buses travelling between the new rising towns of the district. She always had one reply. "Never mind about buses. What this town needs is a real hotel. A proper hotel with dining-rooms and dance room perhaps and good beds. All you've got is that potty Temperance place and the "Station Hotel" and that's a joke."

She was right, but he was not interested. Hotels—let somebody else build the hotels. He kept his eye on the motor car.

By 1901 Rufus Chamberlain also had a motor car. Guided by his father, now on the verge of the eighties and still wearing the same straw-hat, Rufus had made money by investment. Bruno distrusted investment as exemplified by stocks and shares; was uneasy except when his money lay in concrete things, property, land, gas-works; but occasionally something in the stock-market was too good to miss and he bought when Chamberlain bought. By 1901 Chamberlain was by far the more prosperous man.

One night, when he came to supper and stayed on, talking over the whisky, until past midnight, Mrs. Shadbolt brought the conversation round to her own dream, the dream of that hotel she had often spoken about to Bruno.

"When is somebody going to have the sense and initiative to put one up?"

"Castor's a funny place," Chamberlain said. "People eat at home."

"And what," she said, "do visitors do? Have meals sitting on the pavement?"

"They go back to Orlingford," Bruno said.

"Back to Orlingford." She was mildly disgusted. "Good money coming into the town and you let it go out again and then call yourselves business men."

To her there were no obstacles to that hotel except the cautious, provincial-blunted minds of the two men with whom she argued that night for two more hours. Bored by Castor, turned back on herself by friendlessness and the commercialized days that added up behind her like the infallible amount on an adding machine, she longed for some new and if possible big emotional outlet. Like many women she had dreamed of ending her life in a neat, fried-egg and steak-and-chips little boarding-house at the seaside, catering for the August Bank Holiday crowds and perhaps an occasional retired winter visitor. That dream no longer seemed possible; it was replaced by the hotel.

"You fall over yourselves," she said, "to start a gasworks and put your money in new shares. Anything new, and you're crazy to be in on it. But when it comes to one of the oldest things in the world, somewhere where a visitor can have a bed, you H'm and Ha like a pair of old maids."

It was true. They knew it. But it was not business, they said. It was not business.

That drove her beyond argument. "One of you is crazier than the other, but I don't know which it is." She felt that they had minds of iron, which only white heat could affect. For a moment she was angry, then she got over it, and suddenly she began to flatter Chamberlain.

"If it had been anyone else I would have understood it. But you. With your brains and personality and business instinct. You of all people. Why don't you do it?"

"Problem," he said.

"What's a problem to a man like you? Besides, I don't see it. When a thing stares you in the face there's no problem."

"What size hotel had you in mind?" Rufus said.

"About thirty rooms."

"And a bar and all that?"

"A bar, yes, and a lounge and a hall that could be let for dances."

"Where'd you put it?"

"As near the station as you could. On a corner site."

Rufus sat thinking.

"Land's cheap. Building's cheap. Times are good," she said. "You wait another five years and you'll miss the boat."

She went on to flatter Rufus in a warm and persuasive voice that he found fascinating and slightly exciting. She had a way of making him feel a little larger than himself. Gradually she broke through the provincial caution and distrust. "Oh! I agree. I see that," he began to say. "I agree entirely."

And gradually, not that night but on succeeding nights, she won him over. He saw that there might be more in it than a dream. Her voice had some of the same heavy hypnotic effect on him as it had on Bruno. He was drawn over to her point of view less by argument than by the sleepy magnetism of her voice.

Bruno held out.

"Hotels," he said, "are a line on their own."

For a time he remained immovable. At last Chamberlain made a decision.

"If you don't do it," he said, "I shall."

"*We* shall," Jenny said.

That decided him. He had great faith in the Chamberlain instinct, in the streak of intuition, part shrewd, part parsimonious, that had made the Chamberlains for two generations the foremost business people of Castor. He had some idea that a Chamberlain could never be wrong.

And that summer the new hotel, later the "Prince Albert Hotel", began to go up on a waste corner site by the station. In style it looked to be an odd mixture of Gothic and jerry-Edwardian, red brick with stone ornamentation, and somehow it looked stagey and out of place. Mrs. Shadbolt loved it. She chose its red blinds and the heavy red plush suites and cherry wallpaper in the lounge and the palms that stood in the entrance hall and were to go on standing in the entrance hall for another twenty years. It was she who suggested and then staged and made such a huge success of its opening in the December of the same year. Drinks were on the house that night from eight until midnight and she ran about the place like a gay little firefly, intensely excited, marvellous in the black and scarlet that she always loved, her lips slightly painted but painted just enough to set her above the rest of the few women who were there. The place that night was filled mostly with men, young bloods with waxed moustaches and what would now be cissy coloured waistcoats. A few had arrived in motor cars and outside there was a pistol-shot cracking of back-fires as men and girls drove off for an hour of the new sport of spooning on the back seat. The hotel, with its gas-lit red blinds, looked on fire, so that even Bruno, walking about in dress-clothes in the heavy and rather lost way of a monkey dressed up, felt it to be a huge success.

About midnight he was standing at the bar when the porter pushed through the crowd to bring him a message.

"Mr. Arkwright is outside and would like to speak to you."

He went outside on to the steps of the hotel. He saw Julius Arkwright standing in the street below: an older, worn and suppressed Arkwright. He stood by the motor car in which he had driven down from Spella Ho. He looked at Bruno and for a moment he could not speak and then somehow forced himself to speak.

"Caroline would like to speak to you. She sent me down to fetch you."

"Speak to me?" He did not understand it.

"She's very ill," Arkwright said.

Bruno did not speak. They got into the car: Arkwright clenched the wheel like a man who is about to go over a precipice and is aware of it and must resist the shock. "She's very ill," he said again. "She's not going to live."

They drove in silence to Spella Ho. Bruno felt suddenly as though his mind had been boarded up. Behind that boarding, as on a site where there is a demolition going on, his mind was in a chaos. Some part of him was falling to pieces.

Caroline lay on a sofa bed in the smaller lounge downstairs. He went into the room. There was a fire and a small wall-bracket gas-light. He stood and looked down at her. She lifted her face and looked at him and he did not recognize her.

"Hullo," she said.

"Hullo."

"Find a chair," she said. "Isn't there one? I can't see."

He found a chair and sat down. Arkwright had not come in. He looked at her. He remembered the lovely Nordic nobility of the face, the thick strong hair and magnificent shoulders. "You didn't come to see us," she said. He did not answer. He was held in fascination by the change in the face. Thin, terribly tired, it bore no relation to the face he had formerly known. "I wanted you to come and see us," she said. "We both wanted you." The voice, tired but less tired than the face, had in it some of its former intonation. The two women had talked alike, in their golden, teasing fashion, that it was as though he were listening, momentarily, to the voice of Virginia. The impression, remote but very real, hurt him so much that he did not speak again for some time. But in his mind, behind the boarding-up, he felt himself going to pieces, fortitude smashing up, hardness breaking down into misery. "I just wanted you to come this once," she said. "There won't be another chance." He sat and looked away from her.

He sat with her for half an hour. She was dying and knew it, and knew, also, the reason for it. And gradually, without her saying anything of it, he knew also why it was. He saw now how she and Virginia had been component in beauty and vitality; how, as twins often are, they had been dependent on each other for existence. When one dies, he thought, the other dies. They can't go on. They can't live without each other.

He could not speak again. They had been so much alike that he felt, suddenly, that he had been in love with them both. They had created for him a double and doubly beautiful existence and it was now as though Caroline were dying a double death. She had endured the sufferings of two people and he understood as he sat there what sort of suffering it had been. It seemed to double his own.

"I'm glad you came," she said. "We never reproached you. There was no reproach here."

Before he could speak Arkwright and the doctor came into the room. Caroline put out her hand and shook hands with him and said good-bye. He did not know what to say and he went suddenly out of the room.

He walked back to Castor and went home without going into the hotel. He did not trouble to light the gas in the hall but went straight upstairs in darkness. He sat down on the edge of the bed. On the ceiling of the bedroom he could see a dull reflection of light and he got up and went to the window to see what it was. It was the hotel, blazing with light. He went back and sat down on the bed again. He did not think of anything. He felt only that his mind had been shattered by the reverberation of a huge mistake, that the twin fires of self-hatred and remorse were burning him up completely.

CHAPTER III

THE death of Caroline affected him more deeply, in a sense, than the death of Virginia. He felt himself slip backward, confidence broken. He felt relieved of the obligation of ambition and dreams.

The hotel prospered. It was clear that Jenny was right; Castor needed an hotel. And it was the hotel, combined with the death of Caroline, which began to drive something between himself and Jenny. This, for some time, was not noticeable; for a year or two it was not tangible. From the first she ran the hotel. He did not mind this. Without it she would have been driven to despair, and so she dressed herself up in her smart, almost too smart way, right up to the dot of fashion, and went down to the hotel every morning at ten o'clock. She stayed there until ten or eleven or even twelve o'clock at night, superintending service, showing commercial travellers to rooms, serving an occasional coffee or port-wine in the lounge. Castor had not realized how much it needed an hotel; still more, it had not realized how much it needed an hotel with a pretty ex-actress as manageress. On the principle that smart barmaids attract business, they felt that Shadbolt had been very smart himself. The whole district flocked to the "Prince Albert" and talked of Mrs. Shadbolt, who remained chastely and completely faithful to Bruno but who gained the reputation of being a sort of promiscuous tigress who kept, somewhere upstairs in the hotel, a lair where the most terrific affairs went on for those who could pay for them. In a little town like Castor an ex-actress can only be one thing. Castor wanted Mrs. Shadbolt to be a Bad Woman and gossip gradually created her: fast, licentious, common, flashy, wicked, unfaithful. Of the hundreds of stories told about her, ranging from the stories of her own private promiscuity to stories of a bawdy house of ex-chorus girls run in the hotel attics, not one was true. She remained not merely chastely and completely faithful to Bruno, but tenderly faithful. She was fixed in adoration of him as securely as when she had written the letters—"Dear, Dear Bruno"—for which there had been no answer. It remained the same kind of adoration: voluble, demonstrative, a little flashy, very sensitive, expressed magnificently by a body which showed no signs of ageing, expressed so often, and so often without question, that it began gradually to be taken for granted.

She knew nothing of Caroline except that someone had died at Spella Ho and that Bruno had gone to the funeral, a private one, which had been held on the edge of the lake. She had never heard of Virginia. No one ever spoke about her and for the rest of her life she never knew that he had had to make a decision between herself and another woman. No one ever spoke about that either, for the plain reason that no one but himself ever knew of it. So in a sense her adoration, perfect and sensitive and completely faithful in itself, only touched the surface of him. There were things underneath, his early struggles, Louise, Gerda, Mrs. Lanchester, about which he never spoke to her and which she had no idea existed but of which Virginia had known from the first. This shut up some huge part of his life behind a barricade. It was the barricade behind which, at the death of Caroline, his mind had seemed suddenly to break up. It had then seemed temporary. As time went on it became permanent, reinforced and steeled by bitterness. He hid himself behind it: not all of himself, but the best of himself, away from her.

All the time he worked hard. For the next eight or nine years, up through 1902 to 1905 and so up to 1910, he consolidated his position. He was prosperous, held in esteem by his bank. He did not go forward. He watched all the time the progress, in America and France especially, of the motor car; he waited for the moment when he could start his scheme for motor buses, a moment which at that time seemed slow in coming. He bought property; more land. At the close of the century, completely mad, decrepit, and almost helpless in a house of cobwebbed and crazy inventions, Candlestick Parker died, and the sale brought Bruno more land acres along the east side of the town, making a total of almost two hundred acres in all. He remained ambitious, but it was a personal ambition, without ideals. It was the old ambition of pure materialism, the desire to have life in terms of bricks and mortar, land, pounds, shillings and pence. It ceased to have anything to do with politics, with Liberalism and the betterment of the people, with Utopias. He remained a Liberal, but he ceased to speak on Liberal platforms, and might have been a Tory for all he cared about the turn of politics.

By 1908 he was a man of considerable property, but looking round for his friends he found he could count them on one hand: Arkwright, the Chamberlains, Jenny. Then, during that year, Arkwright left Spella Ho. He had played with the place, with its water and gas and telephone, as a child plays with a doll's house, and suddenly he could not endure the solitude of playing with it any longer. Huge sale-boards went up on the outskirts of the estate and remained up, blistering and peeling , for the next six years, the house standing with the same air of sepulchral solitude as it had stood when Bruno had stolen coal from it in 1873. Time seemed not to have touched it at all.

During the following year something else happened. On a windy July day Charles Walker Chamberlain went out of his cupola'd, turreted house and down the hill into the town. He was wearing boots which had not been touched by brush or polish for ten years and the same suit of clothes, never brushed and never mended, in which he had met Bruno out of prison twenty-five years before. He was wearing the old straw hat. The crown was wearing as thin as an ice-cream wafer but for five years now he had painted it at intervals with a Twopenny Bazaar preparation in a tin, Strawpol, Threepence, Makes Your Hat Like New. He was a man of eighty and there had been an occasion, in his middle seventies, when he had almost bought a new hat. Down in the town Clarkson, Draper and Hatter had put out a notice and a box of straw hats, late in

October, after a wet summer: Hats Must Clear 1s. 6d. A week later a dozen hats were left and the notice was much bigger: Positively Must Clear Final Reductions. Hats Half Price 9d. Charles Walker Chamberlain walked by the shop every day and looked at the notice and waited. Clarkson put out another notice: Hats Last Chance Positively Final Offer Here To-day and Gone To-morrow 3d. Charles Walker Chamberlain hesitated, walked home and came back in the evening. The notice hit him in the face: Freemans, Help Yourself. But the box was empty.

Walking down into the town on that hot windy July day in 1908 he felt the streets suddenly too hot for him. He turned and went over the railway bridge and up out of the town. Up on the higher ground the hot wind gusted across the green wheat that came down in those days to the very edges of the streets. It lifted Charles Walkes Chamberlain's straw hat from his head and bowled it across the street and under the wheels of a brewer's steam wagon coming down the empty hill. Charles Walker Chamberlain ran forward like a child retrieving a ball and that afternoon the *Castor Argus and Free Press* carried headlines which were in a sense his epitaph: *Unknown Tramp Crushed by Brewer's Lorry*, and it was not until late that night that Castor, and Bruno, knew that Charles Walker Chamberlain was dead.

CHAPTER IV

"But they move, Bruno. They move about. Like ordinary people. You see them walk upstairs and in the street and sit down and eat and everything. They're real and it looks as if it's raining all the time, only it isn't."

"Move? How's it done? Sort of magic lantern?"

"No, no. They've moving pictures."

"Slides?"

"No, no. It's a long strip of something. With pictures on

it. It goes through a camera and they show it on this white cloth. It's wonderful."

He did not understand it. Jenny had been to London and had come back with the story of a cinematograph show. It was the year. 1910. He had heard of the cinematograph, understood that it was a great invention, but had put it down as one with the phonograph and the typewriter, as a specialized toy which could never influence and benefit the masses as the automobile would. He did not understand how anyone could become excited over what seemed to him moving magic lantern slides. "Next thing you'll be taking me to a Band of Hope."

"You've got to see it!" she said. "You've got to. It's wonderful and you've got to see it. You've got to come up to London to-morrow."

"Got to, got to!"

"Please, Bruno. Yes, please. Please. Once you've seen it you'll feel just what I feel about it."

"And what's that?"

"That we've got to have one in Castor. We must. It's the great thing of the future. It's a miracle. We've got to have one in Castor."

"You mean a theatre? Charge people to go in?"

"Yes. They're opening everywhere."

"It sounds daft."

"It isn't daft. You said the hotel was daft."

He was slightly impressed by that. She talked of the cinematograph all that night. He went down to the "Prince Albert" to play a hundred up at billiards and there she was, in the bar, telling the world about it. She talked about it in bed, saying: "You needn't build anything. You could hire the Public Hall of the old Corn Exchange at first and hire chairs and it wouldn't cost much." He listened, as he always listened, magnetized by her volubly insistent voice, but it seemed to him an entirely trivial thing. There couldn't be money in it. He had made his money out of necessities, gas, houses, land. The thought of making money out of luxuries seemed to him crazy; it was risky and it might even be unlucky. "But you must come. You must see it. At least you can do that," she said.

He went with her to London on the following day. He saw what she had seen: people flickering on a screen, movement, life, antics of a comedian; the film broke, they sat in hushed darkness and he said in a loud voice, "Where was Moses?" and the audience tittered. It still seemed to him a trivial thing. "Just a craze," he said, "that'll die out." She was depressed by his indifference and he felt the proximity of something painful. He felt also that they were far away from each other. Sitting in the darkened cinema they sat on the outer edges of another darkness. He felt it for the first time.

They came out in silence. In the vestibule she let loose a shriek and left him and almost embraced a man who stood talking to the pay-box girl. "Mike! Mike! Mike Livesey!"

The man stared at her and felt her shoulders with his hands, as though he could not believe in her.

"Italian," he said. "Italian. It's Italian."

"All tied up in a box with bows on."

"All tied up in a box," he said. "Well!"

He stood back and she looked up at him: sallow side-lined face, hook-nosed, heavily creased, slightly scornful, the face of a tenth-rate actor who had been touring for twenty years under the impression that he was first-rate.

"You seen the show?" she said. "Isn't it wonderful?"

"Seen it?" he said. "I own it. It's mine, I run it."

"You? You run it?"

He nodded.

"How's it go?" she said. "You doing all right?"

"Packed. Packed night after night. And no dead-heads either. No Wood family!"

She turned and snatched Bruno, who stood reading old play bills nailed on the dirty walls of the foyer. "Please, Bruno." She brought him forward to Livesey. "My husband. Mr. Shadbolt," she said. "Mr. Livesey."

"Husband?" Livesey said. "Well!" He shook hands with Bruno. "Well! Come into the office."

They went into Livesey's office. Livesey took cigars out of a drawer, gave one to Bruno, playfully offered the box to Jenny. "Wouldn't be the first time! Remember?" She began laughing, swung back into memory. Bruno sat silent, playing with the unlit cigar. "Like old times," Livesey said. "And you married! Well!"

"We were in the same company," Jenny said. "Me and Mr. Livesey. Years ago. Before I knew you."

"And," said Livesey, "what days!"

"What days! Oh! What days."

Bruno bit the end off the cigar. They were talking about a world he did not understand. He was shut out.

"You like the show?" Livesey said to Jenny.

"Like it? I came yesterday. I came all the way to see it again to-day." She began to talk excitedly, telling him as fact things which really existed only in imagination: how, above all, they were planning to show pictures in Castor. "You think there's something in it? More than a craze?"

"We opened twelve months ago," Livesey said. "Never had a dead house yet. They're opening everywhere."

"But is it going to develop?"

"This thing," Livesey said, "is only in its infancy."

They talked on. Bruno, shut out, did not listen. He did not like Livesey. He did not like the cigar, which he had not cut properly, and which would not burn.

"You like to see the operating room?" Livesey said.

"Sounds like a hospital."

More laughter. "This way," Livesey said.

Bruno followed Jenny and Livesey and went into the small roughly-fitted operating room at the back of the theatre. The operator was re-rolling film on a spool. The room was hot, the naked electric light hard to the eyes. Livesey and the operator explained how things worked, switched on the noisy projector, and Jenny was thrilled. Bruno did not speak. More and more he felt himself shut out. He felt that the thin end of the wedge driven between himself and Jenny by the hotel and the death of Caroline was struck a blow that afternoon that drove it in almost to its extreme depth. He did not know why this was; the reason for it was not tangible. He only knew that he did not like Livesey, the operating room, the conversation, the reaching back into the past to a life which he sometimes felt was being discussed simply in order to shut him out.

"Well, if you start this thing," Livesey said, "let me know. I'll put you in touch with the proper people and I'll get you an operator sent down until you get a man trained."

"That's wonderful."

"Anything for a lady," Livesey said.

"I could kiss you, Mike. I will kiss you."

She kissed Livesey. Bruno did not do or say anything. The kiss had in it nothing but a splash of playfulness, but he did not like it. He felt it to be the act of a woman who had suddenly become partly a stranger to him.

They went home on the late night train. Before that they went to another motion-picture show and for the two hours in the train she talked of nothing else, of what they had seen, of Livesey, of the imperative necessity of opening a show in Castor without delay.

"Yes," he said, "and who's going to run it? You expect me to stand at the door to sell tickets?"

"I'll run it," she said. "Who do you think? It's my profession. It's what I was born to."

"If you think you can fill any hall in Castor with that thing, six nights a week, you're on a bad egg."

"Well, we'll run variety turns with it. Perhaps you'll tell me now I don't know anything about variety?"

"I never said that."

"You're trying to tell me what I do know and what I don't know."

"No."

"Pardon me. First you tell me I'm wrong about the hotel, now you tell me I'm wrong about something else."

"I don't say you're wrong," he said. "But it's my money, whether you're wrong or right."

"Keep your money," she said. "I don't want it."

"If you start this thing you'll want it."

"Why? Why your money? Why yours in particular? Other people have got money. Mr. Chamberlain has got money."

He was silenced by that, knowing it to be more than ever true. Rufus had inherited what was then the largest fortune ever left by any man in Castor, an estate of ninety thousand pounds. She said: "If you won't listen I'll borrow from Mr. Chamberlain. He'll lend me the little I want."

"Borrow?" he said. "Borrow? By God I'll see you don't borrow."

In that way, by emotion and talk and by threats which he knew she would not hesitate to carry out, she won him over. It was against his judgment and his will. He felt himself not won over, but in actuality driven farther and farther away from her.

The result was that in the September of 1910 a converted Corn Exchange was opened *Motion Pictures Twice Nightly*, *Living Cinematograph*, which to him meant nothing but which to her was like the fulfilment of a dream. He contrasted that stuffy, bare-floored, darkened building and the ambition it represented with the ambition once inspired in him by Virginia: "Shadbolt's Fighting Speech Extra", the town-house, his frock coat, the carriage waiting to take him to the House. As if to make the memory of this frustration more bitter the motion-picture house was a huge success. He had a theory that there was profit in necessity. It did not occur to him that there could be profit in the huge latent demand of the people for luxury. In Castor there had never been any theatre except Irish's Travelling Vaudeville and shows like it, once or twice a year. The cinema struck down at the latent demand for cheap pleasure like a drill striking down at oil. Enthusiasm spouted up and welled over, filling the converted Corn Exchange five nights of the week and overflowing it on Saturdays: tired, excitement-hungry factory workers booing villains and shooting with cowboys, thrilled by Mrs. Shadbolt's improvised Rossini-Sousa stuff rattled out on a hired piano. In the interval, and before the first performance, she sold tickets, and no performance began until she took her seat at the piano stool in the darkness, under the screen. She worked hard, the cinema replacing the hotel, both thickening and making more permanent the wedge already driven in between herself and Bruno.

By the beginning of 1911 it was clear, and clear even to Bruno, that the Corn Exchange would no longer do. She would not let him rest for a moment from her excited talk, at first merely insistent, but later almost threatening, of a new cinema, now on the scale of a theatre, with a stage and a circle and an orchestra pit and plush seats that tipped up. She wanted this theatre near, at best opposite, the hotel, reasoning that commercial travellers bored by Castor society would welcome such handy entertainment as a godsend, that each could not fail to be an attraction for the other. He knew that she was right, but it was something which did not touch the best in him at all. He did not care about it, could not arouse in himself any enthusiasm for something which, compared with the ambitions of the past, seemed a very cheap and pointless thing.

Whenever he wavered, during this time, she held over him the threat of Chamberlain. "All right. If you're so mean, I'll go to Mr. Chamberlain. Mr. Chamberlain will listen to me." He did not attach any great importance to this frequent and gradually more frequent use of Chamberlain's name. But it drove him at last to do what she wanted.

He built in 1911, on a site opposite the hotel, the Victoria Variety Palace and Cinema. It matched the hotel: raw, solid, ornate, brick. As with the hotel, she designed it; she planned its future, organized its staff and the six months ahead bookings of variety turns which were to be sandwiched in between the films. She arranged its gala opening, with tickets of invitation, a six-reeler, five variety acts by London artistes and something which Castor crowded to see more than any one thing: an act by herself. The legend of her dancing in the eighties was a story which had never died down, and people took tickets that night less to see the six-reel film and the London artistes and the interior decorations than to see the wicked Mrs. Shadbolt appear in her true colours and where she really belonged at last. When she appeared that night she was a woman of forty-five, almost forty-six; she looked more than ten years younger. She was as slim and firm breasted as when Bruno had first seen her in Irish's Travelling Vaudeville; and in the short skimped red skirts and pale flesh tights, with the grease paint colouring her face, she looked very little over thirty. But the audience was disappointed. What they saw was not something wicked at all, but a rather ordinary dance by a woman who had not danced for fifteen years, who was out of training and practice and who had forgotten the best she had known.

After her dance Bruno came on to the stage and made a short speech. He was wearing a frock coat and a top hat. She stood by his side, half his height, slim legs as beautiful as ever, looking like a young woman. He began to speak. She nudged him and whispered "Your hat", and suddenly he remembered and took off his hat and held it in his hand.

As he took off his hat a man at the back of the audience took his pipe out of his mouth and leaned over and spoke to his wife, behind the back of his hand.

"Shadbolt begins to look old," he said.

CHAPTER V

IT was true: he had begun to look old. At the same time he had not begun to feel old. He did not feel any older than he had ever felt. But the wedge driven between himself and Jenny by the hotel and the cinema and most of all by the death of Caroline began to be thickened suddenly by age. He was fifty-eight. But now it was she, and not he, who was conscious of it.

She began to spend less and less time at the house which, two years before, she had adored so much. She left the house about ten o'clock every morning and went to the hotel. She spent half an hour there talking to the cook or the barman or the office girl, nervously smoking many cigarettes, and then went across the road to the cinema, still frowsy and dead and still unswept but with that stale odour of theatre about it that she loved. She spent two or three hours there in the office. She totted up the previous night's receipts, dictated letters to the office girl and nervously smoked many more cigarettes without knowing she was smoking. About one o'clock she went back to the hotel, had a hasty tray-lunch in her office and then showed herself in the dining-room. The traffic of commercials was the same, week in, week out; she talked to first one and then another, was familiar but held them at a slight distance, smoked their cigarettes and listened to their borderline smutty stories and yet never permitted any nonsense. She was popular, but what had been true of her for ten years was still true of her: she was constantly faithful to Bruno. No one believed this, and commercials who had tried hard to seduce her or even kiss her on the stairs or in the bedrooms which she took them to inspect told fantastic stories of her as a promiscuous lover, one against another, afraid to admit defeat. She looked promiscuous: dark, passion-burnt eyes, slim swinging hips, firm breasts accentuated by her thin black dresses, the excited nervous way she smoked one cigarette after another. She stayed at the hotel all afternoon, and about four o'clock again showed herself in the lounge, where one or two commercials would be back again, reading the racing results in the afternoon paper and having a cup of tea before catching the five o'clock train. At five-thirty she went back to the cinema, saw the first house safely started at six, went back to the hotel at half-past, back to the cinema at eight-fifteen, and so on, backwards and forwards across the road, until the closing of both places at ten-thirty. Long after official closing time she still stayed on at the hotel, still pouring out emotion in the form of energy, the nervous strain of it making itself felt in that continued chain-smoking of scores of cigarettes. She got back to the house about midnight, spent a noisy half hour in the bathroom over her toilet, and then spent five minutes over a final cigarette while sitting up in bed. By that time Bruno was asleep, tired after his own long day. She sometimes woke him, by accident or design, and kept him awake for another half hour, talking, or she woke him for no more purpose than to satisfy something which even the hotel and the cinema close-ups could never satisfy. Still young and vigorous, she still asked for regularity in passion. All the time he felt himself shut more and more away from her.

Suddenly, in 1912, she got bored with the hotel and the cinema and the whole of the life she had cut out for herself in Castor. She was tired; emotion needed new outlets. She spent moody, angry days, smoking madly. "Let's get away for a while," she said at last. "The South of France or somewhere. We've never had what you'd call a holiday. Let's go to Paris and then on to Nice."

The moment was a bad one. He was on the verge of realizing a dream he had planned and cherished for more than ten years: The Castor and District Omnibus Transport Company. With a garage proprietor named Caleb Nichols he had already drawn up a deed of partnership and they had on order two double-decker buses of the London type. Nichols was a man of experience, had opened the first garage in Castor, had run the first huge Schneiders and had been almost the only man in Castor who had not laughed at Arkwright's inelegant, stinking vehicle in 1897. He was a man of inexhaustible devotion to the internal combustion engine; he remained up all night, struggling with the plugs and valves and magnetos of his ancient chariot Schneiders as other men might sit up for women or sick children or books or devotion. The motor car was his altar. He was exactly the man Bruno needed. In a fortnight Castor would see the first two buses, to be followed by four more buses, of the Shadbolt and Nichols Company. They would run in a rough triangular course across the river valley, Castor to Orlingford to Lingborough, Lingborough to Castor, and reverse, a route which two railways had not touched and now never would touch. The whole venture was revolutionary to a growing but still little town like Castor, still five and even ten years behind the times in thought, morality and progress, still a Victorian town with an Edwardian label pasted on it, even though Edward was dead. For its success it depended utterly on the energy of Shadbolt and Nichols. To Bruno all talk of going for a holiday, even to Brighton, was as pointless as talk of going to the North Pole.

Jenny was furious. "All you think about is that damned company. Work. Nichols. All I ever hear all day is Caleb this, Caleb that. All you think about is making money."

"No," he said. "Not quite. But this is important. This is something I've waited ten years to do. Longer than that. Ever since I was a kid and tried to run that carrier's round to—"

"Oh! For God's sake!" she said. "If it's not money you're talking about it's something you did thirty years ago."

"You talk like it yourself. Everybody does."

"Well, let's live in the present for a bit. Go somewhere. Do something. Time was when you were glad enough to run over half the country after me. Now it's too much to take me for a holiday."

"It's not too much trouble. And I will take you. But not now. I can't. Not till this thing is through. In six weeks."

"Six weeks."

"That's not long. The latter end of August."

"Not long! I'll go scatty."

She smoked furiously.

"You smoke too much," he said. "It's bad for your nerves."

"Smoke too much!" She got up and threw down the cigarette, let it smoulder on the carpet.

"Smoke too much. Interfere with my personal tastes! Say what I must do and what I mustn't do. Go on! Say it! Do it!"

He put his foot on the cigarette and walked out of the room. She followed him, shouting.

"You know it's right. You know it's right or you wouldn't run away from it."

He walked upstairs, hard, phlegmatic, a million miles away from her. She raised her face, screamed.

"Why don't you answer? You know it's right. You know it's right. You know it's right."

He went into his bedroom, out of sight. She ran upstairs, in a frenzy at his non-resistance. She wanted to quarrel. Her nerves, stretched for weeks, began to break. As she came upstairs he came out of the bedroom and went into the bathroom, locking the door. Frenzy leapt into fury. She ran along the landing and began to beat on the bathroom door with her fists, shouting, calling him names. He turned on the basin tap and washed his hands. Her voice shrieked above the sound of running water. He did not answer but suddenly turned on and lit the geyser, the long fall of water loud in the empty bath. She beat on the door with the flat of her hands. She kicked it and shouted with uncontrolled nervous frenzy which he heard even above the noise of water. "You're just a miser! A mean, self-centred, rotten miser. That's all. That's all you are a miser I know it now a miser I've thought it for years and now I know it. A money-grabber. A cheap money-grabber. That's all. Just a jumped-up cheap money-grabber that's all that's all. I know it now. I've thought it for years and now I know it!" He did not answer; took off his coat. He hung his coat on the door and undid his collar and took off his tie. He sat down on the bath-stool and took off his boots. Slowly, deliberately, not speaking, he took off the rest of his clothes and got into the bath, keeping the hot water running. He sat still, watching the water rippling its small tide up between his thick, ugly, slightly bowed legs. She had not finished kicking the door and almost weeping now, she yelled "Mean is bad enough. But mean and ugly that's what you are ugly that's what you are just mean and old and ugly. Old and miserable. Old and ugly that's all you are that's all you are." He sat silent in the water, looking at his feet sticking above the water. Ugly feet: he knew that. Toes crossed and twisted and curled over each other. Ugly feet: ugly because as a child his boots had had to last until the cramped feet could be cramped no longer. He looked at the slightly bowed ugly legs. As a boy he had wondered why his legs were not straight. He knew now. Rickets had bowed them out, sent him walking on ankles of gristle, given him that slight waddle in his gait that he still had. All that she was saying was true. It did not affect him. He took the soap in his hands, watered it. Bubbles rose between his fingers. They were fingers of whose ugliness he had never had any doubt. All she was saying was true. "Old and ugly and just too mean and miserable to spend a penny! Too mean and miserable why don't you answer why don't you answer something? You know it's true that's why you know it's true!" She was crying now, nerves broken, voice weaker and more bitter. He sat calmly soaping his hands and looking at his old ugly feet. Her voice did not produce in him a single moment of anger or suffering. He sat behind a barricade unconsciously built up ever since the death of Caroline and now complete. Nothing she said could ever affect him now.

She went away at last and he remained in the bathroom for almost another hour. When he came out the house was quiet and she had gone. He poured himself a whisky and before finishing it got on the telephone to Caleb Nichols, saying that he was coming round, in about ten minutes, to see him. He went round, and stayed there, at Nichols's garage, until two o'clock in the morning. It was a great occasion: the two new double-decker buses were due to arrive at midnight from Yorkshire. They did not arrive until almost one o'clock. Nichols brought out whisky, and the two drivers, Nichols's two men on night-shift and Bruno and Nichols himself had a celebration party on the upstairs deck of one of the buses. They all got slightly drunk; and when Bruno went back home at three o'clock in the morning he had already forgotten that there had been trouble with Jenny.

And that night, while he sat drinking to the success of The Castor and District Omnibus Transport Company in Nichols's garage, she was unfaithful to him for the first time, at the hotel. She was unfaithful with Rufus Chamberlain. Chamberlain came into the hotel every night between eight and nine o'clock. His mother had outlived his father by only six weeks and he had arrived at much the same point of boredom with that huge turreted Frenchified house as Jenny had arrived with the cinema and the hotel. He had begun to talk of selling the house and, with typical Chamberlain meanness, of taking all his meals at the "Prince Albert", where as a shareholder he was entitled to discount off the bill.

He went into the hotel that night about nine o'clock without any intention of talking about these things. He had three or four drinks and read the local paper. As always, there was nothing in it, and he got up at last and went into the lounge to look for a magazine or a woman or a crony to talk with. There were only two men in the lounge, and there was only one woman. "Hallo, Mrs. Shadbolt," he said. They all stayed talking until ten o'clock. At ten o'clock the two men left, but he stayed on, talking to Mrs. Shadbolt. She sat on the edge of a table, swinging her legs, with their pale dove-coloured stockings and scarlet clocks. He was a man of fifty-five, but, like her, he looked almost ten years younger: fresh-faced, smart, with the full fleshy handsomeness of good living. She sat swinging her legs and the movement carried a ripple up through her whole body, tight under the black dress. He sat watching her, fascinated, and began to tell her suddenly of the idea he had: of coming to live and eat at the hotel.

"Well, and a good idea," she said.

"I get fed up with that great empty house," he said. "Four servants to one man."

"Well, why don't you come?" she said.

"I was going to talk to you about it," he said. "Discuss it."

"As far as I'm concerned," she said, "there's nothing to discuss. All you've got to do is to choose your room and say when you're coming and that's that."

"Simple."

"Simple's the word," she said.

She sat swinging her legs, gave an extra swing and jumped off the table. "Like to look at a room now?"

"Is it all right?"

"It's our hotel," she said, "isn't it?"

They went out of the lounge and through the passages which had become permeated now with thick warm odour of beer and stale cooking and the dust on the topmost leaves of the artificial-looking palms, and went upstairs to the bedrooms where, she said, Number Eleven had the best view. They went into the room, still fitted like all the hotel with gas, but now in darkness. She made no attempt to get a light but went to the window and stood looking at what view there was: many lights sprinkled over the lower darkness of the town. There was the view, she said, and in daylight you could see the woods. Chamberlain came and stood beside her. He stood close to her. She did not speak and suddenly she was aware of him, not with mere alertness, with the alertness of an inner part of herself. She felt that he was waiting to move. In the darkness she suddenly felt curiously alight, as if a large aperture had opened up before her bored and stifled emotions. Suddenly he did move and she let him hold her, without troubling to speak. He began kissing her and she let him do that too without any protest, feeling the immediate cancellation of all her tired distress. She felt emotion flood her from the lips downwards, her lips literally wet, her whole body leaping up out of passivity.

The back of her dress was fastened with press-studs. Chamberlain put his hand on the top stud and unfastened it and pulled and felt the slitting open of the dress as the rest of the studs pulled away.

"Simple," he said.

"Simple's the word," she said. She held him desperately.

From that moment Chamberlain began to take the place of the hotel, the cinema and Bruno himself. At first, on that first night especially, she did not take it so seriously. She looked upon it as an act of revenge. It was a desperate remedy in a desperate moment. She did not think of repeating it. When she did repeat it, at first rather against herself, then willingly, then as an everyday act of emotional ritual, it was just as she had once done with the hotel, the cinema and Bruno himself. She thought of nothing else; thought rushed out on the same terrific surging current as emotion.

Bruno did not know of this. For five or six weeks he did not even know that Chamberlain had given up the house and taken his things to the hotel, to eat and sleep there. When he did it did not surprise him. The "Prince Albert" was the place for Chamberlain, who had always kicked his heels in that fantastic house on the hill.

In the same way he did not notice any change in Jenny. Since she already spent ten and twelve hours of the day away from home, another hour or two or even a night did not seem to matter. It could not lengthen the distance between them. He was too absorbed, also, in his own affairs, in the sight of his two red buses, soon afterwards six red buses, making their erratic time-table between the towns and villages. She in turn was not interested in this. That did not surprise him either. She had never been interested. That first half-year The Castor and District Omnibus Transport Company could have declared an interim dividend of twenty per cent. Bruno saw no reason to declare it or even mention it, since only he and Nichols were interested. He contemplated later, an issue of shares. At the end of 1913 he declared a dividend of twenty-five per cent and made an issue of ten thousand shares. He became the biggest omnibus company in a radius of forty miles. Twenty red buses made a regular and more frequent service to more towns and villages. Nichols's crazy barn garage was pulled down and there went up in its place a lofty concrete cavern in which buses roared like beasts, as drivers stepped on accelerator pedals in the early morning. All this time, in room Number Eleven, at the "Prince Albert", things were going on which the chambermaids and then the boots and then the commercials and finally the whole of Castor knew about. By the end of 1913 he was almost the only adult person in Castor who did not know that Chamberlain and his wife virtually lived together at the hotel.

Just at that time, with his interest in the bus company settled enough to make him take things a little easier, he suddenly remembered that Jenny had wanted to take a holiday. It was the moment when he might have found out about her, except for one thing. There appeared in the *Castor Argus and Free Press* an article on some excavations being made at that time on the site of Roman encampments three miles out of the town. "It is quite evident," the article said, "that the name Castor itself is Roman, i. e. *castrum*, a camp, and it is equally in evidence, from the finds made at the Orlingford Road excavations, that what attracted the Romans there were the rich deposits of iron. Iron ore had been found in such large quantities in the digging that it has been a veritable nuisance to Mr. Wicklow, who is in charge and who somewhat facetiously remarked to our representative,

"When we next dig here it will be down a pit-shaft."

When Bruno read that article it was as though he had been shaken out of a deep soporific. He remembered Parker, Parker's intense and slightly insane experiments with steel in that impossible and yet not wholly impossible condenser in the backyard of a house that itself had been built out of great blocks of sepia-coloured ironstone. He remembered what had finally shaken his faith in Parker. He remembered how he had once talked to Charles Walker Chamberlain about those experiments for a harder steel. "Ever hear of Bessemer?" Chamberlain had said. "Bessemer did more with steel than Parker ever thought of doing before you were born." It did not now seem to matter that Parker had searched in a mad way for something different, not only a harder steel but a lighter and even rustless steel. It seemed only to matter that the land Parker had sold to Bruno must be rich in iron.

The idea acted on him like an explosion. He got his car and put in it a pick and shovel and drove out to the land that same afternoon. He had already seen, in a field that he had let for grazing for twenty years, the hollows, over-grown now with grass and harebell and thyme, made by Parker's crude workings in the fifties. And what he did there that afternoon was as fantastic as anything Parker had ever done. He began to dig for iron. It was as though he expected to unearth it in ready stiffened pigs. He work-ed as he had so often worked in the past, out of ignorance. Ignorance drove him on where knowledge, even a little knowledge, would have kept him back. Through ignorance he got a sort of crude faith, not only in himself and an idea, but in the land on which, that afternoon, he shovel-led and dug like a navvy. He worked with the same indomitable blind energy as he had walked from London through the snow. Nothing, he thought, can stop me now, nothing is going to stop me: as though he had only to move enough earth to strike layers of iron as a man might strike a waterpipe. Iron, he thought, iron. Parker was right. Parker must have been right. He remembered how disappointed he had been at the non-fulfilment of his own dream of the single-line railway coming through these same fields. Now it seemed like a blessing. His eye went over the land, to the south, towards Orlingford, and he saw how that line must cut through the Roman site and end on the northern edge of Orlingford, by the railway, where iron-furnaces had reddened the night sky for forty years. What was mined and smelted in Orlingford could be mined and smelted by him in Castor. He was going to do it. How he was going to do it he did not know; but, he thought, I am on that same belt. The iron is the same. The Romans knew. Parker knew. Parker was right. Occasionally, as he dug, he got out a lump of what seemed to him almost raw iron, a blue lump, slightly burnished in appearance, that seemed as heavy as lead. He carried these lumps to his car. As he went across the field to the road and stood in the road he could see Spella Ho. The house was empty; he would look at it for a moment, white and solid and beautiful in the shadows of the trees in the afternoon sun, and once he had a feeling, as he had once had long before, that something between himself and the house had to be set right. It was as though he had something to make up to it. He still did not think of it as having anything to do with affection, but the thought of it saved him from any danger of losing faith in what he was doing. He went back and drove the pick down into the iron-seamed earth with a tremendous blow; it snapped the pick-shaft at the junction of wood and metal as though it were rotten.

He gave up then and drove home. He felt a little sobered, and did not know quite what to do. Ignorance had brought him so far, and now he felt at a dead end. He took a lump of iron ore indoors and put it on the dining-room table and then, for the third or fourth time, read the article in the weekly paper. Reading it, he had a sudden idea. He got on the telephone and rang through to the offices of the paper. At eleven o'clock that night he was still drinking whisky with Mather, the chief reporter, and on the following Friday there appeared in *The Castor Argus and Free Press* another article: By our Expert: "The metallurgical potentialities of the eastern side of the valley have long been the subject of speculation, but it has remained for Mr. Bruno Shadbolt, the inaugurator of so many of the town's progressive enterprises, to put that speculation to the test. Recent exhaustive tests by London experts have established the fact that the valley is richer in ore than was hitherto thought. It now transpires, also, that South Wales interests are watching developments with the closest attention and an announcement of the greatest public interest may shortly be expected. Far-sighted prophets who have visualized the town as one with immense industrial possibilities may shortly be congratulating themselves on their vision."

There was no announcement. The Frome and Taylor Consolidated Iron and Steel Corporation, head offices in Yorkshire, controlled the output and furnaces at Orlingford; and, they said to the Castor reporter, tests tell us that we have sufficient workable ore here to make it unnecessary to consider touching another inch of land for fifty years. They filed the article. Copies of it were sent to another forty concerns in Yorkshire, London, and South Wales. One filed it. Bruno waited. While waiting he got down from London an expert whose report confirmed all that the article had ever said or that he had ever felt. That report, circulated too, "is the greatest possible vindication of Mr. Shadbolt's judgment and faith. We are sure," *The Castor Argus* went on, "that the citizens of Castor will await developments with the keenest interest."

The citizens of Castor, momentarily switching from gossip of Chamberlain and Jenny to talk of Bruno and iron, awaited developments. Bruno himself waited. Ignorance and faith had brought him so far. Now they held him again at a dead end. Nothing happened.

He waited for months and might have gone on waiting for years except for one thing: the declaration of War. In January of 1915 the article in *The Castor Argus*, pure puff at the time of writing, was turned up in the London offices of South Wales Amalgamated Iron and Steel, then already being harassed by a government department that was itself harassed by the necessity for an increased output of munitions. They sent down an expert to Castor. He came back with samples of ore and in twenty-four hours delivered a report almost identical with one that lay in Bruno's desk at the gas-office and which he had not troubled to take out. The expert pencilled in the top right hand corner of the report: "Offer five thousand," afterwards explaining this: "He's a queer bird. He apparently has no notion at all of what mining for ore means. He told me himself how he dug it out with his own hands." In fourteen days South Wales Amalgamated had opened negotiations with Bruno.

He went to London. He got up on a dark January morning to catch the first train at 7.19. The maid got his breakfast, which he ate alone. Just before departing he went up to Jenny's bedroom. She was still asleep. He held open the bedroom door and let in the light from the gas-globe on the landing. The light woke her and he said: "I'm going now. If I'm not home to-night it will be because the negotiations haven't finished. But as soon as they're over and the deal's through I'll telegraph. Then you come up."

"Come up?"

"Yes. To London. Celebrate."

"Eh?" She was frowsy with sleep; still half in another world.

"Celebrate. Have a bit of a holiday. Forget the War and everything."

"Holiday? It's a bit late to talk about that, isn't it?"

"Why? I'll telegraph. As soon as it's over I'll telegraph."

He went to London with one idea in his mind. "Talk

big," he thought. The offices of South Wales Amalgamated were in the City; solid, mahogany-furnished, gloomy, giving him glimpses back into the days when he had tramped an even gloomier London, looking for work. He hated London. It filled him with a notion of revenge. It did something to me, he thought, that no other place ever did, that not even Castor ever did. For a long time, at the first interview, he did not say much. He nodded when they told him how, in their opinion, the report of their expert was less satisfactory than they had hoped. He did not say anything at all when they said, "Such a concession as this is bound, at least, to be problematical," At three o'clock in the afternoon they offered him five thousand. He went and looked out of the window. "Now," he thought, "is the time to say something."

After about five minutes he went back to the table. He sat down and looked at each of the three Amalgamated Steel directors in turn. "Gentlemen," he said, "you are talking out of the backs of your necks."

Now they were silent.

"You seem to take it for granted," he said, "that I'm going to sell. I don't know that I shall sell. I don't know that I shan't develop it myself. If the concession isn't worth more than five thousand, it isn't worth more than ten thousand to develop. I could do that."

In their minds they had a figure of twenty thousand. They said: "Call it ten thousand."

Bruno said: "The War looks like lasting another two or three or even four years. If it does the price of iron and steel will go up to somewhere you've never seen it before."

"No one can foresee that," they said.

"I foresee it," he said. "Another thing. Frome and Taylor foresee it. They've opened up nearly a mile of new workings since October last year."

They did not speak.

He said: "I've got every reason to believe that Frome and Taylor would pay double your price merely to prevent your ever coming into that valley."

"Our price," they said, "is fifteen thousand."

They talked all that afternoon and met early on the following day. The news of War was black; the people depressed. He argued with South Wales Amalgamated all morning and met them again in the early evening; he took them by stages, from one deadlock to another, to a figure of forty-five thousand. This was their offer at the end of the second day. He rejected it; said, "Its exploitation as building land would bring me that." They smiled at this, and he surprised them by saying: "All wars are followed by a boom." In the middle of the third day, when the machinery of discussion had begun to turn more smoothly under the oil of a bottle or two of champagne, he threw in a spanner. He began to talk about royalties. Through the whole of the discussion it had been their aim to prevent him ever thinking of royalties. They knew suddenly that they had under-estimated him; felt that it would have been better to have begun with fifty and finished at sixty, rather than to have begun at five thousand and finish by talking of royalties. They offered sixty thousand, and he said: "At your anticipated rate of output that would be the royalty for about ten years." They were slightly indignant; asked how he could have the barest notion of their anticipated output. He said: "I know what the output of Frome and Taylor was for the year ending July 1914. That was in a twelve-hour-a-day shift. Now they're on a twenty-four. So will you be." He was bluffing, in part, but they were not sure of it. They were impressed by the stubborn, aggressive quality of his answers, by which he gradually induced in them a feeling that he was doing them a great favour. "You seem to think iron ore can be picked up like pebbles," he said. "My God, the country's crying out for it. It's a national need."

It finished on the fourth day. His talk of royalties, kept up to the last, frightened them. They agreed at ninety-eight thousand. It was a price that, to both sides, seemed terrific at the moment. Later, as the War went on and the price and demand for steel rose to the heights he had predicted, they thought of it as a god-send.

He went straight out of the offices of South Wales Amalgamated Steel and telegraphed Jenny. "All done at a hundred thousand could you catch four-twenty will meet you St. Pancras. Bruno." It was then about half-past two. He went back to his hotel and changed his room for a double, with bath. He gave the page-girl five pounds. "Pound for yourself. And get some flowers with the rest and put them in the room." He went down to the barber's saloon and had a shave and a trim and then had a bath in the bath-annexe of the new double room. He felt immense. "I've gone through with it," he thought. "I've done it. I've gone through with it." He took a taxi to St. Pancras.

The train came in at six-fifty-five. It was crowded with soldiers going back from delayed Christmas leave; there were many women. He waited at the barrier, feeling very happy, thinking perhaps this is what we wanted, something like this, we've been apart, now it will be all right. Soldiers and women filed off the platform. It was empty at last. She had not come.

It didn't give her a lot of time, he thought, the telegram. She couldn't get the four-thirty. She'll get the six. Just to make sure he went to the Public Telephone and put through a trunk-call to the house. The line was congested, the connection poor, so that the answering voice sounded throttled.

"Has Mrs. Shadbolt left?"

"Yes," the maid said. "She left about five."

"That's all right," he said.

He rang off and went out of the station. He had two hours before the train was due. He found a bar. "What will it be?" the barmaid said, and he said: "What's new?" "The moon for one thing," she said, "but you can try a gin-and-it." "What's that?" he said, and she told him. "Gin and Italian." Funny, he thought, coincidence. He would tell her about it. "You're a drink now, Jenny-and-

Italian." He saw her laughing about it; felt happier than he had felt for a long time.

At eight-seventeen the train came in and he was there to meet it. He saw the same procession of soldiers and women, with the same result. She wasn't there. He could not understand it. He left the station and walked up and down the streets outside it, alone, miserable, accosted by tarts, the smell of fish-and-chips, exactly as he had walked and been accosted thirty years before. As though it had lain rancid in his mind all that time the bitterness of it all rose up again, mingling with the new bitterness, souring everything. A hundred thousand. What is it, he thought, unless there's somebody to tell it to?

He went back to the station and met another train, the last. It was as he expected. She was not there and he went back to the hotel. The page-girl had arranged the flowers very nicely: pale mauve early tulips, great branches of lemon chrysanthemums, many small bowls of violets. He took off his jacket and sat down, and then after about five minutes the doorbell rang and it was the page-girl. "Flowers are not over-plentiful and there was some change," she said. "Fifteen and threepence." He looked up at her, attracted by her small, young, fresh face. "You keep it," he said. And suddenly he thought how he would like her to stay, with her tight little figure filling out the plum-coloured page-suit; it was war-time, and perhaps she was that sort of girl. He felt immensely lonely, tired. "You stay with me," he said. She went out of the room.

He went back to Castor on the following day. He felt the separation between himself and Jenny to be complete. The deal with South Wales Amalgamated seemed a completely barren thing.

He arrived home in the early afternoon. When he got into the house he could hear the bath-water running. He went upstairs. "Is that you?"

"Oh! Mr. Shadbolt." It was the maid's voice. "I didn't know you were coming."

"Is Mrs. Shadbolt in?"

"No, Mr. Shadbolt."

Funny, he thought, taking a bath in the afternoon. He went downstairs. She's at the hotel he thought, and rang through. No, Mrs. Shadbolt wasn't there. Mrs. Shadbolt hadn't been there all day.

He waited for the maid to come downstairs. When she came down she looked hot from the bath; it accentuated her look of scared guilt.

"What time did Mrs. Shadbolt go yesterday?"

"About five, Mr. Shadbolt."

"To catch the train?"

"I don't know."

"Didn't she say anything?"

"No."

"Nothing at all?"

"No."

"Did she say you could have a bath!"

"No, Mr. Shadbolt. I'm sorry."

"No? Hasn't she been in all day?"

"No."

He sat down at the telephone again. He did not know quite what to think or do. He felt that he had to speak to someone, and he rang back to the hotel. "Mr. Chamberlain isn't in?"

"No," the office girl said, "Mr. Chamberlain isn't in."

He put down the telephone. Turning, he saw the maid's face. It was scared as though he had caught her in some fresh act of guilt.

"You know something," he said, "don't you?"

"No."

"What is it? Come on. Tell me. What is it?"

"I don't know anything," she said.

She began to cry; great blubbering tears spread like glycerine on her hot face. She knew what all Castor already knew, and after a time she ceased crying enough to tell him what it was. In a moment he too knew that Jenny had gone away with Chamberlain.

CHAPTER VII

"THE land will not be split, ladies and gentleman. The land will not be split away from the house."

He was sitting at the back of a large upstairs room at the "Prince Albert" on a winter afternoon in the year 1923: a man of seventy. Spella Ho was changing hands for the fourth time in his life. Voices of people numbed him; the voice of the auctioneer rose like the voice of a schoolmaster or a preacher.

"It has always been the wish of Mr. Arkwright that the land should not be split away from the house. House and land, ladies and gentlemen, will only be sold together. Fourteen hundred and fifty acres and the house. Will you start me? Do I hear somebody start me? The house and the two home farms. They all go together. Will you start me, will somebody start me? Do I hear twenty thousand?"

"You don't," a voice. Laughter.

"Well, what do I hear?"

"Five thousand."

"It's an insult, ladies and gentlemen, a disgrace. Six thousand. It's a most unique opportunity. More improvements have been put into this property by Mr. Arkwright than into any house in the district. The lake alone is unique. Seven thousand."

"You ought to knock something off," a voice said, "for the soldiers playing football in the lounge."

Laughter. "True," the auctioneer said, "the use of the house as a war hospital might have knocked a little paint off the walls. But that adds to its history. It is a house, ladies and gentlemen, with a very long and extraordinary history."

Bruno sat staring into space. What was happening seemed to have no relation to him. History? He heard the voice of the auctioneer raising the bids, running them up, false and actual, between long pauses. They rose to twenty thousand, but the face of the auctioneer remained twisted, in pain. Such a price did not mean anything. Voices buzzed about Bruno in comment, the voices of curiosity, pettiness. He sat looking into space. He was not bidding; did not mean to bid. The thought of buying the house did not occur to him. He had come out of a sort of curiosity himself. "Twenty-three thousand," the auctioneer said, and he heard the bidding rising again, reaching the thirties, halting, then stopping altogether. In the long pause that followed he experienced a feeling of relief. It was flat, without pain or exultation. He was glad, in a simple way, that no one had bought the place. It did not mean any more than this.

He went out of the room and downstairs with the crowd, no one speaking to him until he reached the corridor below, with its eternal dust-bloomed palms and smells of beer and stale cooking, smells now steeped into the flesh and bone of the place. A voice said then: "Should have thought it might suit you, Mr. Shadbolt? Man with a large family." The man laughed at his own joke. Bruno laughed too, did not say anything, and went out of the hotel.

It was about two o'clock, the afternoon dull already, the red cinema lights Now Showing *Foolish Wives* Twice Nightly already shining in the dull air across the street. He walked away from the hotel, a bus pulling up outside the cinema, the voice of the conductor "Prince Albert! Palace! Any more fares please?" bitterly shot out into the cold air as the bus went past him. His bus, his cinema, still his hotel. He walked along the wind-dried pavement back to his house, completely shut off now from the street by the limes and chestnuts and cypresses, pruned to make a screen. It seemed to him that the air had in it a feeling of snow. He walked steadily, upright, still smart, without an overcoat or stick. Age had hammered character into his face, so that it had a hammered-out, impressive sparseness, almost without flesh. It was no longer ugly; age had similarly hammered out its crudities; it had the permanence of bronze. He went out of the street into the garden and it was only then that he remembered what had been said to him at the bottom of the stairs. Remembering it, he stood still. It was as though he had struggled for seventy years through the darkness of recurrent stupidities simply to arrive at the revelation of a single moment. Why hadn't he bought it? He went on to the house, inside, into the drawing-room. He suddenly wanted to buy it, was suddenly as scared as a child that sees a toy in a shop-window and wants it and cannot wait and is afraid in another day it will be gone. He picked up the telephone and called the auctioneers, Killick and Franklin, and said, "Is Mr. Killick in?" and the clerk said "No, Mr. Killick isn't back yet from the auction." He asked for Mr. Franklin and in a moment Mr. Franklin came and Bruno said, bluntly: "Spella Ho. What's the reserve on that?" Mr. Franklin asked who it was, and Bruno told him. Mr. Franklin said: "Fifty-five thousand, Mr. Shadbolt." "The asking price?" Bruno said, and Mr. Franklin said: "Yes, Mr. Shadbolt, Fifty-five thousand, the asking price. Knock five off." Bruno said; "I'm coming down. Whatever happens don't do anything. I want the key. I'm coming down."

He went out of the house again and down into the town and into the offices of Killick and Franklin, speaking to Mr. Franklin a moment and getting the key. "Yes, consider it an offer," he said. "I'll be back in an hour and talk more then." "Cold weather, Mr. Shadbolt," Mr. Franklin said, and Bruno said: "Cold?" as though suddenly he did not know what time of the year it was.

Furnaces belched smoke from the huge complicated mass of South Wales Amalgamated works as he walked out of the town on the east side. Rows of flat-fronted workers' houses dug red-blue teeth into the countryside, the road to Spella Ho going up almost under the shadow of the condenser. He heard the clank-clock-clank of shunted trucks down in the sidings, saw small armies of ant-men filing out from the seven-to-three day shift, dispersing down the hill. Steam-smoke hung momentarily in the dark air, before evaporation, like snow; and beyond, and already in ten years it seemed a long way beyond, he could see the uplifted arms, black against the sky, of the river-diggers, hoppers swinging up out of the gulleys, spewing down the clay-blue, iron-brown earth that looked in reality black in the lightless afternoon air, making a new sky-line, like alps in miniature, of the naked earth. In ten years he had often stopped to look at this; had reckoned it an achievement. Now there was no time, and, he felt, no need to stop. He walked straight on past furnaces, stacks of pig-iron standing like the coverings of iron dug-outs in the yards, and past the last of the flat-fronted houses, in ten years down almost to slum level, that were cut off as with an axe by the boundaries of Spella Ho. He did not stop until he got half-way up the slope, and then he turned and stood for a moment and looked back, seeing the town below. He saw it stretching now from the mass of South Wales Amalgamated over towards the corresponding puffs of snow-steam, like a twin reflection, that came from Ebbw Vale on the far side of the valley. Almost all that lay between was now the town, its blue, dead face smoke-powdered in the still air. Gasometers, six in number now, stood like some vast arrangement of pillbox defences, dull crimson, at the foot of the hill up which buses crawled like toys drawn up on invisible strings. In a sense they were things spawned out of his endurance and courage. In the creation of almost all of it he had had some part.

And standing there he saw it all, suddenly, as he had not seen it before. Standing between the house and the town he stood between much that had been created by twin forces in himself. Looking down, he could see the huge, more than tangible mass of his material endeavour for almost fifty years: the sprawling record of his undefeated ignorance, courage and strength. Looking up, he could see nothing but the house. It did not seem to have changed in fifty years by as much as an inch of lichen on the lime-stone. There was no record, except in his own mind, of things that had happened there. There was no record of the best in himself.

He went on and unlocked the main gates at the end of

the avenue; the familiarity of the key, the same as in Mrs. Lanchester's time, troubled him. He tried not to think of it. Memory forced itself on him with bleak insistence: Louise, the daily journey with her, in secret, the testing of the locks of every hay-choked and rusted gate in the place. He walked up the avenue under the bare limes, the massed claret twigs almost the only colour now in the dark air. He had driven away from the avenue gates with Gerda. There was no record of it. It might not have happened, he thought. He had seen Virginia and Caroline biking down the avenue and coming a cropper in the summer grass, skirts high over pink bloomers such as you now saw displayed in every tuppeny shop in the world and whenever almost a woman sat down at all. There was no record of that moment of terrific unconventionality, or of the two lovely golden creatures. No record. A gasometer had a record. It keeps on, you record it in figures. Pig-iron has more permanence than a woman. It lasts for ever; the stones of a house last with it. What happens to us? he thought. There's no record for us.

He stood on the terrace. It had begun suddenly to snow a little, not fast. For some reason he did not want to go into the house. He walked round it. A ton or two of coal was still piled in the yard behind the kitchen, and it was as though he had gone back fifty years. He recalled his mother, dying of a cancer of honesty, trying to make him honest: he could recall the death-coldness of her hands. There was no record of her except that bitter unforgettable coldness. He walked away from the coal, on which soft dabs of snow had begun to make their mark like bird-droppings, and went round to the west side and again to the front of the house. He remembered the breaking of the windows, Chamberlain. He recalled Chamberlain and Jenny; had no emotion about it.

In the same way he had no emotion about the house. Now, after fifty years, it was about to be his and he did not know what to think of it. If there was any grief attached to it, it did not touch him; familiarity lessened the force of grief in the same way as it lessened the force of pleasure. He remained on the terrace a little longer. It was snowing faster, the sky darkening and letting fall huge slow gobs of snow, without wind. He looked at the immense frontage of the dead house and remembered wondering, fifty years before, how any human soul could live in so large a place. Now I'm going to live in it myself, he thought. Now I shall know.

When he unlocked the front door of the house and went in at last it was almost too dark to see. He had no matches and had some idea that the gas had anyway been cut off. He stood at the foot of the stairs and looked up, feeling the apple-smooth polish of the banister rail that swung up out of sight like a mahogany snake. He could smell a faint odour of carbolic, perhaps carbolic soap. Hundreds of wounded men had lain for four years in the rooms, matrons had tramped the corridors, concerts had been given, doctors had pronounced life extinct, and bright blue figures had been wheeled away on wheel-beds, and there was no record of it except the chipping of plaster on the walls, here and there a naughty drawing of a nurse half sponged off a wall, and a smell of carbolic soap.

He stood in the hall, swinging the key, looking up. He could see the white figures of the cherubim and seraphim in the painting flying across the ceiling. He thought for a moment of going upstairs, then changed his mind. Plenty of time, he thought.

He went outside and locked the door and stood on the terrace, for a minute, before going. Already he thought: I own it, it's mine, this is what I wanted. Snow was falling more quickly now. He saw it settling like wool on the unmown grass of the lawns. He saw it gathering almost like smoke in the distances, one with the steam-smoke let off by South Wales Amalgamated and the chimney smoke of the town. Between the town and himself the lake reflected the sky. Snow and falling darkness gave everything, the lake, the iron-works, the town and the fields between, a strange appearance of distance. It seemed to him for a moment that he had climbed a long way up; that now, at last, and for one moment, he stood on top of the world.

BOOK SEVEN

SPELLA HO: 1931

CHAPTER I

THE full heat of afternoon hung over Spella Ho as he came out on the terrace some time before three o'clock on a day in July 1931. Heat shot back from the white flag-stones almost like light from a mirror, tiring the eyes. He went to the edge of the terrace and looked down on the park. Patches of dark tree-shade mottled the scorched, almost faun-brown grass like the flank of a deer. Far down was a white blot. Someone was down there and had been down there all day.

He went down the steps of the terrace and out into the park and across it, to find out who it was. Whoever it was, they were sitting down; they, he thought, because there seemed, as he got closer, to be two people, two slim white objects. Then as he got closer he saw that there were two objects but only one person: a woman, with an easel. She was facing towards the house. He walked down to her: an old man, rather slow but erect, dressed in a pair of cream-white flannel trousers tied with a fancy green waist-band of paisley pattern, a panama hat and no jacket over the white shirt. In those smartish white clothes, the trousers relics of a period when he had tried to out-flash Chamberlain, he looked impressive, a man by no means defeated by time, and almost aristocratic. Age had hammered dignity into his face, a kind of ironic handsomeness beaten out of the big-boned ugliness.

He went down to the woman and then, as he got nearer,

saw that she was not a woman, but a mere girl, about twenty-three. She was wearing a pretty pink-striped washing frock and no hat, hair blonde in the sun. She had seen him coming but she did not do anything. She fixed her eyes on the house and then on the easel and went on working.

When he came up to her and stood looking she still did not move at all but she spoke. "Good afternoon," she said. "Is it all right?" It was a quick, self-reliant little voice, certain as an electric bell. "I mean my being here." Her eyes looked straight at him, frank and slightly disconcerting, clear as ice. "Is it all right? I came up to the house and asked this morning and they said you were out." Her legs, bare up to and beyond the knees, stuck out from under the easel.

"Yes," he said, "it's all right."

"Thanks," she said.

"Painting?" he said.

"No, pencil. Just a sketch."

"The house?"

"Yes," she said. "Who sweeps the chimneys?"

He laughed and said, "When they're swept at all it takes a week but they're never swept. Mostly I've got gas fires. They're better. They save trouble."

"That's good," she said. "There's enough smoke from that rotten town now."

He did not say anything to that, but watched her drawing. He felt fascinated by her sitting there bare-headed in the sun and in a way she reminded him of Virginia and Caroline: hair just as blonde, with the same frank teasing quality in the eyes and the friendly humour in the high little voice. Then he did speak. "Had any dinner?"

"Oh! yes. I bring sandwiches."

"Come from Castor?" he said.

"Oh no. Oh! God no," she said. "No fear." She blew, making a face. "No. I come from Cambridge. But I'm making drawings of the big houses in the country. Sort of holiday task.'"

"What's wrong with the town?" he said.

"What's right with it?" she said. "Look at that. For one thing. Look at it."

She turned and looked over her shoulder and he knew what she was looking at: South Wales Amalgamated, condensers black against the sky, the claw motions of the river diggers just visible in a gap between the trees. He heard the clack-clock of trucks shunting down on the sidings, a roar of steam in the hot silence and the echo of it, mocking, as though from the other side of nowhere. "What do you call that?" she said.

"Well," he said. He did not know what to say. There had been times when he had called it his biggest achievement. "I don't know," he said.

"Well, I do. Hideous."

He had an answer for that. "You wouldn't get far without steel," he said.

"Yes, but to put it there. Just to plank it down. Like that. In front of this house. The one next to the other. You see any sense or reason in that?"

"Yes," he said. "I do. The iron was there before the house."

"That makes no odds."

"The iron is as important as the house."

"Is it? Well, anyway, I'd like to meet the man who did it."

"I did it," he said.

She made another face and pulled at her dress, at the arms and breast, as though it were sticking to her skin. "I was hot enough before I said that," she said. "Now what do I do?" She was grinning. He just smiled, stood looking at the firm little figure tight and alert under the washing dress. "You say what you like," he said.

She smiled, quietly and rather gently, in apology. She looked suddenly a creature of character and affection: at once radiant and downright. No nonsense about her, he thought. Then she said: "You'd better tell me what else you've done before I put my foot in it again."

"Well," he said, "the gas-works."

"God!"

"The cinema and the hotel."

"Not the 'Prince Albert'?"

"Yes."

"Perhaps you'd better not tell me any more," she said. "I'm liable to go off the handle. You see, among other things I'm interested in town-planning. And if there is one town that makes see me red it is this."

"Fifty years ago it wasn't much more than a one-street town," he said. "And one-eyed at that."

"Better to have kept it one-eyed," she said.

"How?" he said. "Why? It's given people things. Light, money, comfort. When I was a kid we had farden rush-lights. No comfort. Nothing. Not even a school here."

"Yes, I know. No one denies progress. But you've planked something down that's going to go on being an eyesore for ever. What about that?"

"We didn't know we were going to plank it down."

"It just happened?" she said.

"It just happened."

"I know," she said. "A bit here, and a bit there. A street and then a hotel, and then something else. Anyhow. No plan. I know. Terrible."

"We seized opportunities."

"Opportunities." She blew her little habitual sigh, half of disgust, half despair, "Didn't it ever occur to you to make it beautiful while you were at it?" she said.

"I don't know. I don't think so."

"Didn't you ever do anything beautiful?"

He did not answer. There was nothing he could say to that. If he had done anything beautiful there was no record of it. There was no record of beauty, he thought, and affection, love, happiness, things like that. I can't tell her that. It's private, inside me. It's the same for everybody, he thought now, as he had once thought before. Everybody is shut up; part of everybody is shut away from everybody else. Not speaking, soon not thinking, he sat watching her in the sun. She had an air of sudden permanence: flesh brown and strong, hair thick-curled almost like blonde marble in the golden perpendicular light. He looked in admiration at the soft, naked legs, the warm arms, the fine pink-polished fingers. Thought, moving more like the glass slide of a dream, became in its effect cloudily panoramic, so that he saw her in a series of non-existent pictures: coming back to the house, staying there for tea, talking, sketching some other part of the house, staying the night. The pictures slid across his mind; woke speculative ideas that seemed like part of his former self. If I'd been younger, he thought, I know what I should have done. I should have kissed her and tumbled her into the grass and run away with her. Things like that. Perhaps she could come back for tea? The paintings on the stairs: it's just possible, he thought, that she'd know all about them, would like to copy them. In that case she could stay the night. I could ask her. She could come back and I could talk to her. I like the way she talks. It's a long time since I talked with anybody.

Sirens spat out from South Wales Amalgamated, signalling the three o'clock shift, cutting the thick hot silence. They woke him from the empty-eyed moodiness of speculation. He saw snow puffs of steam in the sky, heard the echo mock itself in the distances.

"How's that?" she said. "You call that beautiful?"

"It's hot," he said, "if that's anything. Wouldn't you come back to the house and have some tea?"

"Tea? What time is it?"

"That whistle," he said, "that's the three o'clock shift." Between the split-second interval of saying this and of her reply he experienced a feeling of the acutest loneliness. It seemed like the sudden concentration of years of loneliness. He was a man without friends; he had seen and known that for a long time, but now he felt it. He felt it with a sudden sharp despair that was almost terror. He felt so alone that he craved suddenly for the companionship of a strange person out of another age and another generation. She could come back. Nothing to do but sketch. She could sketch the house. Her voice struck him back into reality:

"Three? Not already?"

"That's the three shift just off," he said.

"Oh! good God," she said. "I've got to get the train at three-forty. It's taken me twice as long as I expected. It must be the chimneys."

"You're welcome to a room at the house," he said. "If you want to finish. You could stay the night and work tomorrow."

"Stay the night? He'd skin me."

"Who would?"

"My boy-friend."

"Oh! yes," he said.

She worked for another ten minutes because he said, "You'll just do the town in twenty minutes and then you can get a bus." During this time he stood looking at her and then at last she packed up the easel and camp-stool. She folded the easel into a long attaché case, and carried the stool in the other hand. "You can go down through the park," he said. "A short cut. By the lake." And she said: "Oh! yes, I came that way this morning. By the two gravestones on the edge of the lake. Where the two women are buried." He did not speak. She gave him a friendly little smile and tried to hold out one hand, but both hands were full, and he shook hands by grasping the hand that held the attaché case.

"Good-bye," she said. "It's a lovely house. And thank you."

"Come and look at it again sometime."

"Perhaps. I can't tell." She turned to go. Facing the South Wales Amalgamated and seeing the black mass of steel and the claw motions of the river diggers above and beyond the trees, she turned and pulled a last funny little face, friendly, ironic. "If there's a war I hope they'll bomb it to bits."

"It may be you," he said, "instead."

She had begun to walk away as he spoke. She did not hear, and he was glad. As she walked down through the park in the hot sunshine she seemed suddenly like the personification of all youth. Distance lengthened between them rapidly as he turned and walked away towards the house, and once he turned and looked back. She was already far down in the park, going towards the lake that lay with glass-dead tranquillity in the great heat and unbroken light of full sun. At that distance she might have been anybody and she became for one second the personification of all the women he had ever known.

At the bottom of the park, by the lake, she herself turned and looked back. He was about to go up the steps of the house. He went up them. She saw him walk along the terrace, solitary, diminutive, white in the full glare of the white sun. She set her attaché case and stool on the ground, to rest a moment and change hands. Then she stooped quickly to pick them up, because, she thought, that's the only train and I can't bear to miss it, and when she looked up again it was all she could do to make out his white figure against the great sun-white front of Spella Ho.

He had become one with the stones of the house.

DATE DUE

GAYLORD			PRINTED IN U.S.A.